TOM CLANCY

OATH OF OFFICE

★

MARC CAMERON

P9-CCZ-222

BERKLEY
New York

BERKLEY
An imprint of Penguin Random House LLC
1745 Broadway, New York, New York 10019

Copyright © 2018 by The Estate of Thomas L. Clancy, Jr.; Rubicon, Inc.;
Jack Ryan Enterprises, Ltd.; and Jack Ryan Limited Partnership
Penguin Random House supports copyright. Copyright fuels creativity, encourages
diverse voices, promotes free speech, and creates a vibrant culture. Thank you for buying
an authorized edition of this book and for complying with copyright laws by not
reproducing, scanning, or distributing any part of it in any form without permission.
You are supporting writers and allowing Penguin Random House to continue to
publish books for every reader.

BERKLEY is a registered trademark and the B colophon
is a trademark of Penguin Random House LLC.

ISBN: 9780735215979

G. P. Putnam's Sons hardcover edition / November 2018
Berkley international edition / October 2019
Berkley premium edition / November 2019

Printed in the United States of America
1 3 5 7 9 10 8 6 4 2

Cover art by Bose Collins
Cover design by Eric Fuentecilla
Maps by Jeffrey L. Ward

PRINCIPAL CHARACTERS

UNITED STATES GOVERNMENT

Jack Ryan: President of the United States

Mary Pat Foley: Director of national intelligence

Arnold "Arnie" van Damm: President Ryan's chief of staff

Scott Adler: Secretary of state

Robert Burgess: Secretary of defense

Mark Dehart: Secretary of homeland security

THE CAMPUS

Gerry Hendley: Director of The Campus and Hendley Associates

John Clark: Director of operations

Domingo "Ding" Chavez: Assistant director of operations

Jack Ryan, Jr.: Operations officer and senior analyst

Dominic "Dom" Caruso: Operations officer

Adara Sherman: Operations officer

Bartosz "Midas" Jankowski: Operations officer

Gavin Biery: Director of information technology

Lisanne Robertson: Director of transportation

OTHER CHARACTERS

United States

Dr. Cathy Ryan: First Lady of the United States

Will Hyatt: U.S. Air Force Reaper pilot

Michelle Chadwick: United States senator

Randal Van Orden: Professor of astrophysics, U.S. Naval Academy

Alex Hardy: U.S. Naval Academy midshipman

Russia

Nikita Yermilov: President of Russia

Maksim Dudko: Yermilov's aide

Erik Dovzhenko: Russian SVR officer stationed in Tehran

Colonel Pavel Mikhailov: Antonov 124 pilot, Russian
   Air Force

Elizaveta Bobkova: Russian SVR operative stationed in
   Washington, D.C.

Europe

Hugo Gaspard: French arms dealer

Lucile Fournier: French assassin

Urbano da Rocha: Portuguese arms dealer

Iran

Reza Kazem: Leader of the Persian Spring

Ayatollah Ghorbani: Lesser Ayatollah in Iran's ruling council

Parviz Sassani: Major, Islamic Revolutionary Guard Corps

Maryam Farhad: Dovzhenko's Iranian girlfriend

Ysabel Kashani: Iranian academic; Jack Junior's former
   girlfriend

Atash Yazdani: Iranian aeronautical engineer

Sahar Tabrizi: Iranian astrophysicist

Cameroon

Chance Burlingame: U.S. ambassador to Cameroon

Adin Carr: Diplomatic security agent assigned to Cameroon

François Njaya: President of Cameroon

General Mbida: Cameroonian general

Sarah Porter: Wife of deputy chief of mission, Cameroon

Sean Jolivette: F/A-18 Hornet pilot, USS *George H. W. Bush*

Any man who tries to be good all the time is bound to come to ruin among the great number of men who are not good.

—Niccolò Machiavelli

I

1

In Mother Russia, secrets did not stay secret for long. Information was strength. Informing was ingrained. It was nothing short of miraculous that Colonel Pavel Mikhailov of the 224th Air Detachment, Military Transport Aviation, had been able to hide his sins at all.

The tribunal convened by his superiors had been a lengthy and embarrassing ordeal. But he was better for it, wasn't he? *Bez muki net nauki*—no torture, no science. No pain, no gain, the Americans said. Now he'd gotten back his wings—and he wasn't about to do anything that would jeopardize them again. He would be careful. He would be precise. Above all, he would be sober.

Flashlight in hand, the fifty-three-year-old colonel walked beneath the drooping wing of the monstrous Antonov An-124 cargo plane, taking comfort in the smell of jet fuel. A light wind tousled his thinning gray hair. Rosacea that never seemed to go away anymore pinked the round apples of his cheeks. The night had turned out chilly, but the day had been a pleasant one for spring in Moscow, and the black tarmac was still giving up its warmth. Colonel Mikhailov wore small foam earplugs to protect his hearing, but the whine of the auxiliary power unit and the hydraulic squeal of machinery were muffled music to his way of thinking. He played the flashlight under the broad surface of the swept wing, then carefully checked each of the twenty-four tires, as complete and thorough in this preflight as if he were still a pink-faced cadet at Gagarin Academy.

He'd never wrecked an aircraft, or even had a close call, but as his commanding general said, no matter how skilled a pilot he was, one could only show up for work "looking like a bag of ass" so many times before people began to talk. Ironically, his superiors had not begun to worry until after he attended his first weekly meeting of Alcoholics Anonymous. The Russian government had long been wary of AA—secret meetings and deference to a higher power other than the state lent credence to the general lack of trust in any program created by the West. But more than that, it was Mikhailov's new attitude that bothered them.

Vodka was as much a part of the Russian psyche as great-coats and poems about troika rides.

In 1858 the government attempted to refill the state coffers drained by the Crimean War by tripling the price of a bucket of vodka. Peasants took oaths of sobriety to protest this tax. Temperance movements swelled as formerly sotted citizens swore off anything more potent than beer—and that just would not do. The Army intervened with crushing aggression on behalf of state alcohol interests, flogging the protesters and using funnels to force vodka down their throats. Temperance groups were outlawed, and more than seven hundred protesters were arrested as rebels.

If Colonel Mikhailov was suddenly worried about

handling his liquor, perhaps everyone else should worry as well. Perhaps he was a rebel.

Three decades of service had given Mikhailov guardian angels in high places, men who had flown with him in Afghanistan in the eighties, who still held some measure of loyalty, though they had risen to loftier heights. Skilled pilots with Mikhailov's experience were hard to find—and he told himself he was better while in his cups than half the kids in today's Federation Air Force when they were flying sober.

The disciplinary hearing had been excruciating. Listening to one's numerous shortcomings was difficult enough when drunk. A clear head made it nearly unbearable as the panel of generals ticked down the list, fault by disgusting fault. Those well-placed friends didn't stop the panel from threatening to have him cashiered, but even through the fog of shame he knew better. Had they wanted to take away his pension, they would have simply done it, not threatened it.

Though at times he felt a bucket would have been the perfect vessel from which to drink more vodka, Colonel Mikhailov managed to keep his mouth shut during the process. He did precisely as he was told, and he eventually earned back his wings—wings that brought with them enough trust for this mission.

He'd flown his Antonov 124 to Zhukovsky Airport from Migalovo the day before. The runway at the 6955th home base was adequate for the enormous bird, so long as she was empty, but load her up and it was a different story. Seventy-four thousand, three hundred fifty-two kilograms heavier than it was the day before, the An-124 now needed substantially more runway on takeoff than Migalovo provided. Zhukovsky was located some thirty-six kilometers southeast of Moscow along the Moskva River. It served not only as a civilian international airport, but also as home to Gromov Flight Research Institute, which added to the security protocols needed for sensitive missions like this one.

Apart from the performance and security reasons for changing airports, the two-hundred-kilometer flight served as a shakedown run for the crew of six—four of them new to Mikhailov. He had flown with one of the two engineers before, but the other, along with the radioman, navigator, and first officer, were not from the 224th. Substitutions like this happened, especially on this type of mission, but the An-124 community was relatively small, and he was surprised he'd never met any of these men. Had he stood on firmer ground with respect to his wings, he would have asked more questions. Mikhailov knew his reputation as a skilled pilot was unmatched in the notoriously tricky Antonov, but his reputation as a drunk was just as well known, even outside the military. The new crew members observed him carefully during the preflight briefing for any evidence of alcohol.

He'd arrived early this evening, used his identification card to badge his way through the concentric layers of gates, doors, and armed security personnel, making it to his airplane in time to watch the onboard overhead cranes and powerful winches load the two twenty-meter-long wooden crates through the tail door. His flight manifest noted that the contents of each box were *osoboy vazhnosti*—of particular importance—what the United States called Top Secret. Their destination was Sary-Shagan in central Kazakhstan, making the classification somewhat moot. Sary-Shagan was a missile test facility, so there was no question as to what these were. There were no markings, other than computer barcodes, but dosimeters affixed to the fore end of each crate left little doubt that the items inside were nuclear. As pilot-in-command, he had to be informed that each item weighed a little over thirty-seven thousand kilos. The length and weight narrowed it down a bit, some kind of medium-range missile, surely a new model, since they were on their way to be tested. Mikhailov was paid to transport, not to deduce.

It didn't matter to him what he carried, so long as he was flying.

Attachment points on the missiles themselves protruded through small cutouts in the wood along the length of the crates, allowing the Antonov's internal crane system to load each item through the massive rear cargo door and nestle them all securely in the bay.

There was room to spare.

Mikhailov had moved a battalion of soldiers, huge military trucks, tanks, other aircraft, even a rescue submarine. He and his fellow pilots were fond of saying they were capable of transporting the Kremlin, so long as the weight was correctly distributed.

The loadmasters would stow the massive tow bar in the rear cargo area after the Antonov was pushed back; then they would stay behind in Zhukovsky, leaving the unloading of this cargo of particular importance to their counterparts at Sary-Shagan.

With his preflight inspection completed, Colonel Mikhailov walked up the open aft cargo ramp, hugged the wall to pass the secured missiles, and climbed the stairs to the upper deck. The rest of the crew had already taken up their positions in the cockpit. They bid him the customary welcome deserving of a colonel and pilot-in-command, and he settled himself into the left seat. No matter how many times he climbed in behind the yoke of any aircraft, he still felt a sense of wonder that heated his belly like . . . well, like a good drink.

He put on a pair of reading glasses, ready to perform his portion of the pre-takeoff checklist, while the first officer, an imposing and broody man named Cherenko, read point by point from a laminated card. A civilian—or just as likely an FSB pilot—he wore dark slacks and a white shirt with three yellow stripes on the black shoulder boards.

A secondary warning light for the fire-suppression system in the cargo hold had not been replaced as per Mikhailov's order the previous day, but he made the decision to wait until they returned to Migalovo. The remainder of the checks were unremarkable.

Mikhailov turned to the navigator seated behind him, who'd already received clearance and instructions for takeoff from Delivery Control. "Flight time?"

"Three hours and thirty-seven minutes, Colonel," the navigator said. "Winds are on the nose most of the way. A Ural Airbus 320 coming in from the south reported heavy turbulence at flight level one-nine-zero."

Mikhailov nodded, unperturbed. "Very well," he said. "Let us be on our way. I know a woman there who makes very good mutton stew."

"It is probably Kazakh horse cock," First Officer Cherenko said and chuckled as he stowed the preflight checklist in the binder beside his seat.

"Whatever it is"—Mikhailov shrugged, deciding he did not like the man—"the stew is delicious." He checked his watch—0104 hours—and leaned forward, adjusting the radio to hear the latest flight information service broadcast. He listened to the recorded message play all the way before giving a nod to the first officer. The trip from Migalovo the day before had established that Mikhailov preferred to let his copilot run the radios while he flew the airplane.

"Ground," Cherenko said. "Antonov 2808 ready to taxi with information Bravo."

"Antonov 2808," a male voice said. *"Hold short Runway One-Two, monitor Tower on one-one-niner-point-five."*

Military pilots spoke in Russian among themselves, and, to the consternation of pilots transiting from other countries, the tower sometimes did as well. But English was the international language of aviation, and this airspace was controlled by civilians. The tower controller put them in line behind an Il-76 heavy, cautioning them of wake turbulence from the departing giant.

"In line behind the heavy," Cherenko responded. "Antonov 2808."

A moment later the forty-six-meter, four-engine Ilyushin Il-76 lumbered down the runway, leaving invisible vortices of whirling wind behind it.

The controller spoke again. *"Antonov 2808 clear for takeoff on Runway One-Two, fly runway heading until five thousand feet. Contact Moscow Departure."*

Cherenko read back the instructions as Mikhailov pushed the throttles forward slowly. The airplane began to shudder in place as he babied the four Lotarev D-18T turbofan engines for almost five full minutes before he released the brakes and began his takeoff roll. Slowly, steadily, the great bird picked up enough speed to heave herself off the runway.

"Positive rate of climb, Colonel." Cherenko's voice came over the intercom in Russian now, eyes on the altimeter. "Landing gear up."

The massive Antonov was a touchy bird, but in Mikhailov's capable hands more than a half-million pounds of airplane, fuel, and secret cargo flew with remarkable grace.

Air traffic controller Svetlana Minsky licked chapped lips and pressed slender fingers against her headphones—as she was wont to do when she grew nervous. Her idiot boyfriend had convinced her to stop smoking, and she was feeling it tonight. A motivational poster tacked to the wall above her said in Cyrillic: *The same hammer that shatters glass forges steel.* The notion would have been hilarious had it not been so sad. The hammer that was Air Traffic Control was plenty capable of shattering steel. And anyway, Minsky was far too busy doing her job to be reading bullshit motivational posters. She and the dozens of other controllers on watch inside the windowless blue room of Moscow Center took care of the airspace for seventy airports in and around Moscow. Tonight was extra hectic, and she cursed her boyfriend for stealing her cigarettes.

The agitation in her gravel voice was apparent over the radio, earning her a side-eyed warning from her supervisor, who sat birdlike at a row of desks behind her, in the middle of the bullpen.

She watched a numbered blip appear on her radar screen as the sweep came around.

A new voice to go with the blip crackled in her headset. Thickly Slavic, the English would have been almost impossible for anyone but another Russian to understand. *"Moscow Departure, Antonov 2808 leaving eight hundred feet for five thousand."*

"Antonov 2808, radar contact. Continue climb as directed."

The Short-Term Conflict Alert on Minsky's computer showed a second Antonov, also with the Russian Air Force, bypassing Zhukovsky on a heading that would intercept 2808 at present speed and altitude. The planes were still eight miles apart. This gave her three miles before she'd have an "incident"—when two planes got closer than five lateral miles or a thousand feet of altitude.

Minsky dealt with other aircraft for a time, and gave a phlegmatic cough when she turned her attention back to the two Antonovs. All the open miles in the sky and these two bastards were determined to fly directly into each other.

Minsky wanted to curse almost as bad as she wanted a cigarette. *"Antonov 2967, amend altitude to one four thousand, turn left thirty degrees for separation of company traffic departing Zhukovsky."*

There was no response.

This was not unheard of. Pilots bumped radio knobs, switched to the wrong frequency, or became engrossed in some conversation with the flight deck. Sometimes they merely fell asleep.

Six miles apart.

Minsky tried again, repeating her command for 2967 to change altitude.

No response. The term to describe an aircraft that didn't respond over the radio was NORDO, but she didn't take the time to use it.

"Antonov 2808, maintain one six thousand, turn left thirty degrees without delay."

Closing in on five miles. This was too close to becoming an official "incident."

Both airplanes now climbed toward eighteen thousand feet, converging on the same point southwest above the Moskva River.

Minsky consoled herself that only one of them had to move out of the way.

The pilot answered with a read-back of her instructions. *"Maintain one six thousand, turn left thirty degrees, Antonov 2808."*

Minsky snatched up a small rubber alligator her boyfriend had given her to combat the stress of not smoking. She began to squeeze it, as if trying to obliterate the stupid thing from the world. She sighed in relief at the read-back as the number representing 2808 on her radar screen moved from its original path, following her instructions.

Inexplicably, the radar blip that was 2967 moved as well, directly toward 2808 in heading and rate of climb.

Minsky didn't waste time on the NORDO airplane.

"Antonov 2808, turn left thirty degrees immediately."

In the parlance of air traffic control, "immediately" meant exactly that. The pilot should not take time to disengage the autopilot or fool with the heading bug. He was to grab the yoke and turn the airplane the very moment he heard the command.

Antonov 2808 acknowledged, but did not alter course.

Fifteen feet away, across the dimly lit room, the "snitch" on the supervisor's computer alerted him that there was a problem at the same moment Minsky reached up and snapped her fingers to get his attention. He rolled his chair across the blue industrial carpeting, eyes wide when he saw the two blips on the screen coming closer.

Minsky didn't expect him to help, she just wanted a witness that she was doing everything by the book.

"Try the other one," the supervisor whispered.

The conflict alert alarm sounded on her radar, signaling two minutes until a midair collision. The Americans called an incident like this a "deal"—certainly the most supreme of all understatements, Minsky thought.

She tried again.

"Antonov 2967, turn right thirty degrees, immediately. Maintain flight level one-niner-zero. Break. Antonov 2808, turn left thirty degrees for separation, company traffic three miles off your right wing. Break. Antonov 2967, turn right immediately."

Nothing.

Minsky crushed the rubber alligator in her fist, smacking it over and over against her desk. She could have been singing "Bayu Bayushki Bayu" to these idiots for all the good it was doing.

Then, blessedly: *"Left thirty degrees, Antonov 2808."*

The blip began to alter course with each radar sweep.

Minsky released a pent-up breath. *"Thank you, 2808. 2967 is NORDO."*

"We will attempt contact," 2808 replied.

Minsky allowed herself a moment to rub strained eyes with the heel of her hand, but a string of expletives from her supervisor snapped her back to attention. Antonov 2808 adjusted course as directed, but the second bird moved right along with it. At their present course and altitude, the two airplanes would very soon become a fireball over Russia.

Minsky continued to give voice commands. Her supervisor typed the identical flight instructions into the Sintez computer system, sending them to the aircraft via electronic message. At the same time, other traffic was diverted far away from the area. The second Antonov seemed bent on a midair collision. She watched in horror as the two blips on her screen grew closer with each sweep of the radar, squawking the ident numbers of their respective transponders.

"Antonov 2967," Minsky said again. The pleading ran like a fissure of softer stone through her granite voice. *"You must maintain altitude and present heading."* She repeated the same in Russian, just in case.

The targets momentarily froze into what was called a "ghost track" as the confused radar and computer processors worked to reacquire the two airplanes.

The supervisor groaned, leaning in almost on top of Minsky for emotional support. His voice cracked. "Twenty seconds. Then we will know."

The high perch of the Antonov's flight deck gave 2808's crew a terrifying view of the belly of the aircraft above as it overflew them, bearing down like an eagle swooping on her prey. Colonel Mikhailov cursed through gritted teeth, pushing the yoke forward as the other plane flew directly overhead at four hundred feet, matching course as if shadowing in a tight formation.

The instruments flickered momentarily, along with the cabin lights. Mikhailov heard the flight engineer seated behind him say something unintelligible, but his hands were full and he didn't have time to check in.

"I have the airplane," Cherenko said from the right seat.

Mikhailov's head snapped around. "Negative, it is still my air—"

The cold steel of a pistol barrel against his neck caused the colonel to freeze. Very slowly, he lifted his hands from the yoke.

"You have the airplane," he said.

He half turned to see the first engineer, unconscious in a heap on the floor, drugged or struck in the head. It was impossible to tell. The engineer he did not know held the pistol in a sure hand. Smiling serenely.

The second Antonov continued to shadow them. The transponder blinked off and then came back on, flashing a completely different ident number.

The radio squawked and a new voice came across as the second plane peeled away, wings lifting into the night.

"*Moscow Departure, Antonov 2808. We are in the clear. 2967 passed directly beneath us.*"

The radioman behind Mikhailov spoke now. "*Moscow Departure, Antonov 2967. Sorry about that. We experienced an intense electrical storm that had us all flying blind. We have it worked out.*"

"*2967, do you wish to declare an emergency?*" the female

controller asked, her voice strained from the near miss on her watch.

"*Captain advises negative,*" Cherenko said. "*We will land in Saratov and perform required systems check. Antonov 2967.*"

The controller gave him a telephone number to call to "discuss the matter further." A report would certainly be logged. He acknowledged receipt but did not write anything down.

Mikhailov started to lower his hands, but the engineer prodded him with the pistol until he rested them on top of his head.

"So," Mikhailov muttered, "we have become 2967 and they are now us." The radioman continued to speak with Departure, and Mikhailov felt the airplane bank sharply to the right, heading almost due south. He looked at his first officer, pained at the stupid futility of all this. "There are other ways for them to figure out who we are."

"True enough," the engineer with the pistol said. "But with the right equipment and the right people supporting . . ."

"What could you hope to gain? The missiles will be useless without the launch-control devices."

"That is true as well," the radioman said, smiling down at the two leather briefcases at his feet.

Mikhailov felt as if his insides had broken.

"I see," he said. "What will happen when the other airplane reaches Kazakhstan with no nuclear missiles onboard?"

"It will fly in that direction," Cherenko said. "Unfortunately, the same electrical storm we just experienced must have damaged that aircraft's navigation and com-

munication systems. It will drop out of radar contact somewhere over the wooded hills of the Bashkiriya forest and
be lost en route. I can assure you, that plane will not be
found."

"Then what is our destination?"

Cherenko glanced sideways and shook his head. "That,
I am afraid, Comrade Colonel, is no longer your concern.
For, you see, you are supposed to be aboard the doomed
aircraft." He twisted a little farther in his seat to make eye
contact with the radioman seated at the workstation behind him. "Yuri, it is already Thursday—little Friday.
Would you be so kind as to get the colonel some vodka?"

"No . . . I . . . ." Mikhailov stammered. "I . . . do not
drink—"

"My friend," Cherenko said softly. "Do yourself a
favor and have some vodka. It will make what comes
next . . . easier."

2

The President of the United States set a white porcelain coffee cup on a wood coaster at the edge of the Resolute desk. There were those who thought Jack Ryan surely drank from the skulls of his defeated enemies, but in truth, the academic and former Marine much preferred his coffee from a chipped ceramic mug, the interior of which was richly stained from the many gallons of brew that had gone before. He'd make the switch to that mug later in the day, but the first meeting in the Oval Office with a newly minted Cabinet official necessitated the fancy White House china to go with the requisite photo op.

With the photographer gone now, Ryan had moved around to the front of his desk to sit in one of the two Chippendale chairs, across from Mark Dehart, the secretary of homeland security. The upholstered couches and chairs in the middle of the Oval were more comfortable, but they had a way of swallowing people up. Ryan had met with Dehart briefly once before, immediately following the last White House Correspondents' Dinner. That off-the-cuff meeting had taken place in a tiny Washington Hilton anteroom not much larger than a phone booth. It was a bit of an ambush—as interviews with the Commander in Chief often were. Dehart hadn't had the time or the space then to be nervous, but he appeared downright unflappable now. His eyes sparkled with intensity at this first official sit-down with his new boss. Ryan liked that. People who were comfortable in their own skin were more likely to offer honest critiques and advice. And honest critiques from within one's own camp were in short supply when one was arguably the most powerful person on the planet.

This morning, Ryan had blocked out a full twenty minutes with his new DHS secretary. It was an eternity as Oval Office meetings went, especially when the purpose was just a friendly chat.

Ryan gave an approving nod. "I apologize for taking so long to have you in for a visit."

"You're a busy man, Mr. President," Dehart said. He was a fit sixty-one years old, lean, with the hungry face of a triathlete and the crow's-feet of a born smiler. A crisp white shirt accented a deep tan, as if he'd spent any vacation time from his previous job as a congressman plowing fields on his old John Deere tractor. Dehart was born of Pennsylvania Dutch stock; his father and grandfather before him had been dairymen. He had used the "milk money" he'd earned to pay his way through undergrad at Penn State and then for a master's in biology from Carnegie Mellon. A scientist at heart, he was a deep, analytical thinker with a farmer's work ethic. He was honest and well liked by most. In the Machiavellian world of D.C. politics, that meant there were plenty of people who wanted to see him crash and burn because he made them look bad.

Dehart shifted in his seat. He wasn't nervous, he just

preferred to be up and doing rather than sitting and thinking about doing. "Frankly, I was surprised the confirmation went through," he said. "I don't know why, but Senator Chadwick really has it in for me."

Ryan gave a slow shake of his head. As chair of the Homeland Security Appropriations Subcommittee of the Senate, or "cardinal," Michelle Chadwick wielded enormous clout.

"No, Mark," Ryan said and sighed. "Her fight's with me. She just happens to have a scorched-earth policy when it comes to battles, political or otherwise. Honestly, I think I could put *her* name forward for a nomination and she'd disclose some sordid affair just to make me look stupid for trying to appoint her." Ryan took another sip of coffee to wash the taste of Michelle Chadwick's name out of his mouth, and then set the cup down to wave away any lingering thoughts. "Anyway, you made it aboard. Are you ready to hit the ground running?"

Dehart smiled. "I am indeed, sir."

"Had a chance to read your briefing books?"

As secretary of homeland security, Dehart was responsible for, among other things, Customs and Border Protection, Immigration and Customs Enforcement, FEMA, the Coast Guard, and the Secret Service.

"I'm about two and a half feet down the three-foot stack of folders," Dehart said, completely serious.

"Take it from me," Ryan said. "Briefers are like cows, they add more to the pile every day."

Dehart grinned. "The manure simile occurred to me, Mr. President. But my mother called this morning to warn me to keep my flippant remarks to a minimum, first time in the Oval Office and all."

"Sage advice," Ryan said. "So you've read enough to get a feel for what's ahead of you . . . ahead of us. Tell me what scares you."

Dehart inhaled deeply, and then glanced over at the presidential seal in the middle of the Oval Office carpet. He measured his words carefully before looking Ryan in the eye. "Three things, Mr. President."

Ryan raised an eyebrow. "Which three things?"

"Any three, sir," Dehart said. "If they all happen at the same time."

Reza Kazem did as he'd been instructed, more or less. The Russians were, after all, experts in tradecraft. He couldn't see anyone but knew they were with him every step of the way, watching for signs of a tail.

The twenty-seven-year-old Iranian had spent four years at Georgetown earning a bachelor's degree in mathematics and had no difficulty navigating in Washington, D.C. He'd certainly been here long enough to know that there were spies and, more important, counterspies behind every tree and under every stone.

At just under six feet tall, with olive skin and a full head of dark, wavy hair, Kazem did not stand out in a crowd in Iran or Washington—until one looked at his eyes. Deep green, the color of the sea in a gale, they'd garnered him plenty of female attention during his time at Georgetown. A dreamer at heart, he often forgot to eat—especially now, with so much on the line. This gave him a gaunt appearance, which American girls also appeared to like. He enjoyed football—what the Americans called soccer—and ran two miles every morning to stay in shape. He was not particularly strong in a physical sense, but that didn't matter. People didn't bend to his will because he muscled them. He simply told them what he wanted, looked at them with his stormy-sea eyes—and they did it.

Kazem had taken a cab from his hotel to the Metro station at Tysons Corner, where he boarded the Silver train toward Largo Town Center. As instructed, he got off the train at Rosslyn, taking the impossibly long escalator up to street level, where he walked two blocks east to a Starbucks. It was early, and he had to wait in line with all the other morning commuters to buy a cup of coffee and a slice of lemon cake, which he ate outside the doors on the street. The sidewalks teemed with people wearing earbuds, carrying newspapers, drinking coffee, but no one looked anything like an intelligence operative, Russian or otherwise. Whoever was out there must have been highly skilled. Kazem finished the lemon cake—which was moist and as good as anything he'd ever had in Iran, though he hated to admit it—and retraced his steps to the Metro station. This time he took the Orange train that ran parallel to the Silver. At L'Enfant Plaza, he changed to the Blue Line, where he retraced his journey yet again, this train turning south as it sped across the Potomac, through Foggy Bottom—where the State Department was headquartered—and bypassing Rosslyn altogether. Above ground now, Kazem stood, holding on to a steel bar above his head, the train packed shoulder to shoulder. He caught a glimpse of the endless rows of white stones on the hillside at Arlington Cemetery, and the expansive parking lot of the Pentagon. He was indeed in the belly of the beast.

Kazem exited the train at the Fashion Centre at Pentagon City, returning again to ground level and walking east on 15th until he reached the Crystal Gateway Marriott. He made his way through the hotel lobby and down a long, sterile-looking tile hallway into the Crystal City Underground shopping area, redolent with odors of starched shirts and polished shoes—where he was finally supposed to meet his contact.

He pushed his way through the crowds of freshly showered government workers and uniformed military personnel arriving via Virginia transit trains on their way to the Pentagon or one of the myriad other offices in this little corner inside the Beltway.

Kazem found who he was looking for outside yet another Starbucks across from a restaurant called King Street Blues.

She sat at a small, black metal table, situated among a half-dozen other identical tables. Even though she was seated, he could tell the woman was tall, and willowy thin—a long-distance runner often seen jogging on the paved trail along the Potomac between Arlington and Mount Vernon. Amber hair curled slightly at her shoulders, framing high cheekbones and a prominent, but still attractive, Slavic nose. Her charcoal-gray business suit looked expensive, though Reza had never concerned himself with things like women's fashion. Contrary to the rules of tradecraft, he knew his contact's name—or at least the name under which she'd registered at the embassy—Elizaveta Bobkova, first assistant to the Russian economics attaché in Washington. Reza also knew Bobkova worked for SVR, Sluzhba Vneshney Razvedki, the Foreign Intelligence Service of the Russian Federation. More specifically, she was assigned to SVR's Political Intelligence Directorate, Iran Department.

He had met her face-to-face once before, at the national zoo, after going through a similar surveillance-detection run. This morning, two cups of coffee and two slices of lemon cake sat on the table in front of her—exactly what he'd ordered in Rosslyn, the signal that all was well.

Bobkova waved Reza over with a flick of her long fingers, the nails painted bright red. She certainly wasn't trying to remain unnoticed. She smiled broadly and gestured to the chair opposite her.

"I trust your journey went well," she said as he sat down.

Kazem slid his backpack between his feet.

"It did," he said. He eyed the lemon cake. The brisk spring weather had made him ravenous. "May I eat this?"

Elizaveta nodded, and then took a sip from her cup, smudging the dark plastic lid with a darker half-moon of lipstick. "You are remarkably beautiful," she said. "Do you know that."

Kazem took a bite of lemon cake, just as moist as the one in Rosslyn, and let the comment slip by. He needed this woman, so he decided not to say what he was thinking. "Thank you for meeting me," he said.

"Did you see anyone behind you?"

Kazem shook his head. "I did not."

"I thought you might have noticed some of the men who work for me," the Russian said. "They are bumbling imbeciles, all of them."

Kazem knew different.

He said, "Am I to infer from this meeting that your superiors have agreed to help our cause?"

"In a way," Bobkova said. She took another drink of coffee, then swirled the cup around, sizing him up. "As I am sure you are aware, my country has been a remarkable ally of the present regime, but we are certainly not averse to what is happening now. This insurgency, this . . . Persian Spring, as it has been called, is quite . . . remarkable."

Kazem stifled a smile. He'd lived in the United States long enough to know that she was overusing the word.

"Our cause has a groundswell of support," Kazem said. "Demonstrations beyond Tehran—Qom, Isfahan, east to Mashhad and as far south as Bandar Abbas, and countless other cities. Facebook, Twitter, Telegram—the government blocks them all, but we find ways around." He waved his hand as if that were old news. "But you do not care about this. Will Russia provide what we need?"

"This is proving to be . . . remarkably difficult . . ." Bobkova looked up as she spoke, flashing her toothsome smile at a passerby to her left.

Kazem followed her eyes to see a young man in a beige trench coat—like something out of a Humphrey Bogart movie—stumble over his own feet. The man came to a full stop for a brief moment. A new flood of commuters coming in from a recent train outside across Crystal Drive loosed mumbled curses at the man's stupidity, flowing around him toward the Metro station as a river flows around a boulder. The man, likely a few years younger than Kazem, had pink skin that looked as if it had been rubbed with salt. His hair was slicked with pomade. An impeccable navy-blue pinstripe suit was visible beneath the open trench coat.

The pink man licked full, carpish lips as he shot a furtive look back and forth from Kazem to Bobkova. An instant later the spell was broken and he disappeared into the crowd toward the Metro station.

"I think he recognized you," Kazem said. This odd-looking man with scrubbed skin set his teeth on edge.

"Indeed he did," Elizaveta Bobkova said.

"What?" Kazem said, astounded at the flippancy of this woman. "You have me spend two hours avoiding surveillance, when all the while you *planned* for us to be seen together?"

Bobkova patted the table and gave a knowing smile. "My job is one of intricate masquerades. The measures you took this morning were absolutely necessary. If you did not try to lose your tail, the FBI would believe our meeting was of no consequence."

Kazem shot a worried glance over his shoulder. "That man was FBI?"

"Hardly," Bobkova scoffed. "I met him at an embassy dinner a few nights ago. But he is the talkative sort. That serves our purpose well enough. You should be happy. This way the United States will want a piece of the action. I would not be surprised if they begin to airdrop suitcases of money to you at once. That is the way Americans handle things." A mischievous grin perked her lips. "And anyway, it will drive them crazy trying to figure out the why of it all."

Kazem shook his head as if to clear it. "I do not understand any of this," he said. "But you are the expert. As to the other matter, what do you mean by 'in a way'? We have been specific enough in our requests. Iranian intelligence is bad enough, but the Revolutionary Guard is ruthless. There are things we will need to combat their effectiveness. Technical equipment that is imperative to the movement. What does this mean that you cannot help us directly?"

"I can see why people attach themselves to your cause." She was staring into his eyes again. "So very remarkable . . ." She whispered to herself, dreamily, before snapping out of the stupor. She coughed, sitting up a little straighter. "Anyway, I mean just what I say. The government of Russia can provide you nothing directly." Kazem started to protest, but she raised her hand. "But I will send you the contact information for the men who can."

Bobkova was obviously intelligent and wanted him to think she had more information than she actually did. The masquerade of which he was a part made her little games look silly by comparison. He pushed away the uneaten half of his lemon cake and looked hard at the woman. The poor thing had no idea what she was up against, what she had become a part of. Her arrogance was . . . well, remarkable, and it would be her undoing.

"This is just plain weird," an FBI counterintelligence agent named Murphy said, taking a sip from his coffee cup at a table sixty feet up the corridor from Bobkova.

"'Tis indeed, Grasshopper," the senior of the two agents muttered. This one's name was Coyne. He'd been with the Bureau for seventeen years, eleven of those with the Counterintelligence Division. Hailing from Tennessee, he counted his southern roots as a badge of honor and an outward sign of his savvy as a hunter of men.

The two agents watched the Iranian and the Russian with their peripheral vision while they drank their coffees and chatted. They wore neck lanyards with color-coded badges that allowed them access to the Pentagon, like half the other people in the underground shopping mall.

"The Russians have always played patty-cake with Tehran," Murphy said. "I don't get it. Why would Elizaveta Bobkova be meeting with the leader of a group trying to topple the present regime?"

"And better yet," Coyne said, "why did she park herself right where Corey Fite would see her during his morning commute?"

"Corey Fite?"

"Guy with the puffy lips," Coyne said. "He's Senator Michelle Chadwick's top adviser and boy toy. No, Elizaveta's a smart lady. A certified no-shit brainiac. She's the queen of the *maskirovka*, the big show. Crystal City is the Serengeti Plain of counterintel officers. This place has more spooks per square foot than anywhere in the nation. We're everywhere, either training or running real ops. There's no way Bobkova holds a meeting down here if she wants to keep it secret. She wanted to be seen—for sure by Fite, probably by us."

"Why?" Murphy asked. "What's the angle?"

"Skullduggery and shenanigans, Grasshopper." Coyne set his coffee down hard enough that some of it geysered out of the little hole in the plastic lid. "We got the apparent leader of what's shaking out to be a viable Iranian coup sharing cake with a known Russian spymaster—who wants Senator Chadwick to be aware of the meeting. I don't know if they taught you this at Quantico, but if the Iranians and Russians are involved, they are up to their treacherous asses in no good."

3

United States Air Force Captain Will Hyatt pulled his red VW Passat into the parking lot of the twenty-four-hour Walmart just west of Highway 95. People assigned to Creech Air Force Base tended to designate where they lived by the zip code alone rather than saying North Las Vegas. He'd just scored a house nearby in 89149. The kids were loving the new pool. The Walmart was just around the corner, so he'd offered to stop by "on his way into battle" to grab a few things for the twins' birthday party.

Hyatt was sweating by the time he got out of the car, thinking he should have done a few laps himself just to cool off before work. It was early, not even seven in the morning, but heat already shimmered up from the asphalt.

He was in and out in a half-hour—mainly because he couldn't buy anything that melted or went bad during his twelve-hour shift, which was pretty much everything on his wife's list except paper plates and napkins. He'd grabbed a couple of bags of water balloons even if Shannon hadn't told him to. All seven-year-olds liked water balloons, didn't they? Will was only thirty, but it seemed like it was half a century since he'd been seven years old.

Flying drones aged you—and not for the reasons one might think. It wasn't particularly physical. He wasn't pulling any G's. Hell, the MQ-9 would suffer catastrophic failure if it had to pull two G's. He wasn't sweating his ass off in some bunker in Kandahar, or trying in vain to keep his kids' attention over an iffy Skype connection. He got to sit in a comfortable leather chair in a temperature-controlled trailer, and then go home at the end of his shift. He even had the day off tomorrow for the party.

It sounded like he was whining when he said it out loud, but therein was the problem.

Captain Hyatt was home, and yet he wasn't. Not really. How could you loiter over some ISIS shithole for weeks, watching for signs of some high-value target—and then blow that same HVT to hell and then jump into the family Volkswagen and make the hour drive back to zip code 89149 to kiss your kids and try to screw your head on straight enough to keep the wife happy? He wondered if the guys downrange missed the endless list of honey-dos that seemed so mundane, if not downright pointless, next to hunting terrorist assholes.

Shannon didn't understand. To be fair, she probably would have if he'd confided in her, but how do you tell your wife that not actually having to be eight thousand miles away from her makes you sad? "Honey, this coming home at night in between war fighting is about to make me crazy." That was the lamest of all lames. He would suck it up, kill who needed to be killed, and then replace the water heater—or whatever stupid shit happened to break around the house—and he'd be happy about it.

He unlocked his car, feeling the blast of superheated air roll out when he opened the door. This Nevada heat was killing his new Passat. He'd bought it with the retention bonus the Air Force gave him to keep him from jumping ship. He knew guys that were making double his O-3 salary flying for private contractors in the same facilities at Creech.

He waited a few seconds so the car would cool down to what the twins called "subvolcanic," and then threw the flimsy plastic bag onto the passenger-side floor. This shift was 0700 to 1900, the most volcanic part of the day. Hopefully the balloons wouldn't melt into a ball of goo in the parking lot. Balloons. He started the car and backed out, shaking his head. Who gave a shit about balloons, anyway? Hyatt was suddenly sorry for the internal fit of anger. He'd schedule a meeting with the chaplain as soon as he arrived on base. One part minister and two parts listening ear, Captain Willis was a godsend when it came to negotiating the dynamic of war fighting and yardwork.

Traffic seemed lighter this morning—which was weird, because it was the same group that went into shift every day. No one lived on Creech—less affectionately known as Crotch—so the cars coming from North Las Vegas to Indian Springs formed a slow-moving line that stretched for two miles from the gate.

Hyatt parked, leaving his window cracked to protect the balloons, and then, having second thoughts, returned to get the bag and took them inside with him. He wrote himself a note on the palm of his hand so he wouldn't forget to grab them at the end of shift.

His workspace, like those of the five hundred other drone pilots flying from Creech, was a desert-tan air-conditioned trailer tucked in with dozens of other air-conditioned trailers. A sign on the metal door said *You*

Ain't in Kansas Anymore, reminding all who entered that they were operating in a theater more than seven thousand miles away when they sat at their consoles.

He wore a flight suit—a bag, they called it—and a green David Clark headset, and sat in the left of two beige leatherette seats in front of six screens and video monitors that displayed the specifics of his MQ-9 Reaper UAV, located over Helmand Province in Afghanistan at that precise moment. The cameras offered Hyatt a remarkably clear view of the target from twelve thousand feet.

Sensor Operator Staff Sergeant Ray Deatherage sat in the right seat. The workstations were remarkably similar, but where Hyatt flew the aircraft and fired the missiles, Deatherage's job was to operate the onboard cameras and fix the laser on target to provide the missiles with an aiming point. The irony of his name was not lost, but the CO expressly ordered that no one was to refer to him as Death Rage, or Death Ray Deatherage, his skill with the laser targeting system notwithstanding.

The new guy was there, too, sitting in the back of the cramped trailer with his embossed leather notebook that said *Oreo* on the front—like the damned cookie. It was a weird cover for a CIA drone guy, but whatever. Hyatt got paid to fly the Reaper, not second-guess the intel weenies. The movies always made the spooks out to be more sinister somehow than the military, but they were just people. Weird bastards to be sure, but still just people. Brian, if that was even his real name, had been with them ever since Hyatt had sent up a report on Faisal al-Zamil's location. Brian seemed like a nice enough guy, even with his Connecticut accent. But Hyatt knew he was there for only one reason.

A cell-phone number belonging to one of Zamil's wives had been pinging off a tower near Nad Ali for the past month. Hyatt and another MQ-9 had taken turns loitering for days above the compound believed to be her residence. At twelve thousand feet, the woman never even knew they were there. Hyatt thought it weird that he, Deatherage, Brian, and the other Reaper crew were probably six of maybe eight or nine men in the world who saw her without her veil. They watched her hang out her laundry, shake her fist at the kids, or hustle out to the car to go to the market, always escorted by three dudes who were not Zamil, damn it. Sometimes, though, she went to another house some six klicks away. It was thin, but higher thought it worth the time and effort. Zamil was a known supplier of weapons to ISIS, and as such, the high-value target du jour. And this was their only real lead.

Hyatt watched the missus for six days, logging visitors, building patterns of life, noting how often she made the six-kilometer journey to the other compound, and, more important to him, where the kids were at specific times during the day. Most of his shift was during the nighttime in Afghanistan, so the bulk of his images were ghostly infrared images like something out of a video game. But a kid's head poking out of a window helped him avoid collateral damage in the event Zamil did show up.

And then the wily bastard just walked out of the house. He didn't go anywhere at first, he just took a stroll around the inner compound, and then ducked inside. Captain Hyatt had written a report, and Brian, the CIA drone guy, showed up in the middle of the next shift, less than twenty-four hours later. He wore a flight suit like everyone else, but with no nametag, unit patch, or rank insignia, there was no doubt to everyone on base who he worked for.

A good deal of Hyatt's job could be a lot like watching paint dry—but life got a little more interesting once Zamil actually came into the picture. He was wanted directly in connection to an attack that cost the lives of three American soldiers and fifteen Afghans. This would be a preplanned operation. A targeted killing based on evidence. A team of lawyers checked the law, then policy, and then the boxes to say it was okay to pull the trigger. These suits made certain any proposed strike met the laws of armed conflict, the preordained rules of engagement, and the top-secret instructions known as "spins" put in place by theater command. No laser was aimed and no trigger got pulled until the lawyers at the Air Force head shed signed off on all three.

The CIA had lawyers, too, and their own checklist, but they operated under different ROEs and had a little freer hand to pull said trigger when the time came.

That's where Brian came in.

"Movement," Staff Sergeant Deatherage said, toggling the Reaper's cameras to follow Zamil out of his house to a waiting Toyota pickup. The truck had arrived the day before, a green tarp covering a load of something that was stacked in the bed.

Captain Hyatt tapped his joystick slightly. At twelve thousand feet, it didn't have to move far or fast to keep up with the pickup. He shot a quick glance over his shoulder, but Brian held up an open hand. "We have a 'concur' on the death warrant, but let's see where he goes."

"Roger that," Hyatt said, inching along, unseen, the wrath of God more than two miles above this death-dealing asshole who was about to become one with the yellow dirt over which he now traveled.

"Second truck coming in from the north," Staff Sergeant Deatherage said, calling out what all of them were seeing.

"A transfer," Hyatt said, zoned in now. The crosshairs on his console stayed on the Toyota.

The two trucks stopped nose-to-nose in the middle of the deserted road. It was late, a half an hour until sunset. The trucks, along with every rock and pebble, cast long shadows over the orange ground.

"The new guys are wearing *shemagh*s," Deatherage said. "Impossible to ID them."

Brian was standing now, hovering just off Hyatt's left elbow, as if the extra eight feet of distance would help him see the images on the screen any better. All three men watched as Zamil and his second-in-command walked to the rear of the Toyota. The second man was Omar Khalid, who, though not quite to the level of Zamil, was adjudged bad enough by the head shed that he'd be worth qualifying for prosecution. That was the word they used. *Prosecution*.

The men in the air-conditioned trailer leaned forward slightly as the two Afghans they'd identified threw back the tarp.

Hyatt stood up without being told, and Brian slid into his seat. Agency rules of engagement were more permissive. Their lawyers said it was okay to fold unidentified third parties in with the death warrant, if those unidentified third parties were doing something illegal. Nobody wanted these guys running around with a dozen new French Mistral MANPADS. Like its American cousin the Stinger, the shoulder-fired Mistral could wreak havoc on coalition aircraft—especially the MQ-9s, which were sitting ducks if they ventured below ten thousand feet.

By the time Hyatt handed off the controls and Brian plugged in his own headset, Omar had climbed into the bed of the Toyota.

"Master Arm on," Brian said. "Weapons hot."

"Lasers hot," Deatherage said.

"Three, two, one, rifle," Brian said, pulling the trigger. "Missile away."

Standing behind his chair, Hyatt looked at the instrumentation.

The hard work had been the endless hours of waiting, watching, logging patterns. It was largely academic from this point. A single AGM-114R Romeo Hellfire II missile locked on immediately, flying toward the lased target as if on a wire. Traveling at 995 miles per hour, it took just over seven seconds to make the trip.

Zamil and the others were in the process of unloading the Mistrals and pulled the tarp a little farther, displaying the rest of the Toyota's contents the instant before the Romeo turned them to a flaming ball of fire and dust. A secondary explosion—really a series of them that happened almost too fast to distinguish—touched off just after the initial splash.

Hyatt watched the wind blow away smoke and dust.

"Master Arm off," Brian said. "Weapons safe."

"Laser safe," Deatherage said.

Brian sat still for a moment.

"Did you see that?" Captain Hyatt said.

"The secondaries." Brian gave a low whistle. "I know, right."

"That, too," Hyatt said. "I'm going to rewind the video feed a little. I think he had some MICAs."

"French MICAs?" Brian stood now, unplugging his headset and making way for Hyatt.

"Pretty sure," the captain said.

"I call that a well-armed enemy," Brian said. "French Mistrals, French MICAs. I'd like to know where they're gettin' their shit."

"That's your battle space," Hyatt said. He set a course for Kandahar. The guys on the ground there would land the bird, perform any needed maintenance, and then do a refuel so she could jump up on station for another ten to twelve hours.

A few clicks of his keyboard later, the report and relevant video were on their way to Hyatt's commanding officer at Creech. She'd run it up the chain, where it would be reviewed and discussed every step of the way, before being sent to encrypted servers at Langley, the Pentagon, and the director of national intelligence's staff at Liberty Crossing, just to make sure all bases were covered.

Brian put a friendly hand on Hyatt's shoulder. "Not to be a sociopath, Captain, but we did a good thing here. It needed to be done."

Deatherage still had the cameras focused on the carnage of the kill site.

"Yep," Hyatt said. He could get over the splashes, but he didn't get off on talking about them. "Done deal," he said.

Brian took the hint. "What's that written on your hand?"

Hyatt gave an embarrassed shrug. "A note to myself so I don't forget something for my kids' birthday." He took a final look at the smoldering crater that had once been Faisal al-Zamil before he turned his palm upright.

Balloons.

Some terrible god of war he was . . .

4

If Portugal was the westward-looking face on a map of the Iberian Peninsula, then the pinnacled rocks and secret grottoes of the Algarve coast made up the whiskers below a pointed and somewhat pensive chin. The coastal village of Benagil lay in a deep valley, equidistant from the coastal towns of Albufeira and Lagos to the east and west, respectively, one of countless whitewashed jewels on the limestone cliffs above a half-moon beach of honey-colored sand. The proximity to Africa made the Atlantic here seem almost—but not quite—like the Med.

While tourism had certainly come to this tiny village of fewer than three thousand, Benagil still had a robust fishing fleet and boasted a charm reminiscent of a quieter, more innocent Portugal. This naïveté made it an excellent location for Hugo Gaspard to conduct his business. There were enough tourists with money that the arms dealer did not have to go without the creature comforts to which he'd grown accustomed. The local gendarmerie, though intelligent enough, tended to attune themselves to car break-ins or burglaries at holiday villas. The mere idea of an international crime boss completely overwhelmed their radar.

Gaspard had been down to this same beach three days in a row, while he waited for the Russians to show up. He made the mistake of walking the hundred fifty meters down the hill from his Mercedes on the first day. There was parking along the narrow road on the cliffs overlooking the sea, but the corpulent Frenchman was much too fond of fine wine and rich pastries. Walking more than a few meters aggravated his gout—and his heart, and his lungs, and the bone spurs on his heels. Worse than that, walking made him feel poor.

Today, he'd ordered his driver to drop him off near the handicapped parking spot, as close to the trail to the beach as possible. The driver would stay with the car while the other three accompanied him to the beach. One could not be too careful these days.

Gaspard stripped off his loose shirt as soon as he got out of the Mercedes. He would have done it earlier, but his ponderous belly made much movement in the backseat problematic. He'd already changed into his swimsuit in the villa and stepped out of his trousers on the side of the road, throwing them into the car on top of his shirt. The suit, a small triangle of red spandex, would have been considered tiny even on a man of much smaller stature. Gaspard's belly hung low enough that a casual observer could be excused for thinking he wore nothing at all. Gaspard didn't care. He had little to prove—and enough money that he could even buy respect if anyone had a problem with the way he dressed.

His meeting with the Russians was two hours away. The turquoise-and-cobalt water was much too cool to swim, but the air was a pleasant—and a slightly unseasonable—twenty-five Celsius. The cloudless sky made it feel even warmer. He would use the time waiting to work on his tan.

Praia de Benagil was not an incredibly large beach. It could be packed with pale British tourists in the summer, but now, in May, he had the place almost to himself. A few climbers, probably Americans, scrambled up the rock cliffs to the east. A Nordic-looking couple with a small child braved the chilly water, splashing in the surf near three wooden fishing boats that lay on the sand on the western end of the beach, by the walkway up toward the village.

Gaspard spied a slender woman in a black two-piece as he tromped along the beach leaving splay-footed divots in the sand. She had staked her claim in the center of the beach. She lay provocatively on her back, her head propped up on a woven-grass beach bag, the brim of an almost comically huge hat shielding her face while she read a paperback. Gaspard thought she might be a blonde, maybe with a splash of freckles across her nose, but the hat made it difficult to be sure. That did not matter to him. She was a leggy thing, with all the right swells and curves and a minuscule suit that obviously meant she sought companionship. Anyone with a figure like that, who wore such tiny bits of cloth, was . . . well, looking for it.

He would sit near enough to strike up a casual conversation, and see where it progressed. The French were not animals. *He* was not an animal—not any longer, having attained a certain amount of refinement with his newfound wealth. He would be discreet, smooth, the perfect gentleman. If that did not work, he would let her know how rich he was. Whatever method he employed, Hugo Gaspard intended to take this nubile creature to his villa by midafternoon. She could drink wine and eat chocolates while he met with the Russians, and then they would spend the evening together.

It was a good plan. Gaspard was a man of vision—and he could envision it—every delectable moment.

Gaspard's three bodyguards flanked him, gazing outward with the predatory looks he paid them for. Gaspard himself had carried a pistol most of his life—since his time as a thuggish youth running a string of hundred-franc whores in the Bois de Boulogne. His lunatic mother—a prostitute and a heroin addict—had passed to him one single piece of worthwhile wisdom during her short life: *A man who carries many keys may look important—but a truly important man hires someone to carry the keys for him.* Now, having made enough money to buy all the whores in the park, Hugo Gaspard paid others to carry the guns.

Sun glinted off the thick gold chain that nestled among the rolls of his fleshy neck. Lines of sweat dripped down his chest. He nodded at a spot two meters from the woman, standing by while two of his men laid out his towel. It was extra large, to provide coverage from the sand against his sizable breadth. The third bodyguard, a bulldog of a man with a nose flattened by many fights, eyed the young woman suspiciously. His name was Farrin, and his threatening glare was certainly overkill. The woman had not approached them. They were setting up near her. And anyway, she could not be dangerous. She was so young, so deliciously . . . breakable.

"Relax," Gaspard said, loud enough for the young woman to hear. It would not hurt for her to know that Gaspard was a man in charge of other men. "This peach is nearly naked. What harm could she possibly bring to me?"

She glanced up from her book—a mindless romance written in English, judging from the bare-chested muscleman on the cover—and then she looked away, pretending to ignore him. Faint parallel scars on her upper thigh, like a tribal initiation or ritual, became visible as Gaspard got closer. There was a story there, to be sure, and he would have it before the night was over.

Gaspard situated himself on his belly, grunting a little as he wallowed a depression into the sand beneath his towel, enabling him to lie relatively level. Resting his jowls on stacked hands, he could ensure an even tan on his back while still gazing sideways at the young woman.

"Are you American?" he asked, eyes half closed, sleepy from the radiation beating down from the sun and the exertion of walking fifteen meters up the beach.

She raised the brim of her hat and gave him a long look, as if considering whether or not to reply.

"Dutch," she said. "Why do you ask?"

"Your book is written in English," Gaspard said and chuckled. "What do the English know of romance? French romances are much better, both in the writing—and in the flesh."

"You read a lot of romance novels, then?" the young woman asked.

Gaspard shrugged. "It is a logical argument. The French language is a romance of the tongue. Just speak a few words of it and you will see for yourself."

"I am to assume you are French?"

"Oui," he said. *"Tu parles français?"*

She held up the thumb and forefinger of her free hand. *"Un peu."* A little. "I prefer English."

"Pity," Gaspard said. "'Please rub my back with oil' sounds much too forward in English."

The young woman stifled a laugh—a good sign, to be sure. "You are certainly the bold one."

"I have a very important meeting in two hours. That allows me only a finite amount of time in which to meet you, dance around the niceties of social discourse, and then invite you to my villa before dinner."

The woman lowered the book to her chest, still open, and cocked her head to one side. Perfect brunette locks brushing tan shoulders. Not a blonde after all, but, oh, the glorious freckles splashed across her nose. "*Before* dinner?"

The young woman scooted into a sitting position, hugging exquisite knees. Gaspard could plainly see the lines of many scars along her thighs—an automotive accident, or possibly an athletic injury. He could picture her, splashed with freckles while she played football with the local boys. She may have been a *garçon manqué*—a tomboy—growing up, but she was certainly all woman now.

"I see no point in wasting time," Gaspard said. "As I mentioned, I have a meeting in two hours."

She finally closed the book, but kept it clutched in her hand. "An 'important meeting,' you said."

"I said 'very important meeting,' to be precise." Gaspard rolled half up on his side so he could look more directly at the object of his conquest. A line of sand pressed into the edge of his belly where it had escaped the confines of the beach towel. He brushed it off with sausage fingers. Two gold rings caught the sunlight. "No point in beating around the bush—"

"Or wasting time," the young woman said.

"Quite," Gaspard said. "I am already rich, but this meeting will make me richer, I dare say, than anyone you have ever met." He leaned forward, looking back and forth from the sea to the cliffs before lowering his voice. "My meeting is with the Russians."

"*The* Russians?" the young woman said, wide-eyed, mocking him just a little. "All of them."

"You are quite the forward girl," Gaspard said.

She smiled playfully. "No point in beating around the bush."

She scooted across the sand on her knees, extending her free hand.

"I am Lucile," she said.

Gaspard brightened. "A magnificent French name!" Still on his side, belly and chest sagging toward the beach, he took her hand and kissed it. "I am Hugo. *Encantado.*"

"I thought you were French?"

"When in Rome," Gaspard said. "Or Lisbon . . ."

Gaspard's bodyguards perked up. Farrin, especially, grew apoplectic about anything or anyone who got between him and his boss, but Gaspard waved them away. He'd warned them as soon as he'd seen the woman—targeted her, really—that he wanted space, ordering them to keep watch from a comfortable distance of at least twenty meters away. Having bodyguards showed everyone he was rich. Bodyguards who treated him as if he might shatter at any moment only made him look frightened, weak. It was a delicate balance.

Lucile was close enough to smell now, *earthy*, Gaspard thought, like warm rain.

"You are visiting Portugal?" Gaspard said.

"Small talk?" Lucile said. "I thought we were dispensing with such things."

"Touché," Gaspard said.

"Are you well and truly rich?"

The Frenchman smiled. "More money than you could possibly imagine."

"Oh." Lucile scrunched her freckled nose. "When it comes to money, I can imagine quite a lot. Do you really want oil on your back?"

"I do indeed," Gaspard said.

"And you will buy me dinner?"

"Indeed."

She leaned toward her bag. "I have some oil here—"

Gaspard grabbed her by the toes—tan things, painted pink—and thought that his reflexes were still very good. "You must use my oil," he said. Farrin marched over an instant later, shoving a plastic bottle of suntan oil at the woman. It was greasy from recent use.

"Thank you," Gaspard said to Farrin. "Now go away." He released the woman's foot and let his face fall forward, toward the towel. He turned slightly toward Lucile, words muffled. "I know it may be difficult for you to comprehend, but it is possible to kill someone with poisoned suntan oil." He raised wildly overgrown eyebrows up and down. "The process will be easier if you straddle me."

"Are you being serious?" Lucile knelt beside him. "Poisoned suntan oil?"

He wallowed deeper into the sand, head on his hands again, squinting into the sun. "There are people who do not like me very much."

"I find that difficult to believe," the young woman said. She threw her leg across his rump, climbing aboard to pour a line of oil onto the leathery folds below Hugo Gaspard's hairy shoulder blades.

The book lay in the sand beside her right knee—within immediate reach.

5

Domingo "Ding" Chavez stood on the edge of the limestone cliff above the eastern end of the Praia de Benagil, eyes fixed at the small screen on the controller in Bartosz "Midas" Jankowski's callused hands.

"She saw it," Chavez said, gritting his teeth.

"Relax, boss," Jankowski said. "How about you exhibit a little faith?"

"I'm telling you, she saw it."

"That's a big nope," Jankowski said, popping the *p* for emphasis. "I'm keeping the bird in the sun. She didn't see anything but glare." Working the bird—a pocket-size unmanned aerial vehicle called a Snipe Nano—the retired Delta colonel swung his legs easily, as if he were sitting on a boat dock and not perched on the edge of a sheer seventy-foot drop. He was tied in, but that little factoid didn't do much for Chavez's churning stomach.

"You better be right," Chavez said. "The last thing we need is for some beach bunny to tip off the target that we have an eye in the sky."

Chavez had let his hair grow out over his ears, as he often did on ops where he didn't want to look like the former Army NCO that he was. Even absent the military haircut, it was obvious to anyone with experience downrange that

Chavez had been around the combat block. That wasn't exactly rare in this day and age. There were enough warfighters coming home who'd seen the elephant that he could at least blend in at the mall.

Domingo Chavez was in that height range that tall people called short and short people called tall. Good genes and a lifetime of PT gave him an athletic build, even in his late forties—an age his son reminded him was "too old to die tragically young." JP was a good kid, but had he known the dangers his father faced "for reals, yo" on a daily basis, he wouldn't have been such a smartass.

Chavez and Midas had counted four bodyguards, three on the beach plus the guy guarding the vehicles— a gray Mercedes that served as Gaspard's limo and a dark Peugeot they apparently used as a follow car.

The rest of Ding's team was doing some bouldering this morning while they watched. Hiding in plain sight was the only way to operate in these small villages where there was a hundred percent chance that you'd run into your target a dozen times a day. Scrambling around the rocks allowed Chavez and his team to blend in, to be noticed for something other than what they actually were—operatives from The Campus. The off-the-books intelligence organization worked under the guise of the financial arbitrage firm Hendley Associates, across the Potomac from D.C.

Free climbing over the ocean was fairly safe—so long as you knew what you were doing. Chavez did not, so he spent his time at the top, looking down, happy to keep his feet planted on the level. Hands and fingers were made for pressing triggers and slapping the shit out of bad guys— not hanging on to minuscule rock nipples on the face of some cliff. Still, he'd dressed to look the part—nylon running shorts, a tank top, Scarpa approach shoes with sticky soles, and a harness for a small bag of climbing chalk. Midas was dressed much the same, while Jack Ryan, Jr., worked his way up the rock face, shirtless, wearing skin-tight Lycra climbing shorts and pointy La Sportiva climbing shoes that made him look like some kind of ballet dancer. Chavez was just old enough that he would have looked like the creepy old dude in bicycle shorts had he tried for the same getup. Lisanne Robertson climbed with Jack, also wearing Lycra shorts—which she wore much better than Ryan did—and a black sports bra.

Not officially a Campus operative, the former Marine and police officer was the transportation coordinator and in-flight attendant for the Campus/Hendley Associates Gulfstream. Because she often pulled security when the plane set down in hostile situations, John Clark, director of operations—and Ding's father-in-law—folded her into tactical training sessions and range time. She had zero experience running surveillance detection or tailing a target, but she was as savvy as Chavez had ever seen. She was also an accomplished climber, often hitting the rock gym in Bethesda after an evening team PT workout that left Chavez looking for the nearest couch and a cold beer.

Lisanne's voice came over the net, as if she knew Ding was pondering her climbing skill. "I don't think either of them saw it," she said.

"Told you so," Midas said, without looking up from the palm-size controller. "I still have eyes on our arms-dealing asshole—and the girl is still clueless. You gotta learn to trust me, boss."

———

Lucile Fournier used her left hand to distribute the oil, keeping her right hand dry. Clasping with her thighs, she leaned forward, digging into the fleshy back with her forearms and elbows now, paying particular attention to the base of the disgustingly flabby neck—searching for just the right spot. Gaspard's hair was well groomed but longish, the dark curls reaching below his collar, had he been wearing a shirt. *Good.* That would help to hide what she had in mind.

He moaned under her rough ministrations, his alligatored skin shining bronze in the sun.

Plouc, Fournier thought. Such a slob. Gaspard might have money, but he would never have class. But she laughed as though she were oh-so-lucky to be riding on this fat pig. She shot a quick backward glance under the crook of her arm, checking the location of the three bodyguards. As she suspected, they were behind her, slumping on the gunwales of a couple of fishing skiffs that were pulled up on the sand, more than twenty meters away. The black bottoms of her swimsuit had a small rip over her left cheek, and she was certain that all three men, including the more astute Farrin, were completely mesmerized by the flexing muscles of her toned derriere as the rip opened and closed and opened again in concert with her movements.

"Have you been in Portugal long?" she asked.

Gaspard grunted in time to her kneading. "Now . . . you start . . . the small talk . . ."

She ignored the gibe. "Do you know *sebastianismo?*"

"I confess that I do not," he said.

"King Sebastião," she said. "He was also a rich man. Like you, he, too, had an important meeting, his against the Moors. Unfortunately, he was forever lost in the deserts of North Africa. The word *sebastianismo* comes from that. A failed venture—hope for something that can never be."

"Stop," Gaspard said, sounding pained. "Your history lesson depresses me."

"As you wish," she said. "But I do like the word. *Sebastianismo . . .*"

She leaned forward now, kneading with her left arm, pressing her breast against Gaspard's back. Her right hand slipped into the paperback book at her knee and retrieved the MSP derringer hidden in the hollowed pages. A whirring noise above her head, like a dragonfly—or a passing bullet—almost caused her to fumble with the pistol. She regained her composure and brought the gun up quickly before the bodyguards could see it, covering it with a cupped palm. Pistol secure, she turned, looking for the source of the noise, half expecting to see Farrin standing there, ready to blow her head off. *Merde!* She released a pent-up breath. Nothing but a blinding sun. *Maybe it really was a dragonfly.* She willed her body to relax and become more fluid, and then returned to the task ahead.

The Soviet-era Malogabaritnyj Spetsialnyj Pistolet fit her hand perfectly—better, in fact, than the Beretta she customarily carried. The Small Special Pistol had first seen action with KGB units in the early 1970s. Its specialized ammunition utilized a captive piston inside the brass casing that drove a 7.62x37 projectile, similar to that of an AK-47, out a short barrel at a speed just shy of five hundred feet per second. The gases from the detonated propellant—and nearly all the resulting noise—remained trapped inside the cartridge, rendering the MSP very close to "Hollywood quiet." The ballistics were quite limp, something around half of the diminutive .32 auto. But the Russians had proven many times over the last four decades that a Spitzer bullet delivered at point-blank range more than made up for the round's middling performance.

Lucile leaned forward slightly, digging in with her elbow to draw a grunt of pleasure from Gaspard. She nodded to herself. That would be plenty loud enough to cover the noise.

He groaned. "Masterful. Are you certain you are not French?" He clenched his buttocks beneath her groin, making her want to vomit. "I am usually the one to do the riding," he mumbled. "If you know my meaning."

Pistol hidden between her breasts now, Lucile clutched with her thighs to retain her balance and leaned farther forward, lips touching Gaspard's ear. The smell of his sweat was nauseating.

". . . *courir sur le haricot,*" she said. Literally "run on the bean," the phrase more figuratively meant he had gotten on her last nerve.

Gaspard froze, suddenly realizing Lucile was not who she'd said she was.

"*Tu* es *française,*" he whispered, face still buried in his towel. You *are* French!

Instead of answering, Lucile dug deep into the muscles of his back with her left elbow. With her right hand, she pressed the MSP against the depression at the base of his neck, just below his skull, aiming downward. She pulled the trigger in perfect time with the resulting grunt brought on by her elbow.

Gaspard sagged in the sand, all the air leaving his lungs with a heavy, gurgling groan, his brain stem clipped at the base. *Fini.*

Lucile continued to knead Gaspard's flaccid muscles, chatting amiably. This man had never been anything more than a hollow shell, so it was not at all difficult to talk to him when he was dead.

She stopped abruptly as if he'd said something to her, then tugged at the seat of her panties, drawing the body-guards' attention there, away from the blood and bone on the towel where this pig's lower jaw had been. She looked up at Farrin.

"He wants some wine," she said, sotto voce, as if she were letting Gaspard drift off to sleep.

Farrin scowled.

Lucile gave him a *Suit yourself* shrug. "I have a bottle in my car if you want to get it."

The bodyguard gave a toss of his bulldog head up the hill as if to say *Get it yourself.* She knew that's what he would do, if only to watch her walk away in the torn bikini bottoms.

A scant twenty feet below the edge of the cliff where Ding and Midas had set up shop, Jack Ryan, Jr., wedged a knife hand into a rock crevice, made a fist, and used the resulting friction to pull himself closer to the face. The pain against his knuckles was a welcome penance. He'd decided to swear off women for a while, at least the conquest of them. Climbing above him, a perfect triangle of perspiration where tight climbing pants met the small of her back, Lisanne Robertson was making the decision difficult. She was pleasant to climb with and behind, but she was also a workmate and friend, certainly not someone he should be fraternizing with. *Don't dip your pen in company ink,* Clark had baldly warned everyone after Dominic Caruso and Adara Sherman had become an item. It didn't matter. Ryan had had such shitty luck with women lately that he'd decided to remain celibate in the near term anyway.

Lisanne was the better climber and took the lead, picking the route. She moved effortlessly, slowing down for Jack's benefit. He was plenty athletic, getting more than twenty miles a week on the roads around his home in Old Town Alexandria and at least two nights a week with a local soccer league. If climbing were simply a function of strength and size, he should have been able to match this lithe woman pitch for pitch. Fitness was vital, and though Jack's six-foot-plus wingspan definitely helped, it turned out that climbing had a lot in common with ballet.

Lisanne hugged the rock face, stretching her Lycra climbing shorts to reach with an incredibly long leg for a toehold as high as her waist. Directly below her, Ryan behaved as a warrior monk and did the gentlemanly thing, turning away to look down at the beach and their target.

Ryan had little doubt that Hugo Gaspard was here to meet with the two Russians who had just arrived in the village of Carvoeiro, some five kilometers along the coast to the west. According to Dom Caruso, the men might as well have had GRU tattooed on their foreheads. The location of the meeting was still up in the air. Caruso and Adara Sherman kept an eye on the Russians, while

John Clark kept an eye on them, providing countersurveillance and protective overwatch.

As with the lion's share of Campus operations, the road to action had been prefaced with a hell of a lot of reading, analysis, and conjecture—some of it educated, some more along the lines of a WAG—or wild-ass guess.

Hendley Associates' proximity to the Pentagon allowed the Internet gurus of The Campus to strain terabytes of raw data in the way of intelligence information from daily encrypted transmissions from Fort Meade. Mary Pat Foley, the director of national intelligence and confidante of the President, was fully aware of the broad mission of The Campus, but details were kept in house, giving Liberty Crossing—home of the director of national security—and the White House deniability. Sort of.

A transmission grab from Creech Air Force Base had shown eleven seconds of footage from an MQ-9 Reaper drone loitering over Helmand, Afghanistan. The video was grainy, but analysts were fairly certain the guy in the picture had gotten his hands on a half-dozen MICA rockets.

Jack Junior had worked up the report, identifying the ISIS leader in the video as Faisal al-Zamil, a Saudi national—or at least he had been until the Hellfire missile from the MQ-9 had turned him into fine desert shellac. Zamil came from a wealthy family with bank accounts in various locations around Europe. With the help of Campus Internet savant Gavin Biery, Ryan had been able to follow money from an account in Amsterdam to several pass-through shell companies that would have fooled a casual observer—to a mid-level French arms dealer who thought he was more important than he actually was, named Hugo Gaspard. A tap on the Frenchman's Paris phone had revealed the appointment with the Russians in Portugal.

After an unofficial and off-site deconfliction meeting with DNI Foley to be certain that no one from any of her sixteen U.S. intelligence agencies were already birddogging Gaspard, John Clark brought his little team to the Algarve coast—to watch a very tan and wrinkled walrus of a French arms dealer wallow around on the beach with a cute brunette in a black bikini.

"The girl's leaving." Ryan spoke into the cell-phone mic hanging next to his lips. "Our rabbit's meeting must be imminent."

"Maybe," Ding said. Ryan caught a flash of him peering over the edge.

Below, the brunette trotted up the trail toward the road. "She left her bag and towel behind," Lisanne said.

Ding's voice crackled in his ear. "I think she saw the drone."

"Would you stop with that, boss?" Midas said. "She didn't see—holy shit!"

Ryan looked at girl—running faster now—and Gaspard, still hanging out on his towel. All three bodyguards were slouching by the overturned boat.

"What?"

"Jack," Midas said. "You and Lisanne should keep eyes on the girl."

"Roger that," Ryan said.

"Talk to me," Ding said. "What are you seeing?"

Midas held up the drone controller's display. "See right here in the upper corner of the screen? Unless I'm mistaken, that's a chunk of Hugo Gaspard's brain in the sand next to what used to be his face."

Clinging to the rock with one foot and a fist, Ryan scrambled up and over the edge behind Lisanne. On his belly, he looked down toward the beach in time to see two bodyguards running to their boss while the third, a short, stocky man, sprinted up the path leading toward town, pistol in hand.

"She just jumped on a motorcycle," Lisanne said.

"Got it," Chavez said. "A red Ducati, heading west, toward Carvoeiro."

Clark and the others were there.

Ryan grabbed the small daypack that held his gear, running toward the rented midnight-blue Audi A4.

"Go with him," Ryan heard Chavez say, half a moment before Lisanne Robertson slid into the passenger seat and slammed the door. "And keep your commo on. I want real-time COP."

COP was a common operating picture. Their radios had GPS locators that pinged on both Chavez's and John Clark's phones, showing the location of every member of the team superimposed on a map of the area.

Ryan started the car while Lisanne took a plastic case the size of a pill bottle from his backpack and popped it open. She poured the tiny flesh-colored earpiece into her open palm and held it out to Ryan. He took it and popped it into his ear at the same time he punched the accelerator, sending up a rooster tail of gravel from the rear tires. Lisanne handed him a loop of copper wire and attached mic, along with a radio about the size of a deck of playing cards. Ryan put the wire over his neck and switched on the radio, clipping it to his shorts as he drove.

"Check. Check," he said.

The sound of Midas's voice filled his ear.

"Have you, five-by-five."

"Stay with her," Chavez said. "But do not engage."

"Copy," Ryan said. He pressed the accelerator and cut the wheel to the left, fishtailing into a drift that took him from the parking lot and onto the main road without wasting time on the angle. "We should be catching up to her in two minutes."

Ryan turned to Lisanne, who was working with her own radio.

Ryan took another corner at speed, outside, inside, outside, cutting the apex and hearing the tires chatter on the pavement. Still no sign of the red Ducati.

He straightened the wheel, shooting another glance at Lisanne. "You okay with this?" he said. "You're not operational." He regretted how superior the words sounded as soon as they left his lips.

"Fancy driving," she said, putting in the earpiece and ignoring the premise of his comment. "They send you to quite a bit of specialized training?"

"Yep," Ryan said. He slid around another corner, catching a glimpse of the bike, and then the gray Mercedes, disappear over the crest of a hill ahead.

Lisanne settled into her seat. She opened the map on her phone, then turned it toward Ryan, eyebrows up, as if to ask a silent question. He gave her a slight nod. He would drive, she would watch the map and give him the big picture.

"We're still heading northwest on 1273," she said for the benefit of Jack and the others on the team. "Gaspard's bodyguards are right behind the woman, dark gray, late-model Mercedes sedan . . . about one kilometer ahead. She has lots of choices. Hard to say if she's going inland or is going to cut toward Carvoeiro."

Jack swerved left, narrowly missing an elderly man out walking with his little white dog beside a hedgerow. The man shook a handful of mail, yelling as they went past. Jack stayed to the center of the narrow road, working through the possibilities. "Smart money says she'll get out of here after a hit, but if she's working for the Russians, she may be running toward reinforcements. Good chance we'll be heading your way, Mr. C."

6

It was difficult to say if the row after row of white-washed hotels and tapas bars spilled down from the cliffs of Carvoeiro or crawled back up from the sea.

Dominic Caruso and Adara Sherman sat together at a covered table at the Più Grand Café, one of many restaurants located along the road leading down to the beach. Mournful guitar chords poured from overhead speakers, traditional Portuguese fado, prompting Caruso to sigh.

"They must like to be sad here."

"I like it," Adara said. "They call it *saudade*—irreparable loss, longing."

"No kidding," Dom said. "It makes me long for some classic rock. Give me some AC/DC over this stuff any day."

Though they were on surveillance, the chemistry between them was real, so they did not have to pretend to be a couple. Caruso was a credentialed special agent with the FBI, "on loan" to The Campus. He wore a loose cotton shirt with the sleeves rolled up over strong forearms, khaki slacks, and comfortable lace-up Rockports that he could run in.

Adara Sherman was in her mid-thirties, with blond hair that fell just over her ears; her white shorts and navy-blue polo accented her propensity for CrossFit. She'd been

Hendley Associates' director of transportation, dealing with travel logistics as well as physical security of the company G5 when it was on the ground. It was the position now held by Lisanne Robertson, a fact that gave hope of eventual promotion to the latter. Sherman was a former Navy corpsman and always had at least a small tactical medic's kit within easy reach. The relationship between her and Caruso had happened naturally, and, so far at least, they'd proven they could work together without any issues. Caruso told himself that at times like this the fact that they were a couple made the op even more believable. Clark and Hendley weren't altogether happy about the work relationship, but neither of them tried to put a stop to it. The heart wanted what the heart wanted, even in the intelligence community. There were plenty of operational couples in the FBI and the CIA, though they rarely worked on the same cases. Even Mary Pat Foley, the director of national intelligence, and her husband had been spies together back in the day.

Their table at Più Grand gave Sherman and Caruso a direct line of sight to the covered balcony on the second floor of a tapas bar and restaurant called Casa Ibérica. There had been no time to put listening devices in place. In fact, it was little more than luck that they had such a good visual. The two Russians had arrived a half-hour before, first getting a table at a small restaurant across the street from Dom and Adara called the Bar Restaurante O Barco. John Clark had walked past, aware that they were probably checking for a tail. He was proven right five minutes later when the Russians stood and dropped their menus on the sidewalk table, apparently unable to find anything to their liking. They walked down the ramp to the beach, on the sidewalk just feet away from Dom and Adara, before returning to get a table at Casa Ibérica, up the switchback hill from the promenade of shops and restaurants above Carvoeiro Beach. Guarding against another turn-and-burn by the Russians, Clark sat down across the street on the same level as Adara.

"Eyes wide," Clark said into the mic on the neck loop under his shirt, as if muttering at his menu.

Dom toyed with a shrimp in his *cataplana*, a seafood-and-pork stew. "Copy. Our friends are just sitting there, chatting over their beers."

Adara paused for a beat, waiting to see if Clark responded or if Lisanne came back with a sitrep on where they were with the fleeing motorcyclist.

"I'm thinking they're either in the dark about Gaspard," she said, "or they are complicit to the hit."

Jack's voice crackled over the net. "She's heading right toward you. Makes me think they're probably involved."

"Maybe," Clark said with a whispered grunt. "I don't see any countersurveillance, but guys like this will surely have some. We do."

Adara took out her phone and raised it to take a couple of photos of Dom with the sea behind him. She handed him the phone and let him take some of her. Like a giddy couple on holiday on the Portuguese coast, they put the phone on the table between them and scrolled through the photos, paying special attention to anyone behind either of them that looked out of place. Two men behind Caruso caught their attention. Both were young, rawboned, with shaggy blond hair. Their clothing was just ill-fitting enough that it looked like it had been purchased by a distant aunt who'd never met them—or an

SVR quartermaster. One of them hid discreetly behind a menu and the other turned his face.

"Watch this, John," Adara said. She motioned a waitress over and asked her to take a photo before sliding her chair around beside Dom. Again, the men ducked their heads.

"Got 'em," Clark said. "Somebody's cage just got rattled."

Farrin Galle pounded on the dashboard with his left hand, his right touching the butt of the Steyr GB pistol at his belt. He was originally from Belgium. Seven years in the French Foreign Legion's elite 2e Régiment Étranger de Parachutistes had ingrained in the bullish thug enough tactical sense not to draw his weapon during a chase. There was too much of a chance the handgun would be dislodged during even a minor fender bender. And anyway, shooting was too good for the bitch. What he really wanted to do was cut her up in tiny little pieces and then step on each piece before feeding them to the crows. It wasn't that she'd killed his boss—there was no love lost for Hugo Gaspard—but this woman had had the balls to kill him right under Farrin's nose. There was no way to keep something like that a secret. Word would get out. Good work would dry up and he'd be forced to protect low-level drug dealers, or worse yet, some prima donna actor. No, this little brunette bitch was dead. If he managed to kill her, that might salvage his reputation, at least a little.

"Want me to run her over, boss?" Yves, the man behind the wheel, said.

"That would be most welcome." Farrin nodded at the

fleeing Ducati, now fading into the distance. "But would you not have to catch up with her to do that?"

Instead of answering, Yves stomped on the accelerator.

Farrin glanced in the side mirror. The dark Audi loomed larger as it gained on them. They were likely in league with the assassin. Louis and Alain would make short work of them.

Alain's voice crackled over the yellow FRS handy-talky in the seat between Farrin's legs. He snatched it up.

"Go."

"We're in position, boss," Alain said.

"Take them," Farrin said. "And make an example of it."

"Black Peugeot," Lisanne said. "Coming up behind us fast."

"I see them," Jack said through clenched teeth. He swerved the rental car back and forth, keeping the Peugeot from moving up alongside. He had a Smith & Wesson M&P nine-millimeter in his daypack, but shooting from a moving vehicle at another moving vehicle with a pistol was not just a last resort, it was a waste of meager ammunition. Beyond that, there was little point in relying on 128 grains of lead when he had three thousand pounds of metal at his fingertips.

The guys in the Peugeot didn't understand the concept, because the passenger rolled down his window and leaned out, aiming over dark sunglasses to open up with some kind of SMG. Both Lisanne and Ryan ducked instinctively when a couple of lucky rounds thwacked into the trunk.

"We're taking some fire," Lisanne said, her voice matter-of-fact, describing the offending Peugeot over the net for the rest of the team.

Jack rolled his shoulders to keep them loose, willing himself not to squeeze the wheel as he continued to swerve the Audi across both lanes. "So much for blending in. Someone is bound to call the cops."

"Hang tight." Ding's voice broke squelch on the radio. "We're three-quarters of a mile behind them and gaining."

"They're resorting to spray-and-pray," Ryan said. "But I like their odds if they have enough ammo. Good chance they'll get off a lucky shot by the time you can close the gap." He shifted in his seat, settling in deeper behind the wheel, reaching a conclusion. "I'm going to try something."

Ding inhaled so deeply his mic picked up the groan. "Jack . . ."

"Trust me," Ryan said. The machine gun clattered behind them again, this time shattering the Audi's rear window. "I think they're going to try and PIT us."

Lisanne craned around to look over her shoulder, and then up at Ryan. Her head cocked to one side, dark brow arched. "So what's your plan?"

Jack turned and gave her a quick wink.

"I'm going to let them."

Yves slowed the Mercedes on the outskirts of Carvoeiro. "She disappeared, boss," he said, pushing a lock of blond mop out of his face and gulping back the croak of failure.

"This I can see," Farrin said. He slammed a big hand into the dash, a blow he really wanted to deliver to Yves, but that would have made the imbecile run into a utility pole. "Get out!"

"Boss?"

Farrin's voice grew quiet. "Get out of the car and switch seats. I will drive."

"They won't get a chance to actually PIT us," Jack explained to a slack-jawed Lisanne Robertson—and the others holding their collective breath on the net.

"Nah," Lisanne said. "They'll just put a few bullets in our skulls."

"There's that," Jack said, watching the car behind him grow larger in the rearview mirror after slowing down for a sharp left curve. The guys in the Peugeot had to get lucky only once. For this to work, Jack had to do everything right.

The PIT, or pursuit intervention technique, allowed the driver of one vehicle to use his front quarter-panel to untrack the rear wheels of a second vehicle while traveling at highway speed. When done correctly, the vehicle on the receiving end simply spun out of the way, allowing the vehicle initiating the PIT to continue driving, or, as in the case of the guys in the Peugeot, turn around and murder Jack and Lisanne while they sat stuck helplessly in the ditch.

Lisanne leaned forward, craning to see around a white stucco building as they reached the junction with Route 124–1. Lagoa and Portimão lay to the right. To the left were Carvoeiro and the sea. "I can't see left," she said. "But I've got a good view toward Lagoa, and the bike is nowhere in sight."

Ryan punched the gas, shooting around the corner to the left as the black Peugeot rounded the corner fifty meters behind them.

"Turning toward Carvoeiro on 124–1," she said over the radio, her calm voice belying her wide-eyed look.

Jack brought the Audi out of another tight turn and mashed the accelerator to the floor on a relative straightaway. Houses gave way to tree-covered limestone hills on either side of the road. If he was going to do anything, this was the place. "You know the OODA Loop?" He asked without looking up.

"Of course," Lisanne said.

The OODA Loop described the steps the human brain had to go through in order to take action— Observe, Orient, Decide, Act. An interruption of the process meant starting over—or a costly mistake. Disorient someone, they had to observe again, before making a new decision. Change things up as that decision was being made, and the original action was often executed, even if it was wrong.

"Well," Jack continued. "I'm gonna throw a wrench in their loop."

Ding came over the net again. "Can you make it into town? I show you just a couple of klicks out."

Another volley of fire answered the question. More rounds popped against the Audi's trunk.

"Not likely," Jack said.

He tapped the brakes, bringing the speed down to just below seventy miles an hour. His serpentines back and forth across the winding two-lane grew less pronounced, allowing the Peugeot to inch up on the left side.

Lisanne slid down in her seat so she could just see out

the side mirror. "Now we're down to the nut-cuttin', as my father used to say. Jack . . . guy on the right is lining up for a shot."

"I'm counting on it," Ryan said. He kept an eye on the Peugeot in the side mirror, holding his breath as the passenger leaned all the way out to take careful aim in the buffeting wind. The guy seemed sure in the knowledge that since Jack was trying to run, he'd just keep running.

Twenty feet away, fifteen, then ten, the shooter leaned half his torso out the window.

Jack stomped the brakes hard, coming just shy of locking them up. He let off immediately so he maintained control, but the damage was already done. The Peugeot sped past. Metal screamed against metal, catching the hapless shooter and smearing him between the two vehicles with a sickening thump and dragging him out the window of the Peugeot.

The decision for his next move already made, Ryan floored the accelerator again before the other driver could reorient. He nosed the Audi up next to the Peugeot's rear tire. Tapping the brakes slightly caused the Audi to squat, stabilizing it as he cut the wheel toward the other car. At nearly seventy miles an hour, it required little more than a kiss to untrack the Peugeot, but Ryan started his PIT aggressively, giving the other car a solid nudge. He straightened the wheel immediately after impact. The Peugeot fishtailed to the right, continuing to spin around in front of the Audi, crashing against a low limestone wall facing the other direction and flipping up on its side. Steam poured from the radiator.

"And . . . they're done," Lisanne said. She rose half

out of her seat so she could get a better look as they flew down the road toward Carvoeiro.

"Son of a bitch!" It was Midas on the radio, obviously passing a piece of the dead shooter in the road. "That had to hurt."

"You guys okay?" Ding asked next, checking on his troops.

"Good to go," Ryan said, breathing for the first time in thirty seconds. "But the Ducati is in the wind."

7

Ryan cut left on a cobblestone road that led into the hills just before entering Carvoeiro proper. Distant sirens said the Guarda Nacional was responding to the accident from several directions. The lack of a rear window as well as an untold number of bullet holes in the Audi's body made police contact a certainty if they were spotted.

Lisanne took the moment of relative calm to change out of the tight climbing shoes and into a pair of Brooks runners from her daypack. They rode on in silence while they worked through the quiet neighborhood of vacation rental villas and down the hill toward town, leaving the radio net to the others. Ryan figured he had a good fifteen minutes before the two or three Guarda units stationed in Carvoeiro broke loose from the scene and came back into town to look for a dark Audi. Human nature would make them want to stare at the mangled body, at least for a short time.

Ryan made a slow right on Rua do Cerro. Trees lined the quiet street, lush and green with new spring foliage. Low limestone walls, thick hedges, and dazzlingly white villas made him wish he were here on vacation instead of on an op.

"This is incredible," Lisanne said, her voice hushed as if she were in church.

Ryan stopped at the bottom of the hill, at the intersection with the larger Estrada do Farol. Midas and Ding were to the east, waiting to pick them up so they could abandon the Audi, which had been rented under a false ID.

"What do you think?" He looked at Lisanne. "Keep looking or turn left?"

Chavez answered, "Get your ass over here."

"Copy that," Ryan said, making the turn. He hadn't gone a half-block before Lisanne gave an excited bounce in her seat, humming with sudden emotion.

"On the left," she said. "Red Ducati."

Ryan slowed, peering up a cobblestone drive alongside a white three-story building with a bar and restaurant on the ground level and two floors of apartments above. The fuel tank and front tire of a red Ducati Monster peeked out from behind a rock wall in back.

"We might have her," Ryan said, giving their location over the net. "She could be in one of the upper apartments."

"Or the next building," Chavez said. "Or across the street, or just maybe she's abandoned her bike and is at this very moment hauling ass to Lisbon."

"Your call, boss," Ryan said. "But we're sitting right here. I think I should try and get a plate number off the bike. I'll drop Lisanne off here so she can watch the front, then I'll drive up, take a look, and be down the hill in a flash. I'll pick up Lisanne and we'll be outa here in two minutes, maybe less."

"Two minutes," Chavez said. "We'll head your way."

———

Dominic Caruso asked the waitress for a touch more Foral de Portimão, an inexpensive local red that she'd recommended. Adara reached across the table and gave his hand a squeeze, prompting him to follow her gaze over his shoulder.

"Our friends on overwatch are starting to get antsy," she said, once the waitress had poured the wine and left.

Clark came over the radio. "I see that."

Adara smiled at Dom, chatting away about the weather, the beach, anything but a surveillance on a couple of Russian spooks. She gave a play-by-play so he didn't have to turn around. "One of them just clouded up like he saw something he didn't like . . . He's standing now. I think he's about to head across the street . . . Nope. Scratch that. Now he's sitting back down."

"Must be in commo with his Ruski friends," Dom said. He scanned the balcony for anything out of the ordinary. "I think I see what's going on."

"Care to enlighten us?" Clark said.

"There's a new player," Dom said. "Tall, jeans, tan sport coat with the sleeves pushed up like he's auditioning for a remake of *Miami Vice*. Dark hair cut over his ears. Big honking watch I can see from here. He was just standing in the doorway watching a minute ago. I thought he was looking for someone. He's making his way toward the Russians' table now. There's no one else seated at that end of the balcony. That must be what spooked our friends here."

"One of Gaspard's men?" Clark offered.

"Could be," Dom said. "He's sitting at the table with the Russians. Hard to tell from this distance, but they don't look very happy to see him."

Urbano da Rocha made his move the moment he received the call from Lucile. He'd had no doubt of her abilities, but things happened, and he did not care to be caught in a meat grinder between Hugo Gaspard and the two Russians who were about to become his friends.

"Hallo," he said, giving the two men the closest thing to a benign smile a man like him could muster. "Would you mind terribly if we speak English? I can manage in Russian, but in this sort of back-and-forth, mistakes could be made, leading to unfortunate events."

Neither Russian smiled. They did not appear to be startled as much as dyspeptic, bothered as they might be bothered by a fly that had just flown onto their pudding from a manure pile.

"Who are you?" the elder Russian said, curling a long upper lip.

"My name is da Rocha."

"I do not know you," the Russian said.

"What you mean to say," da Rocha said, still smiling, "is that you do not know me *yet*."

"It would be better for you if you left us alone," the younger Russian said, flicking his hand. He had a ridiculous bowl cut and an ill-fitting suit that made him look like a runaway child who had climbed out the window of his nursery.

Dealing with Russians was tricky business—especially

the brutish ones—and what Russian did not have a little brute in his DNA? These two cretins would certainly have a difficult time with subtlety, so da Rocha decided to get straight to the yolk of the egg.

"Hugo Gaspard is dead."

The Russians looked at each other. Bowl Cut's tongue darted out, tasting the air.

"Who is this Gaspard to us?"

Da Rocha shrugged, ignoring the sidestep. "I am here to take his place. With, I might add, much better terms than anything Gaspard could have provided . . . God rest his soulless black heart. I can provide you with all the hardware he could, plus—"

Long Lip gave a curt nod and then dropped a wad of cash on the table for their unfinished meal. "If you will not leave, then we will."

Da Rocha suddenly brightened. "I have military contacts who can vouch for my bona fides, if that makes a difference."

Long Lip pushed away from the table. "Mr. da Rocha," he said. "We will be in touch if we are interested. Any attempt by you to make contact with us would be a grave error on your part."

"Very well," da Rocha said and sighed. "I had hoped you might be more reasonable."

"I mean what I say," Long Lip said. "Do not contact us again."

Da Rocha picked up a breadstick from the table and dipped it in the nearest bowl of half-eaten pasta. "Oh." He chuckled, speaking around a mouthful of food. "Make no mistake. The next time we meet, you will beg to hear about my terms."

———

Da Rocha gave the Russians a moment to leave, not wanting to press them too much for the time being. He'd had nothing to eat, but left twenty euros on the table anyway, buying a little goodwill from the waiter who'd watched him sit down with the Russians.

He had to force himself not to hum as he made his way inside and then quickly down the stairs to street level. A silver Porsche 911 R drove down from Encarnação, directly past the Guarda Nacional depot, and pulled to a stop along the curb. He opened the door and slid into the passenger seat, leaning across to kiss the blond woman behind the wheel. She wore large sunglasses and a sheer white wrap over a two-piece swimsuit. A brunette wig lay draped across the console between them.

Lucile Fournier shifted into second gear, keeping the roaring 4.0-liter engine caged as she drove north through town on 124–1. "The Russians did not accept your proposal?"

"They did not," da Rocha said. "But I am not really surprised. They do not know us. It is only a matter of time. Soon I will be the only one left who has the connections they need."

"If I do my job," she said.

"Precisely." Da Rocha stuffed the wig behind his seat. "Speaking of that, it went well, my darling?"

"Easy," she said, pretending to spit. "Hugo Gaspard was a very nasty man."

Da Rocha raised a brow. He reached across the Porsche's black leather interior to caress the back of her neck. "And if they are not all such nasty men? Will it be so easy then?"

"It will, my love." She shrugged, shifting into fourth when she reached the edge of town. The 911's engine growled. "I am a very nasty woman."

"Indeed you are," da Rocha said, his hand dropping to her bare knee. "In so many wonderful ways."

Lucile gave the top of her head an absentminded scratch, the itch no doubt brought on by covering her blond locks with the mesh of the brunette wig. "What do you think it is?"

"What what is?" Da Rocha thrummed his fingers on her thigh.

"Arrête!" She pushed his hand away. "None of that until you concentrate. I am talking about the job, this thing the Russians want."

"I honestly do not know," da Rocha said. "It is enough that Hugo Gaspard believed it would set him up for life. The Russians must be trying to move something that will bring an incredible amount of profit."

Killing Colonel Mikhailov had not been easy, but even that was preferable to this interminable waiting. Cherenko was a pilot, and a damned good one. He was meant to be in the air, not lying on a bunk in Oman under a clattering swamp cooler. Babysitting was not the work of a pilot. He could have gone swimming, but these people probably flushed their toilets into the sea. He'd never been fond of the ocean, preferring air currents to even the bluest of water. And this water was brown, a dusky, foamy mess like wet concrete that made it impossible to tell from a distance where the sand ended and the sea began. When the wind blew hard, it picked up enough sand that air and earth and water all seemed to combine into a single ugly element. In an airplane, he could have gotten above such nastiness.

One could read only so much news. Most of it was lies anyway, even from his own country. He laughed at that—especially from his own country. What little truth got out was incredibly depressing. As if there was not already enough to worry about in Russia, Cherenko was assaulted daily with stories of missing children, brutalized women, and all manner of plague from every corner of the world. This deadly strain of flu in North America was particularly chilling—if the stories about it were true. Perhaps an island off the coast of Oman was not such a bad place to be after all.

The most eventful portion of the mission had so far been the midair ballet south of Moscow. After that, it was just a series of stops and starts to disrupt any trail. They spent one night in Erbil, Iraq, offloading a couple of crates to establish a reason for their flight and give American intelligence an opportunity to take a few photographs of the airplane while it sat on the tarmac. Russia sold many weapons, including T-90 battle tanks, to Iraq, so the presence of a large transport aircraft was hardly noteworthy. The tail numbers had been changed to those of 2967 when they put down in Saratov for "systems check." They'd also used the opportunity to pass Mikhailov's body to a waiting GRU cleanup man while still inside Russia for later transfer to an area of the mountains nearer the presumed crash site. They could have dumped him out at altitude, but it would have been problematic if some hiker, or even a military patrol, found the body of a Russian Air Force colonel a thousand kilometers from where his aircraft was supposed to have gone down. Conspiracy theories abounded around vanished aircraft, especially those thought to be carrying nuclear material. There was no point in pouring petrol on the flames.

Landing at the island airbase of Masirah hadn't been too much of a problem, considering the Antonov's established record of recent electrical problems. There were few airports in the world that would not allow an aircraft to land with a declared emergency. Oman and Russia were not exactly friends, but they were not enemies, either. One million dollars in medium-denomination bills weighed approximately fifteen pounds. The largesse of a twenty-pound briefcase along with some whispered words about rare antiquities bought a blind eye from even a neutral acquaintance. What did the Omani base commander care if the Russians smuggled a little statuary and art out of Iraq? Cherenko had half hoped the Omani colonel would tell them to move on, or, at the very least, become nosy so they would be forced to fly somewhere else. At least then he'd be in the air instead of loitering on some shithole of an island waiting for further instructions. But the greedy old fool was too busy counting his money.

Cherenko grunted to himself, struck with a sudden idea. He rolled half over in his bed, the oval armed forces ID tags he wore around his neck falling to the side as he reached for his black leather briefcase. He pulled out the small tablet computer and stuffed the ID tags back inside his T-shirt before situating himself against the grimy pillows. Checking his personal bank account would help to pass the time. If converted into cash, it would weigh considerably more than fifteen pounds.

———

Dmitry Leskov picked a bread crumb off his longish upper lip and stared up at the headliner of the rented Toyota sedan, happy to be out of the fishy-smelling restaurant. A major in the 45th Guards Independent Reconnaissance, an elite Spetsnaz brigade of Russia's Main Intelligence Directorate, he'd never been fond of seafood. Give him a good borscht and maybe a few buckwheat blini with smetana and onion any day. He cared for none of this stuff you had to pry out of its shell to get in your mouth. He and Captain Osin had served together in Chechnya and Ossetia. Disguised as civilians, they'd distinguished themselves during the intervention in Ukraine, earning the trust of their GRU commanders for exceedingly delicate missions on behalf of the motherland.

"This da Rocha character is certainly pompous enough for our purposes," Osin said, pushing blond bangs to the side of his face before starting the car. He was a capable soldier, Captain Osin, his penchant for farm-boy haircuts notwithstanding.

"Maybe." Leskov gave a noncommittal shrug. "But I don't like him. We still need to talk with Don Felipe. He's no smarter, but certainly more trustworthy. We should mark the Spaniard off our list before we take a gamble on this one."

"And we will," Osin said. "You do have a nose for these things. Perhaps da Rocha is CIA, or American military."

"Perhaps," Leskov said. "But I doubt even the Americans would stoop to killing Gaspard. Yuri said he was indeed murdered by a woman while sunbathing on the beach. Odd that they would assassinate him so publicly."

Osin grimaced. "At least we don't have to spend another minute with that pig." He nosed the Toyota into traffic as he spoke. "It is ironic that da Rocha would work so hard to be involved in our project, all things considered."

Another shrug. "Ironic indeed."

Leskov nestled down in his seat and closed his eyes, suddenly exhausted. These delicate missions for the motherland were becoming more tedious by the moment. This one would require a great deal of cleanup—and since it was extremely close-hold, that cleanup would fall to them.

Lisanne Robertson walked across Estrada do Farol after Jack dropped her off. It was still early in the season, with few outsiders on the street, but the bus stop in front of the hotel portico gate gave her an inconspicuous place to wait. She kept her back to the stucco pillar, scanning the area while trying to keep an eye on the Audi as Jack made his way up the lane toward the motorcycle. There was always a chance it was just another Ducati, unrelated to the assassination, but she agreed with Ryan. They were here. Why not check it out?

She couldn't help but wonder about him. He was a nice guy. Smart, kind eyes, good heart—the traits her mother had told her to look for in a man. The fact that he was rugged and athletic didn't hurt. Still, they worked together.

She turned to look to the south just in time to see a blond man jump out the passenger door of a gray Mercedes ten feet away. He kept a black pistol close to his body, half hidden by a leather jacket, and hooked his hand toward the car, barking an order in French to get in.

She raised her hands and stepped forward, closing the gap as if to comply. Shorter than the man by a head, Lisanne knew he probably underestimated her. A drastic mistake on his part.

Boot camp at Parris Island and the police academy had only honed the natural affinity for fighting that she'd inherited from her father. She bowed her head when the man reached her, eyes wide, looking as subservient as she could.

"You killed the wrong person, bitch!" the blond man said, still speaking in French. He reached to shove her into the waiting Mercedes.

She sidestepped, moving into him rather than toward the car. Her left hand parried the pistol away as her right shot upward, catching him under the nose with the heel of her palm. She rolled up and over, intent on peeling the big thug's nose off his scowling face. He backpedaled, striking out with the pistol instead of firing it. Wasting no energy on excess movement, she brought her right hand down, delivering a hammer fist to the bridge of his already injured nose.

The blows were painful but not incapacitating—and the man had been in a fight or two himself. He snatched her wrist as it went by his face, jerking her sideways and throwing her backward. She hit the pavement hard, landing on her butt, stupidly trying to catch herself. A wave of nausea washed over her as something snapped in her wrist.

"*Salope!*" the man spat, aiming the pistol at her face— just before Ryan roared across the street and plowed into him with the Audi.

Ryan kept going, dragging the body past the bus stop, through the gate, and into the hotel courtyard. The

Mercedes sped away, abandoning the big Frenchman. Tires squealed as Ryan threw the Audi into reverse and shot out into the street, reaching across to fling open the passenger door. Lisanne scrambled in and he drove east down Estrada do Farol.

John Clark's voice came across the net after Ryan brought everyone up to speed.

"Dom and Adara, stay with me on the Russians. With Gaspard dead, they are our only remaining lead. Ding, you link up with us as soon as you pick up Junior and ditch his ride."

"Copy that," Chavez said. "Midas got a screen grab of the girl from the mini-drone footage. I'll send it off to Gavin and have him try and get an ID."

"Finally," Clark said. "Some good news."

Lisanne flipped the switch on her radio, changing it to push-to-talk mode so she wouldn't broadcast to the rest of the team. Teeth clenched, she was obviously in pain, her face pale. She cradled her right wrist in her lap but reached across with her left to touch Ryan on his hand where it rested on the steering wheel. "Thank you, Jack," she said. "I gotta tell you, you're a pretty handy guy to have around."

8

Some people were born spies. Others found themselves deceived by the lure of international travel. Erik Dovzhenko was shamed into it by his mother.

The slap of Dovzhenko's scuffed leather shoes pinged off the concrete walls of the stairwell, sounding like a handful of coins dropped into a wishing well. Wishes were wasted in Evin Prison. The Ministry of Intelligence, or VAJA, made certain of that. The Islamic Revolutionary Guard Corps stomped out any hope they missed.

Dovzhenko paused mid-step, taking a contemplative sip of his coffee—a third of it milk—and steeled himself in the sterile quiet. He was already exhausted and wanted to sit down right there on the stairs, but he was on camera so there was no point in that. Stopping to drink some coffee was one thing. Sitting down to think would surely spawn questions he did not care to answer. Russia and Iran were allies, but the IRGC mistrusted even those in their own ranks—especially now. A moment of weakness or indecision would be seen for what it was—a lack of commitment. So Erik Dovzhenko took another drink of his coffee and hauled himself downward with the metal banister. The journey to section 2A, subbasement 4, of

Evin Prison was not an easy one to make, and he needed all the help he could get.

He was an experienced, if uneasy, professional, fifteen years with the Sluzhba Vneshney Razvedki—the SVR—half of the Russian version of the old Soviet KGB that worked mainly outside the motherland. If FSB was the Russian equivalent of the American FBI, SVR was the CIA. Dovzhenko had the dark, wavy hair of his Azeri mother, which he combed straight back with pomade. He'd inherited his father's handsome, if somewhat brooding, Russian face. That along with his olive skin and dark hair made it difficult to tell just exactly where in the world he was from. Such ambiguous ethnicity came in handy for an intelligence officer, and he sometimes wondered if his mother had not married his father for the sole purpose of having a child who could easily melt into a crowd virtually anywhere in the world. Dovzhenko was a fit one hundred ninety pounds and just under six feet tall, with square shoulders and massive boxer's hands. His thumbs were on the large side, which had prompted a combatives instructor at spy school in Chelebityevo to comment that they would be good for gouging out the eyes of an opponent in battle. Dovzhenko had done some grisly things during his fifteen years with the SVR, but so far, he had yet to poke out anyone's eyes with his thumbs.

He should have been promoted by now, certainly further along in his career than watching the goings-on of IRGC thugs in the belly of an Iranian prison that stank of shit and moldy bread. His mother was the spy in the family, using her knowledge of Azerbaijani and other Turkic languages in service to the KGB in the early 1980s. She had good stories and told them often, joking that she had started pushing Erik toward the clandestine life while he was still "hanging on the tit."

As far as Erik knew, she'd not been employed since the KGB was dissolved, but, as she often said, there was no such thing as a former KGB officer. You were always active, just waiting to be called back into service. No one called. Erik could tell she missed the action, the excitement. He supposed that was the principal reason she pushed him toward the SVR—so she could live vicariously through the exploits she knew he would have. His father had been a teacher. An unassuming and gentle man who sat in his chair with his nose in a book while his wife skulked around the house with an old Makarov in her pocket, drinking a potent Azerbaijani mulberry liquor called *tutovka*—or, worse, cheap Russian vodka in a bottle with a tearaway foil lid. There was no need to replace a cap once Zahra Dovzhenko tucked into a bottle.

His mother's drunken tirades alone had been enough to push Erik out of the house. She still had enough contacts that she was able to get him recruited. He was athletic and smart, and he found he had an aptitude for the work, though he never really enjoyed it. There was a certain sociopathic nature to spying that always left him a little bilious. He had no trouble walking up to a criminal and punching him in the face—or even shooting him, if it came to that. But he had too much of his father in him to enjoy the lying game as much as his mother did.

Men and women who lied for a living tended to be uncomfortable around those who valued the truth. Erik Dovzhenko was trusted implicitly, but he was not loved—by his peers or by his superiors. In an organization like SVR, not to be loved meant not to be promoted.

While so many of his cohort had already attained chief of station in places like Prague and Berlin, Erik Dovzhenko was stuck in the eternal purgatory of mid-level case officer, descending into the lowest circles of Hell—like here in Tehran.

Six meters above, spring had come to the city. Sparrows flitted and chirped among new sycamore and mulberry growth, grass turned from brown to green overnight, and the snow that blanketed Mount Tochal was beginning to melt. Six meters below, deep in the bowels of section 2A, subbasement 4, things were much darker. Sewage gurgled through open drains. The smell of urine and hopelessness mingled in the fetid air with stale cigarette smoke and the overwhelming stench of the IRGC guards' cologne.

The prison—sometimes called Evin University because of the intellectuals and student activists housed there—could be unbearably hot in summer and bitter cold in winter, adding to the misery of the prisoners. Dovzhenko's white shirt was damp from his short walk across the parking lot in the rain. He customarily wore a brown horsehide jacket, though it made him look decidedly more like the Russian spy that he was. But good jackets were hard to break in, so he'd left it in his car, not wanting the stink of the prison to seep into the leather.

Maryam would smell it, even over the smell of his cigarettes. She was attuned to such things.

Reaching the bottom level, he took a long drink of coffee and pulled open the heavy steel door. It was not locked. No one in their right mind would come down here unless they had to. Dovzhenko almost smiled at that notion. Major Parviz Sassani wanted to be here, but the

IRGC thug only bore out Dovzhenko's theory. The man was good at his job but definitely not in his right mind.

The moans and whimpers of the prisoners met Dovzhenko before he got the stairwell door open—along with something else.

In Lefortovo, the prison in Moscow where this sort of work was undertaken, detainees were kept isolated from outside stimuli. But the Iranians had taken a page from the playbook the Argentine junta had used during their Dirty War. The sounds of traffic driving down from the ski resorts on Mount Tochal, planes flying overhead, and groundskeepers' equipment were clearly audible. Like a medieval *oubliette* or "pit of forgetting," prisoners heard the world above as it carried on around them as if they did not exist. These sounds went only one way—piped in electronically so the prisoners' complaints and the torture itself could not be heard above. The Ayatollah had assured the world that this sort of thing did not go on in Evin. According to the Supreme Leader, the government had built a swimming pool and Jacuzzis in the prison. In Iran, as elsewhere, the biggest lies were more easily swallowed.

He pictured the IRGC interrogator before he saw him, eyes gleaming, spittle flying with each word. The volume varied from maniacal scream to breathy hiss, but the intensity remained the same. The whispers were the worst, under pressure, each word capable of flaying skin.

And it was the same questions, over and over and over again. *Who are the protesters? Where are the protesters? Where is Reza Kazem?*

Dovzhenko followed the anguished sounds to the right, through another door, this one locked, so he had to be buzzed in. Then he took one last breath before stepping through, gritting his teeth and squinting, as if anything would blunt the sights, sounds, and smells of the section 2A interrogation chamber. Two men he recognized from the Ministry of Intelligence stood smoking along the concrete wall to his left. He'd seen them work and knew they could mete out severe torture, but they were generally professional, torturing when they felt it necessary to elicit information or gain mental control of a dissident. Dovzhenko did not know if all VAJA men were the same, but though these two did not shrink from use of the wooden rod or spring cable, they were dispassionate in the application. A more professional security and intelligence service, the Ministry of Intelligence ran the prison, but the IRGC was much more powerful, both in government and the business world. They were seeing to the protesters by edict of the Supreme Leader, and they kept their VAJA counterparts at arm's length so as not to divulge too many of their methods.

IRGC Major Parviz Sassani enjoyed his work—and it showed in his smile, a ghoulish grimace, as if the act of harming another somehow caused pain to leave his own body. Cathartic.

Two young men hung suspended from eyebolts in the ceiling, shoulders displaced, hands purple from the thin ropes biting into their wrists. Their feet were just inches off the concrete floor. Looking more like sides of meat than human beings, they were naked but for gray prison shorts that resembled cutoff jogging pants, soiled with all manner of blood and filth. Their bodies swung hypnotically on the cables, moving, no doubt, from a recent beating at the hands of the three IRGC men. Blood trickled from the largest man's toes, where the nails had been before Sassani pulled them out. The pliers and the nails lay neatly arranged on a wooden desk—along with a couple of bloody teeth.

Dovzhenko shook his head. This was new.

The IRGC goons had turned their attention to a third prisoner, this one not much more than a boy. His name was Javad—seventeen years old, but he looked maybe thirteen. He cried more than the others, babbling pleas for his mother that only seemed to enrage Sassani and spur him on.

Javad was on his back, hands tied behind him so he teetered on his fists, unable to lie flat. Legs up, his ankles were bound to a wooden board set between two posts. Stiff cords kept the soles of his bare feet pointed upward. They were already swollen, black and blue from earlier treatment. Sassani himself swung the three-foot length of willow branch, roughly the diameter of his little finger.

Foot whipping was a favorite of secret police the world over. Parts of the feet could, by necessity, withstand a large amount of stress. Other parts—small bones, the toes—snapped with relative ease. When meted out by an expert, bastinado could cause maximum pain, with damage that was hardly visible but for a little pink and swollen flesh. Turn up the force and it could cripple. This often led to a perverse relief when a prisoner saw he or she was going to be bastinadoed instead of receiving a treatment that left more visible scars and marks. "Perhaps they will only whip my feet and let me go . . ." Such thoughts flew quickly after the first agonizing blows.

Major Sassani used the treatment as a fallback, when he tired of breaking ribs or stubbing out cigarettes on exposed skin. He swung the willow branch from over his head, causing it to whir through the air and allowing the poor boy time to anticipate the blow, doubling the agony.

These three prisoners had been here for the better part of a week, with Sassani getting right to work almost from the moment the doors clanged shut behind them. They had told him everything they knew within the first hour. Even trained operatives eventually talked, but these students leaked like broken vessels, spilling everything they knew at the mere sight of the torture chamber. Through snot and tears and terrified sobs, they confessed to sins from grade school.

In the end, it did not matter.

Javad stopped thrashing after the fifth blow. His feet looked like great purple balloons with toes. Sassani hit him twice more to make sure he was truly unconscious. Satisfied, he tossed the willow branch on the desk in the corner. He nodded to his two IRGC companions and then hooked a thumb over his shoulder at the hanging men.

"Allow this one to rest," he said. "And bring me another. The fat one will do."

The heavier of the two students, a man in his early twenties named Babak, began to whimper. A swollen eyelid fluttered open.

"Comrade Erik," Sassani said, rubbing his hands together in front of his chest like a housefly. "I am sorry that we did not wait for you."

The Russian waved away the comment. Sassani knew full well that Dovzhenko despised him. The feeling was surely mutual—if only because Sassani appeared to hate everyone.

The Iranian was younger by five or six years, perhaps thirty-four or thirty-five. He'd been promoted quickly in the Revolutionary Guard Corps. Dovzhenko supposed the IRGC rewarded cruelty, so long as it was focused in the preferred direction. His own SVR was not so different in that respect, which was likely why Dovzhenko found himself stuck working with the likes of Parviz Sassani. His superiors obviously thought he needed some sort of lesson in cruelty.

Dovzhenko knew little of Sassani's background. His father had apparently been martyred in the war with Iraq, and he was highly regarded by the mullahs and ranking IRGC members. His father-in-law was a ranking IRGC general. He must have learned English in the UK or some commonwealth country, because he spoke it with a British accent—like the devil in an American movie.

Sassani was slightly taller than Dovzhenko, with dark, wavy hair and a coal-black beard he kept trimmed only slightly longer than a five-o'clock shadow. He wore fine suits, even during interrogations, hanging his jacket inside a metal locker along the wall by the door. Several flecks of blood spatter dotted the breast of his collarless white shirt, the tail of which had come untucked during his exertions with the willow rod.

He rolled down his sleeves, producing a pair of gold cuff links from gray woolen trousers, along with a dark blue pack of Gauloises. He stuck a cigarette in his mouth and spoke around it while he fastened the cuff links.

"What do you hear, my friend?" He searched deeper in his pockets until he found a disposable lighter.

Dovzhenko kept his eyes on the IRGC men who were busy tying Babak's feet to the board.

"There are rumors of bombing," he said. "Some sort of government building."

Sassani clicked the cheap lighter, to no avail. "I have heard this as well," he said, giving up. He gave a little chuckle. "At least we do not have the American flu. A plague on the Great Satan for her fight against God."

Dovzhenko wondered how the Iranian squared the earthquakes and illness in his own country, but he kept the thoughts to himself.

Sassani gestured with the unlit cigarette. "What of the phone trackers and computer software your government has promised us? Our technology is fine, but yours is much more precise. I should not have to remind you that we are in a time of national crisis."

"Very soon," Dovzhenko said. He fished the lighter from his own pocket and opened it with a flick. It was a gift from his maternal grandfather, gold, with the eight-pointed star and flame of the Azerbaijani crest.

A cloud of smoke enveloped Sassani's face as he puffed the cigarette to life. He held it to the side, considering Dovzhenko for a long moment. "The precision of your technology would be extremely useful in ferreting out the traitors."

"As I said, very soon." Dovzhenko nodded to the prisoners. "Surely these three have given you viable information by now."

Sassani shrugged. "I suppose. But they are weak." The Iranian wheeled and walked toward the heavy man, who was now strapped to the board, touching the coal of the cigarette to the arch of the man's bare foot. Sassani stepped away from the thrashing and croaked screams.

Bloody spittle drooled from the corners of the man's

lips, down his cheek, to pool on the filthy concrete floor by his ear. Sassani hovered over him.

"I ask you again," the IRGC thug said. "Where is Reza Kazem?"

The prisoner groaned. "I do not—"

Sassani pushed the cigarette into the man's eyelid, bringing more screams and futile attempts to escape the pain.

"Tell! Me! Where!"

The prisoner coughed, wincing.

"I do not—"

Sassani lifted his hand to apply the cigarette again.

"Isfahan!" the prisoner screamed, pulling away, away, attempting to shrink into the concrete. Anything to avoid another injury to his eye. "He is in Isfahan." He began to sob. "I swear it. Isfahan."

The smile drained from Sassani's face when he realized his cigarette had gone out.

A callow guard wearing a green uniform and baseball cap walked in and stood to the left of the door beside the metal lockers, taking in the sights. Unknown to Dovzhenko, this one was young, incapable of growing more than a sprout of facial hair. If the torture room bothered him, he was smart enough to keep that to himself.

Sassani stood and raised a wary brow, as if he'd been caught doing something vile by a younger brother. "What is it?"

The young man braced against the wall. "The court has handed down the sentence," he said. He offered up a folder, which Sassani snatched away.

He read it over, giving a slow nod of approval. "Public hanging."

The IRGC thug nearest the boy, Javad, spoke up. "This

one has cheated the hangman." He gave the lifeless body a shove, causing it to swing in a greater arc.

Sassani scoffed. "See," he said to Dovzhenko. "As I told you. Weak. But he will hang with his fellow traitors, nonetheless, by way of example."

Sassani took the cigarettes out of his slacks and put a fresh one in his mouth. His venomous smile made Dovzhenko sick to his stomach. "May I trouble you for another light?"

Dovzhenko looked on passively as he lit the Iranian's cigarette. There was something at play here. Something Dovzhenko could not quite put his finger on.

Reza Kazem was a troublemaker to be sure, the face of the tens of thousands of students and other dissatisfied Iranians who took to the streets in greater number every day across the entire country. It was natural for Sassani to want to know his whereabouts—but he wasn't hard to find.

9

President Jack Ryan's eyes flicked open at 5:27 a.m., just before his customary alarm. He was exhausted, and could have used the extra two minutes and forty-one seconds of sleep, but Cathy was home. Beside him. Right now. Awake. Conflicting schedules and high-profile jobs made grabbing a few moments together all but impossible. Times like this could not be taken for granted. He fluffed his pillow—they had great pillows at the White House—and grabbed his glasses from the nightstand when he turned off the alarm, before rolling over to face his wife of nearly forty years. She needed glasses as badly as he did, but had yet to put hers on, which was good because it tempered her view of his aging face and bleary-eyed bedhead. Nestling in closer, he caught the scent of mouthwash and Dioressence perfume. Supremely good signs indeed.

Egyptian cotton sheet pulled up to her chin, blond hair fanned across her pillow, Cathy Ryan fluttered long lashes. She began to sing as soon as Jack turned over, in a voice somewhere between Betty Boop and Marilyn Monroe.

". . . Happy Birthday, Mr. President . . ."

Ryan chuckled, kissing her on the nose when she finished the song. "You know it's not my birthday, right?"

Dr. Ryan's eyes flew wide. Her lips puckered in a mock pout. "Really?" For one of the most talented ophthalmic surgeons in the world, she played the part of breathless bimbo incredibly well. Both hands now clutched the sheet on each side of her pouting chin. Her perfectly manicured nails were painted a deep red called I'm Not Really a Waitress. Amazingly, the White House press office had been able to keep the name of the color under wraps.

Her breasts rose and fell beneath the sheets as she heaved an exaggerated sigh. "Darn! If it's not your birthday, then what am I supposed to do with this present?"

Eighteen minutes later, Ryan turned slightly to glance at his bedside clock and heaved a sigh of his own. Cathy's arm trailed across his chest, her leg over his thigh, warm, so they no longer needed the sheet. Soft breaths puffed against his neck.

She chuckled softly.

"What?" he said.

Ryan couldn't see her face, but he'd known her long enough to feel the tensing of her skin when she smiled. "You ever think what it would be like if there was some crisis of impending doom right now and the Secret Service had to burst in here with Arnie?"

"Now would be better than five minutes ago," Ryan offered, considering the real possibility that his chief of staff might barge into the presidential bedroom if the threat was great enough.

"Maybe a little better," Cathy said. "But not much."

Ryan shrugged. "It's different for you, hon. You'd be embarrassed, cover up with the sheet. I, on the other hand, couldn't help but feel a little bit proud. It would be a guiltless way to proclaim, 'Hey, the leader of the free world's still got it.'"

"Oh, you still got it." She nuzzled in closer, shuddering a little. "Anyway, I can't just lie around here all day. I need to get to the hospital."

"I know," Ryan said. "I'll hear it later in the briefing, but you docs must talk about this stuff. Fill me in on the latest expert opinions about this epidemic."

Cathy reached down for the sheet and pulled it up to her chest before collapsing back on her preferred stack of three down pillows. Ryan knew she was envisioning a map of the United States and the number of deaths in each area. If the victim happened to be a child, she'd see the name. Her brain worked that way, recalling pictures of information—pages she'd read, images she'd seen— with a near-photographic memory. Though she specialized in diseases and injuries of the eye, Cathy had been asked by her husband to be the face of the media campaign providing education and information on the recent outbreak of a virulent strain of influenza.

"One hundred and thirty-seven," she said. "That's in the U.S. and Canada. But there are two hundred–plus reported sick enough to hospitalize. We're having some luck with antivirals, maybe even stemming the tide, but it's too early to know for sure. First responders, military, essential personnel, hospital staff—they should all be vaccinated by the end of this week or early next. The CDC is doing a terrific job of pushing out everything we have on hand, basically attempting to throw a bucket of sand on the fire and smother it all at once. The trouble is, Jack, we're going to run out of sand, in the near term at least. We usually recommend vaccinating the very young and the elderly, but this stuff is hitting primarily healthy people in the prime of life, much like the pandemic of 1918."

"The Spanish flu," Ryan said.

"Yeah, well, Spain got a bad rap," Cathy said. "Given that same line of reasoning, they could call this the American flu, since we publish our findings to the world in hopes that everyone can stop it. There were certainly other countries with similar outbreaks in that same year, but Spain was the one that reported the illness." She let her head fall sideways against the pillow, looking directly at him. "As I said, this virus affects a vital portion of the workforce, the doctors, nurses, and pharmaceutical techs who would normally be the ones leading the fight. The 1918 pandemic killed more people than both World Wars combined—almost five percent of the world's population. It was virulent stuff, Jack. And this strain has the potential to be even worse. Unchecked, it'll burn through the best and brightest within months, maybe even weeks . . ."

Ryan groaned.

Cathy nudged him in the arm. "See what I did there?"

"What?"

"I caused you to panic," Cathy said. "That, Jack, is the number one reason this flu is so bad. I don't mean to downplay the seriousness of the illness, but we provide better care today, a generally healthier lifestyle, and the ability to fight secondary infections that killed many of the people in the 1918 pandemic. Unfortunately, we also have a twenty-four-hour news cycle that is yellow journalism gone rogue. The idea that this is the worst, most deadly illness in history—which it is not—is the stuff of pure unadulterated bull hockey. Each new reported case gets thrown up on the crawler at the bottom of the broadcast as Breaking News. Honestly, from a medical standpoint, I'm almost as worried about the flooding in Louisiana and Mississippi as I am about this flu."

Ryan nodded.

"I've gotta tell you, Jack, there is a better-than-average chance more people will be injured in riots than by the actual bug. And that bitch Michelle Chadwick isn't helping matters."

Ryan gave his wife a pat on the thigh. "Probably best we keep your feelings about the good senator between us."

Cathy lifted the sheets, giving the area under them an exaggerated look. "It's just me and you here, boyo," she said. "And besides, I'm allowed a little anger at someone who spews that kind of vitriol at my husband. She held a press conference yesterday accusing you of inaction. You. Can you believe it?"

He gave Cathy another pat on the thigh. This one for his benefit. "I'm ashamed to say it, but I think I'm getting used to politics. The garbage still stinks to high heaven, but I can hardly even smell it anymore."

"Have you noticed that the news isn't even the news?" Cathy said. "It's about how social media reacts to the news. Michelle Chadwick is scaring the crap out of the country, Jack. Isn't it against the law to yell 'Fire' in a crowded theater?"

Ryan shrugged. "She'd argue that there's an actual fire."

"Whatever," Cathy said. "But she's pouring gasoline on it."

Ryan bunted the subject back to the flu.

"I saw the public service announcement you did with

the CDC," he said. "Thanks for lending the trustworthy face of the first lady to the cause. Should keep people home from work and school if they are sick, and, hopefully, get them to the doctor for a flu shot before they get that way. Say, I have an idea. How about you come work for me?"

"You can't afford me."

"I'll reinstate the draft," Ryan said. "Nationalize health care. Press all doctors into government service, especially beautiful ophthalmologists."

"Oh, yeah," Cathy said and chuckled. "That'll go over big with your constituents. I specialized in ophthalmic surgery for two reasons. One, I happen to be good at it. And—"

Ryan smiled, finishing her thought. "And GBSs." Cathy Ryan was an exceptionally gifted doctor, but, as with most docs, he supposed, one of her least favorite parts of med school rotations was what the students called GBSs—gooey butt sores. The list of GBSs was apparently endless, and Ryan had seen far too many photos in medical textbooks over the years. Enough, at least, to understand why his wife had chosen ophthalmology.

Cathy swung her legs off the bed, exposing the arch of her back and the exquisite swell of her hips, now completely free of the sheets. "There's that," she said. "But I'm not a big fan of by-the-ways, either."

"I see," Ryan said, though he obviously did not.

Cathy held a pink terry-cloth robe across her lap but hadn't put it on yet. She turned slightly, leaning on one arm while she looked at the still-reclining Ryan.

"You know," she said, shrugging the robe over her shoulders while she explained. "Patient comes in for something else and then stops kind of like Colombo when the visit should be over and says, 'By the way, Doc, I know I came in for a sleep apnea, but while I'm here, you think you could set me up with some of those little blue pills my friend Bob told me about?'"

"Sounds smart to me," Ryan said.

Cathy stood, wagging her head. "You got no issues, by the way, Mr. President. And anyway, the point is, you got this. You don't need me to work for you."

Ryan sprang sideways, grabbing the tail of her robe and giving it a tug, pulling her toward the bed.

"Jaaackkk," she said, as she walked in place, in a half-hearted attempt to escape. "I really do have to go. Don't you have a meeting about raising taxes or something?"

He held the robe for another half-second, just long enough to let her know he wanted her to come back to bed, but agreed that they didn't have the time. It was a delicate dance, letting such an intelligent woman know he could not possibly live without her—and then doing precisely that for long stretches at a time.

Ryan shot another glance at the clock. It was a sorry state of affairs that he could feel like such a slacker for staying in bed until six in the morning. He let his head fall against the pillow in time for Cathy to turn and catch him looking at her.

She held the robe closed, tight at her neck, sheepishly drawing back her head. "What?"

"I was just thinking," Ryan said. "I hope Jack Junior finds a girl like I did."

10

The Russians were in Seville for less than an hour before they decided to go swimming.

Jack Ryan, Jr., sat on the floor of Midas's hotel room, leaning against the angle formed by a set of white-washed radiator pipes and the wall. A dog-eared paperback copy of *The Great Game* by Peter Hopkirk lay on the rug beside him. The room was pleasant enough, and smelled, as most hotel rooms around the world smell, of instant coffee and the last person to occupy them—in this case, a woman who was overly fond of her Coco Chanel. Even boutique hotels like this one made it far too easy to wake up in some cookie-cutter suite and forget where you were.

It was nearing noon, and Midas was posted a few blocks away in Clark's room to keep watch. According to the retired Delta operator, the Russians were lounging around the rooftop pool, pasty and white in the Spanish sun. They were waiting for someone.

Surveillance could go kinetic at any moment, so this momentary lag was the first opportunity to form up the team to regroup and do a quick AAR for the past few days. Midas listened in over the radio from his post, in virtual attendance.

Clark loved his after-action reviews. Jack certainly saw

the need, but some things that were done in the heat of the moment sounded . . . well, asinine with the benefit of hindsight. Still, Clark was a talented and experienced leader who'd made plenty of mistakes of his own. He didn't use the AARs as a chance to embarrass, at least with no more than a good-natured gibe or two. Honest, open critique benefited the entire team. Serious corrections happened in private. Jack had learned early on that though neither Clark nor Ding would often admit it out loud, they forgave almost any mistake of the head. Mistakes of the heart—errors that demonstrated a weakness in character—would never be tolerated.

Clark sat on the end of the bed. Dom and Adara on the floor at the foot of the leather love seat, while Ding leaned back in the swiveling desk chair, notebook in hand. Jack absentmindedly ruffled the pages of the book with his thumb, like shuffling a deck of cards. Both Clark and Chavez had come to believe strongly in reading assignments—geopolitical, cultural, leadership, even some fiction. Nothing was out of bounds. Essays on intelligence and tactics were favorite topics. DNI Foley, with whom both men had worked extensively at CIA, wrote an in-depth study called *How to Work a Russian Asset.* She had the chops for it. Born Mary Pat Kaminsky, she was the granddaughter of a riding instructor in the house of Tsar Nicholas II. There was even some stuff by Jack's dad. He could almost hear the old man's voice when he read it.

According to Ding Chavez, good intelligence officers were like sharks—they kept swimming or they died. Languages, once learned, had to be practiced consistently or they risked growing stale. Techniques and methods had to be practiced—in the mat room, on the pistol range, or on the street. Some things you could come by naturally—but even those required sharpening with a great deal of practice and study. *Don't practice until you get it right. Practice until you don't get it wrong.* The sentiment had a hell of a lot more meaning when ignoring it could get a friend killed. The real intel types were more bookworm than playboy—though, Jack admitted, the human-engineering side of the job was more interesting than the Chinese or Cyrillic flash cards Adara was always carrying around.

Jack didn't mind the reading. It gave him something to do during the down time—and there was always a good deal of that, hours of sheer boredom punctuated by massive adrenaline dumps big enough to explode the average human heart.

The Russians had gone from their meeting at Casa Ibérica to a small hotel in Lagoa, north of Carvoeiro, where they'd stayed for two days. Lagoa was larger than the tiny hamlets along the coast and marginally easier for Clark and the rest of The Campus to blend into without too much worry of being recognized, so long as they didn't press the surveillance too much. The Russians departed on the afternoon of the second day in a meandering surveillance-detection run that took them six hours to make the two-and-a-half-hour drive east to Seville. The one with the bowl haircut spent a lot of time in the hot tub. His partner sat by the pool and read or talked on the phone. The two who'd been on overwatch stayed in their room, apparently content that their services were not needed between operations.

Ding and Midas had a back-and-forth while still in Portugal on the risk versus benefits of placing a small GPS tracking device on the target vehicle. The device would transmit location information to Campus operatives over a GSM cell signal, allowing them to run a looser tail. The Russians made the decision for them when they came out at the end of the first day and ran a handheld cell-phone tracker over both cars. They weren't especially thorough, but they had a directional antenna, so they didn't really have to be.

They'd have to keep at least one of the cars in sight.

The three Campus vehicles bounded, trading places over the course of the journey, all the way to the EME Catedral Hotel, tucked into the pedestrian district in the shadow of the Giralda bell tower. It was a few blocks from the bullfighting arena along the canal off the Guadalquivir River in Seville.

Clark booked a double at the same hotel, down the hall from the Russians. The others set up at small hotels in the area, none close enough to offer a direct view of their target, but that couldn't be helped. Dom and Adara generally stayed out of sight, since the Russians who'd been working overwatch in Portugal would likely recognize them from the restaurant.

"You with us, kid?" Clark asked, dragging Jack back to the present.

". . . Yes?" Jack gave a wan smile. He hoped there wasn't going to be a quiz on whatever it was that Clark had been saying.

"Outstanding," Clark said, seeing right through him. "Hugo Gaspard was our main objective on this op. But we're already here, so it's worth keeping an eye on the Russians in the near term. Ding, how about you bring everyone up to speed on what Gavin found."

The camera on the Snipe Nano mini-drone didn't have the visual clarity that a cheaper, off-the-shelf model might have, but night vision and the ability to zoom more than made up for it. Midas got several good screen grabs of the female assassin from the footage. Adara's numerous selfies contained some grainy photos of the Russians and the guy who'd dropped in on them at Casa Ibérica. Gavin and his team had been busy enhancing the photos and running them through some facial recognition programs and databases.

Ding Chavez flipped back a page in his notebook.

"The woman who killed Gaspard is named Lucile Fournier. She's French, originally from a little burg outside Avignon. Father was a pharmacist until she literally gave him some of his own medicine and then dumped his body in the Rhone River. She spent two years in what the French call a 'closed education center' for the murder, apparently learning some pretty nasty stuff from a couple of cellmates. She eventually graduated to big-girl prison and, later, a couple of terrorist watch lists. Gavin did some link analysis and found one of her former cellmates was a half-sister to the guy you saw meeting with the Russians—a small-time Portuguese arms dealer named Urbano da Rocha. He's been arrested a couple of times by gendarmerie in various countries, but never convicted. The Cuerpo Nacional suspects he had ties with the Ochoa crime family in Galicia, but, again, nothing that stuck. Other than that, very little information on the guy, except that he seems to be expanding his business. Gavin got nothing back on the Russians."

Midas spoke up, his voice streaming in over the radio. "So we have international arms dealer and fat man of intrigue Hugo Gaspard about to do an unknown deal with some Russians, assassinated by the female associate of another arms dealer, who happened to sit down with those same Russians."

"You're trackin'." Chavez nodded, though Midas was in a hotel room blocks away.

"All right." Clark got to his feet, hands up and together in front of his chest. It was what law enforcement called a "field interview" or "ready" stance, and he looked very much like he was about to draw a weapon or smack somebody. A lifetime of smacking had ingrained the habit.

"One more thing," he said. "This needs to be said, but I'm only going to say it once. We're a small unit. Trust is imperative or none of this works. I know some of you . . . all of you . . . wonder exactly what went on in Texas with the Magdalena Rojas op. It's no secret that I went a little 'off the reservation,' so to speak."

Caruso waved a hand. "I told everyone there was nothing to hear."

"I know you did," Clark said. "And I appreciate it. But you and I both know that's not true. I'm not going to address specifics. You all know as much as you probably should about my past—"

"It's legendary, Mr. C.," Ding said.

Clark scoffed. "I'm being serious."

"So is he," Midas chimed in.

"The point I'm making," Clark said, "is that I'm not going to lie and tell you nothing went on out there. But I'm not going to drill down on the details, either. The sum total of all the unpleasant things I have done in the past should probably remain classified, or, at the very least, unspoken, for the good of all. That does not mean

I don't admit it occurred. Dom knows some of it, but not all. Suffice it to say that I hashed everything out with Gerry. Here's the thing, and the chief reason I bring it up. Gerry Hendley is *my* boss. He did what bosses do and that's between him and me. *I* am your boss. Anyone here decides to color outside the lines, you have to hash it out with me, not Gerry. And I gotta tell you, he's a hell of a lot more understanding than I am."

"Damn, boss," Midas said over the radio, the only one too far away for Clark to smack. "You're gettin' me all choked up with this sweet sentiment."

Never one to explain his explanation, Clark moved on. "How is Lisanne?"

"I talked to her a few minutes ago," Adara said. "She's at a comfortable hotel in Lisbon chasing down a couple of Tylenol with some good Portuguese wine. Her wrist is broken in two places, and she's bummed that she can't be here. But she'll be fine. I was looking at the screen shot of Lucile Fournier we got from the Snipe—not too much of a stretch to think Gaspard's thugs mistook Lisanne for the assassin. Same hair color, pert build."

Ryan scrolled through the images on his phone. "I can see it," he said.

Ding hung his head. "I shouldn't have sent her out there," he said. "She's not op—"

"Heat of battle," Clark said, raising his hand to put a stop to that kind of talk. "She has plenty of training to ride along. Good job getting her out of there, Ryan."

"Thanks," Jack said, kicking himself for leaving her alone in the first place. His track record with women was pretty dismal of late. It seemed like he picked girls who wanted to spy on him, were too busy spying for their own country, or were bona fide evil bitches. He was as red-blooded as the next guy, but had never considered himself a girl-in-every-port kind of guy. He wanted to settle down. Date someone cool. Someone pretty. Someone . . . sane. Lisanne certainly fit that bill. But the idea of asking her out was ridiculous. That definitely qualified as coloring outside the lines. First of all, Clark would shoot him. Second . . . Clark would shoot him.

11

Crescent wrench in hand, Sarah Porter stood up from a vain attempt at repairing the leaky pipe under the sink and watched her cell phone buzz across the kitchen countertop. She looked outside in time to watch three armored personnel carriers roll down her street—Cougars, they called them. She knew this because Rod had pointed it out to her during a Cameroonian military and police parade in downtown Yaounde the weekend before.

She shook her head as the heavy vehicles clinked and rumbled by. No wonder their roads were so crappy. She'd seen plenty of military vehicles over her husband's twenty-one-year career as a foreign service officer. But she'd never been told they were called Cougars, at least this kind. She chalked it up to her "Learn something new every day" list, which grew exponentially each time Rod bid on a new country assignment.

Cameroon was a promotion—at least on paper. Rod was the DCM—deputy chief of mission, second to the ambassador. He'd run the political section in Croatia during the last tour. There had been a lot to love about that posting—delicious food, the Adriatic, no cobras. But that's how Rod's career had worked out, bid on and get a great post, then promote to one that was . . . slightly less great. As a trailing spouse—the common term for following your diplomat other half around the globe— Sarah was used to it. Sort of.

The clatter outside stopped, but Sarah caught a glimpse of another Cougar between the houses on the next street over. She'd accidentally driven up on protests before, when the kids were little, and wondered if this was one of those.

"Are you seeing this, Rod?" she muttered under her breath, happy to have the comfortable heft of the crescent wrench in her hand as she leaned closer to the window to try and get a better look. The doorbell nearly caused her to pee her pants.

She held the wrench behind her thigh and peeked out the front curtains to find June Kim, one of the spouses from the South Korean embassy. The Bastos district of Yaounde was a mini–United Nations, with diplomat families from the many embassies to Cameroon living and working in the area.

June's pleading eyes darted from Sarah to the armored vehicles that now sat eerily silent at the end of the street. "Does your phone work?"

Sarah put the wrench on the counter. Normally an introvert, she was suddenly happy to have company. "Come on in and I'll check. Any idea what's happening?"

"I do not know," June said. "I was on the phone with my husband and it suddenly stopped working." She looked toward the street. "That's when I saw the troop carriers. I do not like this at all."

"The embassy will know." She looked at her watch. "Rod's in a meeting right now. I'll call Post One and see what I can find out." She punched in the speed-dial number for the embassy's main security post. Rod had told her and the kids early on that this was their version of 911 when they were overseas. She smiled as she waited for it to connect, hoping to calm her friend. "Sometimes it's good to be married to the deputy chief of mission." A fast busy. She tried the speed dial again. Still nothing.

Kim turned for the door. "I will go to our embassy. It is probably nothing."

"Probably," Sarah said. "But I'll walk with you anyway."

The two boys ran at the first sound of approaching Army vehicles, diving between two houses, seeking cover behind a tattered boxwood shrub. They'd been watching a football game through the fence, unwilling to cross General Mbida's men, who were posted at the gates. The U.S. embassy was across the street to the northeast. The embassies of South Korea and Tunisia were a few houses away behind them, the Saudi embassy across the street, half a block to the west of the U.S. compound. Jean-Claude was not quite sixteen, Lucien barely a year older. Stains of chicken blood and the preparation of a recent meal provided the only camouflage on their bright yellow T-shirts.

The stucco houses on either side of the narrow alley would have been considered middle-class in the United States, but here in Yaounde, where many Cameroonians earned less than $2,000 a year, they were palaces.

"*Bientôt,*" Lucien whispered.

Jean-Claude strained his ears. The rattling armored personnel carriers had stopped, leaving it quiet but for the periodic cheers and groans from the nearby football pitch and the cluck of a hen with her peeping chicks scratching in the

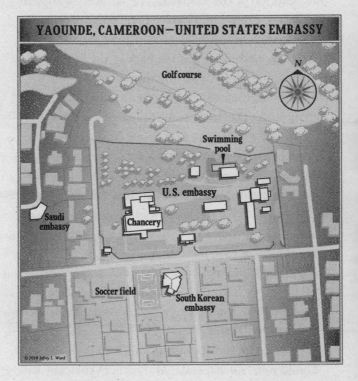

YAOUNDE, CAMEROON—UNITED STATES EMBASSY

Golf course

N

Swimming pool

U.S. embassy

Saudi embassy

Chancery

Soccer field

South Korean embassy

© 2018 Jeffrey L. Ward

dirt behind him. The air seemed heavy, charged with static. Lucien was right. Something was going to happen—*soon*.

The military trucks started up again, rattling their way toward the football pitch. Across the way, on the other side of the embassy fence, a Cameroonian man in a loose white shirt swept the sidewalk. The chancery was open now, receiving those who wanted to fill out paperwork for American visas. Jean-Claude watched the peeping chicks as they disappeared around the back of the house—and thought seriously about joining them.

He watched the two U.S. Marines standing behind the embassy fence. They were young, perhaps just a few years older than he was. They looked more scrubbed than they did treacherous, though they stood ramrod straight and there was an intensity in their faces that made Jean-Claude's stomach churn. He crouched lower, making sure the stubby palm tree hid his silhouette, checking quickly for any green mambas or button spiders—only slightly more frightening than the U.S. Marines.

Jean-Claude peeked around the edge of the shrub. If the Marines saw him, they ignored him—and these men did not look like the type to ignore anyone. He wished he'd worn a better shirt.

"What do you think will happen?"

"I told you," Lucien said. "My brother's company will arrest General Mbida and he will stand trial."

"But the Americans are right there," Jean-Claude said. "If Mbida is so friendly with them, will they not come to his aid?"

"Perhaps," Lucien said. "But my brother does not think so. He says they will be too worried about their own skins to face our military."

Lucien's elder brother was a Fusilier, Cameroon's version of the Marines across the street. He was loyal to the president, and well paid because of it.

"The Americans can't help but stick their noses where they are not welcome. The U.S. President is siding with Mbida to overthrow our elected president. My brother saw the video with his own eyes."

Jean-Claude scrunched up his nose in thought. "If the general was going to mount a coup, why would he be on the football pitch with his sons? It makes no sense."

Lucien cuffed his younger friend on the side of the head. "Stop thinking so hard. Maybe we can see my brother arrest the traitor."

A woman's terrified scream came from around the corner, followed by another, this one higher. Jean-Claude's sister had cried like that when a passing taxi had broken her hip.

Lucien's shoulders began to tremble with excitement, so much so that Jean-Claude was afraid the Marines across the street would see the boxwood leaves shaking.

Loud cracks and snaps filled the air as the armored vehicles drove directly through the wooden fence and onto the field. A voice boomed over a loudspeaker, ordering Mbida's men to lay down their weapons. The boys duck-walked between the houses, closer to the demolished fence, so they could get a better look.

Jean-Claude heard a commotion and turned to see Mbida walking out of the chancery. That made more sense. His children were playing football across the street while he plotted with the Americans.

"I think your brother did not have all the information

about the general's whereabouts," Jean-Claude said, still smarting from the early smack to the side of his head.

Lucien cursed. "It does not matter. He will come out. They have his children."

Sporadic gunfire popped and cracked at the football pitch. Women screamed, men shouted, as more orders boomed from the loudspeaker.

An instant later, three young women tore around the corner, running toward the embassy gate. Arms flailing, knees pumping, they ran as if chased by a wild beast. And indeed they were. A squad of about a dozen men ran after them. One of the men moved to shoot, but another swatted the rifle away. Jean-Claude was not a Fusilier, but he was smart enough to know that firing at someone running toward the American embassy would be the same as firing at the American embassy—bringing the wrath of the U.S. Marines posted there.

General Mbida had run from the chancery steps to the gate and waved the girls forward, beckoning them to hurry inside with him. All three of them were young, perhaps fourteen or fifteen, and all wore T-shirts and shorts, tight to their bodies. Boko Haram used children as suicide bombers along the Nigerian border. Even with the general standing right here, the Marines would never have let these girls near the gate if they'd had on clothing that could have hidden a bomb. The one in the lead was bleeding from a wound to her shoulder. As she ran closer, Jean-Claude could see her T-shirt was ripped. This was Mbida's eldest daughter.

One of the Marines dropped to a knee and aimed his rifle at the pursuing Fusiliers, while the other waved the girls through the gate.

Lucien pounded his fist on the ground, cursing again. "Americans must always play the hero."

One of the two armored MRAP vehicles rounded the corner now, and came to a stop facing the embassy. A man in a colonel's uniform stood in the top hatch and spoke into a megaphone.

"General Mbida is a criminal and a traitor wanted for crimes against his people. Send him out at once."

The Americans did not respond, so the colonel repeated himself. The Marines at the front post had moved behind a colonnade now. Their rifles were still at the ready, though not aimed at anything.

The colonel surveyed the embassy with a pair of binoculars for a moment, and turned to someone inside his armored vehicle before putting his hands over his ears.

An instant later the M2 .50-caliber machine gun mounted on top of the Cougar fired three short bursts at the embassy roof, destroying the antenna arrays.

The colonel spoke into the megaphone again. "You are harboring a known criminal. Send him out at once and we will stand down."

Jean-Claude heard women's voices next, yelling in angry English and something else, maybe Korean. A man barked orders, doors slammed. The colonel ducked into his MRAP for a moment, before stepping back up with the megaphone. "I say again—you must send out the traitor General Mbida without delay." He paused for effect, gloating as if he now held the winning hand. "And please pass along a message to Deputy Chief of Mission Porter. His wife is being well taken care of. For now."

12

The White House steward brought in a breakfast of steel-cut oats and fresh blueberries while Ryan showered and dressed. The cyan-blue tie was a little too bright—and too constricting—for his taste, so Ryan decided to leave it on the bed until the last minute. Cathy assured him the tie matched well with his charcoal-gray suit of worsted wool. A good fountain pen and a nice pair of cuff links were about as far as his style sense went.

Ryan kept a copy of *The Wall Street Journal* folded in his lap while he ate. Reading and eating were natural partners, feeding the mind and body—except at Cathy Ryan's table. But she'd stepped away to take a call from the hospital, so Jack had decided to cheat and wash down his morning meal with a little economic news. His late father, a detective with the Baltimore PD, had imbued in him a fierce work ethic, while his mother had given him an extra measure of guilt for doing anything that felt remotely like he was wasting time.

He tossed the newspaper aside when he heard Cathy coming back in from the bedroom. She raised a suspicious brow, enough to let him know that he might be President of the United States, but she was the undisputed commander in chief at the breakfast table.

The Secret Service special agent posted in the Center Hall of the Residence could tell POTUS was on his way out before he opened the door.

"SWORDSMAN en route to the Oval," the agent said into the mic clipped to the collar of his shirt as the President stepped into the hallway, leather briefcase in hand. The response from the USSS command center was transmitted through the agent's earpiece and inaudible to Ryan.

"Good morning, Nick," Ryan said. "How are the kids?"

"Just fine, Mr. President," the agent said, stepping across the hall to enter the elevator. Ryan knew it was the only answer the agent could give, but it was important for him to know that the boss knew he had kids, and that his wife worked as a nurse. Kindness came naturally to Jack Ryan, and he sought nothing in return, but on a purely strategic note, it was a smart tactic to treat the folks who had his back as if they were something more than furniture.

He gave a polite nod to Andrea Young, the Secret Service Uniform Division officer posted outside the elevator on the ground floor. UD was everywhere inside the White House.

Officer Young had tipped off Rear Admiral Jason Bailey, the physician to the President, that Ryan was on his way down. Dr. Bailey stepped out of his office across from the elevator and adjacent to the Map Room. He was a jovial man, with dark hair, rosy cheeks, and deep lines around his eyes, as if he spent most of his day smiling. Bailey oversaw a staff of half a dozen other doctors and nurses that made up the White House Medical Unit, but he delegated little when it came to the President himself. If there was traveling to be done, Dr. Bailey was the one to go, staying near enough to Ryan that he could reach him quickly, but just far enough away that he would not be caught up in any catastrophic event that might render him unable to do his job. When Ryan was in the residence, Dr. Bailey braved the commuter traffic of Highway 50 from his own home in Annapolis so he could put eyes on his patient first thing in the morning when he stepped off the elevator.

"Good morning, Mr. President." Bailey raised a mug of peppermint tea as if to offer a toast. He canted his head to one side, giving Ryan a narrow eye, probing like a CT scan. "A little extra bounce in your step this morning."

"Is that so?" Ryan shrugged, trying to keep a straight face as he thought about Cathy. The presidency really was a fishbowl.

Ryan hung a right when he got off the elevator, stepping outside to continue his morning commute past the Rose Garden and along the colonnade to the Oval Office. He looked forward to the minute or two of fresh air and breeze. The Secret Service agent opened the door and stepped aside, posting outside the door.

Ryan's principal secretary buzzed the intercom the moment he sat down at his desk.

"Good morning, Betty," he said, waiting a beat. She usually gave him a minute or two to settle in, so something had to be up.

"SAIC Montgomery is here. He'd like a few minutes before your nine o'clock."

"By all means," Ryan said, scooting back from the Resolute desk and rising to his feet. Normally people stood when *he* came into the room, but Gary Montgomery was the Special Agent in Charge of the Secret Service Presidential Protection Division—the hundreds of men and women who kept Ryan and his family safe. If Ryan was going to defer to anyone, it would be Montgomery.

The SAIC of PPD came through the door. He was forty-eight years old, six-three, and built like a linebacker. His dark suit was on the expensive side, cut loose to allow for the SIG Sauer pistol and extra magazines on his belt. No desk-jockey boss, he had to be just as prepared as the most junior post-stander on the protective detail—maybe more so. Montgomery had boxed at the University of Michigan and, apart from any athletic competition involving Ohio State, was generally mild mannered. He possessed what Ryan's father had called "quiet hands" and moved with the confident demeanor of a person whose abilities had been severely tested and found equal to the task. Competent. Calm. Unflappable.

And he wasn't smiling.

Ryan motioned to one of the chairs in front of his desk. "Morning, Gary."

"Good morning, Mr. President," Montgomery said, remaining on his feet and getting straight to the point. "As you know, Secret Service Protective Intelligence has search-engine alerts set up on you, your family, and key members of your administration."

"That's gotta be a load of fun to read," Ryan said, shaking his head.

Montgomery glanced at his watch, the kind of glance that said he was in no mood for lighthearted banter. "A little over an hour ago, no fewer than seven different websites calling themselves news organizations put up what are essentially four slightly different versions of the exact same—"

Betty buzzed the intercom again. "Sorry to interrupt, Mr. President, but DNI Foley just arrived, along with Secretaries Burgess and Dehart. The attorney general telephoned to say he is on his way."

The Oval's west door all but exploded off its hinges as Arnie van Damm burst in. He wore a suit, but his bald head was flushed and sweating, as if he'd just stepped off an exercise bike. It took a lot to rattle him, a savvy political operative.

He shot a hard look at Montgomery. "I assume you are here about—"

"I am," the agent said.

Jack Ryan leaned back in his chair and steepled his hands on his chest, index fingers pointing at his chin. He was the only one in the room sitting down, and judging from the way everyone else shuffled their feet, that wasn't about to change anytime soon.

"You all know Gary Montgomery, the agent in charge of my Secret Service detail," Ryan said. "He was just about to brief me on some information his protective intelligence division has come up with."

The director of national intelligence looked at Montgomery. "That crap on the Internet?"

"Yes, ma'am," Montgomery said.

Fiercely loyal, Mary Pat Foley was one of Ryan's closest confidantes and friends, and, as such, was prone to being a bit of a mother hen. She'd moved up next to his desk as soon as she'd come into the Oval, as if to cover him with her wing. As director of national intelligence, Foley provided an umbrella of communication over the sixteen intelligence agencies of the United States. She'd been a case officer at CIA when Ryan was still an analyst, earning a well-deserved reputation as a crack intelligence operative, unafraid of getting her hands dirty with calculated risks. She gave the Secret Service agent a long look, sighed, and then took a half-step back from the desk, literally yielding the floor.

"Sir," Montgomery said, picking up the offered baton and running with it. "An hour ago, several quasi-news sites put up a video purported to be of you talking to a small group of supporters in a Washington hotel."

"Purported?" Ryan mused.

"Yes, sir," Montgomery continued. "The voice and image sound and look like you, but it's definitely not you."

"The Secret Service would be in a position to know," Ryan said. "What am I *purported* to be saying?"

"You're assuring those present that you are saving enough flu vaccine for those in your innermost circle, including the people you are addressing. The video is just a snippet, only twenty-four seconds long, but most of the websites quote unnamed sources that say more damning videos will be released soon." Montgomery blinked hard, as if he had a bad tooth. "The sites go on to accuse you of turning a blind eye to the flooding in Louisiana and the cholera outbreak there that they—"

Ryan sat up straighter. "I'm going to stop you there, Gary." He looked at Homeland Security Secretary Dehart. "Cholera outbreak?"

"That's why I'm here, Mr. President. Three cases as of five a.m. Central Time."

Bob Burgess, the secretary of defense, grimaced. "Cholera? I thought we eradicated that in the U.S.?"

"Doesn't happen often," Dehart said. "Not since we figured out how to keep our water supply and sewage separate. That said, every major flood or hurricane poses some risk. The area where these cases hit is extremely poor, with a lot of folks still using well water and outhouses."

Burgess turned up his nose. "Outhouses can't still be a thing."

"You'd be surprised," Dehart said, turning to Ryan. "FEMA personnel out of Baton Rouge are at the hospital now. A CDC team is en route. I'll have information for you within the hour."

"But no one has died?" Ryan asked.

"Not yet," Dehart said, his mouth set in a grim line. "But two of the cases are children. The prognosis isn't good."

Ryan closed his eyes. "A cholera outbreak . . ."

"Not an outbreak," van Damm said, glaring at Montgomery. "Three cases."

"I used the websites' language, sir," Montgomery said.

"Go on," Ryan said. "What else does the website language say?"

"More accusations," Montgomery said. "You supposedly have a team of personal assassins to carry out extrajudicial killings pursuant to the Ryan Doctrine. There's a lot of discussion about what they are calling a 'callous unwillingness' to support the students in Iran against their oppressive regime. But the vaccine video is the most problematic, as far as the Secret Service is concerned."

"You mean the one that is the most likely to make people want to kill me?"

"To put it bluntly," Montgomery said. "Yes, Mr. President."

Van Damm slid a tablet computer across the desk. "I've got it pulled up if you want to take a look."

Ryan watched the twenty-four seconds of footage four times. He knew he'd never made such a speech, but even he would have said it was real.

"This video is a clip from an address I gave to a group of public policy students at the University of Maryland a couple of years ago. I'm sure someone's thrown it up on YouTube." He slid the chief of staff back his tablet. "The voice sounds like me, and my lips match the words being said, but as I recall, that particular speech was about European trade."

"Unfortunately," Mary Pat said, "it's getting all too easy to manipulate audio and video. Deepfake, or Fake-App, they call it. There are several types of software that do a believable job. We were playing with this tech several years ago at the Agency. You just need an existing video and some audio files from which to get exemplars. An actor can then sit in front of a camera and microphone and read from a prepared script. The program inputs the mouth movements, facial expressions, and synthesized voice onto the target video. It's CGI and AI all rolled into one."

"Should be easy to disprove," Ryan said. "Since the actual video is on YouTube."

"That's the problem," Foley said. "The real video makes you look good. The doctored one makes you look bad."

"And you think people will believe the bad," Ryan said.

"That's the way it works, sir," van Damm said. "Stir some bullshit in with the truth and the bullshit floats to the top." The muscles in his jaw tightened. "The opening bell in New York won't ring for another hour, but the

London Exchange is already in a freefall. Somebody believes it. And Senator Chadwick is helping things along by providing color commentary as events unfold. Her snarky tweets have already been retweeted thousands of times. This whole shit storm has taken on a life of gargantuan proportions."

DNI Foley made a face like she'd just eaten a whole lemon. "I wouldn't be surprised if she was behind this. Chadwick, I mean."

"I doubt even she would stoop this low," Ryan said.

"Well she's certainly piling on," Foley said. "Especially about the Persian Spring."

"Is that what we're calling it now?" Ryan asked, looking pained.

"Well, she is," Foley said. "And so is just about everyone else."

"All of you have a seat," he said. "I want to get into that."

Special Agent Montgomery braced. "Thank you, Mr. President. I'll be over at the Hoover Building this morning following up on this with a friend at the FBI. Special Agent Langford will be in charge here."

"Gary," Ryan said, leaning forward with both elbows on the desk. "And this goes for the rest of you as well. I can see full well that you've all got your blood up about these posts and twitters . . . tweets. You're pissed. Hell, I'm pissed. But I'll remind you all that when our blood's up it's easy to make mistakes, mistakes the American people do not deserve. It goes without saying, but this Internet garbage notwithstanding, neither the FBI nor the Secret Service is my private police force. We can't go around tossing senators in jail—or throwing them off balconies—just because they say mean things about me."

He was met with silent stares.

"Understood?"

Murmurs now, but none from the heart.

"Understood," Montgomery said. "But I do have to protect you, Mr. President. And to do that, I need *all* the facts. Sometimes protective investigations aren't necessarily prosecutable . . . because lines get crossed."

"Watch the lines." Ryan held up his hands. "But I trust you."

Montgomery left through the door to the secretaries' suite, pulling it shut softly behind him.

Ryan called for a coffee service and joined the others in the center of the Oval, taking his customary chair by the fireplace.

"No balconies?" Mary Pat Foley said. There was an unspoken pecking order in the group, and as President Ryan's oldest friend in the room, she nestled in at the end of the couch nearest him. "You sure about that?"

Ryan turned to Dehart, the newest member of his cabinet. "You'll have to excuse her, Mark."

"I'm kidding." Foley smirked. "But seriously, how do you feel about thumbscrews?"

Ryan gave a wan smile. "Let's talk about Iran," he said. "Most of the stuff those websites said about me is bullshit. We all know that. But Senator Chadwick is right about one thing. I do have serious misgivings about this so-called Persian Spring."

The chief of staff rolled his eyes. "Due respect, sir, but here we go again. The existing regime makes no bones about the fact that they hate us. Throwing U.S. support behind the protesters seems like a no-brainer."

"I agree with Arnie," the SecDef said. "But just this one time."

Ryan tapped a pencil against the knee of his crossed leg. "The trouble with no-brainers," he said, "is that they make it easy for us to stop using our brains. I'm not a big fan of that."

"Can't argue there," Burgess said. "I'm not saying we should follow blindly, but virtually all of our allies are falling in behind the protesters."

"That's a true point, sir," Foley said.

Ryan shook his head. "There's something about this Reza Kazem character that rubs me the wrong way. He's a little too . . . Rasputinesque for my blood. I'd like your people to dig into him a little deeper."

"Right away," Foley said. "And speaking of Kazem, the Bureau puts him meeting with a Russian SVR operative in Crystal City four days ago."

Ryan chewed on the new information. "Which SVR operative?"

"A woman by the name of Elizaveta Bobkova," Foley said. "She's registered as an economic attaché, but there's no doubt she's Russian intelligence. From what I hear, she's quite the up-and-comer in the Sluzhba Vneshney Razvedki." Mary Pat Kaminsky Foley's Russian was flawless—as was her intuition regarding Russian spies. "According to the Bureau counterintel guys, Senator Chadwick's aide saw the meeting."

"Was this aide a party to it?"

Foley shook her head. "Just a witness. They said he looked as surprised as they were. He definitely saw it, though, according to the agents. Seems like sloppy trade-craft for an operative of Bobkova's caliber. Maybe she wanted us to see her."

"No word from the good senator's office?" Ryan asked.

Foley shook her head.

"Why am I not surprised."

"Moscow backs the sitting regime in Tehran," Dehart said. "Why would one of their intel types sit down with Kazem?"

"Hedging their bets," SecDef Burgess offered. "A couple of moderate mullahs are making noise about meeting with the protesting students."

"I know I'm painting with a broad brush here," Ryan said. "But in my experience, there are no moderate mullahs in Iran. There are hardline mullahs and practical mullahs—who are still hardline but understand realpolitik enough to know that certain concessions have to be made for their regime to survive in the near term."

"There is another possibility regarding Bobkova," Mary Pat said. "We see Russia playing nice with Reza Kazem's group, we're more likely to jump on the bandwagon. Not sure why they would want us to, but it plays into your hunch that something we don't know about is going on in the background."

"That sounds about right," Ryan said. "Birddog this for me."

Foley nodded. "Of course."

"With your permission, Mr. President," van Damm said, "I'd like to schedule another meeting on this topic tomorrow. Things are very nearly reaching the boiling point in Iran. We need to keep a weather eye."

"Good idea," Ryan said. "In the meantime, Mark,

you'll check with your people in Louisiana, and Mary Pat, you'll get me more on Kazem and this Russian connection. There is something going on here that we aren't—"

Betty buzzed in for the third time in the past fifteen minutes. "Commander Forrestal is here, Mr. President. He says it's urgent."

"Very well," Ryan said into the intercom.

The deputy national security adviser, United States Navy Commander Robert Forrestal, stepped inside the door and snapped to attention, as he always did when he came into the Oval. He'd changed over from his winter blues to his summer white uniform just weeks before. Ryan thought Marine Corps dress was the classiest uniform that there was, but when it came to the Navy, the summer whites looked especially sharp.

"Good morning, Robby," Ryan said. "And you too, Scott."

The secretary of state, Scott Adler, stepped in behind Commander Forrestal. "I'm guessing you're both here about the situation with the video?"

The two men looked at each other as if surprised by the question. They both nodded.

"Arnie showed me," Ryan said. "I'm sure the networks have already picked it up."

"CNN has it," Adler said.

Forrestal spoke next. "We have personnel in Garoua, in the northern part of the country, as well as air assets in Agadez, Niger. They are aware of the situation and—"

Ryan frowned, throwing his hand up. "I think we're talking at cross-purposes here. Start over as if I don't know anything about this. Because I sure as hell do not."

"Cameroon, Mr. President," Forrestal said. "President Njaya's troops have surrounded our embassy in Yaounde."

"Surrounded?" Arnie van Damm put a hand on top of his bald head. "What the hell do you mean, surrounded?"

Adler gave an exhausted shrug. "Encircled, Arnie. Swarmed. Bum-rushed." He looked at Ryan. Any briefing in the Oval was meant for the President, not the chief of staff. "They were attacked, sir. No casualties reported, but we believe a Cameroonian general has taken refuge with his family in the chancery."

"We believe?" Ryan asked, his voice dropping to a fierce whisper.

"Cameroonian forces destroyed the satellite antennas and appear to be blocking cell transmissions. We're trying to reestablish communications now."

Ryan considered everything that had been said in the past few minutes. He looked hard from Forrestal to Adler. "There was some miscommunication about a situation with a video when you first came in. What video were you talking about?"

The secretary of state spoke next. "A video of you, Mr. President. You and General Mbida of the Cameroonian Army."

Ryan nodded. "Mbida was in Washington three months ago, looking at colleges for his eldest daughter. We spoke briefly at an event . . . I can't even remember where."

"Kennedy Center," Adler said. "You were both at the same performance of *Rigoletto*."

"That's right." Ryan groaned. "Cathy's doing. I just spoke with him for a few moments during intermission."

"It goes without saying that the video is not real, but in it, you are seen assuring General Mbida that you will back him in a coup against President Njaya."

"All right," Ryan said. "Let's get the rest of the principals in here." By that, he meant the principal members of the National Security Council. Those already present in the Oval were principal attendees, but an incident like this called for the chairman of the joint chiefs, D/CIA, and, at the very least, White House counsel. He looked at Foley. "Deepfake? That's what you called it?"

"Yes, sir."

Ryan tapped the pencil on his knee again, working through the possibilities. "Two of these videos coming to light in a matter of hours can't be a coincidence. There's a state actor behind this—and I'm betting it's not Cameroon."

13

It seemed like a great deal of commotion for one man to go fishing.

A phalanx of black ZiL sedans and BMW motorcycles painted militia white and blue blocked each end of Bol'shoy Kamenny and Bol'shoy Moskvoretsky—bridges crossing into the center of Moscow—snarling already horrendous traffic by forcing afternoon traffic to detour to the Ulitsa Krymsky to the west or Ustyinsky to the east. Apart from roving members of the Presidential Security Service, vehicles were now nonexistent in the uppermost arc of the Moskva River south of the Kremlin. Snipers armed with modern Orsis T-5000 precision rifles parked themselves behind powerful scopes on either bridge, scanning the river and adjacent buildings as if their own lives depended on their vigilance. Militia patrol boats to the east and west halted all maritime traffic.

A gaggle of heavily vetted journalists stood with their cameras and recorders on the other side of a rope line, a hundred feet to the east along the concrete embankment. Russians in general thought it foolish to smile for no reason, but these men and women approached the assignment of watching the president of Russia with all the gusto of a press that was free to write exactly what it was told to write. Most of them smoked or drank strong tea from metal thermoses, paying only rudimentary attention to the two fishermen.

Maksim Dudko stood on the bottom of the concrete steps leading down from the Sofiyskaya Embankment, and cast his line with an expert flick of his wrist. He began to reel immediately, drawing a sideways glance from President Nikita Yermilov, who considered himself a purist with his eight-hundred-dollar Orvis fly rod.

Dudko found himself ever in the shadow of his former cohort at the KGB—but the shadow of the most powerful man in Russia could be a very comfortable place. For one, he got to go fishing within sight of the Archangel cathedral's golden domes without having to fight for a spot with some idiot with a stick and piece of string. Dudko retrieved his lure, checked over his shoulder to make certain he didn't hook a roving security man, and then flicked another cast into the foamy brown water. He stopped reeling long enough to dab at his eyes with a tissue. The winds were from the south this afternoon, bringing the sour stench of sulfur dioxide and something that smelled a good deal like burned popcorn from the Gazprom Refinery a scant ten kilometers away inside the Moscow Ring Road.

Yermilov stripped out a few feet more from his reel and began to flick his rod, placing the fly exactly in the center of the eddying current seven or so meters upstream. Purist or not, one had to admit that the president was extremely good at the artistic side of fly fishing. Unfortunately for everyone, that did not mean he could catch fish.

"What are you using today, Gospodin President?"

Yermilov flicked the tip of his rod, whipping it back and forward and back and forward. He let the fly settle on the water for only a few seconds each time—certainly not enough time for a fish to even notice the thing. "My favorite violet leech," he said. "A certain winner at this time of year."

"Excellent," Dudko said, hooking his third perch of the afternoon. The president gave him a withering stare and then glanced quickly at the gaggle of press. They appeared to animate slightly each time a fish was landed.

"And you?" Yermilov said. "A spinning rod, of all things. With what monstrosity are you flailing the water today?"

Dudko smiled. He hadn't survived this long without understanding the president's veiled meanings. They were so deep sometimes as to be positively subterranean. He gave an embarrassed shrug. "I am using a vibrating spoon. In truth, it is not altogether sporting." He continued to reel, pausing for a beat as if mulling something over. "To be honest," he said, "I would not mind giving that violet leech a try . . . if I might trouble you, my old friend." He held out the spinning rod, silver spoon dangling, dripping water—and the tiny jawbone of his last catch.

Yermilov passed him the fly rod without reeling in the line, causing no small amount of concern in Dudko that he might accidentally hook something before the president got the spinner in the water. It turned out to be a nonissue.

Yermilov roared with glee at each fish he reeled in, even going so far as to school Dudko on the proper way to land each bream or roach. "Excellent, Maksim Timofeyevich. I must use this vibrating spoon in Irkutsk in July. The cisco fishing there is superb this year."

"With the added benefit that you can eat the fish," Dudko said.

Yermilov darkened. "What do you mean by that?"

"The PCBs, Gospodin President," Dudko said, wide-eyed now. "Mercury, other toxins. Any fish caught from the Moskva would be full of dangerous chemicals."

"That is nonsense and you know it," Yermilov scoffed, adding to the toxins in the water with a ball of spit he hawked from this throat. "It is perfectly safe to eat fish caught in any waters in Russia."

Dudko gave the bobbing nod of the impotent. "I am sure it is, Gospodin President." He had accompanied Yermilov on his annual fishing trip to Irkutsk to fish in Lake Baikal for the past eight years. It was inexplicable that he would not be invited again this year—but if the president was going to issue an invitation, this would have been the perfect opportunity. And then Dudko had had to make the incautious remark about eating fish from the Moscow River. How stupid of him. He knew Yermilov prided himself on the perfection of Mother Russia—even her toxic fish.

A murmur rose from the press gaggle, giving Dudko a moment's respite from the president's glare. A few of them looked at their mobile phones. Some took calls, nodding sternly, pretending that there was nothing even remotely as interesting in the world as watching the president of the Russian Federation catch fish that he was never going to eat.

Yermilov reeled in another fish, this one a sickly-looking bream with a misshapen dorsal fin. He gave a toss of his head toward the press line. "What are they going on about?"

The security officer nearest the journalists spoke to a woman behind a camera for a few moments, and then turned to stride quickly toward a more mature officer, the man in charge of the president's detail. This one wore a dark suit and buzzed hair that showed the rolls of pink scalp above his ears. Dudko had never seen someone with muscles in their head like Yermilov's lead agent. The elder security man listened intently, still scanning the area while the young man spoke in his ear, and then turned to approach Yermilov. He stopped some ten feet away until the president let go of the rod long enough with one hand to motion him closer. The security man passed him a mobile phone, whispered a few short words, and then took a step back.

Yermilov held the phone as far away from his eyes as possible with his free hand, turning away so the press could not get footage of him squinting. He continued to fish with the other free hand. A smile spread slowly across his face—no small thing for someone who believed smiles were generally the product of a weak mind. At length, he passed the spinning rod to the security man and turned to Dudko.

"Let us walk."

Dudko complied at once, passing the president's Orvis to the same security man, who promptly handed off both rods to the junior member of his team.

Yermilov showed the phone screen to Dudko as they walked west along the embankment toward Kamenny Bridge. "What do you make of this?"

Dudko scrolled through the article, waiting for the president to say what *he* made of the situation before chiming in. He might be able to recover from one slip, but not two.

"There is a lot going on with the United States," Yermilov said.

Dudko offered to return the phone, but the president had read enough. Dudko slipped it into his vest. "President Ryan certainly has his hands full at the moment."

Yermilov stopped and gazed across the river, eyes half closed, the way he did when he was coming to some conclusion.

"Operation ANIVA," he said.

"This is a large step forward, Gospodin President," Dudko said. He knew he had to tread carefully here, but the man did keep him around to offer some modicum of advice.

"Nonsense," Yermilov said, turning to walk back toward the security team and the press gaggle, making it clear that there would be little more in the way of discussion. Dudko had said exactly the wrong thing.

"Think of it," Yermilov said. "Floods, disease, an embassy under siege, and citizens who are finally aware of the great Jack Ryan's duplicitous ways. One of his own senators has accused him of going after political rivals. He is much too busy to bother with a little military exercise, even if it happens to involve Ukraine. And what can anyone do once we have control? It is rightfully ours in any case. We have our Russian citizens there to think of."

"This is true," Dudko said.

Yermilov stopped, peering directly into Dudko's eyes. "You believe me responsible, don't you?"

As far as Yermilov was concerned, "me" and the Rodina—Mother Russia—were one and the same.

"It is not my place to think of such things," Dudko

stammered, almost hearing the doors to Lefortovo Prison slam shut behind him.

"No," Yermilov said, offering slightly more shoulder as he walked. "It is not. I will tell you this, though, our Black Sea bots would make short work of Ryan's reputation. Whether it is us or not, I am more than happy to take advantage of the situation."

Already drowning, Dudko threw away any flotation he had. "But President Ryan, sir, he already suspects our activities on the Internet."

Yermilov wagged his head from side to side. "Jack Ryan will do what Jack Ryan will do . . ."

Had the army of Russian Internet bots, run out of various warehouse locations around the Black Sea, been involved, Yermilov would surely know about it, for there was little that went on inside or outside Russia of which he was not aware.

"Byla ne byla." Yermilov shrugged. Literally, "There was, there was not," the proverb more figuratively meant "Let the chips fall where they may." It was a brash sentiment for the most powerful man in Russian, but had worked well for him up to this point. "Besides, his own citizens are questioning his so-called Ryan Doctrine for what it is—state-sponsored murder."

They walked slowly along the river, reaching the security men again. Former KGB mongrel that he was, Yermilov was still a political animal. He took a moment to wave at the press before taking back his own fly rod.

"I think there is a fish on there, Gospodin President," the young security officer said as he handed it off.

"No," Yermilov said smugly. "I am quite certain there

is not." A moment later he began to fight a fish. "Look," he said to Dudko, ignoring the security man completely. "I have caught another. Sorry to say it will have to be the last. I have much to take care of."

"Of course," Dudko said for at least the hundredth time in the past hour. "That is a nice catch there, sir."

"You take the fish," Yermilov said, holding the stringer up and foisting it on his aide so the media could see his generosity as well as his faith in the Moscow River. "You can tell me how they tasted tomorrow."

"I will make some calls," Dudko said.

Yermilov leaned away. "To whom?"

"The generals," Dudko said. "To begin Operation ANIVA."

Yermilov waved away the thought. "Do not trouble yourself, Maksim Timofeyevich. Colonel Grokin will contact the necessary players."

"I . . ." Dudko paused, looking helplessly at the wall of stone that Yermilov's face had become. He bobbed his head again. "Of course, Gospodin President."

Dudko's guts twisted. The muscles in his face began to twitch and he had to move his jaw to make them stop. And just like that, he was on the outside looking in, with that fool Colonel Grokin contacting the necessary players. And now the wily old yes-man would probably get an invitation to go fishing in Irkutsk as well. Dudko had to do some-thing. A grand strategy that would bring him back into good standing. He was good at strategy—a master, really. That's why Yermilov had kept him around, wasn't it? He'd had a dry spell. That was all. But what to do now? This thing with the American President had some promise. There were Russian fingerprints all over it, though the

Americans who hated Ryan had certainly kept the ball rolling, so to speak. Yes, this might provide a way back into Yermilov's good graces if Dudko played his hand correctly. By the time they climbed the concrete steps up the Sofiyskaya Embankment to Yermilov's waiting ZiL, Dudko had begun to see the way before him. The armored sedan was set up in vis-à-vis fashion and he started to climb into the rear-facing seats across from the president.

Yermilov stopped him. "You must take home your catch," he said. "One of my men will give you a ride."

Yermilov gave a flick of his hand, like a cavalry officer signaling forward, and the motorcade sped away. Dudko found himself standing on the sidewalk with a plastic bucket full of fish and a lone member of Yermilov's security team.

"Your residence, Comrade Dudko?" the young man asked.

"Yes, of course," Dudko mumbled, preoccupied in the fog of his nascent plan that swirled in his head.

This could work. He would make the call as soon as he dropped off the poison fish and returned to his office. One of the benefits of being in the inner circle for so long was that he knew things about people.

Elizaveta Bobkova would not be happy about his proposal. No, she would yowl like a cat over a bathtub, trying everything to scratch and claw her way out. But what could she do? He knew too much about her, and as chief SVR officer of Washington Station, she had far too much to lose.

14

President Ryan decided on a preliminary briefing while he waited for the rest of the NSC principals to arrive. Still in the Oval, he leaned back in his chair and closed his eyes, pulling up the image of West Africa. He'd always had a knack for geography, but the deployment of more and more American troops to join the hunt for Boko Haram terrorists had drawn lines in his mind that were crystal clear. Cameroon had more than its share of violence and corruption, not to mention a president who had done away with term limits and declared himself the winner of each election over the last two decades. But they were still ostensibly U.S. allies in the region.

"How many people do we have in the embassy?"

"They're slotted for fifty-one direct hires," the secretary of state said. "Some of those are bound to be off at conferences or out of country on home leave. Many of the diplomatic corps live nearby so some of them might even have gone home for lunch. Without communication with the embassy, I'm still trying to find out how many families are in country. I will know more on that before lunchtime here."

"Make it an hour," Ryan said.

Adler folded his hands in front of his belt. "I will, sir." There was no *I'll do my best*. That was a given. The prodding meant he could pass along to foreign service officers who worked for him that the President of the United States put their people, their families, as a top priority.

Ryan groaned. "All right. Let's have it all, Robby."

The deputy national security adviser referred to his notes, making certain to get the facts straight in his bottom-line-up-front brief.

"At 1258 hours local time, State Department Ops received a call from one of the administrative staff at our embassy in Yaounde, stating that they were under siege by Cameroonian military forces. The connection was lost after approximately forty-five seconds. The deputy chief of mission's wife—her name is Sarah Porter—was at home a few blocks away. She was apparently taken hostage by the military forces involved. Her condition or whereabouts is, as of yet, unknown. Apparently General Mbida fled pursuing troops through the embassy gate along with at least one of his daughters. Six armored Cameroonian military vehicles arrived just moments behind them but remained outside the fence. That is all the information we got before contact was broken. Efforts to reestablish communication with anyone inside the embassy compound have proven fruitless to this point."

Ryan leaned forward in his chair, mentally bracing himself for what was about to come next. "Casualties?"

"Unknown at this time, Mr. President. Contacts at the South Korean embassy report small-arms fire. They're buttoned up tight for the moment, but they have dedicated an analyst to keep us up to date on what they're seeing—which up to now is not very much."

Ryan said, "Let's open some back channels through neighboring countries. Get things rolling right away."

"We have DEA personnel in Lagos and Homeland Security in Accra," Forrestal said. "One of my Annapolis classmates is an NCIS special agent stationed in Douala, on the coast. I've reached out to him directly but have yet to make contact. And the two hundred seventy-eight men in Garoua to the north."

"Good work, Robby," Ryan said, stifling a groan. He was groaning far too much lately, and didn't want to do it without thinking if the cameras happened to be rolling with hot mics. "So that's the *what*. How about the *why*? This seems like a drastic overreaction to a grainy video."

Forrestal looked at Scott Adler. His job was to brief and offer analysis when called upon to do so, but the embassy fell under Foggy Bottom's purview—and the Commander was happy to let the secretary of state jump in.

"We're still in the guessing stages," Adler said. "But President Njaya has been hounding us to publicly take his side against the separatist movement in the English-speaking areas of the country."

"Okay," Ryan said. "I realize we're early in the process here, but I need eyes on the ground. Some kind of intelligence. What's the size of the Marine guard force there?"

Forrestal glanced at his notes. He'd been briefing Ryan long enough to know he would ask about fellow Marines. "The NCOIC and five watch standers," he said.

"Maybe they run a split shift," Ryan observed. "Could be they're not all on duty. Find out the number for the NCOIC and for the Marine House in Cameroon." He turned to Burgess. "On second thought, you handle this, Bob. I want someone stratospheric in their chain of command to call and remind these Marines not to rush in and get themselves killed. We need intelligence, not martyrs. This is not the hill I want them to die on."

Cell phones were customarily left in a basket outside the Oval, so Burgess opened a drawer in the base of his chair, retrieving one of the secure landlines to make his call. He cupped a hand over his mouth, speaking in hushed but forceful tones to convey the gravity and necessary speed of the situation. He hung up less than a minute later, giving the President a nod that it was done.

Forrestal said, "Two MQ-9s are in the air now from Garoua. They should be on scene in the next ten minutes."

"Good to hear," Ryan said. "Let's get the feeds piped into the Situation Room."

"Already being done, Mr. President," Burgess said.

"Bob," Ryan said. "Any of those sons of bitches who've attacked American soil so much as point an antiaircraft weapon above the tree line, and we dust them."

"Understood."

"The Task Force Darby CO"—Forrestal referred to his notes—"Major Workman, is discussing the situation with his host counterparts there in the northern part of the country."

"Eighty-seventh Infantry out of Fort Drum is running the show along the Nigerian border," Burgess said.

Ryan gave a nod of approval. "Tenth Mountain. Good."

Burgess continued. "Major Workman feels confident at least some of the Cameroonian Rapid Intervention Battalion will give him a straight answer. They've spilled blood and shed blood together fighting Boko Haram. There's some trust there going both ways."

"If they even know," Ryan said. "BIR forces working

daily alongside the U.S. military are not likely to be in the loop on any attack. Are you telling me the Cameroonian military chased one of their own generals into our embassy and nothing hit any of our tripwires?"

Every U.S. mission overseas had emergency action plans that included highly classified benchmarks that would elicit specific responses. These benchmarks were known as *tripwires*. Molotov cocktails on a car parked across the street might cause an increased uniformed guard presence. Lob one over the fence and stronger measures would kick in. Certain tripwires—coups, nearby terrorist attacks—might call for anything from the evacuation of nonessential personnel all the way to the destruction of documents and closure of the embassy.

"None, Mr. President," SecState Adler said. "This happened all at once. No warning. No tripwires."

Forrestal said, "Initial reports indicate most locally hired security forces have walked away in the face of the military vehicles."

"'Most'?" Ryan said.

"Korean witnesses say there are two out front with the Marines."

Ryan took a deep breath. "I'm trying to imagine our Marines allowing people to run into the embassy, even a general."

Forrestal paused for a moment, like he had uncomfortable news. "The Korean diplomat I spoke to indicated the Marines taught a big self-defense course to local women and girls. This is only a guess, but General Mbida's daughter could have been part of that class. According to the South Koreans, the Marines recognized them, saw they were in danger, and let them in."

Now Ryan let go with an honest-to-goodness groan.

"What about Diplomatic Security?" he asked. The regional security officer would be the senior law enforcement and security expert at the embassy.

"The RSO is a guy named Carr," Adler said. "He was a SWAT officer with Albuquerque PD before he came on with State. I pulled his record before coming over here. He's apparently kind of a badass. He's been with DSS for fourteen years."

"We could use a few badasses over there right now," Ryan mused. "Cameroon . . . That's Ambassador Burlingame. Right?"

"Correct, Mr. President," Adler said. "Chance Burlingame. He came over from USAID a couple of months ago. He's got a lengthy history with the foreign service in Africa."

"What's his status at this moment?"

"Outside the embassy," Adler said, shifting on his feet as he did so. No one in the room liked to admit that they did not have a clear answer to one of the President's questions. "We are still checking. But according to the staffer who made the original call to Ops, the badass RSO is with him."

15

Adin Carr loved his job, but he didn't care much for the title of regional security officer. His father was a cop, his brother was a cop, and he was a cop—not a security officer. The title of RSO was absent from his business cards and he introduced himself simply as Special Agent Carr. No one in Africa—or anywhere else other than the big-dog diplomats at Foggy Bottom—cared anyway.

"You, Mr. Ambassador," Carr said, dodging a centipede the size of his hand as it undulated across the dirt trail, "are one heck of a runner."

He adjusted the fanny pack on his waist to keep it from flopping as they headed down the wooded trail. The Glock 19 he carried inside the small nylon bag wasn't a huge weapon, but he didn't have a lot of extra padding and the ten-kilometer course up the hill behind the embassy and around behind the Hotel Mont Fébé gave it plenty of time to give him a hellacious bruise on the point of his hip if he wasn't careful. He was tall, a little on the gaunt side, with the dark copper complexion of his Navajo mother. A desert rat at heart, he'd grown up on the reservation near Blanding, Utah, and would never get used to humidity like that of West Africa. Carr subscribed to the maxim that golf was a good walk spoiled, but the course behind the embassy offered a great place to run without getting run over by some crazy taxi driver. Better still, it was manicured and relatively well drained after the last week of constant rain. There was the off chance that some rascal would try and rob him during the run, which was the point of carrying the Glock.

He'd started calling the bad guys "rascals" when he was RSO in Papua New Guinea, the assignment prior to this one. The word had a quaint connotation in the United States—mischievous. But in PNG, the masked bandits would hack you to pork chops with a bush knife if they didn't shoot you in the face with a homemade shotgun.

Carr's mother was from the Two Rocks Sit clan, daughter of a long line of Navajo holy men. She believed in skin walkers, curses, and all manner of witches and spirits, but those highland tribes Carr met in PNG took it to an entirely new level. Those rascals burned women to death for sorcery on a regular basis. As with most assignments, he and Linda had made many friends in PNG, but the three years in Port Moresby had been an eternity, with him worried about his wife every time she went to the store. Cameroon was poor, rife with political corruption, and pretty much looked as if the whole country had just been carpet-bombed. But it was a picnic compared to their time in PNG. It was sure as hell better than going back stateside. He'd already been told he would be tapped as a supervisory agent at WFO—the Washington Field Office—on his return and he wanted to stay away from D.C. as long as possible. Besides, he and Linda were in this for the adventure. Africa was a good place for that. Black mambas, bush cobras, rampaging elephants, Boko

Haram—there was plenty to love. He'd heard the rascals were a little more civilized in Cameroon, but the ones he'd seen still carried big bush knives, and he didn't intend to find out how eager they were to use them. Especially not with the ambassador in tow.

The last chief of mission had contracted malaria and returned to Iowa. Burlingame had been in Cameroon for only two months, but he wasn't new to Africa, having worked for the U.S. Agency for International Development in several other countries. The ambassador was an inch or two taller than Carr, well over six feet, with sandy blond hair that he kept just long enough to part. He carried himself well, and, as anyone who'd spent any length of time on the continent, understood that unpredictable things happened for one simple reason—*TIA*.

This Is Africa.

"Adin," Burlingame said, hardly even breathing hard after five and a half of their six-mile run. "What do you say we add a couple of klicks to our run tomorrow."

"I'm heading to Botswana tomorrow to teach a class at the regional police academy. I'm game for Friday." Carr shot his boss a grin. "But you might keep in mind that I not only have to run, I have to be in good enough shape to fend off a deadly forest cobra while you escape if we get into trouble."

Burlingame chuckled—something the previous guy rarely did, even before he got malaria. "Then who am I supposed to run with while you're gone to Botswana?"

"You could stay inside, where—"

Emergency sirens that Carr had mounted on the embassy walls stopped him in his tracks. Painfully loud, the wailing sirens pulled double duty, warning everyone on the compound that something bad was going down, and, it was hoped, scaring some sense into any vandals who might be trying to pull a Tehran.

Carr ducked sideways, toward the shadow of some trees, grabbing Ambassador Burlingame by the shoulder of his T-shirt and dragging him along.

"A drill?" the ambassador asked.

Carr crept forward, keeping an eye peeled for the whip-like form of any Jameson's mambas as he pulled aside the greenery for a better look at the embassy grounds.

"Nope," he said. "Not a drill."

"How can you know?"

"Because I'm the one who schedules the drills."

The scene came into view for both men at the same moment, and their reactions were 180 degrees apart. Burlingame gasped, bolting forward, ready to run head-long to the fence. Carr yanked him back, keeping him in the safety of the trees.

Burlingame attempted to pull away. "I have to get down there."

"Hang on," Carr hissed, taking a better grip on the ambassador's shirt. He was fully prepared to tackle the man if he had to. "We won't do anyone any good if you're caught up in whatever this is."

Burlingame's chest heaved. "Your people gave no in-dication?"

"None," Carr said, still concentrating on the melee below. Three women he recognized as embassy spouses had been swimming with their kids in the pool not far from the back fence when the sirens went off. Embassy staff drilled with their families for all sorts of disasters and emergencies. Even the kids had scrambled out of the pool and were now running toward the chancery. Six heavy Camaroonian MRAP vehicles had taken up strategic positions outside the fence.

"A siege," the ambassador whispered.

An embassy staffer Carr recognized as Karen from Human Resources leaned out an upper-floor window with what looked like a satellite phone, before ducking quickly back inside when she saw the MRAPs. Carr thought it odd that she'd risk leaning out for a call until he saw the demolished antenna array on the roof. They'd heard a couple of booms before they came around the mountain, but they'd been muffled by the thick foliage and Carr had chalked them up to aircraft or a distant military drill.

His hand dropped to the fanny pack, tapping his own Glock to make sure it was still there. He had one extra magazine with fifteen more rounds, giving him thirty-one in all. The pistol made him feel a little better, but it was hardly enough to mount a counterattack. In addition to the sidearm, he had a folding Benchmade knife, a small Streamlight flashlight, and a cell phone. He went for the phone first.

"Good idea," Burlingame said. "Maybe someone in the chancery can tell us what's going on."

Carr tried the security office first, got nothing but a fast busy signal. The troops that had rushed the embassy had likely jammed the towers. They'd probably cut the landlines as well.

Carr lowered the phone.

"Cell phones are a no-go," he said. "We need to get you to a secure location and find a landline or satellite phone to call this in."

The ambassador took several deep breaths, trying to

calm himself. "What the hell, Adin? Did Cameroon just declare war on the United States?"

"It looks that way, sir," Carr said. "We need to go."

"We can't just leave."

"That's exactly what we're going to do, Mr. Ambassador."

Burlingame gasped, pointing downhill.

"Damn it!" Carr hissed.

Sarah Porter, the wife of the deputy chief of mission, was dragged from one of the MRAPs and shoved into a waiting jeep. Her hands were cuffed behind her.

"Mrs. Porter . . ."

Burlingame grabbed Carr by the forearm. "We have to follow that jeep."

"Sir," Carr said. "Mrs. Porter is awesome. She's like that really cool aunt that most of us had a crush on when we were kids. But my first priority is your safety."

Burlingame gave him a side-eyed glare. "I can tell you want to go after her. I'm just giving you an excuse. An order, really."

Carr weighed his options. There were several friendly embassies in the area, but there were also a lot of unfriendly-looking military vehicles patrolling around them. No, the Peace Corps offices were a better choice. They weren't secure, but they were close, less than two kilometers away on the east side of the golf course. They'd do their best to see where the Army took Mrs. Porter, and then he'd stash Ambassador Burlingame at the Peace Corps offices until he got a handle on what was going down—or the cavalry arrived.

"You're the boss," he finally said.

"Maybe Boko Haram infiltrated the military, do you

think?" Burlingame asked as they moved, peering through the foliage toward the compound.

"No," Carr said. "It looks like a coup or something. If it was Boko we'd be hearing a heck of a lot more gunfire."

"At least it's political, then, and not religious."

Carr ducked to the right, hopping over a decaying log that looked like a good home for a snake. "Mr. Ambassador," he said grimly. "To some people, politics is a religion."

16

Reza Kazem and his men—seven in all—pressed their chests into the muddy soup, shoulders hunched against a steady downpour, rifles out in front ready to deploy quickly if the need arose—which it would, and very soon. Countless silver waterfalls, born of the heavy spring rains, streaked the gunmetal mountains, turning gullies into streams and streams into rivers.

They carried long knives and assorted versions of the venerable Russian Kalashnikov, some with folding stocks, some with blond wooden furniture, others with a plastic that reflected distorted images of their nervous faces. Guns were not easy to come by, and target practice drew unwanted attention even out of town. Their kit, it seemed, had been cobbled together by someone who looked at a magazine photograph of the gear an insurgent should have. A few of the items, like the coil of para cord dangling from one's belt, were generally superfluous. Others, like the three metal carabiners clipped to Raheem's load-bearing vest, looked ridiculous and posed a real danger to the mission. Still, Kazem left the men to their own devices when it came to gear. The blood of a revolutionary coursed through the veins of every Iranian—even, or especially, those who had grown tired of life since the last one.

Kazem had wanted bad weather. Officials tended not to bother with too much of anything that required them to get out of their vehicles in this kind of rain. The storage facility outside Tehran was a plum assignment, absent the frequent skirmishes farther south in Baluchistan. The hiss of rain and skittering rockslides dampened any noise of approach, but even now, the sound of laughter spilled from the tin guard shack inside the gate.

"This makes no sense," Raheem said from Kazem's left. The mosquitolike whine in his voice made it difficult to be sure if his cheeks were wet with rain or tears. "I only count four guards."

"Do you wish there were more, brother?" Kazem asked, locking eyes with the other man.

"No . . . I . . ." Raheem looked away as if to shake off a trance. "Something is not right. Our information said there would be at least eight on duty and as many as ten."

"Thanks be to Allah that there are so few, then," Kazem said. "It makes our job all the easier."

Kazem looked at the other men, all fresh and eager, but, more important, they had to fall under his spell. Raheem, who always grew nervous before a rally or event, had shown a strong heart in the past. Too much independence was problematic.

The likelihood of success was directly tied to the plan's brazenness—and to the fact that Kazem had more than a little help from the inside.

"Do you think the fence is electrified?" Raheem asked.

The man to his right scoffed. His lips were only a few centimeters above the water and he came close to blowing bubbles when he spoke. Basir was older than the others, with six years in the Army. He was the only one of the group, including Kazem, who had military experience. Incredibly strong, he had powerful forearms and a thick neck from hours of *pahlevani*, an ancient Persian sport that was a mixture of grappling, weightlifting, and dance. "Why would they bother electrifying the fence?" he said. "There is nothing here to steal except trucks and uniforms."

"And yet here we are to steal the uniforms," Raheem muttered. He moved his rifle aside and reached to wipe the rain out of his face, oblivious to the fact that his weapon was now submerged in muddy water.

Kazem and Basir exchanged glances. This man should go in first.

Kazem said, "Few people would want to take a uniform that would get them thrown in Evin."

"And yet we do," Raheem said. "So others might as well. Which is why they might have electrified the fence. Perhaps others have thought of how easy it would be to approach a storage facility of this type. Perhaps they have gun emplacements hidden along the perimeter."

"Or perhaps they have dragons, brother." Kazem chuckled, patience washing away with the rain. He put a night-vision monocular to his eye and played it up and down the fence line. Dozens of vehicles of all shapes and sizes, some white, most green or desert tan, were lined up in neat rows under camouflage tarpaulins rigged between metal scaffolding so as to make them less visible to passing surveillance satellites.

Raheem's whisper became frantic, and the water around him buzzed from his trembling. "I am merely saying we should take our time. The soldiers will eventually see us."

"And so they shall," Kazem said. "But we must be bold, decisive in our movements. Even now, our brothers pay dearly in the basements of Evin Prison. Do not forget that."

This brought solemn nods and whispered prayers from the sodden men.

"Very well," Kazem said, making one final sweep with the night-vision device. "It is time—"

He paused, focusing on two sentries trudging along the inside of the fence beyond the warehouse. Their heads were bowed against the rain, the glow of a cigarette visible under each man's hood. "It seems as though you were correct, Raheem," Kazem said, passing the monocular to the left. "They do have enough sense to deploy sentries."

Raheem's vindicated smile bled from his face at Kazem's next remark.

"Brother Raheem, you are with me. Basir, you lead the attack through the front gate. They will assume your truck has broken down in the rain and let you in. You must cut them down quickly when they check your identification, before any one of them has a chance to hit an alarm." He turned to his left.

Raheem touched Kazem with a trembling hand. "With you?"

"Yes," Kazem said proudly. "You had a feeling about the sentries. The honor of taking them should naturally fall to you."

Basir and the rest of the men were already on the move by the time Raheem fished his rifle out of the muck. Kazem forced a smile and clasped his hand on the idiot's shoulder, hoping to imbue in him a little courage, if not good sense. The AK-47 was durable to the extreme, but mud down the barrel would cause even it serious issues.

It did not matter. The fool would never have a chance to use it. Today, he would die as a martyr. Reza Kazem would make certain of that.

17

The assistant director of the FBI's Criminal Investigative Division kept her face forward but shot a sideways look at Gary Montgomery. Black, shoulder-length hair bobbed as Ruth Garcia picked up her pace, coming into a straightaway around the rubberized track in the shadows of the outdoor mezzanine of the J. Edgar Hoover Building.

Challenge accepted, the Secret Service agent muttered to himself—or he would have, if he'd had the breath to mutter. His wife always told him he was built for comfort, not speed—and she was right enough. A large man like him had to dig deep in order to run neck and neck with a freaking gazelle like Ruth Garcia.

Both agents were dressed in running shorts and T-shirts, Garcia's a dark blue raid shirt with FBI emblazoned across the back in tall yellow letters, while Montgomery's was gray with an understated USSS five-pointed star. The shirts were avatars of personality for their respective agencies—and the agents who wore them. Where Montgomery preferred to stand in the background, Garcia was brilliant and outspoken. She spoke four languages, including the Vietnamese of her maternal grandparents, along with Tagalog, and Spanish from her father's side. Her scrappy attitude and incredible investigative mind propelled her into rapid advancement, seeing her make special agent in charge of the Tampa Field Office before her fortieth birthday. That was followed by assistant director five years later—no small feat for the mother of two.

Montgomery had met her years before during a law enforcement pistol competition in Florida. She'd beat him by the equivalent of half a bullet hole, the ragged circle in the center of her target being a quarter-inch smaller in diameter than the ragged circle in the center of his.

Montgomery's actual Bureau counterpart was the special agent in charge of the Washington Field Office. WFO would handle the investigation of a threat to the President in tandem with the Secret Service. The SAC of WFO was a competent guy, but Ruth Garcia was Montgomery's longtime friend. Friendship plus competence plus access to the FBI's vast investigative apparatus were hard to beat. Even Montgomery's wife knew he had a professional crush on this woman. She was smart, she could shoot. And she could run, damn it. She certainly outranked him, but being the special agent in charge of PPD held tremendous sway, even across agency lines, so no one in either agency said anything when he hopped lightly over the chain of command and bypassed WFO to go straight to his friend. It didn't pay to screw with the guy who rode the Schwinn Airdyne in the White House gym next to the President.

"Big guy's going easy on you," Garcia said, as if reading Montgomery's mind. She downshifted once again to kick up her speed a notch. "You're getting soft in this cushy assignment."

Montgomery hunched broad shoulders, leaning forward slightly to match the new stride. He'd called her that morning, hoping to set up a meeting about what he saw as online threats to the President's character, and the President himself. She'd suggested that they could chat during her midmorning "jog." He should have known better. Another couple of laps of this and he'd be looking for a place to puke.

Secret Service HQ had a decent gym, better than most, but, as usual, the Feebs took things to an entirely new level. Climbing ropes, free weights, machines, heavy bags, mats for defensive tactics, and the rubberized track on which Montgomery was now surely leaving divots, took up much of the secure outdoor mezzanine level overlooking 9th Street in downtown Washington, D.C. Since the track was protected from the rain but open to the wind and outside temperatures, the workouts were bracing and more real-life than plodding along on some treadmill watching cable news.

Mercifully, Garcia ripped through only two laps before slowing to a more manageable trot.

"I'm guessing you have some theories about all this," she said, hardly even breathing hard.

"I do," Montgomery managed to say. "These . . . kind of . . . hit pieces . . . come out . . . all the time . . . But this . . . feels . . . differ . . . ent . . ."

Garcia gave him another side eye, slowing even more. "Tell me if you need to sto—"

"I need to stop," Montgomery blurted. He tried to walk but ended up bent over at the waist instead, hands braced on his knees. "How . . . far was that?"

"A little over four miles," she said, grinning.

"Shit." Montgomery coughed. "I should be able to run four miles."

"At a seven-minute pace? Awfully fast for a sixty-year-old."

"I'm forty-eight . . . thank you very much." The spasms in Montgomery's lungs began to subside. "Can we please get back to saving the President?"

"I don't know what to tell you," Garcia said. "Cyber-crimes has a pile of intel regarding bots and propaganda warehouses all over China, Eastern Europe, and the Persian Gulf. The Internet is the battleground for the new cold war. This audio and video manipulation is relatively new—at least the level of sophistication we're seeing here. Five years ago, I would have told you a state actor was behind this particular video, but with computers being what they are today . . . this could be some middle school kid working out of his parents' basement in Bethesda."

Montgomery rubbed his eyes, chasing away the last of the stars. "Our protective intelligence guys told me the same thing." He shook his head. "Wouldn't a kid go for the laugh? This threat of hoarding a flu vaccine is killing the stock market, not to mention terrifying everyone."

"You obviously don't know teenagers," Garcia said. "They find other people's pain hilarious." She gave a crooked, crazy-eyed smile, looking like she knew just such a child. "Anyway, I spoke to Legal first thing this morning. They're going to run it by the U.S. attorney for eastern Virginia, but so far they don't see a crime here. Public figures have to take a certain amount of pelting with rotten fruit."

"I know," Montgomery said, hangdog.

An eerily familiar voice caught his attention from the

television mounted on a concrete pillar above the free-weight area. The voice was female and husky, like Anne Bancroft with a three-pack-a-day smoking habit. It took Montgomery only a second to recognize it was Michelle Chadwick, the senior senator from Arizona.

"*. . . impossible to say if these allegations are true at this juncture, but I can assure you my office is addressing this. Sanctioned assassinations, covering up epidemics, hoarding vaccine for the elite . . . Any one of these is a serious breach of the public trust . . .*"

The agents rounded the corner and stopped to watch.

The crawler on the bottom of the screen said this was a taped press conference given by the senator an hour before.

"Listen to her," Montgomery said. "Those Internet stories are awfully damned convenient."

Garcia looked up at him, her brow knitting over narrowed eyes. "You really think she's behind it?"

"Probably not," Montgomery said. "But she's sure as shit happy about it."

"And piling on," Garcia said.

At forty-six, Senator Chadwick was young to be on her third term in the United States Senate. She was a bony woman, gaunt even, with high cheekbones and an aquiline nose. Auburn hair draped her head like a helmet. It was common knowledge around the Beltway watercooler that the twice-divorced senator had leapt over the bounds of propriety with a staffer named Corey Fite, deciding the #MeToo movement pertained only to powerful men and their subordinates. Fite had not complained as of yet, and Chadwick's fellow senators didn't want to rock the boat and screw up their own quasi-consensual relationships.

Her grandfather had made his first million as a Scottsdale real estate man when he came home from World War II. Still, she came from new money so far as the East Coast aristocrats were concerned, and the chip on her shoulder was a heavy one. Jack Ryan was rich—much richer than she was. The President came from blue-collar roots and made his money instead of inheriting it, which only served to infuriate her all the more. She consistently referred to him as a Washington blue blood, going so far as to affect a boarding-school lockjaw as if she were clenching an FDR cigarette holder in her teeth when she spoke of him.

". . . past allegations of lying to Congress, an extramarital affair, insider trading, though unsubstantiated."

"Past allegations." Montgomery came up on his toes, ready to rip the television off the pillar. "How about exonerated," he spat. "Unsubstantiated my ass . . . That's just another way of saying he's hiding something."

"Let's walk," Garcia said.

"Hang on."

". . . allegations of silencing anyone who gets in his way, politically or otherwise, are incredibly troubling," Chadwick went on, *"but perhaps even worse is Ryan's utter disregard for our allies in the Persian Gulf. My colleagues in the Senate and I intend to move forward with strong measures condemning the brutal crackdown of the Ayatollah against peaceful students who only want a better life."* Chadwick looked directly into the camera, working it like the actress she was. *"I say to you, Mr. President, do not just sit on your hands. Do something . . ."*

A growl erupted deep in Montgomery's belly. "You want somebody to do something?" he said. "How about I—"

Garcia jabbed him with her elbow. "I know you weren't about to threaten a United States senator right in front of an assistant director of the FBI."

Montgomery forced a smile. "I plead the Fifth."

Arnie van Damm sat down beside Mary Pat Foley on the couch in the private study just off the Oval Office, and then sprang back to his feet half a moment later, cursing at the open laptop computer on the corner of the desk. The meeting with the principals of the National Security Council was over for now, everyone having gone their respective ways, coming up with information, options, plans—tasks Ryan would need to make decisions about.

Ryan slouched in the soft chair across from the couch, legs stretched out in front of him. Cathy said slouching was decidedly unpresidential, but this was his slouching room, away from the media and the peephole into the Oval from the door to the secretaries' suite.

This thing in Cameroon left him feeling helpless. There was still no word on the deputy chief of mission's wife—which meant she was still likely a hostage. Hell, the embassy was surrounded by troops, which meant that for all practical purposes everyone inside was a hostage. Ryan wanted to send in a battalion of Marines and bayonet every last son of a bitch that got in their way— but that was the reason people took hostages, wasn't it. To keep from getting bayoneted from the start. It was usually just postponing the inevitable.

Across the office, van Damm was taking a break from worrying about the hostage crisis to shake his fist at a video of Senator Chadwick's earlier press conference. He sat down again, the veins on the side of his neck pulsing above his collar. "She's crossing the line, Jack."

Ryan looked up, jarred from his thoughts about Africa. "Not quite. Notice how she couches all her remarks and tweets under the guise of wanting to find the truth?"

Foley squinted at the computer like her face hurt. "Intimidation of your political opponents? Where did she get that from?"

Ryan shrugged. "Beats me."

"What does she have against the administration?" Foley asked.

"I'm telling you," Ryan said. "It's me personally. For some reason, she finds me the ultimate villain that must be thwarted. Sometimes I think she's evil—and other times, I think she truly believes I am."

Van Damm leaned his head back, giving an exhausted sigh. "Yeah, but your own private goon squad?"

Ryan rubbed his face, suddenly very tired. "She's not a hundred percent wrong there. I mean, they're not goons, but you know what I mean."

Foley said, "Due respect, Jack, but that is not what she means. The Campus is a scalpel. She's talking about some sort of Robert Rogers's Queen's Rangers. Wanton killers. And anyway, we shouldn't even be talking about it."

"Why?" Ryan asked. "So I can have some kind of deniability? That's not me and you know it. I'm all for separating myself from day-to-day operations, but I will not relinquish the responsibility for the group's existence."

"Jack." Foley's tone rose in pitch, fearing the path the conversation was taking. "Secrecy is par—"

Ryan put up hand. "Don't misunderstand me, Mary Pat. I get the need for secrecy. But you and I don't . . . can't pretend I'm not aware of what's going on. There's a difference between executive privilege and lying—even to ourselves."

Foley started to say something, then shook her head, thinking better of it. "Yes, Mr. President."

"In any case," van Damm said. "If you two are done with your existential crisis, let's get back to what to do about Senator Chadwick. I hate to say this, but maybe you should respond. Clear your name."

"Not a chance, pal," Ryan said. "She wants me to engage her, but I'm not getting down in that mud. I will, however, entertain a press conference to discuss any fears about the flu vaccine."

"She's resurrecting tired allegations about your investments and the SEC," van Damm said. "Everyone knows you were cleared of all wrongdoing."

"Not everyone," Ryan said.

"Chadwick does," Mary Pat said. "Bringing the investigation up without clarifying that, leading people to believe otherwise, that's an outright lie. Someone should prosecute her."

"For what?" Ryan scoffed. "Making me cry?"

"Okay, the vaccine thing, then," van Damm said. "Fomenting panic with half-truths has got to be illegal."

Ryan shook his head at the chief of staff. "Listen to yourself. Don't you find it more than a little ironic that you want to get behind a revolution that would bring freedom of speech to Iran when you're trying to throw Chadwick in jail for speaking her mind?"

18

The crowd on Keshavarz Boulevard, west of the roundabout known as Valiasr Square, numbered more than two thousand. At least a third were there to protest the hangings. The Nīrū-ye Entezāmī-ye Jomhūrī-ye Eslāmī-ye Īrān, or NAJA, Iran's uniformed police force, had set up a broken skirmish line in front of the ones who were brave or foolish enough to be vocal in their protests, but Erik Dovzhenko was certain there were even more among the spectators. He doubted the protesters would use violence in the demonstrations. That would only give the NAJA an excuse to respond with violence of their own—as if they needed an excuse. There would be no rubber bullets here. The slightest act of civil disobedience would be adjudged a capital offense. The riot squads were dressed for battle—"hats and bats," the Americans called it. It would take little more than a cross word, an unholy wink, to bring two hundred hickory sticks down on the protesters' heads in a "wood shampoo"—another American term Dovzhenko found a better description than anything he had in Russian.

Three crane trucks manufactured by Tadano of Japan sat idling in the gray drizzle, blue plastic nooses dangling from their booms, empty for another few moments.

Dovzhenko stood on the roof of a cinema across the street, along with two IRGC minders, watching the scene below through his personal pair of Leupold binoculars. A drizzling rain matted the Russian's hair and dripped from the tip of his nose, prompting him to turn up the collar of his horsehide jacket and snug it tighter against his neck. He couldn't muster the enthusiasm to wipe the rain out of his eyes.

Down on the street, IRGC executioners readied the condemned at the rear of a waiting van. Given the recent groundswell of protests, officials had seriously considered holding the executions behind the secure walls of Evin Prison. But when the chance for civil unrest was weighed against an opportunity to make a public show of force—the show of force won out. The Guardian Council and the Supreme Leader himself had agreed. The observations of justice would be good for everyone who attended the execution. Protest the regime and you got the rope. In public. In front of your friends. In front of your parents. The West could go piss up the rope you were hanged from if they did not like it.

Any of the nearby parks or sports complexes would have offered more room for people to witness the hangings, but though the authorities were cruel and inflexible in the theocratic rule, they were not completely stupid. The intersection at Valiasr Square would provide choke points their troops could exploit and high vantage points for snipers and observation, making it much easier to control.

Dovzhenko's assignment, along with the two IRGC men with him on the roof, was to scan the thousands of people who milled three stories below and watch for any protesters hidden in the crowds. The Supreme Council of Cyberspace had already banned Twitter and Facebook, and recently followed Russia's lead and blocked the popular messaging app Telegram. Other social media platforms had been slowed to a debilitating crawl. Instagram posts from the Ayatollah still went out, but that was about it. Cellular service in downtown Tehran had been cut, leaving any would-be protesters unable to communicate for two hours preceding the hangings.

At last count, more than a thousand dissidents had been killed by police and IRGC thugs over the last three weeks at various rallies across the country. While publicly urging peace, the Supreme Leader made it abundantly clear in private that he was prepared to wipe out tens of thousands to ensure the survival of the theocracy. In Iran, God did indeed move in mysterious ways.

Dovzhenko played his binoculars from face to face in the crowd. Some looked appropriately horrified at what was happening in their country. But many stared sleepily at the simple metal chairs and black body bags that had been readied below the cranes. Theirs was a numb half-interest, something to do before taking the kids to the park or evening prayer. After all, they weren't the ones being hanged.

The chief justice, a *mujtahid* well versed in Islamic law and chosen by the Supreme Leader himself, stood on a wooden platform and read the sentence over the loudspeaker. He'd been chosen for a reason and knew what buttons to push to get the crowd going. The accused were all guilty of *mofsed-e-filarz*—spreading corruption on the earth, a crime often attributed to pimps and abusers of children. What good citizen would not want their streets rid of corruption? Members of the crowd—many of them likely Basij militia who'd been ordered to attend—began to cheer at the sentence that had become a sermon. They goaded others into joining them. The pious *mujtahid* raised his arms, inhaling the applause.

Babak, Javad, and Yousef did not even have to leave their cells to be convicted. That crime alone assured a death sentence, but the council of mullahs sitting in judgment tacked on the capital crime of blasphemy for good measure. The sentence did not matter to Javad. His heart had stopped in the subbasement of Evin Prison under the brutal hand of Major Sassani.

The Ayatollah's trusted Islamic Revolutionary Guard Corps would carry out the execution. Sassani decided that Javad, too, would be strung up with his comrades, a grisly reminder that even if you were already dead, a death sentence from the Supreme Leader would be carried out without deviation.

Dovzhenko lowered the binoculars, feeling his stomach roil. Even the heartless KGB had customarily surprised condemned men with their execution—just another trip to the interrogation room, a walk down a long hallway that turned unexpectedly left instead of right, and ended with a bullet behind the ear before the poor addled soul knew anything had changed. Hose down the walls and bring on the next one. Neat and tidy, and humane in its brutality. These IRGC animals were medieval in their methods. There was no merciful breaking of the neck at the end of a drop. The Americans were fond of calling people Nazis—but the way the Iranians did this was just that, the Nazi method of hanging. A length of heavy rope or blue plastic cord was affixed to the boom of a construction crane and then tied around the victim's neck. He or she was then hauled upward to strangle slowly. If they were fortunate, the cord cut off the carotid arteries' blood flow to the brain. More often than not, the victim danced and twitched during the long haul upward, choking to death over long and excruciating minutes.

Dovzhenko was no stranger to brutal tactics. God above knew he'd been party to much for which he would someday have to answer. The two students quivering at the back of the van—and the one already splayed beside the body bag that would eventually hold him—had been betrayed by someone. Many had been murdered across this country, but those deaths had all been during confrontations with the police. Arrests were made, hundreds rounded up, but Dovzhenko read the statistical reports, and to his knowledge, there had yet to be any other trials. No, these three men had been singled out, plucked from among a thousand others. Why? To make some kind of point? They were not even Reza's mid-level lieutenants. Someone had convinced the Supreme Leader that the benefit of their death would outweigh the unification their martyrdom would bring to the movement. There was something here Dovzhenko was not seeing.

He himself had convinced more than a few to betray their friends. Even though his mother had pushed him into intelligence work, Dovzhenko turned out to be gifted. Getting others to betray their compatriots was the bread and butter of such work, by smooth talk or heavy-handed coercion. Lie, blackmail, threaten—it did not matter so long as the secrets flowed to the presidium in Moscow—and Erik excelled at every facet. There was a necessary heartlessness to it, a willingness to rape the mind of another human being without going completely amok. Sociopathy within bounds, they called it, a sterile medical word to make themselves feel atoned. Any SVR officer with a soul was left nothing but a dried husk in no time at all. Those without, took a bit longer.

The squeal of cables outside the balcony slowed Dovzhenko's gallop of runaway philosophy, and he drew himself back to the scene on the streets below. He forced himself to watch the three blindfolded men rise as if taking flight, jerking kicks causing the two who were still alive to twist. He played the binoculars down to the chairs where the executioners stood at parade rest beside the prison slippers that had fallen off the men during their struggles. Parviz Sassani stood at the edge of the crowd, wearing civilian clothing so he could blend in. Those on either side of him shouted halfhearted chants of *"Allahu Akbar,"* but the major said nothing. He was too busy smiling.

Dovzhenko scanned past Sassani, freezing at the face of a bald man behind the IRGC commander. His breath caught in his throat, enough that the IRGC man beside him gave him a quizzical look. Dovzhenko coughed to cover his sudden surprise. This was unexpected. General Vitaly Alov of the GRU. There had been no mention of the general coming to Tehran in the cables. With ostensibly the same goals, the SVR and the GRU often found themselves at cross-purposes, if only because of jealous turf wars. A visiting general from the military intelligence agency would surely have Dovzhenko's chief of station up in arms, and yet he'd mentioned nothing about it. Curious indeed. Alov was in the open. It was difficult to miss his bald head shining in the rain among a sea of black hair and scarves.

Dovzhenko passed the binoculars to the IRGC thug on his right. They were good binoculars, fifteen-power. He'd had them for years, a present to himself on his first assignment to the Russian consulate in Los Angeles. But they were tainted now with the sights he'd just witnessed. He never wanted to look through them again.

"Where are you going?" the youngest IRGC thug asked.

"To mingle with the crowd," Dovzhenko said. "Gather intelligence. That is what intelligence officers do."

He smiled as if he were still a coconspirator in this idiocy, swallowed his disgust, and then wheeled, cursing in Russian under his breath as he pushed open the roof-top door. He used his forearm to wipe the rain from his eyes, feeling as if he couldn't touch his face until he washed his hands. At times like this, there was only one person in the world who could make him feel human. Maryam Farhad was the most intelligent and tender woman he'd ever known. It was hardly fair for a man with his job to want to spend time with her. She was his life-boat in this sea of shit—and he was dragging her under.

19

The killing would occur in the sand, less than a block away from where John Clark sat on Calle Adriano in the shadow of the great bullring of Seville. He was relaxed, sitting back in his chair, a folded edition of *El País* on the sidewalk café table. Jack sat across from him, not quite as accustomed to death, but experienced enough that he did not startle anymore. It was quiet here, reminding Clark of a side street in Manhattan or northern Virginia—except for the odor of bulls and horses.

El sol es el mejor torero, Spaniards said: The sun is the best bullfighter. And they were right. Clark watched the Russians from the comfort of the shade, while the low sun shone directly across the street, all but blinding them. There was a new man at the table now. Clark couldn't see his face, but hadn't recognized him when he'd first come up to join the Russians with the long lip and the farmboy haircut. This new man was tall, paunchy, without much of a chin. Dirty-blond curls stuck out from beneath a tan beret. A powder-blue sweater draped over his shoulders, one sleeve tucked neatly into the tube of the other in front of his chest, the way Clark had seen men do in South America and Europe but rarely in the United States. The man carried himself like a local, sitting with his back to the sun so the Russians got the brunt of the blinding. He'd arrived twenty minutes earlier, greeting each Russian as if he'd been expected. Clark guessed that he'd probably picked the meeting spot—using the sun to put them off balance. It was much too early to eat dinner, but the café was a good place to link up and grab a drink before they went into the bullfight—where refreshments would cost double what they did outside.

Ding and Midas were a block away, nursing a couple of beers in front of the Hotel Adriano. Dom and Adara waited in reserve in an Irish bar around the corner, still staying out of sight to avoid being recognized by any of the Russians who might have seen them in Portugal.

Everyone was connected via their radios and earbuds, using push-to-talk switches rather than voice-activated, so they could chat among themselves without cluttering up the net. They could easily flip a switch on the radio itself and render the mics on their neck loops constantly *hot*, obviating the need to reach into their pockets and hit the PTT each time they wanted to transmit.

Both Ryan and Clark were dressed in khaki slacks and casual lace-ups with rubber soles that provided good traction. Long experience had taught Clark that he was bound to do a lot more running than he did shooting. He wore a pair of simple suede desert boots that were probably half as old as Ryan. Long-sleeve shirts, slightly tailored, made them look a little less American—Ryan's charcoal gray and Clark's white. John's wife, Sandy, always joked that he had to be extra brave to wear white shirts on an operation, since the guys wearing white in the movies always seemed to die before the show ended. It was amazing that she could still joke about that sort of thing—but, he supposed, it was her way of coping. Everyone had to have some mechanism. Sandy's was her sense of humor. There was rarely a time when she wasn't grinning—at least with her eyes. It was a good thing, too, because one of them needed to look happy, and Clark's smiles always looked a little forced—except when he watched his grandson play ball.

Clark had never really stopped paying attention to the Russians, but someone practicing a few notes on the trumpet in the nearby bullring jerked him fully into the here and now of the street.

Absent the colorful splash of the purple jacaranda trees along the banks of the canal off of the Guadalquivir River just two blocks away, the knotted sycamores of Calle Adriano were set against muted buildings painted amber and rust. Siesta time was over, and people were up and about, preparing for the bullfights that would begin in less than two hours. There was room in the arena for twelve thousand, and hundreds of locals hustled like bees on the streets and sidewalks surrounding the centuries-old Plaza de Toros de la Real Maestranza de Caballería de Sevilla. Vendors rented cushions for the stone benches and sold roasted nuts, beer, and *gaseosas*. Ticket scalpers prepared to haggle with frugal locals and earn their losses back on eager *turistas*. Carriage drivers checked horses' hooves and folded blankets customers would need once the sun went down and the evening grew chilly.

Shafts of bright light cut rapierlike down the east-west alleys, leaving those on the east side of the road still in sunglasses and low hats, while Clark, and those experienced enough to choose a table on the west side of the

street, received welcome shade. Inside the bullring, afi-
cionados paid much more for seats in the shade, or *sombra*, than in the eastern, or *sol*, side of the ring.

Clark had already purchased two tickets in the *sombra*,
in the upper boxes, for a hundred and twenty euros apiece.
This high vantage point would give them a good view of
the Russians, no matter where they sat. None of the team
had been eager to go in and watch the bullfights—each
offering various reasons. Adara had already made plain her
disgust for the practice, and appeared ready to gut anyone
who thought otherwise. The others were more taciturn,
but no one was excited about it. For Clark, the problem
was the horses. His rational brain said they should not be
any higher ranked than another animal, but they were,
and to a lot of people. Seeing horses blindfolded and gored
while the picadors went after the bull's shoulders with the
spear, well, he could do without that. But the Russians
and this new Spaniard looked as though they were going
in. Someone had to follow them.

Clark didn't mind at all when Jack Junior drew the
short straw. He and Ryan Senior went way back, certainly
further than either of them wanted to remember, but he
didn't get to work directly with the kid very often. Junior
was a good deal like his dad. A little more off-the-cuff
than Senior, who had more of an analytical bent. Sometimes. Both were incredibly brave, which meant even
more when you considered how smart they were. It was
easy to appear brave if you were too dumb to realize what
kind of danger you were really in.

Clark took a sip of his San Miguel 1516. It was less
boozy than the other beers on the menu, leaving him
able to drink a little more and still stay on his toes.

"It's tough being your old man's kid," he offered, suddenly nostalgic.

Ryan gave a half-smile and took a drink of his own beer. The kid was absent his usual easy smile. Life seemed to have beaten it out of him of late. "I don't know."

"Yes, you do." Clark shrugged. "This business is hard enough on someone who's not the firstborn son of the immortal Jack Ryan. You doing okay?"

"I'm fine," Jack lied. It was obvious he was not.

"You don't have to tell me," Clark said. "But it's my job to ask—as your boss and your friend. I'm just saying, you're a little young to be circling the drain like a dead spider."

"Is that what I'm doing?"

"I got a nose for these things. You need to get your legs under you, son."

Jack eyed the men across the street. "You think Beret Guy is another weapons dealer?"

"That would follow the pattern," Clark said. He'd let the kid change the subject for now, but they'd come back later and get to the root of his angst—insofar as such a thing was even possible.

"The Ruskis must have something they're trying to move," Jack mused. "Or maybe buy."

"They look official to me," Clark said. "I'm going with option number one."

Jack sipped his beer again, looking up and down the street at the steady stream of people heading for the arena. "Have you ever been to a bullfight?"

"I have," Clark said. "Wasn't what I'd call pretty."

"I read online they give the bull drugs, put Vaseline

and other stuff in its eyes before the fight so he's all messed up and disoriented."

Clark took a long, slow breath. "You read that *online* . . ." He took another drink of his beer and then pointed at Jack with the neck of the bottle. "Let me ask you this. If you were going into the ring with a thousand pounds of meanness and you wanted to make absolutely sure it charged where you directed it to charge, wouldn't you want it to be able to see?"

"I guess I would," Ryan said.

"Not to say they don't do a number on the poor bastards," Clark said. "But I wouldn't trust a damned thing I read on the Internet."

"So you *are* bothered by it?" Jack asked. "The bullfights, I mean."

"You know me, Ryan," Clark said. "I'm not one to engage in long philosophical debates. But I've thought some on this. Commercial beef cattle are customarily finished out in pens where they do nothing but eat and stand around on mountains of their own shit until their appointment with a captive bolt gun in the slaughterhouse—which usually happens sometime between eighteen months and their third birthday. The Spanish fighting bulls that make it into the ring live as near-wild animals until they're graded and sent to fight at about four years old, at which point they have one bad day."

"So you're saying these bulls have a chance?"

"Not a chance in hell." Clark shook his head. "I mean, a thousand-to-one shot, maybe, if the bull displays such incredible courage that the crowd begs the guy in charge of the fight to pardon it. But for all practical purposes, the bullfight ends with a couple of feet of sharp steel stuck between the bull's shoulder blades and the dead carcass getting dragged off by a team of mules like the ones you saw clomping down the street a few minutes ago." He leaned forward, swirling the rest of his beer in the bottle. "You ever read *The Dogs of War*?"

"Sure," Jack said. "You assigned it to us."

Clark smiled. "I guess I did. Anyhow, take it from an old man who's rapidly approaching his use-by date, Forsyth summed it up about right. I want to go out with a *bullet in my chest and blood in my mouth, and a gun in my hand*. If I was a bull, I'd take a few spears to the shoulders to get an extra year on the range and a chance to use my horns. It'd be better than getting prodded up some alley with a hot shot in my ass so I can walk into a captive bolt." He leaned back in his chair and took a drink. "But that's just me."

"I'd pick herd bull," Jack offered. "If I got to choose. A few more years with the added benefits of tending a harem of cows."

"You young guys." Clark shook his head. "I'd imagine every steer once aspired to those same goals. But the odds are pretty grim. My way, I get to keep my nuts and have a chance to hook the guy who's going to kill me . . ." His voice trailed off and he tipped his beer bottle up the street. Jack's eyes followed slowly.

"That can't be good," Ryan said.

Clark reached into his pocket and pressed the PTT switch on his radio. "Heads up," he said. "We've got company. Lucile Fournier—who is now as blond as Adara—is about twenty yards from the Russians and closing."

20

Normally, the act of simply crossing the street in Tehran was so dangerous that locals referred to it as "going to Chechnya." Authorities had blocked the streets to control protesters during the hangings, so Dovzhenko was able to cross as if he'd been in a city that gave two shits about the lives of its pedestrians. He walked four blocks south, under the tall sycamores that lined the shaded walks of Valiasr Street, named for a twelfth-century Shiite imam. The crowds soon thinned to the usual mix of people returning home from work in the rain. Dovzhenko would never have known there had been a hanging if not for the incandescent images of the kicking boys that still burned in his brain. He'd not eaten anything since the bread and tea he'd had for breakfast, but even the tantalizing smells of saffron and five spice drifting out of the shops could not tempt him.

The drizzle abated by the time he reached the white subcompact car the embassy had assigned him. Dovzhenko threw his leather jacket in the backseat, which was hardly large enough for a briefcase, let alone a person with legs. He took a moment to light a cigarette before wedging himself in behind the wheel. It was illegal to smoke while driving in Iran, but the law was seldom enforced, and, anyway, Dovzhenko was much too disgusted to care. The pitiful little vehicle did not help his mood at all.

The Tiba—"gazelle," in Persian—was anything but fast. It resembled a bloated peanut or, perhaps, a Volkswagen Beetle that had been left to melt in the sun. Those sentiments were surely too harsh, but Dovzhenko had too much experience with the little things to be rational. He'd been issued one the year before, during an assignment in Moldova. SVR recruiters tended to draw more romantic images of the life of a clandestine intelligence officer when they spoke to potential trainees. Dovzhenko knew better. The intelligence life was rarely a flashy one. Savile Row suits and Aston Martin sports cars drew unwanted attention. Utilitarian ruled the day, but this, this was ridiculous. The eighty-horsepower monstrosity was more reminiscent of Baba Yaga's cauldron than a car. It was outside the bounds—for even a Russian spy. Dovzhenko was not alone in his assessment. The English-speaking clerk in the Tehran embassy motor pool had gone so far as to dub the little cars "Axles of Evil."

But it got him to Maryam's, so Dovzhenko kept his gripes to himself.

Maryam Farhad lived in Shahrak-e Gharb, an upscale neighborhood in the northwest part of the city, far from the drug rehabilitation center where she worked to the south, where homeless addicts hung in the shadows whispering, *"Darou, darou . . ."* Medicine, medicine. Selling drugs, even the green stuff, was a tremendous gamble. A usable amount of cannabis might be overlooked by the authorities, but as little as five grams of hash oil was a capital offense. As far as Dovzhenko could tell, the government had decided to combat the exploding opioid problem by handing out so much methadone that it, too, was now sold illicitly. Whatever Tehran's master plan, he was glad Maryam didn't live among the lost souls to whom she'd devoted her life.

Dovzhenko could have taken Valiasr Street north and then gone west on the Hemmat Expressway, almost to her doorstep—but he did not have the stomach to see the execution site again, and he wanted to shake any tail Sassani might have on him. IRGC trusted no one. It was the nature of spies. Liars were always the most suspicious of others. In this case, Sassani had good reason. Maryam was a single woman, a Muslim—and Dovzhenko was not. His position in the SVR would save him from execution, but their affair would surely get him expelled from the country, not to mention the black mark it would place on his record. Dovzhenko told himself it did not matter what happened to him, but the consequences to her would be swift and violent. A brutal whipping, re-education, or, if a judge got it in his head that she was corrupting the earth—Dovzhenko had seen the pit behind the walls of Evin, the hole used to bury men up to their waists and women to their necks, the smooth stones the size of apples arranged in neat pyramids for easy access. Officially, Iran had done away with stoning. What a joke. The members of the Guardian Council did whatever they wished. If stoning went against an official edict, they simply issued a new one, granting themselves permission. World opinion didn't stop them. It just moved the behavior indoors.

Dovzhenko worked his way north, tamping back images of what could happen to his girlfriend. They were both accustomed to risk. SVR had no rules prohibiting the consumption of alcohol, even in a Muslim country, provided one kept to oneself and did not overindulge. But attending one of Tehran's numerous underground parties on anything other than official business was not only frowned upon, the prohibition against it was noted specifically in the documented rules new members of the Russian delegation had to sign upon arrival.

Dovzhenko found one on his second weekend, in the basement of a flower shop right in Shahrak-e Gharb, less than a mile from Maryam's apartment. Enforcement by the morality police against these parties, where alcohol flowed and bodies swayed to Western music, came in fits and starts or not at all. Two of the young people at the first party he'd attended were supposedly sons of prominent mullahs. No one wanted to get crossways with them, so for the most part, the gatherings went unmolested.

He'd seen Maryam Farhad fifteen minutes into his first visit. She was about his age, a few years older than most of the college-age kids who smoked and drank absinthe and explored the heady stuff of free thought, even if it was in secret. Dovzhenko had worn his best shirt, open at the collar. Unlike most of the young men at the party, he was old enough to know that wearing a little less cologne and no gold chains caused him to stand out as being more mature. Maryam had smiled at him as soon as she'd removed her coat. Her hips swayed to the music before she'd taken two full steps—as if she'd contained them as long as she possibly could. She wore a silk blouse, tight enough across the chest to pull the buttons just a little and expose an inch or two of lace underneath. This happened all the time in Russia or the U.S., but in

Iran, where women wore mandated headscarves and ill-fitting clothes, the look was scandalous.

One of the male officials at the embassy had lamented what he called the *nos–grudi paradoks*—the observation that the Iranian women with whom he was acquainted who possessed decent breasts also had extremely large noses. Conversely, the more delicate and beautiful the nose, the more barren the landscape when it came to bosom. Dovzhenko had dismissed the sentiment as *nekulturny*—boorish—but was ashamed to note that Maryam Farhad was a beautiful exception to this apparatchik's imagined paradox. And as boorish as it was, the thought of her body only made him want to see her more.

But they had to be careful.

Now he used the slow pace of the stop-and-go traffic to keep an eye out for any telltale signs that he was being followed. He felt reasonably sure he was clean by the time he turned west on the Hakim but took the time to get on and off the highway twice, one eye on his rearview mirror, the other on the evening traffic. It seemed that every other car was a Porsche, each a testament to Iranian resiliency in the face of Western sanctions.

He'd seen nothing out of the ordinary in his mirror since leaving Valiasr. It took several cars to conduct rolling surveillance, even against an untrained target. And Dovzhenko knew the tricks. He'd be able to smoke out any IRGC goons like cheap cigarettes.

He got off the Hakim Expressway at Pardisan Park, a collection of wooded trails and unfinished gravel pits that served as home to monkeys, rabbits, and strange, small-eared wildcats that Maryam called cute but Dovzhenko thought looked alien. They'd come here once before, never holding hands but walking side by side, thrilled and terrified at the notion of getting caught socializing as an unmarried couple. They spoke of her love for opera, of great books, and Rome, where he had spent time but she had not.

He drove around the park twice now, as if he were lost, then stopped to check his rear tire at the top of a gravel hill with a good 360-degree view.

Clean. Or as clean as one could be in a place where toxic air turned a white shirt yellow inside a month's time.

Maryam's apartment was on 2nd, a dead-end street. Dovzhenko parked the Tiba in a business parking lot on 5th, giving him more than one exit, and walked the block and a half. He enjoyed the walk. Recent rains and the near-constant breeze here in the north kept the air cleaner than in other parts of the city.

Dovzhenko let himself inside with his key. The apartment was well appointed like much on the hillside. Garbage washed downhill, so most things were nice here in the north of Tehran. Still in his damp leather jacket, he slumped in a living room chair and lit a cigarette. A driftwood sculpture dominated the center of a glass coffee table. Pictures of seascapes covered the freshly painted walls. He'd thought it odd at first. Maryam didn't seem to care so much for the water, and then other inconsistencies cropped up over the course of his visits. It had once taken her several minutes to find the closet where she stored extra toilet paper. And then she could not locate the five spice. This rose petal–based seasoning was ubiquitous in Iranian kitchens, and misplacing it was akin to a Russian wife saying she couldn't remember where she kept her tea.

Maryam had finally admitted that the apartment was not actually hers, but borrowed from a friend who was traveling. Recalling that conversation now made Dovzhenko feel guilty for smoking, and he stubbed out the cigarette in a clay ashtray beside the driftwood center-piece. He slipped the extinguished cigarette butt into his jacket pocket, a habit drilled into him by his mother before he even went to training. She could have warned him not to smoke instead of teaching him to erase the clues of his presence, his saliva, his particular brand of cigarette—but such were the lessons of a mother who was also a spy.

A metallic rattle drew his attention to the door. His hand drifted to the 9x18 Makarov in his jacket pocket. He sometimes felt a little outgunned by the larger SIG Sauer .45s the IRGC carried, but the little Makarov had been around since the Cold War, was still issued—and he could shoot it with deadly effect.

He relaxed a notch when Maryam came through the door and pushed it shut with her lovely hip. She flipped the deadbolt while she juggled a briefcase and a canvas bag of bread and vegetables. At thirty-seven, she was a year younger than Dovzhenko. She wore a fashionable pantsuit of dark blue, loose enough to hide the swells and curves that he knew were underneath. With most of her body covered, he was immediately drawn to her eyes— and what eyes they were, wide and round and the color of mossy agate—not exactly brown, but not quite green. She reminded him of the American actress Natalia Wood. Dark hair, damp from the rain, peeked from the front of

TEHRAN—MARYAM FARHAD'S APARTMENT

N

Pardisan Park

HAKIM EXPRESSWAY

Parking lot

5th Street

4th Street

3rd Street

Apartment

2nd Street

© 2018 Jeffrey L. Ward

a compulsory headscarf that matched her blue slacks. *Ya rusari ya tusari,* she often said. A scarf or a beating.

He rose quickly, taking the bags.

"Any trouble?" he asked.

She'd not had to walk far, but the morality police often patrolled the areas around the metro stations and grocers at this time of the evening.

"None," she said, voice husky, matching the earthy intensity of her eyes. "I used Gershad to get me past the idiots quite unmolested."

Dovzhenko would have laughed had it not been so tragic. Gershad was an app used to avoid the Gashte Ershad, or morality police. Similar to mobile applications that warned of a radar trap, users of Gershad posted locations where they had seen the chador-clad women and uniformed officers. Icons of bald, bearded morality goons appeared on a map of the city. To Maryam and other women who wished to wear their scarves pushed back an extra inch or enjoy a cup of tea with a male acquaintance, the app was as normal as using a GPS to navigate to an unknown address.

"I found fresh cucumber and tomato—hothouse, this early in the year, but they looked nice." She kissed him, grabbing him by the belt buckle when he turned for the kitchen.

"What a cold little hand," he said, quoting her favorite opera.

She scoffed. "You are aware that Mimì dies in *La Bohème*?"

"I know," he said. "But I do not feel like being happy today."

She pulled him closer. "Do you feel like being hungry?"

"Not really."

"Nor do I," she said. "Not for hothouse tomatoes, anyway."

She turned for the bathroom, as she always did when she got home. He joked that she was conditioned to pee as soon as she saw her own front door. When she came out a moment later, she was minus the *rusari* and her jacket.

"That is much better." She sighed, tripping out of her shoes as she led him by the hand into the bedroom.

21

Later, much later, Dovzhenko lay with one hand behind his head, the other tracing the small bumps of Maryam's spine. She sat hunched forward, arms hugging the tangle of sheets that was pulled over her knees. Shoulders bare, she was beautifully exposed down to the twin dimples at the small of her back. An engraved pendant was suspended on a silver chain against her breasts. Usually one for quiet banter, she was silent now, which meant she had something important on her mind. Dovzhenko continued to run his fingers along her skin, and gave her time to think.

At length, she leaned against the headboard and lifted the necklace over her head. She held up the pendant, letting it swing to and fro as if to hypnotize him. "Do you know what this is?"

"A flower," he said, giving a little shrug. He let his hand slide down her side to touch her knee.

"It is an inverted tulip," she said. "A lily, actually, that grows on the mountains above us. We call it *ashk-e-Maryam*—Maryam's tears." She took a deep, shuddering breath. "I tell you this because I want you to know me."

Dovzhenko sat up beside her and put a finger to her lips. "I know enough to be happy."

"You Russians," she said. "You are so fond of fairy tales that you shy away from real life."

"I am being honest," Dovzhenko said. "I know you well enough."

"No," she said, pulling away. "You do not. But I know you . . . what you do." She rolled to reach for her cigarettes on the side table, flicked open the metal case, and then held out a trembling palm.

He gave her his lighter and then sat back again, eyeing her.

"Okay, then," he said. "What do I do?"

"Do you think I am stupid?" She picked a fleck of tobacco from her lip and blew a cloud of smoke at his face, clicking the lighter open and shut, open and shut. "Any Russian who stays in Iran for as long as you have is either a scientist or a spy." She gave him a wan smile. "And you are not quite boring enough to be a scientist."

"Maryam—" Dovzhenko began to trace a circle on the hollow of her hip. "I am merely an adviser to your government science programs. I am telling you the—"

Her words came softly, like the chirp of a distant bird, but they silenced Dovzhenko all the same. "You would be a beautiful man if you did not lie."

She suddenly slipped down among the sheets, more on them than in them, on her side now, cigarette held in a cocked hand, over her shoulder, as she looked directly into his eyes. "Oh, fire of my heart, you have a pistol in your jacket, along with a small radio, and a leather truncheon. That does not seem typical for an adviser, even in Iran."

Dovzhenko stared at her, stunned.

"So what now?"

Maryam's breast brushed against his arm as she fell away. She put the cigarette to her lips and stared at the ceiling.

"It is better to be slapped with the truth than kissed with a lie," she said.

Dovzhenko groaned. "True enough."

Her head fell sideways against the pillow, looking at him. "Then here is the slap."

"Maryam—"

"What do you know of me?"

"You are a kind soul," he whispered. "You work with drug addicts—"

She put a finger to his lips. "Stop it. Be honest with me, if that is even possible for a man in your job. Where were you tonight, immediately before you came here to the apartment?"

"The executions," he whispered.

She nodded thoughtfully, eyelids trembling as she took another drag on the cigarette. "I thought as much," she whispered. "They were friends of mine, you know. Those boys." Tears welled in her eyes. Looking up at the ceiling, she threw an arm across her forehead. "You must arrest me now—take me to the Evin dungeons to string me up and perform your interrogations."

"Merely knowing someone is not a crime," Dovzhenko said, aware that as a practical matter, this was not the case in Iran or Russia.

"I am a part of it," she whispered into the crook of her arm. "All of it . . . involved enough in the planning of this movement to get myself hanged. For a while, it seemed as though freedoms might win out, but with the help of their IRGC attack dogs, the Guardian Council will always win . . . no matter what we do. I am so tired, my love. Those monsters murdered my friends, and for what? For doing what thousands of others are doing. So go ahead and report me, arrest me . . . Better yet, shoot me now. I am beyond caring."

Dovzhenko swung his feet off the bed and walked naked to the chair where he'd draped his leather jacket. He retrieved the radio and clicked it on. Static and chatter came over the speaker, Sassani and his operatives out working the streets, hunting.

"*Sepah!*" Maryam gasped, using the colloquial name for the IRGC. Her face drew tight, as if she'd not been quite sure how deeply he was involved with Iranian authorities until now.

He pushed the radio toward her. "Take it," he said. "You may turn yourself in if you wish, but I would never give you over to those animals."

She stubbed out the cigarette in the ashtray beside the bed and collapsed against her pillows, sobbing.

He nestled in close to her. "I am truly sorry for your friends."

"Did you . . . ?"

He shook his head. "No," he said. "I am not an interrogator." He did not mention that he had been there to see almost every bloody, bone-crunching second of it. She was too fragile—for now at least. Some slaps of truth were too brutal. "How did you know them?"

"I told you." She sighed. "I am part of it. You have all the evidence you need to hang me. If I am wrong about you and you turn me in, then I will die of a broken heart before a noose can touch my throat."

"I would never." He was surprised at how the truth sounded so like the lies of his past.

"It does not matter," she said. "These young people are exceptionally brave, but they need guidance, someone to lead them."

"Like Reza Kazem?" Dovzhenko said.

She rolled her eyes. "Reza Kazem. He speaks the right words, but there is more wind than substance. Something is off with that one, I will tell you that much."

"You have met him?"

She turned to the side table and retrieved her mobile, stretching beautifully, causing Dovzhenko to catch his breath when the sheet fell away. She rolled over beside him, mobile phone in both hands, and then entered a password with her thumbs, following that with a longer code to bring up her photos.

He nodded at the screen. "You are aware that government agencies have ways around these passwords."

She shrugged and pushed the phone toward him. "I told you. I am too tired to care."

Dovzhenko needed a cigarette, but he wanted to look at the phone first—not for evidence, but because he was curious. On his back, he held the phone above his face, shoulder to shoulder with Maryam while he scrolled through the photos one by one. Smiling students, a bouquet of spring flowers, more flowers. The fifth photo made Dovzhenko sit up straight against the headboard. He zoomed in to get a better look, and then turned to stare down at Maryam.

"What?" she said, incredulous. "I already said I knew them. Are you suddenly angry with—"

He put a hand on her arm, tenderly, he hoped. It only frightened her, and she jerked away.

"This man." Dovzhenko turned the screen so she could look at the photograph. "Have you seen him before?"

She shrugged. "Kazem? I have. Several times."

"Not Kazem," Dovzhenko said. "The other one. The one standing behind Javad."

She shook her head. "Erik, you scare me . . ."

"This man is Vitaly Alov, a general officer of the Glavnoye Razvedyvatel'noye Upravleniye, the GRU, Russia's Main Intelligence Directorate."

"You Russians are everywhere," she said. "I did not pay any attention to him when I took the photo."

"May I get a copy of this?"

"Of course," Maryam said. "But that does not seem wise. Will that not leave a digital trail, linking you to my account?"

He turned to smile at her. "Very good," he said. "I do not plan to send it to myself directly. I will post it on a dummy auction account on eBay, untraceable to me or anyone connected to me. I will be able to access it without downloading it and leaving any tracks."

"That sounds much more spylike," Maryam said. She sat up beside him now, leaning in so her arms intertwined around his elbow, lips buzzing against his shoulder. "Is this General Alov your boss?"

He shook his head, working Maryam's phone to post the photograph of Alov and Kazem. "No. I am SVR. The GRU is a different entity altogether." He tapped the phone against his palm. "I cannot understand why a Russian officer would meet with the leader of your protest movement. Officially, my government backs the—"

On the table beside the bed, Dovzhenko's radio suddenly crackled with static, causing both of them to jump with a start. Parviz Sassani's toxic voice spilled over the airwaves.

Dovzhenko had a passable understanding of Farsi, but Maryam translated anyway.

"*. . . Units three and four, come in from the north on Prioozan. We will approach from the south, blocking any escape . . . Third floor, number . . .*"

She looked up at Dovzhenko and they both mouthed the same words.

"They are coming here."

22

"She's fifteen yards out," Clark said into the radio. "Blond hair, shorter than Adara's. White knee-length shorts, black T-shirt. She's getting plenty of attention."

"She's wearing sandals," Jack noted. "Looks like she's not planning to run."

"Okay," Clark said, lips just inches from his beer. Passersby would think he was talking to Ryan. "I have da Rocha now. He's coming in from the other direction. No weapons that I can see so far. Ding, Midas, start to drift his way in case they split up when we go inside the plaza. I'd like to keep eyes on da Rocha. Adara, Dom, you two ease this way but hang behind a little. I haven't seen any Russian countersurveillance yet, but they're out there. I'm sure of it."

Jack tapped the table to get Clark's attention. "Fournier's carrying something."

"My friends," da Rocha said, striding purposefully up to the seated Russians. He kept his hands in the open so as not to alarm anyone who might be lurking in the shadows. "What a small world it is, meeting you twice in one week."

Both Russians pushed away from the table and stood, as did the Spaniard.

Da Rocha's mouth fell open in mock astonishment. "Do my eyes deceive me, or is this Don Felipe Montes?" He took a half-step toward the street, forcing the Spaniard to turn into the sun to look at him.

Montes gave the Russians a wary glance. "This man is a friend of yours?"

"A mere acquaintance," da Rocha said, still driving the conversation. "And a hopeful business partner, to be sure." He turned to glance at Lucile, who'd stopped a few steps behind the Spaniard. "In any case. I will not bother you any longer. I am only here by chance. It seems as though my taxi dropped me off in the wrong location. Is the bull arena somewhere nearby?"

The Spaniard stifled a grin and pointed west. "You are standing in its very shadow, señor."

Da Rocha looked across the street and scratched his head. "I expected it to be larger," he said. "Are you certain? Where would one go inside?"

Montes rolled his eyes at the Russians, who had yet to say a single word, and then stepped sideways, away from the Russians. He took da Rocha by the shoulder and pointed down a narrow cobblestone pedestrian alley that ran adjacent to the Plaza de Toros.

"Down there?" da Rocha said.

"Follow the crowd," Montes said.

Da Rocha stepped away, throwing a glance at the Russians as if to say "Watch this."

Lucile Fournier walked forward, passing the little crowd by the curb as she touched Don Felipe with her mobile phone.

The Spaniard gave a little jump, like she'd given him a shock. His jaw moved back and forth as a hand shot to his collar, trying to get more air. Da Rocha sprang to help, assisting the man as he stumbled backward to collapse into his chair. He remained upright, eyes open, arms trailing down beside him. Those seated at nearby tables might have thought the poor man was just winded, or perhaps overcome by the brightness of the sun.

Da Rocha patted the man's arm, as if checking on a friend.

"What have you done?" the Russian with the long upper lip said. Da Rocha had correctly identified him as the leader.

"A demonstration," da Rocha said. "The newest in shellfish toxin. Not all armaments need to include facial recognition or advanced GPS—though I certainly have that as well if you want it."

Both Russians glanced nervously up and down the street, wanting to put distance between themselves and the dead Spaniard but unsure of what would come next.

"Shellfish toxin?" the Russian with the odd haircut asked. "How would you even know he is allergic?"

Lucile laughed out loud. "Monsieur, everyone is allergic to this shellfish toxin."

"Amazing," da Rocha said, "how quickly it worked. Wouldn't you say?" He dropped a business card on the table in front of the Russians. "We both know that you are in the market for someone with certain skills and contacts. I assure you, a business arrangement with me would not disappoint you." He patted the dead Spaniard on the shoulder. "As you can see, I am very resourceful."

Clark had to concentrate to keep from jumping to his feet. "Everyone stay put," he said. "The guy in the beret was just hit. Anyone hear a shot?"

No one had.

"This was something else," Jack said. "Poison, maybe."

"Ricin?" Midas mused.

"A little too quick for that," Clark said. "She jabbed him with something, though. The Russians are moving now. Da Rocha and the woman are coming toward you, Adara. See if you can figure out where they are staying. But be alert."

"Ballsy," Ding said. "That makes two that we know of who she's killed in front of a large and hostile audience."

"Yeah," Clark said. "Like I said. Everyone keep your heads on a swivel."

He nodded at Ryan, who left a couple of euros on the table to pay for their beers. The Russians walked east on Calle Adriano, toward their hotel, leaving the dead local and the bullfighting arena behind. For the time being, at least, they seemed to have lost their taste for blood.

23

Dovzhenko sprang out of the bed, hopping on one foot as he put on his slacks. He was already buttoning his shirt before he realized Maryam wasn't moving.

"What are you doing?" He slipped the Vostok watch over his wrist, shoving his feet into his shoes. His socks went into his pockets. There was no time to put them on. "Get up! We have to go."

A lock of dark hair fell across an agate-colored eye. "You are the fire of my heart," she said. "But if they find us together, we are both dead. They will only interrogate me."

"No!" Dovzhenko grabbed her arm, dragging her across the sheets. She didn't struggle, but she didn't help, either. It was like dragging a dead woman. He felt like crying. "They would not dare harm a Russian intelligence officer. We are allies."

Her eyes were half closed, sleepy, trancelike. "You could tell them I was your prisoner. Perhaps you could go a little easier on my feet with the truncheon . . ."

"Why are you doing this?" A sob caught hard in his throat. "Please come with me."

"Where?" She tore the pendant off her neck and handed

it to him. "Please go. You must escape so I can see you again, even if I am in a cell."

"I won't leave you."

She sighed. "My love, if you do not, we will both be killed. Our only chance is for you to go. Now."

Dovzhenko stuffed the silver necklace in his pocket and then, exasperated, kissed her hard before sliding open the rear window.

"I'll be right back."

He switched off his radio and vaulted over the rail, letting his body extend fully so he could drop to the next balcony below. He repeated the process twice more on the second- and first-floor balconies, dropping the last few feet to land among a hedge of thorny shrubs. Tires squealed around the corner as a vehicle turned quickly off 2nd Street and came to a stop in the parking lot out front.

Dovzhenko ran south without looking back, cutting between dark apartment buildings and vaulting several fences to put some distance between him and Sassani's men. Two minutes later, he turned to the east through a neighborhood of large single-family homes, toward his parked car. Motion lights came on in nearly every yard, blinding him. He narrowly avoided tripping headlong into a backyard pond. He reached his car in less than five minutes, hands on his knees, wheezing for air. He really needed to stop smoking. His hand darted to the pocket of his slacks.

His lighter!

He checked his jacket, feeling like he might pass out at the cold realization that he'd left the lighter at the apartment. Sassani would surely recognize the Azerbaijani crest.

The clatter of gunfire tore at the night.

Dovzhenko choked back a scream. Jumping behind the wheel, he started the little Tiba and threw it into gear, pointing it toward Maryam—and the gunfire. He willed the gutless car to go faster. He had to get inside and retrieve the lighter before Sassani found it. If he could not, then he would at least have the pleasure of shooting the son of a bitch in the face before they arrested him.

D ovzhenko parked and jumped out of the Tiba, sprinting up three flights of stairs.

A young IRGC thug stopped him at the apartment door. "What are you doing here?" It was the same one he'd given the binoculars to, a foolish gesture that only made him look odd—and in the intelligence world, *odd* was very much akin to guilty.

"I received a tip," Dovzhenko said, forcing his breath to slow. "I could ask the same question."

"We have also received a tip." Sassani strode around the corner, sleeves of his collarless gray shirt rolled up, a tight pair of black leather gloves stretched over his hands.

Dovzhenko shouldered his way past the door guard, biting his tongue when he saw Maryam's arm trailing off the bed. A rivulet of blood ran from the crook of her elbow to drip from the tips of her fingers. He bit the inside of his cheek to keep from giving himself away.

"I am confused, comrade," Sassani said, head cocked to the side. "Why did you not call us?"

"It was merely a tip," Dovzhenko said. "I am as surprised to see you as you are me." He moved around the room, touching as much as he could without looking too obvious. His fingerprints were everywhere. The sunken divot from where he'd sat on the couch to smoke was still in the cushion. He glanced at the ashtray—and thought of the cigarette butt in his pocket. He and Maryam had made love twice—and she'd never gotten out of bed. *He* was all over this place.

Sassani looked him up and down for a long moment, like a dog looks at a piece of meat it cannot quite reach.

"She resisted?" Dovzhenko heard himself ask, the words hollow, distant though from his own mouth. It was only then that he noticed one of Sassani's men holding a bandage to his arm.

"The bitch shot me," the man said.

Bravo, Dovzhenko thought. He'd not known Maryam even had a gun. He moved into the bedroom as if he owned the place—a skill at which Russians were particularly adept. Intelligence training had taught him to swallow his emotions, to lie with his eyes in order to make his words believable. Seeing Maryam's bullet-riddled body was impossibly difficult, but he dug deep and somehow mustered the wherewithal to appear appropriately shocked at the scene, without breaking down completely.

"What a waste," he said, forcing himself to approach the bed so he could look for his lost lighter. If it was on the floor, he could find a way past this. If it was tangled in the sheets, he was doomed.

A cursory search revealed nothing, and he leaned over the bed, swallowing the fury that threatened to overpower him.

Most of Maryam's wounds were to her chest, but there were two to her neck. Blood soaked the sheets and mattress underneath. But when he squinted and blocked out the worst of it, he could almost imagine she was just asleep.

Sassani's eyes burned holes in the back of his neck. He closed his eyes, controlling his breathing before turning to face the IRGC thug.

"The whore was with someone," Sassani said. "Just before we arrived."

Dovzhenko stared at the man, playing out the scene in his mind. The Makarov pistol held eight rounds in the magazine and one in the chamber. The little 9x18 was stout enough to do the job, but few pistol calibers were optimum as offensive weapons. They often took time to neutralize a threat. Sassani and three of his men were in the bedroom. Two shots for each of them gave him one to spare. He would shoot Sassani first, once in the face, following up with two shots apiece to the other three. Then Dovzhenko would put a second into Sassani's groin even if he didn't need it, because he'd called Maryam a whore. Rather than reload, he'd grab one of the SIG Sauer .45s and shoot the other three IRGC thugs as they came in to investigate. He might even make it as far as the Russian embassy—where his own people would take him into custody.

"Sir," one of Sassani's men said from the side of the bed, "look at this." He held up the gold lighter.

"Thank you," Dovzhenko said, snatching it away. Only bluster and bravado would do now. If he acted guilty, they would smell it. "It must have fallen out of my pocket when I looked at the body."

Sassani regarded him with a narrow eye. He said nothing but gave the other officer a small nod, as if to say "Carry on. We will talk later."

"An autopsy will be performed, as a matter of policy," Sassani said, lips pulled back in a tight smile. "As I said, she was with someone. DNA tests will tell us the ethnicity of her lover."

"A wise course of action," Dovzhenko said.

He looked at Maryam's lifeless body. It was a mercy that she'd been spared the torment Sassani and his men would have meted out. Rape, bastinado, burning— nothing was too base for these men.

"You know," Sassani said. "She is not even the name on the lease for this apartment." He turned to the man that stood nearest the bedroom door. "What is her name?"

"Maryam Farhad, sir."

"Ah, yes, Maryam," Sassani said. "A pious name for a whore."

Dovzhenko suddenly found himself extremely tired. "How did you find her, then?"

"As I said, a tip, just like you. We were lucky. I think we should talk to the actual owner next, don't you?"

"A wise move." Dovzhenko groaned inside. He had never met Maryam's friend, but he knew now that he had to find her and warn her. "I need to piss," he said. "I won't touch anything."

"By all means," Sassani said. "Piss. I don't care."

Dovzhenko started to turn for the bathroom but paused at the bedroom door as if he did not know exactly where it was.

Maryam's jacket lay on the floor where she'd dropped it earlier that evening. He flushed the toilet, using the noise of swirling water to cover the jingle of her keys as he lifted the jacket to his nose, breathing in the smell of her, blinking back tears. He pulled himself together, then found what he was looking for in the pocket, before gently returning the jacket to the floor.

"What is wrong?" Sassani asked when Dovzhenko came out of the bathroom. He was still grinning. "You look as though the weight of the world is on your shoulders, my friend."

"We are not friends," Dovzhenko said.

"That," Sassani said, "is becoming more obvious to me by the minute. But for argument's sake, why is that not so? Because I killed a whore?"

"Her?" Dovzhenko remembered he was a spy in time to scoff. "She is nothing. This is a nasty business we are in, and sometimes we must both do nasty things. The difference is you enjoy it too much."

He turned his back on the IRGC men and walked toward the door. There was only one way forward for him now—a way that, if he were honest with himself, he'd been considering for some time. But first he had to find a woman named Ysabel Kashani.

24

M andy Cruz considered "going blue" and activating the flashing light in the doll-sized outhouse to let the forty-four other watch-standers know she was leaving her desk to use the restroom and they needed to remain on station. Colloquially referred to as Ops, the State Department Operations Center was located just down the hall from the secretary's office, beyond a set of frosted doors and two armed guards. In the shadowy world where diplomacy and intelligence merged, secrets were compartmentalized behind countless locks, and Ops held one of the biggest keyrings in government. Those on watch were call takers, dispatchers, facilitators, problem solvers—and intrepid detectives who were trained to birddog a task until it was accomplished. If the secretary needed to speak with a specific ambassador who could not be located, someone from Ops found out where he played racquetball, where she golfed, or if he or she enjoyed a long lunch at the hotel with a significant other. More than once there had been heavy breathing on the line when she finally got through. But Cruz didn't care. People had to live their lives. Her business was to answer when they called, find them when they were needed, and connect them with the boss.

Just fifteen minutes earlier, Cruz had taken the *S* icon representing the secretary of state on her computer screen and dropped it into a box with the icon for the foreign minister of South Korea, connecting the call. Someone else took notes on the conversation, but, generally speaking, Cruz could figure out the gist of what was going on by the information that passed across her desk. Five minutes after the call with Korea, Secretary Adler's box had dropped in with an icon representing Foreign Minister Tinubu of Nigeria. Two minutes after that, the group supervisor had set up a special Cameroon Task Force and briefed everyone in Ops. Cruz was pulled from her regular duties to focus on the embassy takeover.

Nine minutes after Task Force Cameroon was up and running, Cruz's headset chirped. She clicked her computer mouse to answer the call.

"Hello, Ops!" the voice on the other end of the line said, relieved, as if coming up for air. "Special Agent Adin Carr in Yaounde, Cameroon. The ambassador is safe. I'm talking on a stolen cell phone, so we are not, I repeat, not, secure."

Cruz hit another icon on her screen, notifying her group supervisor that she had a priority caller on the line having to do with Task Force Cameroon.

"Special Agent Carr," Cruz said, "I'm connecting you with the secretary right now." She dropped the icons but stayed on the line. The call would be recorded, and in this situation, all involved stayed on to ensure the call wasn't fumbled or dropped completely.

The secretary came on the line an instant later, asking the question the agent surely wanted to hear. "Adin, this is Scott Adler. What do you need first?"

———

The chief of staff, secretaries of defense and state, and the director of national security stood in the middle of the Oval in the closest thing to parade rest they could muster while holding their leather folios.

"They're moving her," Adler said. "Carr will get back with us as soon as he can."

Ryan's desk line buzzed and Betty's voice came over the speaker.

"Mr. President, I have President Njaya of Cameroon on the line."

Ryan put the phone on speaker. "François, thank you for taking my call."

"Of course, Mr. President. These are most concerning reports I am hearing."

"That's putting it mildly, François." Ryan cut to the chase. "I need Mrs. Porter released without delay. We can discuss the embassy after she's safe."

"I understand, Jack," Njaya said. "I, too, am concerned for the safety of Mrs. Porter. These military officers who have taken her have so far shown restraint, but I am not sure how long that will continue."

"What could they hope to gain, François?" Ryan asked, playing along with the farcical game. "Your military has mounted an attack on United States soil."

Njaya huffed. "Jack, I would not go so far as to say it was an attack—"

"Put the shoe on the other foot."

"I see," Njaya said. "I do not dispute the fact that your embassy is American soil. The men who surround it are merely angry at the aggression against the sovereignty of Cameroon. I am sure this can all be sorted out."

"Have you been able to figure out why?" Ryan asked. Njaya knew exactly why. It may have taken on a life of its own now—matters with rogue militaries usually did— but Njaya had certainly ordered it. Ryan didn't want to play his hand. Yet.

"This I believe I can answer," Njaya said. "A teacher at a secondary school here in Yaounde discovered your very disturbing video on the Internet.

"You are a smart man, Jack," Njaya said pithily, animosity creeping into his voice for the first time. "Perhaps we should stop playing games. In this video you pledge your support to General Mbida and the Anglophones. How could you do such a thing, Mr. President? I would have contacted you directly to work it out, but once my supporters became aware of this video, they began to act of their own accord. It will take some time for me to restore calm."

"That video is obviously doctored," Ryan said. "You cannot believe everything you see online. Surely you know that, François."

"Come, now, Mr. President," Njaya said. "It is your face and your voice."

"Have your people take a look at the metadata. They will prove me out."

"I will do just that," Njaya said.

"And your military?" Ryan asked. "What are they going to do? Before you answer, I will remind you that the United States has been your partner against Boko Haram for many years."

"As I say, Mr. President," Njaya said, "I am sure we . . .

they will get this sorted out very soon. In the meantime, it would go a long way to bringing this matter to a close if your embassy personnel would send out Mbida."

"There's a big difference in someone asking for asylum and someone being held against their will. Before we talk about anything else, Mrs. Porter must be released."

"But I do not know where she is," Njaya said, barely concealing his duplicity. "Do you, Mr. President?"

"François," Ryan said through clenched teeth. "I would think these rogue members of your military would not want the United States as an enemy."

"It would seem to me," Njaya said, "that it is you who cannot afford another enemy. What with everything else you are facing, the influenza, loss of public trust, I should think you would want to clear up this unfortunate incident quickly, before lives are lost."

"François," Ryan said, seething now. "They do not want to test me."

"Oh, Mr. President." The gloating smile was evident in Njaya's tone. "One of your own senators has already accused you of bullying those who do not agree with you."

Ryan's face twitched. Mary Pat Foley, the only one in the room brave enough to approach him at the moment, stepped up to pat a hand on his arm for support. He waved her off, nodding that he was all right.

Njaya, uncomfortable with the silence, spoke again. "I am telling you, Jack, this is not my doing."

"I understand," Ryan said. "And I assure you, François, help is on the way. You will not have to take care of this alone."

"Jack," Njaya said. "You must not act unilaterally."

"Oh, I'm not," Ryan said. "Not at all. Our countries

have had a mutual aid agreement to fight Boko Haram for many years. You have already invited us."

"Come, now, Jack—"

"We're losing the connection, François."

Ryan ended the call. He took a deep breath and then put both hands flat on the desk in front of him.

"We're attack plus five hours and so far we have, what, two UAVs and one DSS agent on station? I want all of you thinking about options. Everything's on the table. DevGru, Delta, the 82nd Airborne . . . hell, an entire Marine Expeditionary Force. Let's get Task Force Darby headed south. Whatever it takes to get this woman out safely and protect our embassy. Am I clear?"

Van Damm said, "The Hostage Response Group fusion cell is—"

Ryan pushed away from his desk. "Arnie," he said, after a deep, deliberative breath. "I fully understand the need for the HRG. But I want action. Coordinated, yes, but not just coordinated planning."

"Understood," van Damm said.

"Very well." Ryan stood and shrugged on his suit jacket. "I'll be right behind you."

"Mr. President," Foley said, hanging back as the others filed out toward the Situation Room. "Would it be possible to have a momentary word?"

Ryan smiled. "We've been friends long enough for me to recognize an intervention when I see one. You don't want me to go in there and bomb the hell out of Cameroon because Njaya's a smarmy piece of shit."

"The thought had occurred to me, Jack," Foley said. "And honestly, none of us would blame you. Though that wouldn't make it the right thing to do."

Ryan stifled a chuckle. "My old man always said that handling anger was like climbing stairs. Everyone gets winded, no matter how good a shape you're in. It's how fast you recuperate that matters. I might get hot, but I won't boil over." His eyes narrowed. "I promise you, if I use force against François Njaya and his military, it will be overwhelmingly violent . . . but completely dispassionate." He waved her toward the door. "Now go keep the Hostage Response Group in line until I get there. I'll be there in a minute."

Alone, Ryan turned to look past his own reflection in the center window behind his desk and onto the South Lawn. He shied away from the spot when anyone else was in the Oval, particularly the White House photographer. The whole look was too derivative of JFK, but it was a good thinking spot, damn it.

Apart from the comparison of climbing stairs to getting angry, Ryan's father had always encouraged him to take a hard look at what he was angry at and admit to himself that it was most usually himself. The plain truth was that Njaya, for all his gloating, was right. Ryan was in a bad spot. The influenza, the flooding with attendant public health issues in the southeast, this business with Michelle Chadwick, and now an embassy under siege, all added to an already full threat board. The United States had many enemies that would love nothing more than to sit and watch her torn apart—and then swoop in to pick up the pieces . . .

"One thing at a time, Jack," Ryan said to his reflection. He had capable hands working on the influenza epidemic and the flooding. Secretary Dehart was on his way to Louisiana to provide a firsthand report. That left Cameroon—with a diplomatic security agent literally hiding in the weeds, and two MQ-9 Reaper drones hovering over station.

"Unmanned aerial vehicles," Ryan said. Low and slow, but they did the job.

Some argued that UAVs sanitized war . . . made it too easy for politicians. If they saved American lives, then Ryan had no problem with them. Ordering Americans into harm's way could never be sanitized. Every bomb dropped, every trigger pulled, did damage, on both ends of the weapon. Ordering multiple deaths, or even one, should never be an easy thing. Some people needed to die, but Ryan was not a man to drag it out. Jack Ryan was no shrinking violet; he'd rather be done with it—whatever *it* was.

Adin Carr crouched behind the rusted box of an old semitrailer beside the man he should have been protecting. Together, they watched a squad of four soldiers, armed with French FAMAS rifles, escort Mrs. Porter into a dilapidated warehouse on the western edge of the city. They'd put a cloth bag over her head and tied her hands behind her back for the move. The apparent leader of the group, a man with a bald spot that looked like an appealing target, gave her a shove that sent her to her knees. Carr had to grab Ambassador Burlingame to keep him from rushing into the open.

"Patience, sir," the DS agent whispered.

"I thought you said you wanted to act," Burlingame said. "So let's act."

"We will, sir," Carr said. "But we have to be smart about it. These guys outgun and outnumber us. Good chance we get Mrs. Porter killed if we go in without a plan and some backup. As much as I'd like to go in with guns blazing, we need to call in and let Ops know where she is so they can send the cavalry."

"Who do you think?" Burlingame asked, eyes locked on the warehouse. "FBI Hostage Rescue, Navy SEALs?"

"You know that old story about FBI HRT being formed?"

Burlingame shook his head.

"The FBI director watched a demonstration of Delta, saw all their gear, and noticed they didn't carry any handcuffs. When he asked why, one of the Delta guys said, 'We put two rounds in their forehead. We don't need handcuffs.' The FBI went on to create the Hostage Rescue Team, but they carry handcuffs."

"In that case," Burlingame said, watching the guy with the bald spot yank Mrs. Porter to her feet, "I'd just as soon they send Delta."

25

Erik Dovzhenko's windshield wipers had no inter-
mittent setting. They simply worked when they felt
like it, wiping away enough rain now and then that
he could mostly see to drive.

Dovzhenko rubbed his eyes with a thumb and forefinger as he drove, trying to clear the fog from his head. He'd
fled straight from Maryam's apartment toward Imam
Khomeini International Airport, pounding on the steering wheel, screaming at the windshield in between his attempts to call Kashani and warn her.

No answer.

Highway 7, the main north-south freeway through
Tehran, was still relatively busy for the late hour, and he
floored the Tiba's sluggish accelerator in an attempt to
merge with the river of red lights and thumping traffic.
In the end, the driver of a crane truck, much like the
ones used to hang the students, took pity and slowed to
let him on.

He'd never met the woman, but he'd heard Maryam's
side of the conversation when they spoke on the phone,
and knew this to be the correct number. The IRGC would
eventually get it from Maryam's phone records. Such

information would not have been difficult to obtain in Russia. Dovzhenko imagined Iran would not be much different. The Persians were meticulous in their recordkeeping. He smacked the steering wheel again, hard enough to hurt his hand. One could not run from a cancer as pervasive as the Sepah. They had connections in every government office, most every business, and, through the interconnecting circles of Iranian society known as *dowreh*, to most families as well. There were IRGC fingers in every pie.

There was no point in going back to his apartment. Dovzhenko had what he needed—his Russian diplomatic passport and money. The rest he could buy or steal.

It was better that he keep moving, to get out of Iran as quickly as possible. That meant abandoning his post. He could feign illness.

Dear Comrade Chief of Station, I am much too ill to continue working, because my dissident Iranian girlfriend was murdered by our corrupt allies.

No. Spies did not call in sick.

And this business with General Alov, whatever it was, complicated matters—a high-ranking member of the GRU general staff meeting with the very people trying to overthrow the ruling mullahs. People had been shot for stumbling into situations that were far less strange.

Dovzhenko knew it was time for him to leave. Not just Iran, but the SVR. Russia. But defection was not easy. Even forgetting the emotional trauma of leaving his country behind, the Americans would not trust him. They would see him as a dangle—a double agent meant to provide misinformation. And anyway, what would he have to offer? The Americans would want someone they could use, not a burned spy who'd been caught up in an affair with a dead Iranian dissident.

A horn blared, pulling him from his anguished stupor. He looked sideways and caught the flash of white teeth in the headlights as the driver of a black sedan cursed and shook an angry fist. Guilty, he saw IRGC operatives everywhere. His hands convulsed on the steering wheel, startled that they had found him so quickly. Then the black sedan sped up, just another driver on Highway 7, pissed that Dovzhenko had drifted into his lane.

The Russian wiped his face with one hand while he kept the Tiba steady with the other, settling deeper into the seat as he focused on the road. He could not afford to have an accident now, or to get stopped by a traffic policeman for erratic driving. But he could not stop. A dog like Parviz Sassani would be relentless in his pursuit. Going to ground, even for a moment, to think, to make a plan, would only do half his job for him.

Sassani would be tied up for a few hours with the remainder of the investigation at Maryam's apartment. She was naked, a sight most of these men did not often get to see. A painful sob caught in his chest. They would take their time collecting evidence and taking lurid photographs, all in the name of thoroughness. The most devout in any religion, Dovzhenko had observed, were often the last to see their own perversions.

He locked the Makarov and his two-way radio in the trunk of the Tiba, which he abandoned among hundreds of similarly ugly sedans in the Number 3 parking lot west of the starkly lit Novotel airport hotel. The sky bridge through the metro station took him across the road to the main terminal where a tired-looking man at the Emirates ticket counter tapped the requisite keys to book him on the next flight to Dubai.

Last-minute airline travel by people who paid with cash and had no luggage was a sure sign of something illegal, so Dovzhenko switched gears, pretending he was the hunter instead of the hunted, as if he were chasing someone and simply had to get on that flight. He exuded the official swagger they taught so well in SVR training—the look that said his business was of the highest import and that it would be extremely dangerous to know what he knew. The ticket agent looked over his diplomatic passport, read between the lines—though incorrectly—and issued his boarding pass so Dovzhenko could continue chasing whatever miscreant he was chasing.

He made it through security quickly, though the screeners were on high alert because of the recent student unrest, not to mention the ever-present threat of Jundallah terrorists for an independent Balochistan.

The flight to Dubai would leave just after one in the morning, leaving him a two-hour layover before he could catch a flight to Kabul. He couldn't remember the last time he'd had anything to eat besides a cigarette. The hangings had pressed a fist to his gut that made food unthinkable. He and Maryam had thought to eat late, but then . . .

He needed to put something in his stomach, even if he didn't feel like it. Most of the shops here were closed anyway, so he decided to wait until he reached Dubai. The airport there was a riotous crossroads of cultures that was almost, but not quite, Muslim. The same way Vegas was almost, but was not quite, America. Or maybe they were both the real faces of the culture and the rest of UAE and USA were the façades.

Dovzhenko's diplomatic passport would get him into most countries without a visa, but a record would still be made. Cameras, though, were ubiquitous in Dubai. Whether in the open or tucked behind the virtual aquarium at passport control, facial-recognition scanners were everywhere. Dovzhenko would be careful, but all he could really do was hope for the best. It would take time for Sassani to pursue a formal inquiry with his superiors, and he would need proof to do that. Wouldn't he? Unless the chief of station saw Dovzhenko's absence as prima facie evidence that he was guilty of something. In which case, he would be detained the moment he got off the plane, if not before it even took off.

It couldn't be helped. Just another reason not to dally.

He alternately cursed for not shooting Sassani when he had the chance, and then consoled himself that he needed to stay alive in order to warn Ysabel Kashani. Sassani would pull out every stop to hunt her down, to find out her connection to Maryam. It was the way he worked, hopping from friend to friend, acquaintance to acquaintance, using his whips and torches to extract the next person who might have something to do with this uprising. Women, it seemed, were the faces leading the crowds of late. Ysabel Kashani was a friend of Maryam's and a woman, which made her doubly suspect, though she was guilty of nothing beyond letting her friend stay at her apartment.

Dovzhenko had seen a few photographs of Kashani but knew little about her, other than she came from a wealthy family and that she and Maryam were friends. He guessed that the two women had met at the university, or possibly the treatment center, both working to help those affected by the torrent of opiates flooding the country from Afghanistan. Kashani was out of the country for the moment, doing something with the United Nations Office on Drugs and Crime. But she was still well within the reach of the IRGC. The Sepah had men all over the Middle East, Africa, and Asia—Dubai, Damascus, Pakistan, and certainly western Afghanistan. Vast networks of paid informants that linked them to virtually every border guard in the Middle East and Central Asia.

What they did not have was Maryam's notebook.

Ysabel Kashani's address was written boldly on the second page, along with several phone numbers. Her office with the UNODC was on the outskirts of Herat, less than a hundred miles from the border with Iran. The government in Tehran would have a record of her employment, but, as with any bureaucracy, Sassani would have to know where to look in order to find it. As long as Dovzhenko got to her before she crossed a border or hit some other checkpoint that entered her passport number into a computer, he could get her out.

Dovzhenko sat down in a plastic chair and waited for his flight to board. It wouldn't be long now. He would fly to Dubai, then on to Kabul where, even with his diplomatic passport, he would have to explain himself before catching the one-hour flight to Herat. He'd been there before, several times, overseeing the transfer of weapons to the Taliban on behalf of the Russian government.

It was often difficult to find enough food or medicine in Afghanistan, but years of war had made weapons another story. Dovzhenko had no doubt he'd be able to find a gun. Maybe even from the Taliban. Guerilla fighters generally preferred rifles, but they would have everything, from ancient Chinese grenades to Claymore mines if the price was right. And there would be some pistols—maybe an American Beretta, but even an old Tokarev would do.

Dovzhenko closed his eyes. He was too exhausted to think clearly, but in too much emotional agony to sleep. He sniffed away tears and steeled himself by thumbing through the notebook. His throat tightened, until he could hardly breathe, at the sight of Maryam's precise handwriting—like an architect's or perhaps a teacher's. He traced Ysabel Kashani's mobile number with the tip of his finger. A note written directly below it in flowing Persian said something like *secondary contact*. Her mother? Dovzhenko slammed the little book closed and bounced it nervously on his knee. Ysabel would not be difficult to find. Sassani would simply identify her family and then go ask them where she was on some false pretense. He could say he needed to talk to her about anything. She was not hiding. She had done nothing wrong, so she had nothing to fear. One of Sassani's female troops would do it, so as not to arouse suspicion, saying she was an old friend.

The overhead speaker clicked, then crackled with a barely understandable call from the gate agent for early boarding. If he was going to warn Kashani's secondary contact, it would have to be soon. Lost in thought, he nearly dropped the phone when it began to buzz in his hand.

It was Sassani.

Dovzhenko snapped a greeting, wanting to appear normal. "It is late."

"It is indeed," the IRGC thug said. "A busy night for us both, no?"

"True enough," Dovzhenko said. He looked up and

down the concourse, suddenly feeling a thousand eyes crawling over him. He glanced down at his chest, half expecting to see the dot of a red laser from a weapon sight.

"Where are you?" Sassani asked. "I had hoped to get your assistance with something."

This was a first.

There was a better-than-average chance Sassani was standing in his apartment right then, so Dovzhenko went with a less verifiable lie.

"I went for a drive."

Across the concourse, the gate agent lifted the mic to his lips to make another boarding call. Dovzhenko lowered the phone and hit the mute button an instant before the speaker boomed.

"Too bad," Sassani said, still unaware. "I am on my way to the dead whore's autopsy. This would seem a good opportunity for me to gain from your scientific experience."

Maryam's autopsy. The concourse closed in around him. Dovzhenko found it impossible to speak.

"Are you still there?" Sassani asked.

Dovzhenko took the phone off mute.

"I am sorry." He summoned his last ounce of concentration in order to conceal his feelings. "The mobile signal cut out. An opportunity for what?"

"Your knowledge and experience," Sassani said flippantly. "But we are fine without you. I only thought to extend the invitation. In case you are interested. The hospital is off Valiasr Street in the event you decide to change your mind. I find autopsies to be extremely revealing."

"I am exhausted," Dovzhenko managed to say.

"Next time, then," Sassani said. "Sleep well, Comrade Erik."

Dovzhenko ended the call. The IRGC didn't need him talking to track his phone, but it would certainly make things easier.

Dovzhenko punched in the number for Ysabel Kashani's emergency contact as he slogged toward the gate, wondering if Sassani would have the authority to turn a plane around once it was in the air.

A female voice answered on the third ring.

"Balay," she answered, mumbling, woken from a sound sleep.

Dovzhenko spoke passable Farsi, but his Russian accent was evident, making it sound especially gruff.

"Ysabel Kashani?"

The voice softened. "Ysabel is not here."

"Where is she?" Dovzhenko demanded, hoping to incense the woman at this late hour with his forceful tone. "I must speak with her at once."

The woman whispered a few frantic words to someone beside her now, hoarse, strained, just as Dovzhenko had hoped. *"He wants to talk to Ysabel."*

A male voice came on the line. "What is the meaning of this? Who are you, calling my home at this hour?"

"Who I am is none of your concern," Dovzhenko said. "Where is Ysabel?"

The man hung up. With any luck, the call had spooked him enough to keep his mouth shut about the whereabouts of his daughter or niece or whatever Ysabel Kashani was to him—at least until Dovzhenko could get to her and warn her.

26

Lucile Fournier glared at da Rocha's reflection in the mirrored lobby walls while they waited for the elevator door to open. Elevators were apparently one of the few places on earth where she was not a picture of calm. Hand inside the gauzy black cover-up she wore over her blouse, she stood on da Rocha's right, keeping her own gun hand free, bouncing on the balls of her feet, grossly out of sync with the canned music pouring from the overhead speaker. An audible chime signaled the car's arrival and da Rocha stepped aside, allowing Lucile to enter first.

She wore the same shorts and T-shirt she'd had on earlier, during the business with Don Felipe. Da Rocha outweighed his curvaceous assassin by seventy-five pounds and towered above her at a little over six feet four inches tall. Still, he found himself mildly terrified every time she came near him. She'd been attracted, she said, to his coarse, bottle-brush hair that stuck out in all directions if he didn't keep it short. He knew differently. If Lucile Fournier was attracted to anything, it was the prospect of violent death. It appeared to make little difference if it was someone else's or her own, it was the notion that fascinated her, and the more violent the better. She seemed like a moth to the flame of the life da Rocha offered, begging for assignments that were incautious at best, and often appeared suicidal to anyone who did not understand how meticulously she planned her operations. There were, of course, always variables. It was for this uncertainty that she seemed to hunger most.

And da Rocha gave her plenty of opportunity to feed.

Urbano was baptized into violent action at the hands of his father, breaking the bastard's neck with an ax handle in a fight over the car. His job delivering groceries paled in comparison, and he'd sought work as an errand boy for the Ochoas, a mid-level clan in the Galician mafia that ran prostitutes and drugs from northern Spain down into Lisbon. Fistfights and a brutal reputation had seen him move up quickly in the organization. He'd earned a nod from old man Ochoa himself when he'd stabbed a rival clan member for trying to recruit some of their girls in Porto. The mob boss became a stand-in for the father young Urbano had killed and welcomed him into the next level of the family business. By the time he was twenty-six, da Rocha had a crew of his own, responsible for receiving cocaine shipments inbound from Colombia and cutting them up for dispersal to the hungry European market.

He was in charge, surrounded by men who respected him and women who answered his every whim—and he had a lot of whims. Life was good. And then he'd run across a load of Russian-made 9K38 Iglas meant for the return trip to Colombia on the same transport ship that brought in his coke. He recognized the sleek, bazooka-like weapons immediately from playing Battlefield 2 with the guys on his crew. He'd always had a thing for weap-

ons of any kind—but had this been a simple load of Kalashnikovs, he would have let them go with no more than
a passing glance. The Iglas were a different animal altogether. Igla—meaning "needle"—was an advanced man-
portable air-defense system, or MANPADS. There were
newer models, but the Grouse, as NATO called this one,
was a highly sophisticated piece of machinery in its own
right. There were those in the Middle East and elsewhere
that would pay handsomely for them. Da Rocha calculated correctly that he could get upward of $25,000 U.S.
for each unit, earning him a quick half-million after ex-
penses. These came with no overhead, but for the time
lost dumping the bodies of the smugglers off the Douro
Point lighthouse.

He found the glamour and excitement of dealing in
armaments much more appealing than pushing drugs
and pimping whores. It was a heady feeling, this shaping
nations. Working with governments had downsides, to
be sure, but in the long run, even a shaky regime was
more stable than the best cartel—and you didn't have to
worry quite as much about ending up in a barrel of acid
if you sold to both sides of a conflict. Though such a
thing was not out of the realm of possibility.

At first, da Rocha paid a tribute to Ochoa for working
in the old man's territory. It was paltry compared to what
he was making, and he paid it for the same reason a man
shooed away a fly instead of using a newspaper and rid-
ding himself of the nuisance once and for all—it was
simply too much trouble. Then the old man had gotten
greedy and demanded a piece of the action. Da Rocha
killed him and every member of his family, but rather
than taking over the business, he left it to the three

Ochoa lieutenants to fight over—a battle that would surely consume them for years.

Next he started to work on his competition. Lucile had worked for a minor dealer in the south of France, a human stain of a man who possessed no charm or charisma. It had taken little more than a wink to get Lucile to cut his throat and come to work for da Rocha.

There was, he supposed, always the chance that she would do the same with him. She was certainly capable of it. But that was what made it interesting.

The elevator was incredibly slow, the canned music accompanied by the noise of banging cables and sliding counterweights. Lucile appeared to hold her breath during the ride, and gasped audibly when the door hissed open on the third floor. A thick Russian man was waiting outside the elevator. A metal railing behind the Russian came up to just below his belt. Lucile hummed under her breath, a tune da Rocha knew she always hummed when she was thinking of how best to kill someone. She gave the Russian a wicked smile, surely pondering how easy it would be to give a little shove and send him crashing to the floor below. He smiled back, surely with murderous thoughts of his own. The tattoo of a dagger rose above his collar indicated that he was *bratva*—Russian mafia. Da Rocha had no doubt a man like this would have an abundance of other ink under his shirt. The rose impaled by a dagger was a badge of honor, meant to intimidate and let others know this one had done time in prison before he'd turned eighteen.

The man grunted and tossed a glance over his shoulder before turning and walking down the hall without a word.

Da Rocha exchanged glances with Lucile, and the two followed dutifully. This meeting was, after all, what they'd been working toward for the past three months.

Rose Neck halted at the door to room 314, a suite, from the looks of the placard, and gave two sets of three sharp knocks in quick succession. Da Rocha was surprised the man hadn't patted them down as soon as they got off the elevator, but when the door opened he understood why.

The Russian with the odd haircut waved them inside with a flick of his hand.

"Disrobe," he said, while they stood in the cramped alcove next to a vanity and mini-fridge. A curtain made from what appeared to be the bedspread hung from the ceiling at the end of the entry, blocking da Rocha's view of the room's interior. He caught the odor of something he could not quite put his finger on, but the order to take off his clothes put his mind on other things.

"If we are going to strip," he said, "perhaps it is time I learned your name."

"You may call me Gregor," the one with the bad haircut said. His thickly accented English made it sound as if he were talking around a mouthful of food.

Da Rocha's eyes narrowed. "Is that your name?"

"No," the Russian said. "But you may call me Gregor just the same. Now, please to undress. There will be robes."

Da Rocha put a hand on his belt and then stopped, canting his head to one side.

"Why?"

"Guns, listening devices, all of those reasons," Gregor said. "You have proven with devastating effect that a man in your line of employ has access to many weapons. Perhaps you have technology that could defeat our scanners."

"I see," da Rocha said, smiling at Lucile. "My dear, you take the bathroom first."

The Russian stepped sideways to block the door. "You will undress here," he said. "Is safer for all of us this way."

Lucile pushed a lock of hair off her forehead. "May I remove my pistol?"

The Russian produced a heavy foil envelope approximately a foot square and held it open. Da Rocha recognized it as a Faraday bag, designed to stop electrical signals from getting in or out. "Put in this." Gregor's eyes narrowed. "But very slowly."

Lucile grabbed the diminutive Beretta Nano from a holster inside her waistband under the tail of her T-shirt, letting it dangle between her thumb and forefinger before dropping it in the bag.

"I do not need a pistol to kill you," Lucile said through a serene smile.

"I am sure they know that, my dear," da Rocha said.

"You make killing complicated," Gregor said, leaning in to encroach on Lucile's body space ever so slightly. "Silent pistols, specialized toxins . . . Why you go so much trouble?"

"Oh, mon petit nounours." Lucile smiled, batting her lashes. "It is no trouble."

The Russian glared down at her, clicking his front teeth as if chewing on his next words. If he understood that she'd called him her teddy bear, he didn't mention it.

"Mobile phones," he said at length, and then put the Faraday bag in the mini-fridge once they'd dropped their devices in. "Now your clothing, if you please. Shoes as well."

Both Rose Neck and Gregor watched with rapt interest as Lucile stepped out of her shorts and then her underwear without so much as a fumble. They took particular interest in the thin white lines that scarred her legs. Parallel and roughly an inch apart, there were nine of them, from the hollow of her hip well down her thigh on each side. Some might think she'd cut herself, but da Rocha had seen them before, and knew the wounds had come from a straight razor when she was only fourteen. Her own father had tried to mark her as his property. Lucile had dosed his beef broth with some sleeping pills she'd found in his kit—and then done a little work on him before enlisting a boyfriend to help dump him in the river. Her young age and the horrific wounds on her legs had kept her from doing more than eighteen months, and all of that in what the French called a "closed school."

Completely naked, she gave a little twirl to demonstrate to the Russians that she was in control of the situation. "See," she said. "No weapons, but for my naughty bits." Gregor retreated a half-step when she shoved the tiny ball of black silk that was her panties out toward him. "Shall I put this in the bag, or do you wish to hold on to them for me?"

Rose Neck gave a crooked grin. Gregor hooked a thumb toward the top of the minibar. "There will do."

Da Rocha shot her a sideways glance, which she returned with a little *C'est la guerre* shrug.

He followed Gregor down the short hallway with Lucile close in behind him. Rose Neck brought up the rear.

It was only when Gregor pushed the makeshift drape aside that da Rocha was able to identify the smell that had previously eluded him.

———

The floral scent of oranges mixed with the aroma of horse manure from the carriages of Barrio Santa Cruz drifted up on the hot evening air to Ding Chavez's perch inside the third-floor window of La Giralda, a block south of the Russians' hotel. During the day, the centuries-old minaret turned Catholic bell tower was one of the most visited places in Seville—and in all of Spain, for that matter. The tours stopped at five p.m., giving Chavez and Caruso the stairwell all to themselves. The night watchman was a big-bellied man who appeared to believe that as long as he watched the base of the stairs, there was really no reason to expend the effort to check out the space above. The biggest danger the operatives faced now was being seen by one of the hundreds of tourists milling around on the cobblestone streets below, snapping hundreds of photos in the dusk that they would surely delete later. To avoid detection, Chavez wore dark clothing and stayed well away from the opening.

He stood behind the eyepiece of what looked like a tripod-mounted SLR camera. Dominic Caruso was a few feet to his left, also back from the adjacent window, with a similar setup. An infrared beam from Caruso's laser microphone was aimed directly at the Russians' terrace window. If things worked as they hoped, conversations occurring inside the room would cause the window to vibrate, modulating the light from the laser when it bounced at an angle to Chavez's receiver and digital recorder. He'd picked up a few terse phrases when they'd first come on station twenty minutes before, mainly jokes about Spanish women and bitching about the Seville heat.

There had been another sound, like the squeak of a twisted balloon or duct tape coming off a roll. Then nothing.

Clark and Adara, who was now sporting a curly auburn wig and nonprescription glasses, had set up shop two rooms down from the Russians, monitoring the cameras and GSM listening devices they'd installed under the metal railing three feet from the door to the junior suite and against the glass of the fire extinguisher on the wall outside the elevator halfway down the hall.

Midas and Jack sat at a sidewalk table of a tapas bar near the hotel entrance, almost lost among the crush of tourists as they nursed a couple of local beers and nibbled on thin slices of rich *ibérico* ham.

"Okay," Clark said over the net. "Jack, Midas, time to scoot over to da Rocha's room and do a little snooping. Be alert for anybody he's got babysitting the place."

"Roger that," Ryan said. "On our way."

"We'll give you a heads-up when they leave the room," Clark said. "Ding, how about a sitrep?"

"They can't be that quiet," Chavez whispered into the mic on his neck loop. He shot a sideways glance at Caruso. "You bump the laser?"

"Nope," Caruso said, his words muffled by the pair of binoculars he used to peer at the Russians' hotel window. "I'm good on this end. I have eyes through a small crack in the blinds, and you're not gonna believe what they're doing in there."

27

D a Rocha's hands shot up, as if to fend off an attack. A guttural, animalistic growl escaped his throat.

Clear plastic sheeting covered the floor and hung from the ceiling along the far wall, tacked up and fixed to the floor with black gaffer's tape. Lucile ran into his back, her skin hot against him.

"Merde!" she spat when she saw the plastic.

Gregor stepped aside and gave a sinister chuckle.

"Relax," the Russian with the long upper lip said from inside the room. "Is not what you think. Is makeshift bubble, not kill house. That is, unless you decide you no longer wish to work with us—in which case, we can repurpose our antisurveillance material . . . if we need to, say, dispose of your bodies."

"No," da Rocha said, hoping his face looked far more nonchalant than he felt. "That will not be necessary. My fervent hope is to work with you. I have, after all, been chasing after you like some sort of lovesick teenager. Have I not?" A series of deep, purposeful breaths began to slow his heart rate from the sudden shock. For a moment, he'd been certain he was about to have his brains blown all over a sheet of plastic. He'd used the technique himself, to protect his own carpet and furnishings from the blood of an unfaithful mistress.

The idea of a bubble was ingenious, really. Many secure intelligence facilities, including the American CIA's newest headquarters building in Virginia, were constructed on the same principle, a building within a building. Music or white noise could be played in the dead space between the two layers, making surveillance with laser or microwave devices next to impossible and rendering even the most sophisticated wall- or appliance-mounted electronic bugs ineffective.

All the furniture had been pushed to the walls, outside the sheeting, the queen-size bed tipped against the inner wall, creating a secure box of plastic, absent anything but four throw pillows. The light coming through the plastic was diffused and flat, giving the sterile "room" a surreal, otherworldly feel. The three Russians in their dark sport coats, with da Rocha and Lucile standing naked as Adam and Eve, would have been laughable but for the severity of the Russians' faces.

The Russian with the long upper lip handed each of them a white terry-cloth robe. "Please," he said. "You may call me Vladimir."

Da Rocha shrugged on his robe, which was a little too snug in the shoulders, tying the knot in front. Lucile put on hers but left it open in front, her breasts parting it like hands through a theater curtain.

"Please sit," Vladimir said, gesturing to the pillows on the floor with an open hand. "To begin, I have to say that your ability to neutralize your rivals at will . . . is impressive, if uncalled for. We have done our research on you, Mr. da Rocha. It seems as though you may be able to be of service to my employers. I must impress on you the sensitivity of what we discuss . . . and the danger of violating our trust."

"I understand," da Rocha said without hesitation. "I'd hoped the route I took to gain your attention might prove I am serious, and certainly no friend of the authorities."

"Perhaps," the Russian said. "But the authority of a higher bidder, more money, if you will, often causes lines of trust to blur."

"I hope our business arrangement will continue far into the future," da Rocha said. He caught the hint of an eye roll in Gregor. It was a micro-expression that would have gotten the man shot if he'd been da Rocha's employee, but he ignored it for the time being. The long-lipped man called Vladimir was the decision-maker in this group, so da Rocha focused all attention on him. "I value trust as well. You have no worries in that regard."

"Outstanding," Vladimir said. "Shall we cut right to the meat of the matter?"

Da Rocha's shoulders relaxed a notch, while at the same time, his guts churned at being so close to securing the deal. "I would appreciate that."

The Russian's head bobbed up and down several times, as if he were just now choosing his words. "Very well. I represent a group of businessmen who wish to move a sensitive product to a group of people in a . . . shall we say, politically volatile region of the world."

"I have routes in place for such movement," da Rocha said. "Some are better than others, depending on the end point."

"Iran," Vladimir said, eyes focused intently on da Rocha, studying his reaction.

"That will be no problem," da Rocha said. "I know of several covert airstrips in western Iran where the IRGC allows certain types of cargo to come in so long as they are paid a tidy—"

"The Revolutionary Guard—or anyone in the Iranian regime—cannot be a party to this."

"They will not be," da Rocha said. "We pay them to leave us alone."

Vladimir shook his head. "This is large cargo. A sea route would be better."

"Also possible," da Rocha said, undeterred. "Where is the cargo now?"

Vladimir gave him another long look. "Muscat," he said.

"Okay." Da Rocha pictured the Gulf of Oman in his mind. No matter their cargo, smugglers were experts in languages and geography. "The trip from Muscat to Bandar-e-Jask is eminently possible, less than two hundred fifty kilometers, I believe. But I have access to large transport aircraft. I could have, say, an Ilyushin 76 in Muscat in a matter of hours with no problem."

The Russians looked at each other.

"All right," Vladimir said. "How you move the cargo makes no difference to me, so long as it gets moved. The buyers will take possession as soon as it reaches Iranian soil."

"We have not discussed money," da Rocha said.

"That is true," the Russian said. "We have not. There are two . . . parts . . . to this cargo. We estimate the wholesale price of each one to be fifteen million American dollars."

Da Rocha blinked hard to try and mask the growing twitch in his eye. The incessant demand and uncertainty of supply of weapons in the black market often made for exorbitant prices. Buyers paid a handsome premium so someone else would run the risk of going to prison. A two-hundred-dollar Bosnian Kalashnikov could go for over two thousand in Mexico. Still, he had a hard time picturing a deal where he could come out on top after laying down thirty million dollars on the front end.

"That is a great deal of money for me to pay for something sight unseen," da Rocha said. "I am not even sure what the buyers have agreed to."

Vladimir raised an open hand. "You must excuse my understanding of English. 'Wholesale' was not the correct word. My employer would pay *you*, not the other way around."

Da Rocha struggled to remain composed. "You will pay me to take these items off your hands? What is the benefit in that?"

Vladimir rubbed his eyes. "The benefit is of no concern to you, my friend. Let us just say that my employer wishes to assist the cause of a friend without becoming personally involved."

"I see," da Rocha said, though he did not—not quite, anyway. He'd learned years ago when running women and drugs for Ochoa that product never went out for free—something was always expected in return.

"We pay you to move the items," Vladimir said. "To act as a go-between. To be the . . . face . . . of the transaction."

Da Rocha leaned on one arm, trying not to slip on the

plastic with his sweating hand. His legs were getting sore from sitting sideways on the floor. "I have many shipping routes and mechanisms," da Rocha said, turning up the bravado like the salesman that he was. "I can move anything from palletized crates of rifles to the largest helicopter gunship. Whatever your cargo is, it will be no problem, but how will I know the retail price if I do not know what I am shipping?"

Vladimir took a quick breath through his nose. "Two things, Mr. da Rocha. The retail price is also set at fifteen million per item. So you will be paid twice."

Da Rocha tried to remain impassive, but he was certain that the notion of sixty million caused his eye to twitch even worse. For a time, he'd thought he might be dealing with some rogue separatist group, but only states dealt in that kind of money, and not for conventional weapons. "Forgive me for being blunt, but is this cargo . . . nuclear in nature?"

Vladimir looked down his nose. "Is that a problem?"

"No," da Rocha said honestly. Death was death. He might as well sell nukes as sarin gas or computerized guidance systems.

"Outstanding," Vladimir said, raising his hand again. "You will be well paid, but I cannot stress enough the importance of your discretion. Without it, there can be no future business."

Future business, da Rocha thought. That was a promising sign. "You will not be disappointed," he said. "That French fool Gaspard was fond of whispering into the wind to make himself feel more successful. It was from him that I first heard of your interest in doing some sort of business."

Vladimir smiled serenely, sickeningly so. "Then we are both fortunate." He pointed toward the doorway. "You should begin immediately. Please provide your account information to Gregor on your way out. He will give you the details."

Da Rocha clambered to his feet on wooden legs, numb from being in the same position too long. He reached down to help Lucile, but she ignored him, not out of spite, but as a practical matter, to keep her own hands free.

She asked, "When will the cargo arrive in Muscat?"

"It is there now," Vladimir said. "This transfer must occur quickly."

"I will make arrangements tomorrow, then," da Rocha said.

"Tonight," the Russian said.

"There were two things?"

"Ah," Vladimir said, standing alongside the other Russians. "I must tell you the other reason my employer is willing to pay such a great sum. There is a high likelihood this particular route of yours will eventually be discovered by the authorities."

"Discovered?"

"Yes," Vladimir said. "Exposed. Burned. Will that be a problem?"

"Not at all," da Rocha said, his pocketbook feeling heavier already.

28

Midas left for da Rocha's hotel first, leaving Jack to pay for the tapas and beer. He would follow up two minutes later, watching for any sign of countersurveillance.

The Russians were pros and had decided on a modest hotel, the size and quaintness of which made tight surveillance difficult. Da Rocha, on the other hand, was in this for no motherland. When it came to priorities, God and country came in far behind the lifestyle of playboy international arms dealer, and the more flamboyant the better. Gold jewelry, fast cars, and five-star hotels. He'd booked a deluxe room at the Alfonso XIII, less than ten minutes south on the far side of the Alcázar palace and gardens.

"We're on-site," Midas said over the net. "How we looking back there, bud?"

"Clean so far," Ryan said. He worked his way around a crowd of elderly couples getting directions from a carriage driver who'd stopped in the middle of Avenida de la Constitución, the horse standing hipshot and head down. This gave Ryan a chance to slow his pace and cross the street as if to make a turn, watching to see if anyone followed him, all while keeping an eye on Midas. At one point, Midas slowed, giving Jack time to step into a small shop to check his six o'clock while he bought a pack of gum. He could not count the number of pocketable snacks he'd purchased over the years to give him an excuse to slow down and watch while on surveillance-detection runs.

"Good deal," Midas said. "I'll hang out in the lobby for a minute and see if anyone comes in behind me. A guy just stepped out of the security office. Looks like DVRs instead of flesh-and-blood watchers. Maybe we caught a break on that front."

"Maybe," Jack said, doubtful even as he spoke. Breaks were for bones. It was a rare mission that actually went better than planned. "Walking through the front door now."

Ryan strolled past Midas as if he were a guest, trotting up the marble steps and through the tiled archways leading to the Moorish upper lobby. It was redolent with tobacco and floor wax, and the muted lighting made it reminiscent of an old-world palace. Ryan pushed the call button on the rich mahogany paneling and took the time to look around. This place was like the White House, only bigger, and absent the somber air. The doors opened to an empty car, and Ryan stepped inside, glad to have the elevator to himself for the trip to da Rocha's suite on the third floor. Spaniards ate dinner late, so most of the guests would still be out exploring the warm Seville nights or trying *pacharán*, the liqueur made from sloe berries and coffee favored in Spain as a digestif. Jack grimaced at the thought. His mom appreciated sloe gin in the winter, but he hadn't inherited her taste for the stuff.

"Clear," Jack said when he stepped off the elevator

and into an empty hallway. The polished wood, arched ceilings, and gleaming tile floors reminded him of the old government buildings in D.C.—built before chintzy cubicles and cheap GSA carpet squares. "Our guy's room is to the right and then on the right, five down."

"Copy," Midas said. "Boarding the car alone now. Be with you—"

"Company!" Jack cut him off, forcing a smile as he pretended to speak into the cell-phone buds that hung from his ear. Two men exited da Rocha's suite, easing the door shut behind them. Jack had obviously caught them between an earlier quick peek into the hallway and their exit. Both men gave a startled jump when they saw him walking toward them. He gave them a nonchalant nod, looking past as if on the way to his own room. He even stumbled a bit, giving them the impression that he'd had too much good Spanish wine. Both men scanned up and down the hall, assessing the situation, and then began to walk toward Jack. Less than fifty feet away, Ryan raised his hand as if to cough, chancing a whisper into the mic on his neck loop. "Two bad guys. 'Bout to get real."

"Twenty seconds," Midas said.

"Gaspard's men," Ryan whispered quickly, and then cleared his throat before lowering his hand. He gave the oncoming men another friendly nod. Ignoring them would have been conspicuous, and the nod allowed him to make eye contact to see if either of them recognized him. One of them carried a laptop, the other was a broad, flat-nosed man who he recognized from Gaspard's gray Mercedes in Portugal. It was a fair bet that this guy was in charge. No matter if it was a mob limo or the U.S. Secret Service, the big boss sat in the back. The driver was a specialist, good at his or her job but not particularly high up in the organization. Security leaders generally reserved shotgun for themselves. Flat Nose gave a sideways glance to his friend, a subtle shift of his eyes that said that hotel guest or not, Jack was a witness, which made him a threat.

Jack felt the surge of adrenaline he always felt when a fight was imminent. Metal detectors at various venues around Seville meant a couple of the team had to travel light—no weapons—or risk losing sight of their Russian rabbits if they ducked inside, an effective way to scrape away an armed tail. Tonight, Jack and Midas drew that duty.

Both Gaspard's men wore loose short-sleeve shirts over T-shirts, untucked and open in front, perfect for breaking up the print of a concealed pistol. The bald man fell behind a step, protecting the laptop computer. Flat Nose put a hand behind his back, walking faster now, less than twenty feet from Jack.

Clark's voice crackled in Jack's earbuds. The comms net was good for about eight hundred meters but got spotty after that. A kilometer away and inside the hotel, the beginning of his message was garbled. *". . . your guy . . . leaving us. Possib . . . return . . . second location . . ."*

Ryan was too close to respond now, too focused on the closing threat in front of him. Even if da Rocha ran straight to his room it would take him eight to ten minutes.

Whatever this was, it would be over long before that.

"**D**ing," Clark said, "you and Caruso head to the Alfonso." He watched da Rocha and Lucile Fournier leave the Russians' hotel room on the screen of Adara's iPad.

Chavez came back immediately, his voice unsteady from running down the stairs at La Giralda. "On the way."

All of them had heard that Jack had seen someone coming out of da Rocha's suite, presumably one of Hugo Gaspard's bodyguards still out to avenge the death of their boss.

"Adara and I will stay here on station," Clark said. "Ding, they're out of comms range over there. Call me on my cell with a sitrep when you get there."

"Roger that." Chavez trotting now. "We should be ahead of them. We're zigzagging southbound on the Plaza del Triunfo and then Miguel Mañara instead of going straight down Constitución."

"The equipment?" Clark asked. The briefcase with the laser and receiving mic was purposely made of nondescript leather, but running with any kind of case was sure to arouse unwanted suspicion from police.

"Left it on the third floor, north corner behind the reliquary," Caruso said.

The fact that the long-distance listening device was an expensive piece of equipment was not the issue. Tech like that was sure to make the news if it was found, and Clark didn't want to spook the Russians if he could help it.

"On my way to pick it up," Adara said. Retrieval of sensitive equipment often fell to her. Sexist though it was, getting past lonely security guards could be a little easier for a pretty woman.

Clark remained in the hotel room, watching the iPad. Where others might wear a trail in the carpet pacing to bleed off nervous energy, he sat motionless on the edge of his chair, hands on his knees, leaning forward slightly as if ready to pounce. A dozen different orders that he

could give his guys ran through his head, things he
would do, methods he would employ if he were in their
shoes. But he held his tongue and listened. These guys
were good. Trust came easy. Patience was an entirely different matter.

Most of the fights Jack had been involved in lasted
just a few seconds—a couple went a bit longer. Six
minutes—forget about it. Adara, the CrossFit diva of the
team, had them doing "Fight Gone Bad" routines over
the past couple of years. These killer cardio sessions con-
sisted of three five-minute sets of assorted jumping, lifting, and throwing that were supposed to mimic the
overall body workout of an actual fight. But even those
dizzying, vomit-inducing routines lacked the shot of
adrenaline and fear that went with facing another guy
whose primary aim was to stab you in the liver.

Jack began to cheat his line to the right as he neared
Hugo Gaspard's men. The chime of the arriving elevator
drew their attention down the hall. Midas barked something unintelligible, forcing them to split their focus and
giving Jack the opportunity to close the distance between
himself and Flat Nose, colliding with the big man's chest
before he could bring his arm around with the pistol. The
Japanese called it *butsukari*—crashing in.

Jack squatted low the instant before he hit the Frenchman, keeping his body centered and pushing upward to
drive the point of his shoulder into the other man's solar
plexus. The second man probably had a gun as well, but
Jack used Flat Nose as a shield just in case that one decided to drop the laptop and engage.

A couple of inches shorter than Jack, Flat Nose had him by twenty pounds—and very little of it was fat. The Frenchman stumbled backward, but only a half-step, like a tree shaken by the ax blow, but certainly nowhere close to felled.

His hand already in position, Ryan slammed a hammer fist to the other man's groin, this time driving him against the wall and pinning the gun hand there momentarily— long enough at least to give the guy with the laptop a side kick to the knee when he made a halfhearted advance.

Midas barreled by at that same moment, performing his own version of *butsukari*, and plowed into the guy with the laptop to smear him down the wall.

Ryan's hand grafted upward, trapping the other man's gun arm while he followed up the hammer fist with three rapid-fire knees. Flat Nose swung wildly with his left hand, catching Jack hard in the ear with a brutal slap. Reeling, Jack staggered just enough to allow the other man to free the pistol and bring it around. It was a small black thing with a stubby, piggish suppressor. A professional thug, Flat Nose didn't have much in the way of technique, but he was extremely accomplished at gross motor skills. He didn't worry about precision accuracy or who he happened to shoot, simply pulling the trigger as the gun arced toward Jack. Two rounds zinged down the hall toward the elevator. Jack got his hands up in time to parry the gun, deflecting a third shot upward so it slammed into a lighting sconce on the wall. Hot gases from the muzzle blast were close enough to sear a line in Jack's cheek, narrowly missing his eye.

Braced by the wall, Flat Nose used it for leverage, pushing off to gain more space to employ the pistol. Jack ignored the left fist that now pummeled his kidney, and attacked the gun with both hands, arcing his knee out and then in, using a hooking motion to stun the nerves along Flat Nose's outer thigh. Ryan's foot slipped on the slick tile floor. This nearly caused him to go down and forced him to put all his weight on Flat Nose's gun hand. The added pressure and resulting dead-leg from the knee caused the other fighter's focus to shift just enough for Jack to yank the pistol sideways, attempting to wrest it from Flat Nose's grasp. The Frenchman cursed, gripping the gun tighter, his finger convulsing on the trigger at the same moment the muzzle crossed his own forehead. The bullet took him just over the bridge of his nose.

Flat Nose fell away, sliding down the wall, leaving Jack holding the pistol. He spun to see Midas standing over the unconscious form of the other Frenchman. A laptop lay beside him on the floor.

Midas put a hand to his swollen nose, dabbing away a bit of blood.

"Throw a head-butt, earn yourself a throat punch," he muttered. "Good trade." His eyes fell to the dead man behind Jack. "You gotta go for the throat, Ryan. I'm not sure playing wild weasel with a handgun can be considered a tactic."

Between the slap to one ear and the muzzle blast to the other, Jack only heard about half of what Midas was saying above the high-pitched squeal, but he got the gist of it.

He moved his aching jaw, unable to remember getting clocked in the face, but absolutely sure it had happened. "We need to get these bodies out of sight."

"Copy that," Midas said. "Eight minutes."

Jack looked at him. "What do you mean eight minutes?"

Midas tapped his own ear. "Your comms are out." He took the next twenty seconds to fill Ding and Caruso in on their present situation.

Ryan used the tip of his index finger to discover his earbud was missing, dislodged during the fight. He made a quick scan of the floor and found the flesh-colored piece of plastic along the baseboard just a few inches from Flat Nose's elbow.

". . . up in two," he heard Ding say as he replaced the tiny device. "They won't be far behind us. Get in touch with Gavin and see if he can image the laptop. Be best if we get it back in the room without da Rocha knowing it's gone."

Ryan helped Midas drag both Frenchmen to the stairwell before anyone happened out of a guest room or off the elevator, then trotted down the hall toward da Rocha's room. There was a tray with a half-eaten room-service order on the floor three doors down the hall. Ryan pulled it over the bloodstains and broken glass from his fight, hoping da Rocha wouldn't notice, and then called Gavin while Midas worked the lock on the room.

"Hey," Biery whispered. Jack could hear another voice in the background.

"Are you in the office?"

"Intelligent Data and Security conference in Omaha," Biery said. "I've never seen so many blond people in my life—"

Ryan gave him a thirty-second sitrep.

"You want me to image the computer remotely in six minutes?"

"Can you?"

"No," Biery scoffed. "But you can drop in the malware from the thumb drive I issued everyone last month. You have it, right?"

Jack took out his keys and popped the endcap off a stubby single-cell flashlight attached to the ring, revealing the thumb drive concealed inside.

Ding got off the elevator, walking quickly to da Rocha's suite.

"Caruso's in the lobby," he said. "He'll give us a heads-up."

Midas looked up from the suite door and smiled. "Got it."

Ding remained in the hallway, walking slowly toward the elevator to keep watch while Jack and Midas slipped into da Rocha's room.

Biery continued to give instructions. Ryan lowered the volume but put him on speaker so he could use both hands. "We're gonna need his password."

"That might be an issue," Jack said.

"Maybe a birthday," Biery offered. "An old pet, a girl-friend? Maybe he has it written somewhere near the computer."

Jack looked around for the most likely spot for the laptop, hoping to leave the computer in the same location and condition Gaspard's man had found it. If da Rocha was unaware of the encounter he'd continue to move forward, giving The Campus a chance to suss out more information about his deal with the Russians. The charging cord lay on the desk, still plugged into the wall. It was a safe bet Gaspard's guy had snatched it from there. Ryan reattached the cord to the computer and picked up the aluminum briefcase from the floor. He used the clip of his ballpoint pen to shim the locks, feeling for the divot on each correct number as he rotated the drum. It took him less than thirty seconds to find the combination. Fortunately, both numbers were the same. Inside, he hit pay dirt with a little red notebook of ideas and passwords. It never ceased to amaze Ryan how many people went to the trouble of setting up an extra-secure password and then wrote it down on a notepad they kept in the computer desk or a locked briefcase, thinking that because it was made from aircraft aluminum and had two locks, it offered some kind of sacrosanct barrier. Ryan pitched the notebook to Midas while he booted up the computer.

"Read me that and then take a picture of it."

Ryan typed while Midas read. He stopped looking at his watch, relying on Caruso and Ding to warn him.

The computer gave a soft chime when Ryan entered the correct password.

On the other end of the phone, Biery recognized the sound at once. "Insert the thumb drive and it will auto-load."

"Got it," Ryan said. "How long will it take?"

"Three or four minutes."

"It had better be three," Midas said.

"Like I have any control over that," Biery said.

"It's working," Ryan said.

"A GSM mic would come in handy right now," the former Delta officer said, snapping photos of the note-book pages for future reference.

"No kidding," Ryan said. There were lots of things that would have been nice—but pockets fill up quickly in tactical intelligence work. Often the only lockpick was a penknife and the only weapon little more than a steel pipe. Next to a flashlight, the item that got the most use was a credit card.

"A GSM mic," Biery said. "Are you kidding me? Did you guys even come to the meeting? This malware is a thing of beauty, a phone-home masterpiece that hides as an innocuous system file and then calls us the moment he logs in and pops up on the network. You don't need a GSM bug in the room. You'll be able to take over the mic and camera in his computer. We'll have keystrokes in real time, see what he's seeing, read what he's writing . . . You can even do things to his files when he's not watching."

"In the lobby!" Caruso said. "Heading to the elevator."

Midas moved toward the door. "Time to haul ass, Jack."

"I called both elevators to stall," Ding said. "But that's not going to buy you much more than a few seconds."

"Thanks, Gav," Ryan said. "Gotta go." He slipped the phone into his pocket and then wiped a droplet of the Frenchman's blood off the laptop as he watched the loading bar fill completely. "This room is full of intel," he said.

"No time," Midas said.

Midas pitched Ryan the notebook, and Ryan returned it to the aluminum briefcase, spinning the locks to the same numbers they'd been on before he tampered with them. Like Clark said, when it came to security it was all in the details. Overkill kept you alive. Ryan made a habit of noting where his combinations were when he left a briefcase unaccompanied, so he assumed everyone else was just as suspicious.

Ryan held up both hands, giving the workspace one

last scan before ejecting the thumb drive and then closing the computer.

"Good to go," he said.

"I hope we put it back in the right place," Midas said.
The door shut behind them and they turned to trot for
the stairs.

"It was a best guess," Jack said. "If we didn't, maybe
he'll second-guess himself."

Midas pulled open the door at the same moment the
elevator chimed down the hall and the doors slid open
with an audible rumble.

They'd just stepped over the bodies of Gaspard's men
when Ryan's cell phone buzzed in his pocket. It was Gavin.

"Don't forget to clear the 'last device' list."

Jack kept his voice to a whisper, still moving down the
stairs. "The what?"

"The computer keeps a record of devices and periph-
erals that are connected to it—video cameras, DVD players, thumb drives. He'll be able to see you were on unless
you delete it."

"That ship has sailed, Gav," Ryan said. "He's already
in the room and we're out of there. How likely is he to
notice it?"

Gavin was silent for a long time. "Depends," he finally
said. "On whether he's more like you or more like me."

"Okay," Ryan said. "What does he have to do to see it?"

"Right-click the mouse," Gavin said.

"Everyone good to go?" Clark said half an hour later,
sitting at a sidewalk café on Avenida del Cid, approximately three blocks away from the Hotel Alfonso

XIII. The thousands of people who'd attended the bull-fights, mostly locals, had returned home but the streets around the Royal Alcázar park were still modestly crowded with tourists not quite wanting to give up on the vibrant Spanish nightlife.

Adara and Caruso sat at the table with Clark, while the others loitered at various points outside the hotel it-self, making it a virtual meeting over comms. Adara had a view of the Russians' rooms over her webcam. Gavin Biery was patched in via radio link.

By "good to go," Clark meant physically. He knew Ryan and Midas had been in a scrap but he'd yet to lay eyes on them. They'd already told him they were fine—good to go—but Clark knew all too well that debilitat-ing injuries had a way of showing up after the adrenaline of the incident wore off. Lucile Fournier had proven she was wicked good at killing people. He wanted everyone on their toes.

Midas said, "My nose is toast, but it's been toasted before. I can still breathe with my mouth shut, and I can't really get any uglier." His tone was light, but they'd all been hurt before, and badly. The entire team took these reports seriously. If someone was operating at half speed, everyone needed to know.

"I'm good," Jack said. "A couple of bruised ribs and some ringing in my ear, but I don't think anything's bro-ken."

"Roger that." Clark moved on, taking them at their word. "So we'll know when da Rocha opens his computer?"

"When he pops up on a network," Gavin says. "His computer will send us a notification. The malware is de-signed to phone home to my system as well as whoever used their device to insert the program. In this case, it was Jack. I'll contact you when I get an alert, just in case Jack happens to be otherwise occupied chasing some piece of tail through the streets of . . . wherever you are in the world."

"Geez," Ryan said. "Is that what you think we do?"

"Well," Gavin said, chuckling, "not all of you."

"Enough of that," Clark said. "Good to have the redundancy. The point is that we've had no phone home from da Rocha's computer as of yet. Maybe there's a problem with the malware."

"I doubt that, boss," Midas said. "Gavin designed it to be robust as well as stealthy. It's late. Maybe da Rocha just went to bed."

Contrary to the public image of the knuckle-dragging Tier One military operator often imagined by the public, Midas and most of the guys in his cohort had advanced degrees, spoke at least two languages, and possessed a depth of knowledge and experience with phone traps, computer forensics, and other surveillance tech. Every Campus operator was accustomed to working with a variety of technical means, but of all of them, Midas was the most likely to trust it.

"Midas is right," Caruso said. "From my vantage point through the window, it looked like the Russians were hanging plastic sheeting. Hindsight allows us to say they put it up to defeat any attempted surveillance, but it must have scared the shit out of da Rocha when he walked in and saw a kill room. Near-death experiences tend to spool up the drive to leave a little posterity on the planet, if you know what I mean. Good chance da Rocha and Fournier are just in there exploring their own mortality."

Adara's mic picked up her scoff.

"What?" Caruso said. "You know it's true."

Ding spoke next, bringing the conversation back on point. "We have some choices to make. Like you said, Mr. C., everybody we've got eyes on is involved in some kind of shit."

"I'm not comfortable splitting up the team," Clark said.

A good long-term surveillance operation on either da Rocha or the man they'd marked as the lead Russian would require double the number of people he had. The relatively small size of the tight-knit team offered the ability to change direction quickly, to lift and shift, but it brought limitations as well.

"Hard to tell if the Russians or da Rocha have the ball here," Ding offered. "We need to follow whoever runs with it."

"Agreed," Clark said. "This da Rocha guy keeps showing up like a bad penny, and it's always bloody when he does. We're looking at the tip of the iceberg here. I want to know what we're not seeing."

29

The morgue was tucked down in the basement at the end of a long hallway—a good place, Sassani thought, for handling the dead, especially dead traitors.

Maryam Farhad's body stayed where it had fallen until the IRGC officer and his men completed a thorough search of her apartment. Ali—the most pious member of Sassani's team—had covered the obscenity, but someone else had pulled back the bloody sheet, leaving her exposed during the search. Sassani thought it better that way. It would incense the men, show them what kind of whore she was, inspire them to work harder to discover her co-conspirators.

After two and a half hours of photographing and fingerprinting, Sassani had ordered the body transported to a small hospital, less than five kilometers north of where he'd supervised the hanging of the three students. He was no monster, but they were, after all, traitors, and their plaintive choking when the cranes made them fly skyward brought him no sadness.

Sassani had come alone to the hospital, glad to be rid of the constant weight of the rest of his team. They were good men, but sometimes he felt as if he were dragging them along. In truth, he preferred his own company over that of anyone else, even his wife, who was always angry about one thing or another.

The smell of paint and disinfectant hit him in the face as the doors to the freight elevator slid open. The fluorescent lighting in the hall had seen happier days. Several bulbs flickered off and on at irregular intervals— something Sassani used to great effect in the isolation cells at Evin. Some were burned out entirely, giving the place a ghostly feel.

Sassani walked slowly down the hallway. Pondering the day before him.

This business with the Russian was puzzling. Dovzhenko had surely known the dead woman. The signs were clearly there—the hollow look in his jowls, the fleeting, not-quite-concealed flash of anger in his eyes. And where had he gone? The Russian was a spy, and spies traded in information. Some of the men had gone out for tea after they'd wrapped up the death investigation. Any spy worth his salt knew that the chatter around tea was as good a place as any to glean intelligence. But Dovzhenko had vanished, to lick his wounds, or perhaps to conceive a clever lie for his superiors to extricate himself from this mess. Sassani was willing to bet that this man was Maryam Farhad's lover. He'd gotten there too quickly, flushed, agitated. Where did a heartbroken spy go in a city that was not his own? He'd not gone home. Sassani had men watching both his apartment and the Russian embassy. No matter, he would turn up soon, and when he did, Sassani would have the necessary evidence to have the Russians turn him over to the IRGC or recall him home to deal with the issue themselves. A delicious thought made Sassani smile. Perhaps he could persuade the Russians to send one of their interrogators to Iran and they could work on Dovzhenko together.

Reaching the end of the hallway, Sassani pushed open the double doors. He did not knock, which drew an irritated look from the woman hunched over Maryam Farhad's body. There were fewer than five hundred forensic medical examiners in Iran, and only a handful with the implicit trust of the IRGC. The number of female doctors in this already small group could be counted on one hand. Sassani knew Dr. Nuri, and realized the necessity of her position. Nuri recognized her importance as well, and pushed Sassani further than he was accustomed, certainly by a woman.

The examination room was well lit compared to the hallway, and felt cramped, with long, stainless-steel sinks, and tables forming an L along the back and left-hand walls. Metal doors, like small refrigerators, checkered the wall to Sassani's right. The bodies of the traitors would be behind three of them, awaiting a cursory glance by a male doctor and a quick burial.

Maryam Farhad was laid out on the metal exam table—more of a large tray, really, with a sort of metal gutter around the edges to catch any fluids or bits of evidence that overran the paper sheet. A white towel covered her ashen body from just below the navel to the middle of her thigh. She had bled a great deal after being shot, but what little blood remained was already pooling at the lowest points, giving her buttocks and shoulders a bluish hue in contrast to the chalky white of her face and belly. A paper tag hung from her toe on a piece of string. The bullet holes—and there were many of them—were cleaner than they were the last time he'd seen her, the effects of the swabs Dr. Nuri had used on the external examination. A rolled towel propped up her head, lifting her chin. The lid of her right eye was half open, as if she were peeking to see who'd just come into the room. Sassani took an involuntary step backward. It was an odd thing, even to him, that he could eat a sandwich while walking the dungeons of Evin Prison, but here in this place, death crawled up his shoes.

The scalpel in Dr. Nuri's right hand caught a glint of light as she hovered over the dead woman's chest. Nuri was a small woman and looked somewhat like a child, standing over Maryam Farhad, who was at least five and a half feet tall, with the touch of extra weight of a woman in her late thirties who chose convenience over nutrition when it came to diet.

The paper cap and shield covered more of Dr. Nuri's face than a *rusari*, which was good, because she made Sassani uncomfortable enough. The blue surgical gown and dark rubberized apron obscured the shape of her body. But a wicked tongue more than made up for her modest appearance.

"You should not be here," she snapped.

"This is a matter of great urgency," Sassani said, unhappy at having to explain himself to anyone, least of all a woman. The fact that she had at least twice his education was of no consequence.

"Have you no shame? Surely the Sepah-e Pasdaran have a female operative they could send to oversee the autopsy of a woman."

Sassani took a deep breath, death and disinfectant and all. "As I said, a matter of great urgency."

Long-handled scalpel poised over the body, Nuri looked up to peer at Sassani, as if to say something else. In the end, she returned to her work, the blade sinking into the bloodless flesh at the left shoulder to begin the large Y incision that would open Farhad's chest.

Sassani coughed. "The cause of her death is more than obvious," he said. "Is that really necessary?"

Dr. Nuri paused her cutting at the top of the sternum. "A postmortem examination can tell the entire story." She glanced at the doors along the far wall, where the other bodies were held. There were twenty of them, five across and four high, with pull handles like the deep freeze in the market near Sassani's home.

The doctor continued. "We may believe we know that the manner of death was, say, hanging. An internal examination can tell us the exact mechanism of death. Did the rope cause the decedent to suffocate, or did a lack of blood flow to his brain cause a stroke first? Such an examination could tell us if forty-one of the fifty-two bones in this person's feet were cracked and broken. If he simply died from heart failure, at least two days before his body was hanged. It is written that even the bones of the living or the dead unbeliever should not be broken."

Sassani glanced at the rib cutters and steel saw in the tray beside Nuri. "And yet here you are, about to break the bones of the dead—for the security of the revolution. I ask again. Is an internal examination of Maryam Farhad necessary?"

Nuri dropped her scalpel into the tray. "If I am not mistaken, you are the one who ordered the postmortem."

"Tell me your findings up to this point," Sassani said, happy to gain back at least some bit of control.

Dr. Nuri stepped away from the body to look at an open folder on the counter behind her, by the sink.

"I have photographed the body from all angles." She looked up at Sassani. "I will tell you, she was quite beautiful in life. You can print them over there if you want to carry photographs of a nude dead woman with you—for evidence. I should say, that might scandalize even a major of the Sepah."

Sassani ignored her. "What else?"

"X-ray findings of four projectiles still in the body are consistent with twelve entry and seven exit wounds—"

"Seven?"

"Yes," Nuri said. "Two of the projectiles likely left the body through the same wound." She pointed to two small holes in the side of Farhad's neck. "See how these may be covered with the tip of my finger?" She cradled the head with both hands, lifting slightly to expose a gaping hole just below the base of the woman's skull. "And this could not be covered with my fist. Your bullets do a tremendous amount of damage as they exit."

"Yes," Sassani said. "That is the purpose of bullets. Is it not? Do you have any information of value?"

"She engaged in sexual intercourse shortly before her death."

Sassani did not try to hide his smile. "So there is . . . evidence?"

"Of course," the doctor said. "That is how I know." She nodded to several test tubes in a metal stand on the counter. Each contained a cotton swab. "There is no bruising, or anything else to indicate that she fought. But I must tell you that does not mean it was consensual."

"Oh," Sassani said, "I am sure that it was consensual. She was naked and smoking a cigarette when we found her."

"A capital crime, to be sure," Dr. Nuri sniped.

"The DNA evidence," Sassani said. He was not about to explain himself to this woman. "I need it now."

"That will take time," Nuri said.

Sassani clenched his jaw. "I tell you again," he said. "This is a matter of great urgency. I must know the ethnicity of the man."

"That can be done."

"Then do it."

"I will begin as soon as I complete the internal examination."

"There is no time," he said. "I need the information at once."

"Major . . ." Nuri cocked her head to the side, as if explaining to a child why he could not have an ice cream. "The science dictates otherwise. Contrary to what you have seen in the cinema, a DNA test simply cannot be accomplished in the space of one hour, or even two. Extraction, the removal of salts and other contaminants, quantification, and then amplification through polymerase chain reaction will re—"

"Spare me the jargon," Sassani snapped. "How much time to you require?"

Nuri's lips pursed behind the clear plastic face shield. She drew a deep breath in through her nose. "I will keep my explanation simple so you can understand what we are talking about. After a number of necessary scientific steps, which cannot be rushed without ruining the entire process, I will be able to separate copies of enough DNA to extract the information you need. These steps will require approximately twelve hours."

Sassani nodded. "I will expect an answer in twelve hours, th—"

She cut him off. "Do you read?"

"Of course I read."

"It is a fair enough question," she said, hiding behind a seemingly genuine smile. "I meant to ask not if you know how to read but if you do. You are a busy man. Imagine a book where all the words are written on transparent paper and then stacked one on top of the other, the letters mixed and superimposed. That is what the DNA will look like at that point in the process. We have equipment that will sieve out the . . . bits of DNA according to size. This will allow me to analyze the data and provide you with your answer."

"All right, all right," Sassani said, growing exhausted. "I only need the man's ethnicity for now."

"I only like the center of a cake," she said. "But I must bake the entire cake to get it."

"You would do well to guard your attitude, Doctor," Sassani said. "Remember that I hold the keys to Evin Prison."

"And I hold the keys to the morgue."

"I will expect a call the moment you have the information." He turned to leave but stopped and spun on his heels. "Or you will not need a key to gain entry into this place."

30

The president of the Russian Federation took a long, contemplative breath and looked deeply into the eyes of each of the five generals seated in front of him. Where the American White House had a quaint Oval Office with cozy furnishings conducive to comfortable fireside chats and quiet conversation, Yermilov's Kremlin office was large, rectangular—as a proper room should be—and furnished with a proper oak conference table meant for getting things done.

For all practical purposes, a large swath of Eastern Ukraine was already Russia. It was certainly *Russian*. All the good citizens there needed to know was that the Kremlin would back their resistance to a heavy-handed Kiev. As far as Yermilov was concerned, he was merely helping freedom fighters return to the fold of their mother country as he'd already done in Crimea. It did not hurt that these regions were sitting on rich supplies of fossil fuel.

"Comrade Colonel General Gulin," Yermilov said, waving an open hand to give the man the floor. "If you please."

The officer stood, straightening his crisp uniform tunic, replete with medals, including the red ribbon with a gold star, the Hero of the Soviet Union medal he'd won during the campaign in Afghanistan. In his early seventies now, Colonel General Gulin had retained an erect military posture. Thick hair piled up on his head as if he'd just removed a hat. Fiercely dark eyes and caterpillar brows gave him the angry-uncle look of Comrade Brezhnev—which made him perfect to bring the rest of the generals and admirals in line for Operation ANIVA.

The general cleared his throat and then looked once more at Yermilov before beginning.

"Malware is already in place at various key locations in Ukraine's banking system and much of her utility sector. Their Navy is little more than a fleet of rusty buckets, allowing us to increase pressure in the Sea of Azov with little resistance. Admiral Bylinkin has stationed the frigate *Grigorovich* in the Sea of Azov. The Black Sea Fleet frigates *Essen* and *Makarov*, along with destroyer *Smetlivy*, are en route from Novorossiysk. Four additional corvettes and three frigates from the Baltic Fleet are currently steaming through the Turkish Straits to take part in our exercise. Within days we will double the mechanized forces in Klintsy and Valuyki. Forces loyal to Russia, already inside Ukraine, will also take part in the exercise, pushing north and west toward Kiev. They will, no doubt, come under attack from Ukrainian forces. On your order our troops will press south across the border to intervene, acting as peacekeepers amid the ensuing violence . . ."

Yermilov's mind drifted as this hero of the Soviet Union went over ANIVA with the rest of the staff. They were all aware of the specifics, but Yermilov wanted them all to know that he was aware—and still behind it. The Soviet action to move nuclear missiles into Cuba was called ANADYR, after a northern town on the Chukchi Sea, on the other side of the world from the coast of

Florida. He'd chosen the name ANIVA for this operation, after the small village on Sakhalin Island, north of Japan—far away from Ukraine.

America's Keyhole and other spy satellites would observe troop enhancements and naval buildup, but Yermilov didn't fret over that. They'd been at this game for years. Yermilov was a better chess player than his predecessors were. He was already two or three moves ahead of Ryan—and with everything going on off the board, the Americans would not even know they were beaten until the game was already over.

"I realize that some of you have concerns," Yermilov said when General Gulin finished. "But they are, I believe, unfounded. Russia has an inherent right to conduct military exercises as we see fit. They do it. We do it. Everyone is happy. Everyone is prepared. Our Russian brothers and sisters in Ukraine expect us to rescue them from the yoke of oppression. It is our duty, is it not?"

A resounding chorus of "Yes" went around the table.

Admiral Bylinkin of the Black Sea Fleet leaned back, lips pursed, as if he'd eaten a sour lemon.

Yermilov's gaze settled on the man.

"What is it, my friend? Do you have something else?"

"No, Gospodin President," the admiral said. "I would only point out—"

"So you do, in fact, have something else to say?" Yermilov interrupted.

The admiral slumped noticeably in his seat. "No, Gospodin President."

"By all means, continue," Yermilov said, now that the man was off balance.

"I realize that Ukraine is not a signatory to NATO,

but considering President Ryan's bluster and bravado, he does not seem to know this."

"Perhaps," Yermilov said. "Ryan certainly has the will. And he does possess the means, militarily speaking. But I do not believe he will have the time. Events on the world stage are unfolding, even as we speak, that will most certainly render Jack Ryan so busy at home that he will have no time to fret over matters abroad, to worry with a country that is not a member of NATO. His hands are full." Yermilov smiled broadly, pushing up from the table to signal that the meeting was over. "It will not be long before he has too much to carry."

At the far end of the office, seated along the wall instead of at the table, Maksim Dudko tapped a pen against the cover of his leather folio binder. The muscles under his right eye twitched with the anticipation.

You have no idea, my friend, he thought. *I will yet be invited on your little fishing trip . . .*

This conversation was far too sensitive to be held in Elizaveta Bobkova's embassy office, even in the wee hours of the morning. Too many ears there. Too many spies, doing what spies did best.

Bobkova had worked for Russian intelligence long enough to know that spies did not customarily murder people from the opposing team, certainly not in their home country. Traitors were one thing, but this just did not happen, at least not on purpose. Still, her orders were crystal clear—follow through or be recalled to Moscow.

After that? That weasel Maksim Dudko said he was in possession of *kompromat*—a file of compromising information in the form of photographs, bank accounts, proof that she was padding her pockets like the rest of them were doing. Stowing away a little money wasn't a crime the president would worry over. However, if such an indiscretion were to leak, Yermilov himself would be embarrassed. In Stalin's day, disobeying an order—or obeying one and making the boss look bad—meant long and brutal conversations with the NKVD while locked in the dungeons of Lubyanka Prison. After a short but detailed confession admitting to treason, if the bones in your legs were still intact enough to hobble, they marched you through the gates of the Communarka killing grounds. Now such matters in modern Russia were handled with a subtler, though equally brutal, hand.

There was simply no way for her to refuse the order from Dudko, no matter how insane. She would take care of this like the professional she was, and then deal with Dudko when it was over. Two could play the game of *kompromat*. A man like him stank with the rot of conspiracy. There would be mountains of dirt. The weasel had actually referred to her as Lizon'ka, the more familiar, diminutive form of Elizaveta. Only her grandfather got to call her that.

But to get that far, she could not be caught—and the Americans were very good at catching.

She'd gone for a long run through Glover Park near the embassy as soon as she'd ended her secure video call with Dudko. The run stilled her nerves and allowed her to work through the specifics of a plan—and choose her team.

The meeting tonight had to happen someplace neutral. A hotel she'd never used to meet another operative, or to administer a polygraph to a potential foreign agent. It had to be someplace not frequented by spies—no small task for an area like D.C., where spying was the national pastime.

Elizaveta had taken three hours to drive out of D.C., picking a random Hampton Inn off Interstate 81 north of Winchester after a meandering journey to Front Royal and through the Shenandoah forest that was sure to scrape off the FBI agents who routinely followed her. There were several who rotated through, but she called them Bullwinkle and Rocky, no matter who they happened to be at the moment.

Once she'd chosen the Hampton Inn, she used a prepaid phone to call and inform her two most trusted men of the location. She'd made no specific plans in advance, so the Americans would have nothing to intercept and no idea where to plant listening devices in advance of her meeting. Even so, she spoke in code, using a one-time pad so only her men could understand. The only way the FBI would have the single-use codebook is if one of these two men had turned. If that was the case, she was lost anyway. Once she was in the hotel room, mobile phones would go in the mini-fridge and all appliances would be unplugged.

If it had been possible to conduct the meeting on the surface of the moon, she would have done so. This assignment was beyond sensitive.

It was madness.

Bobkova had no moral qualms against killing. Some would say she had neither morals nor qualms. She had no problem at all giving some pesky reporter a shove or inducing a toxic reaction in a traitor, but one fact of espionage was so bold as to be outlined in crimson in the operational training manual: Murder of the opposing team was bad business. There was nothing like losing one of their own that galvanized either side into hunting moles and rooting out spies. The FBI would devote hundreds, even thousands, of agents to find the culprit. *Smert shpionam*—Stalin's NKVD motto of "Death to spies"—became an all-too-real possibility. Notions of righteous vengeance gave everyone itchy trigger fingers. Beyond that, the real work would grind to a halt. The added scrutiny after a killing would make intelligence gathering next to impossible. Even if Bobkova was somehow able to hide her involvement in an assassination, expulsion was a foregone conclusion for anyone remotely suspected—and she did not want to leave the West. Capitalism was the "main enemy," but it provided for a comfortable apartment and fresh fruit all year round.

There were ways to stay, but they were unthinkable. Were they not?

She looked at the two men across from her in the dim hotel lighting and slid a sheet of thin onionskin paper across the faux-leather ottoman before leaning back in the rolling desk chair. The men would take a moment to read the instructions. She was ninety-nine percent sure that there were no listening devices in the room, but one percent was enough to blow up in her face, so she remained careful. The fewer words they spoke out loud regarding the actual plan the better.

The men smelled of heavily scented Russian soap and a shellacking of American cologne. The combination might have worked in other circumstances, but the tight confines of the hotel room had quickly taken on the assaultive odor of an airport duty-free shop. They both had mild crushes on Bobkova, and she assumed the cologne was for her benefit. It did not matter. They wouldn't be here long. And Bobkova did not plan to get any closer to either of these men than she already was. Maybe Gorev. He was young and muscular and knew how to shave his ears. But that would have to be later. To do anything now would show favoritism, which would just piss off Pugin. Even he was not entirely unpleasant to look at, not handsome, but he would have been okay with a little grooming.

Both were fit, battle-hardened, and wise to the ways of the street. Experienced intelligence operatives, possessed of the added brutish edge that made them valuable for this type of idiotic mission. She would beat the shit out of that fool Dudko for forcing her into this. If he got her sent back to Russia, she would kill him. Perhaps she would kill him anyway.

Gorev rose from his stool and walked to the bathroom without speaking. He had buzz-cut blond hair and a sad smile that belied his thuggish skills. She heard him flush the toilet. There was hardly any need. The flimsy paper would disintegrate the moment it touched moisture of any kind. Even the humid air of Washington, D.C., would render it unreadable mush in a matter of days. Gorev came into the short hall and leaned against the wall and waited for his partner to finish reading over his own briefing paper for the second time. At forty, Viktor Pugin was older than Gorev by ten years, with dark eyes on a pie-pan face.

Far too many black hairs sprouted from his ears for Elizaveta's taste, but his extra years had brought with them a certain contemplative nature that she respected. He was quick and careful, with just the right measure of each.

She leaned back and folded her arms across her chest, looking at each man in turn, studying them to gauge their mood.

"An interesting choice of objectives," Gorev said, idly bouncing his head softly against the frame of the bathroom door.

Pugin peered at her over the top of his paper, putting a finer point on the matter. "The plan is workable, but the objective is insanity. May I ask where this work order came from?"

Bobkova used her feet to swivel the hotel desk chair while she considered how much to tell them.

"This comes from the highest level," she said.

Pugin gave a soft chuckle. "The *highest* level always has deniability."

She wanted to take a comb to the man's wild eyebrows, but his directness was refreshing. Gone were the days of the Soviet assassin, ready to blindly march out and do wet work for the Rodina with no questions asked, dutifully waiting for some other Soviet assassin to come along and do the same to him if he messed up—or even if he did not. Had killing someone become more difficult? No, that was not it. But getting caught was certainly easier these days.

"It comes from high enough," she said.

31

"Not very subtle." President Ryan tossed a pile of eight-by-ten photographs on the desk and rubbed exhausted eyes. He wore a pair of faded jeans and the gray T-shirt he'd been sleeping in, under a dark blue jacket with the presidential seal on the chest.

Bob Burgess, Mary Pat, Scott Adler, and Arnie van Damm were also present in the Oval. The rest of the National Security Council principals were already scheduled to arrive at the middle-of-the-night meeting, but Burgess had gotten Ryan up early to brief him on developments in Russia.

"They don't have to be," the SecDef said. "It's no great secret that Eastern Ukraine is de facto Russian territory. Crimea gave Moscow fifty percent more claimed coastline on the Sea of Azov, and more of an excuse to patrol it. Yermilov loyalists run a couple of false-flag operations against Russian citizens and he can send in his troops to protect them."

"That makes sense," Scott Adler said. "The Ministry of Defense issued a statement this morning describing this as a combination military exercise and peacekeeping force. I spoke to Foreign Minister Zubov this morning. He assures me there is nothing to worry about."

Burgess scoffed. "I'm sure he did."

Ryan flipped through the satellite photos in front of him again. Russian troops had been on the border with Ukraine for years, but thousands more had arrived in the past ten hours, along with attendant armored personnel carriers and mechanized artillery units. Numerous destroyers and frigates had convoyed off the coast in the Sea of Azov while more appeared to be en route. One photo alone showed the missile cruiser *Moskva*, the destroyer *Priazovye*, and the reconnaissance ship *Panteleyev* of the Mediterranean Fleet moving through the Turkish Straits into the Black Sea.

"How about HUMINT?" Ryan asked, dropping the photos and looking directly at Foley.

"Boots on the ground suggest the same scenario that Bob does. Mercenaries loyal to Russia—"

"Spetsnaz troops out of uniform, dressed as little green men," Burgess said.

"Yep," Foley said, giving the SecDef a side eye for the interruption. "Anyway, these mercenary little green men will likely start moving west and north, taking over radio and police stations until these installations can be 'liberated' by Russian troops. Yermilov's peacekeepers can come in and protect the populace—and, if they are so inclined, see to rigged elections that would certainly show the lion's share of the population wishes they could run back into the loving arms of Mother Russia. Odesa Station hasn't seen any movement yet, but they're hearing plenty of chatter."

"Mr. President," Burgess said. "Yermilov believes we are too distracted to intervene. It is not out of the realm of possibility that Russian troops will roll through Kiev by week's end. These videos, Internet bots, it all points to Yermilov."

"I'm not a big believer in coincidences," Ryan said. "I can't shake the thought that the meeting between Eliza-veta Bobkova and the Iranian protest leader has something to do with this." He looked at Foley again. "Mary Pat?"

"Nothing new yet, Mr. President," she said. "But feelers are out and hooks are baited."

"I recommend a show of force," Burgess said. "Before Yermilov is entrenched."

Ryan nodded. "It may come to that," he said. "Where do we stand in Cameroon?"

Burgess looked at his watch. "Eighty personnel from Task Force Darby traveled down by truck last night from the north. The Cameroonian rapid response troops are naturally worried about their own necks. They stayed behind at Garoua so they won't have to make a decision about who to support in the event of hostilities."

Ryan raised an eyebrow. "I imagine Njaya will see that in and of itself as a decision."

"I'm sure of it," Foley said. "Considering his record."

Ryan looked at the notepad on his desk. It was important to give people involved in this kind of incident a name. "And how about Mrs. Porter?"

Scott Adler spoke next since State was his bailiwick. "The same four men from the Cameroonian Army have been with her for the duration. She's not been harmed physically, though they have been rough on her, according to Adin Carr and Ambassador Burlingame. Water but no food, infrequent bathroom breaks. A lot of verbal abuse. Carr wants to go in guns blazing, and Burlingame isn't any different. Can't say I blame them, and I've been in my comfortable office and sleeping in my own bed. They've been on station for this entire ordeal."

Burgess spoke next. "Two recce teams from Sabre Squadron B arrived in Yaounde three hours ago. They're linking up with Special Agent Carr now." The secretary of defense rolled his eyes and shook his head. "Delta Force soldiers against four exhausted Cameroonian bullies—that should take about a millisecond. They are awaiting compromise authority from you, sir."

"Understood," Ryan said. "If any move is made to harm Mrs. Porter, then they have my authority." He sighed. "Let's see if Njaya is familiar with the Battle of Pharsalus."

"The Battle of Pharsalus?" Foley said, admitting, where others would not, that she wasn't up on her Roman history.

"Caesar's troops versus Pompey's. Pompey thought he had the upper hand, but rather than throwing their *pila*"—he smiled at Mary Pat—"their javelins, as Roman soldiers customarily did in battle, Caesar ordered his legion to march up and thrust directly at their opponents' faces. This tactic so demoralized Pompey and his men that they fled the battlefield." Ryan looked at Burgess. "Our assets in the Atlantic?"

"En route now, Mr. President," Burgess said.

"Good," Ryan said. "Let's move this to the Situation Room. It's time to poke Njaya in his face."

Five hundred seventeen nautical miles off the coast of Liberia, U.S. Navy Carrier Strike Group Two found themselves the closest American muscle of significant size to Cameroon. The 7,542 personnel, one cruiser, two destroyers, and *Nimitz*-class carrier USS *George H. W. Bush* with eighty aircraft had been steaming toward São

Paulo, Brazil, after a brief port call in Dakar, Senegal. Flash traffic from the commander of the Sixth Fleet turned them back to the east.

On the flight deck of the 1,092-foot carrier, Lieutenant Sean Jolivette sat in his F/A-18 and conducted a final left-to-right scan of his cockpit. There were just over a thousand Hornet and Super Hornet pilots in the Navy and Marine Corps. Competition for each slot was more than fierce, giving the men and women who won the opportunity to fly them the bona fide right to a little swagger. Jolivette was twenty-seven years old, five feet nine inches tall, and, like all the others in his squadron, "living the dream."

Both the Hornet's GE F404 engines were running. Each was capable of delivering 18,000 pounds of thrust—approximately one-quarter of the power of a Mercury rocket. He was in his own airplane today—never a sure thing since schedule rotation and maintenance required pilots to fly whatever bird was available when their number came up. Today, however, Jolivette had drawn 420, the nose of which bore his name, rank, and call sign. While the Air Force seemed to go for cool-sounding call signs, Navy tradition dictated pilots keep one another humble. More often than not, call signs stemmed from some embarrassing incident during training. Lieutenant Jolivette earned "Swipe" after a Tinder date during his time at Naval Air Station Lemoore, which, unfortunately, turned out to be with the base commander's daughter. The old man himself had given him the name, a reminder that swiping right didn't always turn out like you thought it would.

Like the other twelve carriers in the U.S. Navy, CVN 77 had the job of projecting American foreign policy around the world—and the four F/A-18s in Lieutenant Jolivette's division today formed the forward force of that projection.

Lieutenant Commander Mike "Gramps" Wertin, the oldest member of the division, was flying 406 from the starboard catapult off Jolivette's right wing. As strike lead, Wertin had briefed the division earlier in the ready room, filling in the blanks left by the Intel O who'd described the mission.

Each F/A-18 had a full warload, including AIM-120 AMRAAM, AIM-9 Sidewinders, and GBU-24 Paveway III laser-guided bombs, along with the wing and centerline tanks for extra fuel. Cameroon had a few old antiaircraft guns, but the intel officer said there was not likely to be any pushback from the ground or the air. Still, when it came to fuel and weapons, Jolivette subscribed to the "Better to have it and not need it" school of thought, right down to the SIG Sauer 228 nine-millimeter pistol in his survival vest.

The assistant Air Boss in the tower—known as the Mini Boss—ran the forward cats, but an officer in a yellow shirt—catapult officers were made famous from their exaggerated dancelike nonverbal communication movements to Kenny Loggins in the movie *Top Gun*—gave the go to launch. Each catapult worked independently, and Gramps's plane was propelled down the deck next in a cloud of steam. All four F/A-18s in the division— Gramps, Swipe, Minion, and Frodo—would join up at an Air Force KC-135 at coordinates roughly a hundred miles off the Cameroonian coast, prior to going what Navy pilots referred to as "in country." The bar attached to the nose gear of Jolivette's airplane was already affixed to the shuttle that would take him down the cat-track.

He was good to go. Martin-Baker of the UK offered a membership in the Ejection Tie Club, featuring a commemorative necktie to those elite souls whose lives were saved during an emergency ejection in one of its company's seats. It was a cool tie, but not something Jolivette aspired to own. Still, he made certain the seat was armed.

He glanced left at the catapult officer, then performed a "wipeout" of the controls, to be certain the fly-by wire computer system and hydraulics that controlled the flight surfaces all functioned as they should. Satisfied, Lieutenant Jolivette turned to salute the catapult officer, who saluted him back, took one final look to make sure everything was good to go, and then dropped to one knee, pointing down the catapult.

Left hand on the throttle, Jolivette reached up with his right to grab the metal bar on the upper right side of the jet's canopy. Six seconds later, the steam catapult worked in tandem with the aircraft's engines, accelerating the jet from zero to 150 knots in roughly two seconds, flinging it off the end of CVN 77 and over the surface of the ocean. The tail dipped slightly as the onboard computer began flying the jet the moment it left the deck. Jolivette felt the sudden lack of acceleration. His right hand dropped from the bar on the canopy to the stick at the same moment he pushed the throttle forward with his left.

The flight deck crew could launch a plane every couple of minutes. Minion and Frodo would follow in seconds. Counting the time it took them to refuel, the four-person strike team would be doing their thing over Cameroonian airspace in less than ninety minutes.

32

President Ryan kept his tone conciliatory, caging his true feelings behind the knowledge of what was about to happen.

"The problem with the United States and our fights is most generally what we call ROE. Are you familiar with that term, François?"

"I am, Mr. President," Njaya said. "Rules of Engagement."

"Exactly," Ryan said. "The rules under which our war-fighters can unleash the devastating force at their fingertips get muddled. In our zest to be the world's police force and protect the weak, we try very hard not to harm civilians, to use a measured response. Our airmen, soldiers, sailors, and Marines often go in with one hand figuratively tied behind their backs. They act as advisers, trainers, and whatnot—when they are in actuality trained very well to inflict maximum damage on the enemies of the United States."

"Mr. President, I can assure you—"

"Hear me out," Ryan said. "The United States tries to fight fair. You know that." His words took on a foreboding timbre, resolute, unyielding. It was the voice he used when Jack Junior had taken the car without permission. The one each of Sally's boyfriends had heard when he'd first met them. Cathy said it sounded like he'd been gargling rocks. "But here's the deal, François, war with the United States will always be asymmetrical. When our men and women go in with clear objectives, they do not falter and they do not lose. Do you understand what I am saying, François?"

"I do, but you must understand—"

"Men loyal to you fired on a United States embassy," Ryan continued. "They took innocent Americans hostage. I am sure you were not complicit in this travesty. And I will help you restore peace to your country. You can have the exact numbers later, but late last night, United States Marines arrived in Niger. About that same time, an additional company arrived in Chad. An undisclosed number of U.S. Special Forces personnel flew in last night as well. No less than eleven MQ-9 Reaper drones, each armed with Hellfire missiles, loiter over your skies. But I find the best way to deal with tyrants is through their pocketbook. Ten hours ago, I issued an executive order to what we call the Office of Foreign Assets Control to—"

"Mr. President, please—"

"You see, there are very few monetary transactions in the world that do not in some way touch an American bank. The OFAC has frozen sizable accounts. But with all the aliases used by your generals, mistakes will take some time to sort out. So far these seized accounts amount to the tune of . . . let me find the exact figure . . . one-hundred-nine-million-three-hundred-eighty-one-thousand-nine-hundred-fifty-three dollars and seventeen cents."

Ryan leaned back in his chair, giving the other man time to do the math. Like most tyrants, he would have a very good idea of how much money he had skimmed from the coffers of his country.

"Mr. President," Njaya huffed. "Your negotiation tactics are brutish—"

"We do not negotiate with terrorists," Ryan said matter-of-factly. "You said yourself, François, these men have acted on their own, outside the bounds of your authority—outside the law. If you have a method of contact, you must tell them to stand down immediately. Tell them you have called the United States to assist you."

"But I did not—"

"Really?" Ryan said, dismissing the notion. "I am sure you did. In any case, that die is cast. Tell your men." Ryan's tone grew darker. "Or as God is my witness, Mr. President, they will face the unfettered wrath of the United States of America. This will not be an invasion of occupation. It will be punitive. Do I make myself clear?"

"Jack—" Njaya was pleading now, as if he might break into tears.

A uniformed Air Force aide whispered something to the chairman of the joint chiefs, who, in turn, spoke to Bob Burgess. The secretary of defense gave Ryan a confirming nod. He held up both hands, opening and closing his outstretched fingers twice.

"François," Ryan said. "If you have a way, I'd suggest you contact your men in the next twenty seconds—"

None of the twelve men had told Adin Carr who they were—though he suspected they were not normally the type to carry handcuffs. They had Special Forces written all over them, but the Diplomatic Security agent didn't really care who they were. They were Americans, and his boss had sent them to help in a matter of hours from the time the proverbial balloon had gone up.

The D-boys, as Carr began to think of them, wore civilian clothing—a mixture of 5.11 tactical khakis and blue jeans, muscle-mapping polos, and loose cotton sports shirts. It took them less than an hour to set up four cameras, three through tiny cracks and holes in the warehouse's metal siding and one through a broken window at the rear of the building. Two showed a clear view of Mrs. Porter, sitting defiantly but still hooded and handcuffed.

Carr had gone from white-hot anger at the moment of the kidnapping to a simmering indignation over the past hours. The sight of Mrs. Porter and the five-gallon bucket they'd had her use as a toilet brought back the rage. They'd made no move to rape her, or even touch her. It appeared that they were just lazy and didn't want to take her to an actual bathroom. They did, however, take every opportunity to make fun of her predicament—like junior high school bullies, kicking someone when they were down.

The bearded D-boys performed their duties with detached perfection, but Carr could tell from the periodic flashes in their eyes that they felt as he did—these guys needed their heads pulled off their necks.

Most of the newcomers carried HK MP5 sub-guns, though two produced Remington 700 rifles with powerful Leica optics. They were short-actions and Carr guessed them to be chambered in .308. He caught a glimpse of a few of the men's pistols, and found they carried an assortment, from 1911 .45s to Glocks similar to his.

The apparent leader of the team, a bearded grizzly bear of a man who identified himself only as "Gizzard," had two flash-bang stun grenades on a load-bearing vest he'd thrown on over his polo. He'd winked when he'd handed Carr an MP5. "I believe in all the force multipliers I can get. Your boss said you're good for this."

The ambassador was more than a little grouchy when he'd not been given a gun as well, but he got over it quickly. Gizzard told both men to grab some much-needed rest. Their orders, the team leader said, were to sit tight and wait.

It seemed like seconds later when Carr's eyes flicked open to Gizzard's gloved hand on his shoulder.

"We're about to go kinetic," he said. "Wait for the signal."

"What's the signal?" Burlingame asked.

Both Carr and Burlingame couldn't suppress their smiles when Gizzard explained.

Carr took up a position behind the rusted semitrailer while two teams of four men—including Gizzard—flanked the door to the warehouse. The remaining four set up at cardinal points, facing outbound to pull security. The kidnappers, apparently feeling safely ensconced inside their own country, had neglected to check outside even once.

Three minutes after the D-boys had taken their positions, the warehouse door opened a crack and one of the kidnappers—the most junior from the looks of him— poked his head out. He was just two feet from Gizzard, who stood on the other side of a small extension of the entryway. Had the man come out another inch, Gizzard could have reached out and touched him.

Instead, the kidnapper took a cursory look as if he was expecting something. Completely oblivious to the presence of the nearby Americans, he sniffed the air a moment, and then ducked back inside.

Thirty seconds later, the air shook with a tremendous

roar. The ground, the trees, the warehouse itself, trembled as four F/A-18 fighter jets ripped overhead in a finger-four formation, turkey-feather exhaust nozzles open. They flew just five hundred feet off the deck at six hundred ninety miles per hour—almost but not quite the speed of sound. Breaking the sound barrier at that altitude would have shattered windows, but a sonic boom would have been too quick. The pilots wanted to maximize the duration of their engine noise. Carr knew it was coming and he still jumped. Watching, hearing, the four jets scream overhead, seeming close enough to touch, was the epitome of "shock and awe."

Three of the kidnappers rushed outside to investigate the terrifying noise. Bald Spot remained inside.

Gizzard gave the one in the lead a rabbit punch in the back of the neck, grabbing him by the shoulder to swing him around and to the ground, like a matador's cape. The next two Cameroonian soldiers in line received similar treatment, and were facedown and flex-cuffed before they had time to cry out.

Gizzard pointed a knife hand at the semitrailer where Carr and Burlingame were positioned and motioned them forward. The ambassador stayed on Carr's tail as he crossed the thirty feet of open ground to the corner of the warehouse.

Gizzard held up a small tablet computer strapped to his forearm, showing the video feed from inside.

Bald Spot had left his weapon against the wall and now paced in front of Mrs. Porter. It was a simple matter for three of the D-boys to breach the door, plow the hapless soldier to the dirt floor.

Carr heard one of the men inside shout, "U.S. Army! We're here to get you out, Mrs. Porter."

Gizzard gave Carr a nod. "It'll be less traumatic for her if someone she knows removes her hood."

Carr and Ambassador Burlingame rushed inside.

"Sarah!" Burlingame said. "It's me, Chance."

"Mr. Ambassador," she said from beneath the hood. Her chest finally gave way to sobs.

Burlingame gently lifted away the hood.

Carr's jaw convulsed when the cloth came off to reveal an ugly black bruise under Mrs. Porter's left eye.

The DS agent wheeled on the downed kidnapper, kicking the man hard in the ribs, rolling him so he was faceup. "You bastard!" Carr screamed, falling on top of the man and pummeling his face with blow after blow. He expected one of the D-boys to pull him off. No one did, so he kept hitting until he got tired—and he was in better-than-average shape.

"You cannot do this," Bald Spot whimpered, when Carr finally let up. "You will be arrested."

Carr hit the man one more time. "Nope," he said. "Pretty sure I've got diplomatic immunity."

Sean Jolivette had once heard a quote from a Lockheed Skunk Works engineer to SR-71 pilots that a sloppy turn started in Atlanta could put the airplane over Chattanooga by the time it was complete. At speeds of Mach 1.7, the Hornet was roughly half as fast as the venerable Blackbird, but it still required a fair amount of finesse to turn. Jolivette bled off speed as soon as he passed over the warehouse coordinates, slowing to best cornering velocity of three hundred and thirty knots. He tensed the muscles against his thighs and gut in the so-called "hick" maneuver, keeping blood flowing to his brain as he took the Hornet into a 180-degree horizontal turn—pulling nearly 7.5 Gs and eating up a hell of a lot of real estate over the ground. Any more Gs and he risked making the guys in maintenance mad when he broke the airplane.

Pouring on throttle, the strike fighters overflew the warehouse once again. Unaware of how things were going on the ground, all four of them repeated the horizontal turn and pointed their noses toward the presidential residence, dropping even lower this time, to do it all again.

Njaya was apoplectic. "You are attacking us!"

As if by magic, Ryan switched to his calmer, more diplomatic self. "What are you talking about, François? My people are there to help you regain control. If the hostages go free unharmed, we can stand down. All this will be forgiven, though, I must caution, it will not be forgotten."

"And the money?" Njaya asked.

"Oh, we'll get that all sorted," Ryan said. "I'm sure the accounts will be unfrozen as soon as every American is released and your troops pull back from the embassy. You can see to the men who have committed these crimes as you see fit."

Njaya gulped. "I will make certain the men who now surround your embassy depart at once."

"That is all I can ask," Ryan said.

"But what of Mbida?"

"He'll be given safe passage out of the country."

There was a long pause on the line. Ryan and the others in the room couldn't help but smile when it was filled with the booming roar of jets overhead.

"I see," Njaya stammered. "But, Mr. President. This entire incident has cost me politically. I am begging you. Do not send your troops into my country. It would make me appear to be weak."

Ryan's voice grew dark again. He spoke clearly and slowly. "You misunderstand the situation, François. I am not going to send in anyone. They are already there, overhead, in your shops, on your highways, behind every building and tree. They are embedded with your rapid response soldiers, whom they have worked alongside against Boko Haram for years."

More silence.

Ryan got a thumbs-up from Burgess that Mrs. Porter was free and safe.

"Very well," he said. "If I can be of any further assistance, please let me know."

He disconnected before Njaya could respond.

Exhausted, Ryan waited in the Situation Room long enough to hear that the Cameroonian troops were pulling back from the embassy. He said good night, knowing the morning alarm was going to come before he knew it, and he made a quick stop by the Oval to grab some papers he wanted to read the next morning before coming in. Standing behind his desk, he stretched, then looked at his watch. He awoke so frequently in different places around the globe that his circadian clock was in constant reset mode. He only paid attention to the time anymore so he wouldn't inconvenience too many others.

Darren Huang, the Secret Service night-shift supervisor, a kid about Jack Junior's age, stood outside the door of the Oval Office waiting to walk him to the residence. Ryan motioned for him to step inside.

"What can I do for you, Mr. President?"

"Hey, Darren," Ryan said. "Still pitching on Saturday?"

Ryan liked to know just a little bit about each of the agents who protected him. Huang was team captain and pitcher on an adult-league baseball team where he lived in Great Falls, Virginia. The agent didn't have the need to know, but two of the other members of his team were case officers at CIA. One of them happened to be Mary Pat Foley's nephew. It was the way of things in D.C. You either were a spy or knew someone who was—even if you didn't know you knew it.

The agent smiled at his boss. "Indeed I am, sir. We're starting off to a pretty good year."

"Good to hear," Ryan said. "I'm going to gather up a few things and hit the head, then I'll be ready. Would you do me a favor and let Special Agent in Charge Montgomery know that I need to talk to him first thing?"

"Understood, Mr. President," Huang said. He stepped outside and shut the door behind him, assuming his pantherlike gaze outward, toward any oncoming threat.

Unbeknownst to Ryan, the agent pushed the button at the end of the wire that ran down his sleeve, and then spoke into his lapel mic to CROWN—Secret Service code for the White House command post—letting the Uniform Division desk officer know that SWORDSMAN wanted to speak with the SAIC.

Ryan had time to get rid of his last two cups of coffee and flush the toilet before his personal cell phone rang.

He let it ring while he washed his hands.

"Jack Ryan," he said, shoving the phone between his ear and shoulder while he dried.

"Good evening, Mr. President."

Shit, he'd woken up Gary Montgomery when he didn't need to.

"My fault, Gary. I meant first thing tomorrow."

"No worries," the special agent in charge said, stifling a yawn. "I can be right there."

"No, no, no," Ryan said. "Please. We can talk about it tomorrow."

There was silence for a moment. Then: "Your call, sir, but to be honest, if it's something important, I'd rather get a jump on it."

Ryan thought about that, nodding to himself. He was the same way. "I have a special assignment I'd like to run by you. It's a delicate matter, the kind that could end a career. And I have to admit this one is very likely to blow up in both our faces."

"Put it that way, Mr. President," Montgomery said, "I'm in one hundred percent."

"Good," Ryan said. "I'll give you a five-minute run-down of what I have in mind, then we can hash out the details when I see you first thing . . . tomorrow."

33

Erik Dovzhenko did a little shopping at the Dubai airport before he headed over to the relatively run-down Terminal 2 so he could catch his Ariana connection to Kabul. He had just over an hour, enough time to grab a few necessities like ibuprofen, Imodium, and Vicks cough drops. Military logisticians, even the notoriously stoic Russian Army, ensured that their soldiers had access to what the Americans referred to as "bullets, beans, and Band-Aids." But intelligence officers—especially those on the run—had to provide for themselves. In addition to his meager first-aid supplies, Dovzhenko purchased two stainless-steel one-liter water bottles, a blue baseball cap with no logo—which was surprisingly difficult to find—and a flimsy-looking duffel bag in an earthen-brown color. It was supposed to be military grade but had far too many straps and loading points that Dovzhenko would eventually have to cut off as soon as he reached a spot outside airport security where he could get a knife. He still wasn't hungry, but he bought a couple of Snickers bars, knowing he'd eventually need the energy.

He filled the two bottles from a water fountain and made it to the gate just in time to make his connection. The inexpensive Vostok Amphibia on his wrist couldn't be hocked to bail him out of a tight spot like the fancy dive watches spies wore in the movies, but it was built like a tank, and was acceptably accurate. His diplomatic passport, a pair of sunglasses, two ballpoint pens, and Maryam's notebook rounded out his entire loadout of gear.

It had always galled him that American currency was so ubiquitous where the ruble was not. But one did what was necessary, and he customarily carried two thousand U.S. dollars divided between his belt and the lining of his leather jacket. He'd change some of it into the local Afghani currency when he arrived at Kabul, but American twenty-dollar bills would speak with a much louder voice.

A young woman with black bangs peeking from beneath a blue hijab greeted him as he boarded. He stowed the duffel in the overhead, keeping the notebook with him, and wedged himself into his impossibly narrow seat. Fortunately, the plane was only about a third full, so everyone had an entire row to themselves. The greasy smell of lamb warming in the galley oven made him wish he'd taken some of the Imodium. He settled himself in as best he could, put on the sunglasses, and pulled the ball cap down low. Exhaustion overtook him, and he was asleep before the landing gear came up—dreaming of Maryam's face, ghostly pale, one eye open even in death, as if to be certain he'd made it to safety.

34

The Afghan customs official at the Kabul airport was a stumpy, heavyset man who looked as if he could not quite commit to growing a beard. He eyed Dovzhenko's diplomatic passport suspiciously, then shunted him off to a supervisor. The second man did not appear to like Russians any more than the first, but waved him into the country nonetheless. The airport was small and the layover was quick, just long enough for Dovzhenko's clothing to soak up the odor of dust and burning garbage that would accompany him for the rest of his time in Afghanistan. He exchanged two hundred U.S. dollars for just under fifteen thousand afghanis—about a third of a month's pay for the average Afghan man. Half an hour later, he was in the air again, flying over mountains that were the same color as his new duffel.

There was one attendant on the Ariana flight to Herat. Unlike the young woman out of Dubai, this one kept her bangs tucked neatly inside her blue hijab.

Anguish and fatigue consumed a great many calories, and Dovzhenko was feeling unsteady on his feet by the time he landed in Herat. Pilots in Afghanistan had gotten used to rapid corkscrew descents to keep from getting shot. Even now, when the danger was minimal around Herat Province, landings were white-knuckle, ear-popping affairs.

The warm naan bread and spiced lamb wraps from the stall outside the terminal caused him to salivate, but he opted for one of his candy bars instead. It was a little too early to be breaking into the Imodium. The sugar seemed to go straight to his cells and, though he felt no happier, he could at least walk in a straight line without looking as though he might keel over. He used the renewed energy to scan the outer terminal for danger.

Dovzhenko had spent enough time in dangerous places to know the threats in this place would come from every direction. Former enemies might act like friends one moment and then revert to old habits if some unanswered insult popped into their minds. A clear head was essential to survival now. There could be no more losing himself to his grief.

His mother had often told him the Tolstoy story about a peasant who went to steal cucumbers from his neighbor's farm. This cucumber thief became so engrossed in thoughts of becoming wealthy from planting the seeds of the stolen loot that he began to daydream others were stealing from him—and absentmindedly shouted to his imaginary guards, "Keep an eye out for thieves!" alerting the real guards. It was his mother's favorite story, and she told it every time she thought Dovzhenko had his head in the clouds. A spy, she said, could not afford to daydream.

In Afghanistan, she was surely right.

Herat was one of the safer cities in the country, which was to say that one might expect to get blown to pieces by an unexploded cluster bomb or be murdered by common criminals instead of having your body torn apart by a blast from a suicide bomber—though that was always a possibility as well. The Taliban generally kept their business to other parts of the country. Around here that was the south, in the scrub-filled wadis below Shindand and to the east where they smuggled opium across the border with Iran. At least that's where they'd been when it had been his job to provide them with Russian Kalashnikovs and F1 hand grenades.

Dovzhenko's taxi driver was somewhere in his early thirties, with the look of a man who had once been muscular and fit but was now muscular and fat. He spoke of politics, the way everyone in Afghanistan talked about such things after half a century of occupation and war. The ride into Herat would have cost around eight U.S. dollars. Dovzhenko offered the man twenty to take him through the city itself and then another five kilometers east through fields of saffron crocus and pistachio trees to the dusty village of Jebrael. The driver kept to the back roads rather than the highway, admitting that the headquarters for his old unit of the Afghan National Army was along the highway. Dovzhenko didn't ask about the bad blood, but it was enough to make the driver spit on the floor when he mentioned the 4th Armored Brigade.

The driver was familiar with the address for the United Nations Office on Drugs and Crime, and, though he appeared to have almost as much bad blood for Russians as he did for his former employer, he took Dovzhenko to the dusty yellow building on the edge of town. The wind was blowing steadily by the time they arrived, sandblasting Dovzhenko's skin and nearly ripping the money out of his hand as he stepped out of the vehicle. The driver snatched away the twenty and headed back the way he'd come without another word.

In front of the building, a boy of twelve or thirteen wearing shalwar kameez, the loose, pajamalike pants and long shirt ubiquitous in Afghanistan, leaned against the wall with his little sister under the swinging wood UNODC sign. They squinted at the new foreigner in the stiff wind. A moment later, a woman in a black chador came out the door and said something to the children. She shooed them past Dovzhenko, her head down. The little girl looked up at him with green eyes and smiled.

Dovzhenko shouldered his duffel and walked inside. The wooden desk in the sparse front room was clean and neat, with a single manila folder in the center. A cup of tea sat on a clay coaster beside it, half full, as if someone had just walked away. A rotating rack full of pamphlets about farming and drug addiction was the only other furniture.

The wind blew the door shut behind him with a loud crack, causing him to drop the duffel and spin instinctively. He released a pent-up sigh, cursing this awful wind.

The sound of a man's voice carried in from somewhere in the back, gruff and confrontational. Dovzhenko opened his mouth to call out, but thought better of it. More voices, angrier now, then the muffled cry of a woman, and the clatter of furniture.

Hackles up, Dovzhenko stepped past the desk and down a dark hallway. His hand went instinctively for the Makarov, reaching inside his jacket pocket before he remembered the pistol wasn't there. Rounding the corner into a concrete storage room, he found two men leaning over the figure of a woman. The men blocked Dovzhenko's view, but he could see a dark blue headscarf. One of the men shoved her against some metal shelving, earning himself a slap to his ear. The other cuffed her hard in the neck, earning himself a kick to the groin.

Dovzhenko gave a shrill whistle, advancing in two bounding steps, and head-butting the nearest man in the nose the moment he turned. A second man, with a thick beard dyed gaudily red, swung at him wildly, a massive fist whirring by the Russian's temple, missing by a fraction of an inch. Dovzhenko gave the man he'd just head-butted a donkey kick to the side of the knee, buying himself a little time. He used the momentum of a spin to plant an elbow across Redbeard's face. The big Afghan fell flat on his back. Dovzhenko kicked him hard, once in the neck and once in the side of the head. Redbeard was out, but his partner was still upright. He hobbled on one leg, spraying bloody mist out the gash of burst skin on the bridge of his nose with each exhaled breath. His chin was up, attempting to stanch the flow. Dovzhenko punched him hard in the throat and then caught him by the face with an open palm, driving up and over, slamming him to the concrete floor. The Afghan's eyes rolled, showing their whites. The spray of blood from his nose slowed to gurgling bubbles. Both men were surely concussed, they might even have cracked skulls, but Dovzhenko did not care. Enraged from the fight, he grabbed the man by the ears, bashing his head against the floor over and over and over. These men had attacked Maryam . . .

Dovzhenko shook his head. No, that wasn't right. *Ysabel.* They'd attacked Ysabel.

He turned to check on her at the same moment a dark blur flew at him. Something heavy hit hard in his chest, driving him backward. Hands in front to ward off another attack, he looked down to see a dagger sticking straight out from his leather jacket.

Screeching like she was insane, Ysabel dropped to the ground, sweeping sideways with powerful legs. Dovzhenko fell, landing beside Redbeard, wondering why the dagger blade didn't hurt more than it did. He yanked it out as he rolled, attempting to evade the woman's lashing feet that seemed bent on caving in his skull.

Dovzhenko had been kicked before by people who knew very well how to kick. Instead of rolling away, he rolled toward her, trapping the lead foot as it plowed into him. He kept rolling, leverage from the weight of his body slamming her backward. She hit the ground with a sickening thud. She tried to scream but managed nothing but a croak.

It was only then, her diaphragm too paralyzed to draw a breath, that she remained still long enough for Dovzhenko to get a good look at her.

Long black hair spilled from a blue hijab. Ebony eyes stared up at him over prominent cheekbones. Her nose wasn't too large, though she probably thought it so, and it had a slight hook to it. The most remarkable feature about her was the scars. With the scarf pulled away he could see many on the bronze skin of her neck. They were not ugly, far from it. A fine white line to the right of a perfect cupid's bow gave her lips a perpetual pout. The rest simply added to the smoldering intensity of her demeanor.

Dovzhenko remembered the dagger and kicked it out of her reach, his hand searching for the wound under his leather jacket.

"You could have killed me," he said, withdrawing

Maryam's notebook, panting. The tip of the blade had nicked his bottom rib, but the cardboard-and-leather cover had prevented it from reaching his heart. He wasn't bleeding badly, at least not that he could see.

"My auntie telephoned to say that a Russian was looking for me." Her English was perfect. Almost, but not quite, British.

"I never told her I was Russian," Dovzhenko said. "Your auntie has a good ear." The aggressive phone call had at least put her on guard, if it had almost cost him his life.

"What are you doing with Maryam's book?"

Dovzhenko closed his eyes. "I am afraid I bring bad news. Maryam—"

The back door creaked open, letting in a howl of wind.

Dovzhenko opened his eyes to find a large Afghan standing on the threshold, the wind whipping the shemagh tied around his neck. The new arrival took a quick scan of the unconscious Afghans on the floor and then shot a glance at Ysabel.

She held up her hand. "I am fine, Hamid."

His gaze then fell to Dovzhenko.

The Afghan's hair was cut close to the scalp, but he had a long black beard, groomed to a great scimitar of a point. Smile lines creased his cheeks and eyes—a rarity in a country that had suffered generations of war. His wide leather belt held a pistol and long knife. A Kalashnikov hung from his neck on a three-point sling with the release tab pulled and the rifle pointed directly at Dovzhenko's chest. The fact that he carried a rifle was not surprising, but a relatively sophisticated tactical sling in a country where many carried their weapons on a length of old carpeting or a piece of rope made Dovzhenko think he might know how to use the thing. He had to be former military, but virtually every fighting-age male had fought on one side or another of one battle or another over the past four decades, so that wasn't much of a leap.

Hamid smoothed the point of his long beard. "The generator is fixed," he said. "They must have damaged it to draw me outside." He motioned for Ysabel to step out of the way. It was clear that she was the employer, but he was in charge of her safety.

He focused on Dovzhenko now. "What is your business?" the man asked in Dari, eyes squinting from the gritty wind that now swirled around the storeroom. Dovzhenko got to his feet and squinted back, but didn't answer.

"What do you want?" Hamid asked again, in English this time.

"I am here to see Ms. Kashani."

Hamid cocked his head to the side. "You are Ruski?"

"I am," Dovzhenko said, staying with English. He raised his hands.

"You should go now."

Dovzhenko took a deep breath. "I cannot do that."

Sand and dust roared outside behind the Afghan, giving him an otherworldly look.

Ysabel spoke now. "He has my friend's notebook." She glared at Dovzhenko with narrow eyes, black as liquid tar. "How did you get it?"

When he told her Maryam's story, Ysabel Kashani fell to her knees and wept.

35

The couch in Major Sassani's office was more comfortable than his bed at home, chiefly because he did not have a nagging woman sharing the other half of it. His wife, Friya, had once been beautiful, if never kind. Now she was neither. Her father was a general in the Corps, which meant Sassani had to keep her reasonably satisfied. But even the general knew his daughter was a shrew. So long as Sassani did not get caught doing anything that would bring dishonor on the family, and thus the general's good name, there was no need to go overboard with kindness or, for that matter, to speak to her at all. She, of course, reciprocated, so Sassani often found himself sleeping on the couch in his office these days.

Sassani had driven to Dovzhenko's apartment after his visit to the morgue and talked to the man he had stationed there. The Russian had yet to return, but he would come home to roost soon enough. Sassani toyed with the idea of accusing the SVR man directly, imagining the delicious flash of fear, the babbling reply of the guilty. Dovzhenko looked down on him, considered him an animal for using techniques that the Russians could no longer stomach. The man's utter contempt for the way Sassani did business was plain in his eyes.

Sassani woke from a dreamless sleep to the sound of people already at work in the bullpen outside his office. His men knew he kept odd hours, and unless the general was going to pay them a visit, they let him sleep until he woke up naturally. Six hours was about as long as he could take on the couch. He stretched, and then rolled to the floor for thirty push-ups. He cheated on the last eight, but the curtains to his office were drawn, so it did not matter. Halfhearted push-ups were better than no push-ups at all.

He opened the curtains and then took a few moments to face east and pray. The piety of a good leader clearly demonstrated, Sassani sat behind his desk to plan his day.

He wanted desperately to spend every moment following leads in connection to Maryam Farhad, and, by extension, the Russian. She was—or had been—up to her slender little neck in this treachery against the regime. He wanted to track down her friend, the one who'd loaned her the apartment. He looked at his notebook. Ysabel Kashani, that was it. But he knew better than to focus too much of his effort on a single case.

This Reza Kazem was a snake and charlatan, wooing tens of thousands with his wickedness. For some reason, the Ayatollah did not want him taken into custody quite yet. It made some degree of sense to use the man as bait to see who committed open rebellion for his cause. Sassani did not say it, but he wondered how many would rebel if Kazem simply disappeared. There were plenty of traitors to deal with. The list of demonstrators identified at the most recent hangings numbered in the hundreds and would only grow as security footage was reviewed. He and his men would begin working on that after lunch, after they'd done complete and careful backgrounds on each known individual. Depending on their family connections and the circles in which they ran, some would be interviewed and given strong warnings to bring their behavior in line with the regime. Others, who had no influential fathers or uncles within their *dowreh* circles, would be used as examples to the others. There were, after all, at least three empty hooks on the ceiling of Evin Prison.

Sassani had just removed the small shaving kit from his desk drawer when his phone rang.

He snatched up the handset. *"Balay."*

"Major." It was a female voice.

"Dr. Nuri," Sassani said. "I expected your call some time ago."

"Rubbish," Nuri said. "I told you it would be at least twelve hours, and it has been far less than that."

"Managing expectations," Sassani said. "A wise move on your part."

"Nothing of the sort. Do you wish the preliminary results via e-mail or fax?"

"E-mail is fine." He looked at his watch. "Tell me what you found."

"Your unknown subject is likely Azeri—"

"That is useless." Sassani's hopes fell. "A quarter of this city is Azeri."

"If you would let me finish," Nuri said. "The man you are looking for is likely of mixed heritage. Azeri and Slavic—Eastern European."

"A Russian?"

"DNA can give you ethnicity, not nationality."

"But he could be Russian?"

"Yes, he could." Nuri groaned. "That is what I said. Slavic. If you have a DNA sample from someone in particular, I can run it and do a comparison. Hair, saliva, something like that would work."

"Thank you, Doctor," he said, forgetting for the time being that he hated her.

He replaced the handset and then picked it up again, ordering the man posted at Dovzhenko's apartment to break in and get a sample of anything with his DNA on it and then run it to the morgue.

The major was smiling when he slid a green file folder to the center of his desk and printed YSABEL KASHANI in block letters on the tab. Her social media accounts showed her to be in London. He'd have one of his men stationed there check it out. Next he completed the appropriate form for a full background and immediate pickup order. He toyed with the idea of calling Dovzhenko's superiors at the Russian embassy but then decided against it. The last thing he wanted was for the Russians to whisk their spy back to Moscow. Dovzhenko deserved more than some administrative punishment, so much more.

Sassani would make certain he was the one to give it to him.

36

Vadek Cherenko excused himself to retrieve something from his room and told his men to oversee the transfer of a dozen wooden crates from the nose door of the Antonov 124 to the waiting Ilyushin-76. The Omani base commander believed they were smuggling antiquities, so it was important that he saw antiquities moving from plane to plane. The missiles would be easily identified, so they were simply left in place, and then the entire airplane turned over to the crew that had arrived on the Ilyushin.

Cherenko could have flown the new plane, but told his superiors he would be more comfortable with another pilot who was more familiar with that particular airframe. He'd known from the moment he'd been ordered to kill Colonel Mikhailov that this operation could have no loose ends. There was someone out there—probably having arrived on the Ilyushin, that had orders to take care of him. It was the way of these things. Kill enough people until you reached a killer who knew nothing of the original operation. Only those who had no idea why they were killing might be safe.

But Cherenko would take himself out of this equation. He crammed the last of his clothing into a small duffel, listening to the whine of the Antonov's engines, feeling the vibration in the thin walls as the plane turned out onto the taxiway. The Ilyushin would follow it out, but Cherenko would not be on it.

The second half of his payment would be deposited in his account once the Antonov was airborne with the missiles and the command-control units. Greed, they thought—whoever they were—would keep him in place until they could silence him as well. But Cherenko was only half as greedy as they believed him to be. It was relatively easy to leave behind five hundred thousand dollars since he'd get a bullet in the ear if he stuck around to see it. He'd already moved the first half of his payment to a new account, unknown to the cretins in GRU. He'd amassed a substantial nest egg, and with it, the first half-million gave him plenty to go into semiretirement in Thailand. He'd pick up a few flying jobs and be set for life.

The others were on their own, but they knew the risks. Yuri Zherdev, his communications officer from the Antonov, the one who'd actually put the bullet in Colonel Mikhailov's neck, was in the most danger. He was young, cocky, with little experience as to the duplicitous ways of men. Cherenko had thought to warn him but decided against it.

"Comrade Major."

Cherenko froze at the sudden voice behind him. He'd not even heard the door open.

He turned.

"Oh, it's you, Yuri," he said, relaxing a notch when he saw his communications officer. "Did our prize get off all right?"

"It did," Zherdev said. "Bound for Iran."

"We cannot be certain of that," Cherenko chided. "Russia can have no part in giving nuclear missiles to the Ayatollahs."

"And still," Zherdev said, "that is exactly what we do."

Cherenko zipped the duffel closed, shaking his head. "Have a care, comrade. Do not repeat that to anyone but me. Now please tell the others I'll be right along. I need to make a quick phone call."

"Will you?"

Cherenko raised a wary brow. "Will I what?"

"Be right along?" the younger man said. "It seems as though you have already moved your funds to another account."

"How do you know this?"

Zherdev sighed. "It does not matter." He took a silenced pistol from behind his back and pointed it at Cherenko's chest.

"Wait!" Cherenko's hands flew up in front of him. "They will kill us all to keep this secret. You know this. None of us is safe."

Zherdev gave a halfhearted shrug. "I believe I am," he said.

"You . . . you, too, have seen things," Cherenko stammered. "That means even you must be silenced."

"I do not think so. You are correct about all the others, but you see, my uncle gave me this assignment. I don't believe his brother—my father in the politburo—would take kindly to him ending me. That's why I am given the job of ending you."

Cherenko began to pant, slack-jawed. "I . . . You . . ." He could have tried to defend himself, but he was a pilot, not a fighter.

Zherdev motioned with the gun for him to turn around. "I'm sorry that I do not have any vodka to offer you. I am told it makes this part . . . easier."

Urbano da Rocha set the phone on the nightstand next to his bed and rolled over toward Lucile, who lay naked in bed beside him.

"We will soon be back in our own bed, my love," he said. "Such as it is."

"Our own bed is fine," Lucile said. "This is foolishness and you know it."

"Nothing of the sort," da Rocha scoffed. "I sell weapons to factions and governments—sometimes both sides of the same conflict. That is how it is done, my dear. If I start deciding who and who not to sell to, then I would very quickly find myself out of business."

"But this cargo is nuclear," Lucile said. "There is grave danger in that sort of business."

Da Rocha traced the angle of her collarbone with the tip of his finger. "You've never worried about danger before. Forgive me, but you kill one with relative ease. Killing a thousand is little different."

"Ah," Lucile said. "But what if we are the ones being killed? It is different then, is it not?"

Da Rocha gave a contemplative nod. "The Russians need us. I believe they are setting up a pipeline to Iran, using us as a cutout so they will have deniability. You heard them. They are trying us out for future business."

Lucile turned, coming up on one elbow. "How do you know this? I think they told you that to keep us in line. You heard them. They fully expect this route to be burned."

"They do," da Rocha said. "And the fact that they told us is a measure of good faith. This route will burn, but we will establish others. The world is a very big place. If Russia wishes to provide Iran with nuclear weapons, they will need a pipeline. Two missiles will only invite retaliation by the West. Even the cretins in Tehran know that."

Lucile fell onto her pillow, staring up at the ceiling, her chest heaving. "It is madness."

"Necessary madness," da Rocha said. "As we have demonstrated so clearly to the Russians, there is always someone waiting in the wings to fill a void. Had we not provided transport, someone else would have. I see no reason why we should not be the ones to benefit. Don't you see, my love? The profit from this will allow us to undercut our competition on other deals, leaving me the last man standing."

"That sounds like a lonely place," Lucile said.

Da Rocha caressed a lock of her hair but gave up trying to convince her of anything. She was deadly and beautiful—but she had no head for business.

37

Dovzhenko left nothing out, including the torture at Evin Prison and Sassani eventually hanging the dead boy's body. He described Maryam's death, going into more detail than he needed to but far less than he still saw when he closed his eyes. He needed her to understand how brutal this man was, to realize that she, too, was in grave danger.

Hamid tied and gagged the two Afghans—though they were still unconscious and it was not likely necessary. Afterward, he stood beside Ysabel with his rifle hanging down in front of his chest on the sling, twitchy, ready, eyeing Dovzhenko. It was beyond unusual to see an Afghan male spending time alone with a woman who was not his wife, especially in ultraconservative Herat. But Hamid had the feel of someone who put a higher value on duty than decorum. Ysabel needed protection, so he protected her, fiercely.

The Afghan listened to Dovzhenko's story with a disgusted grimace and then rolled his eyes, clearly not buying any of it.

"It seems to me that you have made a long journey," Hamid said, "when a phone call would have sufficed."

"Ah, but would it have?" Dovzhenko asked. "You do not believe me now. Do you truly believe you would have trusted me over the telephone?"

Ysabel dabbed at her tears with the hijab, wearing it like a shawl now instead of a headscarf. "So you are the one who called my auntie?"

"I am," Dovzhenko said. "I hoped I could frighten her into being wary when the IRGC made contact."

Ysabel smoothed the front of her dress with both hands and took a deep breath, composing herself. "One needs no warning to fear the Sepah." Another tear, certainly not her last, rolled down her cheek.

Redbeard groaned in the corner but remained unconscious.

Dovzhenko nodded toward him. "Smugglers?"

"Yes," Ysabel said. "You must have passed Fatima on your way in. She traveled seven kilometers on foot just to warn me that some of the local . . . businessmen . . . are unhappy with UNODC attempting to get more poppy fields turned into saffron crocuses." Ysabel sighed, as if this sort of attack happened frequently.

"Smugglers are the least of your worries," Dovzhenko said. "You have to leave, go someplace the IRGC will not know to look."

Hamid gave another grunt. "I still do not understand what is in this for you."

Dovzhenko spoke to Ysabel, ignoring the bodyguard. "Sassani will find you here. I am certain of it."

Ysabel held up a hand to let him know she'd heard enough. "You have to admit how odd it looks that a person who attends torture sessions in Evin Prison, a person who stands shoulder to shoulder with the Revolutionary Guard at public executions, would make the journey to Afghanistan to warn a woman whom he has never met."

"I told you," Dovzhenko said. "He will throw me in prison, too. We have a common problem."

"I have few friends left in government," Ysabel said. "But I will return to Iran and straighten thi—"

"Please!" Dovzhenko said, stridently enough to bring Hamid up on his toes. Ysabel waved him down, a master telling her attack dog to remain calm—for now.

Dovzhenko continued, his passion unchecked. "You must believe me. We have to leave now."

Hamid stepped forward. "*We* do not have to do anything."

Ysabel said, "I'm guilty of nothing but being Maryam's friend."

"But you will confess to much more," Dovzhenko said. "Sassani will make sure of that."

"All right," Ysabel said. "Say I follow you. Where do we go?"

Dovzhenko stood and looked at her, dumbfounded. "Honestly, I am not sure. I cannot go back. That is certain."

"Because you can be associated with Maryam?"

Dovzhenko nodded.

"I knew Maryam better than anyone. You told me enough of the story that I can read between the lines," Ysabel said. "They have evidence that you two were . . . together the night she was murdered?"

"They will," Dovzhenko whispered. "Soon enough."

Ysabel bowed her head for a moment and then looked

heavenward, eyes clenched shut, coming to some painful conclusion. She heaved a heavy sigh. "Listen to me. Maryam spoke to me several times of a mysterious gentleman friend. I have had just such a friend in the past who was, shall we say, in your line of work, so I know something about it. What's more, I'm smart enough to know that if you are a Russian operative assigned to assist the Revolutionary Guard, your coming here will be viewed by your superiors in Moscow as a gross dereliction of duty, if not treason."

Dovzhenko closed his eyes. "That is true."

"So," Ysabel said. "You are running, too."

"I am."

"So you wish to defect to the West?"

"I am so exhausted."

She gave a musing nod. "I take that to mean yes."

Ysabel leaned against the wall, lips slightly pursed, eyes narrowed in thought. Stress and sadness caused her face to flush as if she were sunburned, making the pale scars on her face and neck contrast more than usual. Dovzhenko couldn't help but wonder about the corresponding psychological wounds.

He glanced at the Vostok on his wrist. He'd been here less than ten minutes. She would need a time to process, but they had to move.

Ysabel groaned, seeming to come to some decision. "You risked a lot coming to warn me. I am grateful for that. You cannot go back to Russia, and you certainly cannot return to Iran."

"He could ask the Italians for asylum," Hamid said. "They are the ones running NATO forces for now."

"Whatever I do," Dovzhenko said, "I would prefer to

do it from somewhere else. If only to avoid any of Red-beard's friends."

"At last you speak some sense," Hamid said.

The two men followed Ysabel into the front office, where she retrieved a small daypack.

She draped the scarf over her head in preparation to go outside, and then stopped to stare Dovzhenko directly in the face, as if looking at the back of his skull. "Do you just want to run, or would you turn?"

"Turn?" He knew exactly what she meant but wondered if she did.

"Yes, *turn*. Flip, defect, provide your specific knowledge of what is going on inside the IRGC and Iranian politics to your counterparts in the West."

A cold chill washed over Dovzhenko. The woman spoke not as an aid worker trying to stanch the flow of opium from Afghanistan to Iran but as one who was intimately familiar with the ways of intelligence services. The scars suddenly made much more sense.

Dovzhenko spoke deliberately. "As you might imagine, in my line of work it is extremely difficult to know whom I can trust."

"That is true in any line of work," Ysabel corrected. "At least in things that matter. I know someone who can help us both. He's kind of a *khar*," she said. "But I'm one hundred percent certain that he is a donkey we can trust. I will call him on the way."

A hundred meters down the street from the yellow building that served as the UNODC office, a Pashtun man lay on the rooftop of a nondescript mud building, rendered almost invisible by the blowing dust. He wore the loose shalwar kameez. A flat pakol hat was pulled down over his brow, held in place with a gray headscarf against the wind. He had no idea exactly how old he was, but he guessed it was somewhere around fifty. Dark, wind-battered features made him appear well over sixty, but with the muscle and stamina of a man who walked for miles back and forth across the border with Iran, accustomed to much discomfort and heavy lifting. A pair of Soviet-era binoculars pressed against his eyes. He'd not yet made the pilgrimage to Mecca and could not claim the wisdom of the gray so his scabby beard was dyed orange red. He was, however, wise enough to know that this new man visiting the Iranian bitch carried himself like a Russian. Years of infidel occupation laid bare the subtle differences in the way Russians and Americans carried themselves. Russians acted as if they owned the world. The Americans simply owned it.

He watched the Iranian woman's bodyguard come out and retrieve the old van and drive it up in front of the building, obscuring the view of the door.

The small radio with a whip antenna crackled at the Afghan's elbow.

"Shall we take them now?"

"Hold," the Afghan said. He hadn't survived these decades as a smuggler by rushing into things. They'd come to take the woman, but the Russian added a new dimension. An alternative plan began to form in his mind. It would be lucrative but would take some time to set up. This Russian had somehow bested the two men he'd sent inside to take the woman. He could not be underestimated.

The Iranian woman was a thorn in everybody's shoe. She stirred up trouble with opium producers, made the other women believe they deserved more than they were already given, and walked around a good deal of the time with her hijab cocked to expose half of her head. She was not just a whore but a meddlesome whore. The Afghan would make double the profit, earning from one side to get rid of her and the others who bought her for their pleasure—or to sell again. His tongue flicked out over dusty lips, thinking of all the money.

The woman and the Russian came out next and the van pulled away.

"They are leaving!" the voice on the radio hissed.

"Follow them," the Afghan said. "See where they go. We have much to do."

A motorcycle on the street below coughed to life, followed by another. They both rolled out of the alley farther down the street and rode into the cloud of dust after the taillights of Ysabel Kashani's van.

38

"What?" Ding Chavez lowered his reading glasses when Jack walked into Clark's hotel room. "You look like you took a snap kick to the walnuts."

Ryan made his way to the couch to flop down, only to pop up again and grab a bottle of water from the minibar.

The Russians had gone, so the room at the EME Catedral now served as the command post, allowing team members to meet and plan while slowing their op-tempo and rotating surveillance on da Rocha. At present, Adara was taking a nap, while Caruso and Midas were in the lobby of the Alfonso XIII. They'd sing out if da Rocha or Fournier left the hotel.

"Seriously, kid," Clark asked. "Are you getting sick?"

Ryan exhaled quickly and then took a long drink of water, wiping his mouth with his forearm before blurting, "Ysabel Kashani."

His eyes had a thousand-yard stare, as if looking through the wall instead of at it, fixed on nothing.

Clark shot a glance at Ding, then back at Ryan. "What about her?"

"She's in trouble, John."

"In London?"

Ryan shook his head. "Her Facebook profile shows her in London with a husband and baby, but she's too smart to post photos of her family online. That was all cover. She's in Afghanistan, and she's in trouble."

"**D**amn," Chavez said when Ryan finished recounting Kashani's phone call. "You believe her?"

"Of course I believe her," Jack said, incredulous. "She knows what we do. Hell, she saved my life."

"'Believe' was the wrong choice of word, *'mano*," Chavez said. "What I meant was, is she sure this guy is a Russian spook?"

"If anyone would know, it would be her," Jack said. "She was writing opinion papers on Russia for the university when we were . . . when I met her."

Clark rubbed his chin in thought. "If this Russian wants to turn, he should just go to the embassy in Kabul. The Agency has plenty of competent case officers there who can deal with him."

"It sounds like he has some trust issues," Ryan said. "He trusts her and she trusts me. She's hoping I'll handle it personally."

"Oh, hell, no," Chavez said. "That's too classic. We don't let oppo choose who their handler is going to be. Besides, CIA would get more than a little pissy if we jump into the middle of their bailiwick."

"We're already in the middle of it, Ding," Ryan said, pleading his case. "She called *me*."

Chavez scoffed, mimicking the tone of an answering

machine. "Beep. If this call is in reference to a defection, please hang up and dial 1-800-CIA or go to your nearest U.S. embassy."

Ryan waved him off and turned to Clark. "John, this Russian has been inside Iran for months. He could be a treasure trove of information. You know as well as I do how hard it is to work assets in that country."

Clark looked at Ding. "Can you give us a minute?"

Chavez shrugged, staring for a long moment at Ryan. "I'll go check on the others while you talk some sense into numbnuts."

"I should have known better when I first saw her Facebook page," Jack said, as soon as Chavez was gone and the door shut.

"So," Clark said. "She's not married?"

Several months before, Jack had taken a peek at Ysabel's Facebook page to find a photo of her with a man and a baby, looking happily married and living in London. He now kicked himself for taking anything on social media at face value.

"No husband," he said, "and no baby. She couldn't talk about it much on the phone, but it makes sense. Hell, everyone I know in this business has a fake profile on social media. I was using one when I looked at hers. Listen—"

"No," Clark said. "Do yourself a favor and you listen before you run off half-cocked. I know you feel like you owe this girl for putting her in harm's way."

"They beat the hell out of her, John. Broke her neck trying to get to me. She healed, but that's a little more than 'harm's way,' don't you think?"

"My point," Clark said, his voice even, "is that you

feel responsible for things that were out of your control. The government of Iran has done some serious backsliding in the freedom department since you were over there last. The mullahs are clinging to power tighter than ever, fighting for the very existence of their regime with everything they've got. No one knows who's aligned with who anymore. It's not much of a leap to make the case that someone who felt he owed Kashani, who'd been her lover, no less, might be blind to the possibility of a trap."

Jack was silent for nearly a full minute, studying his feet. The tension of the moment caused him to breathe as if he'd just sprinted up a flight of stairs. At length, he looked up, jaw set with a realization he didn't like. "I can't argue with you."

"Good," Clark said. "Because if you had, I wouldn't have let you go."

Jack's mouth fell open. "You're going to authorize it?"

"Jack," Clark said and sighed. "The mere fact that you came in here and informed me of the call before you just hopped on a plane is light-years ahead of where you were when you and Ysabel were together. I don't like splitting the team, but for all we know, da Rocha could sit here in Seville for another month. You said yourself, this Russian could have a shitload of intel."

"So you don't think it's a trap?"

"You're positive it was Ysabel on the phone?"

"I thought of that," Jack said. "She knew things only Ysabel would know." He closed his eyes. "Personal things."

"Okay, then," Clark said. "I've met Ysabel Kashani. Pretty sure she'd die before she knowingly lured you into a trap. But notice how I said *knowingly* there. Just because she's clean doesn't mean the Russian is. I'll need to run my idea by Gerry and let the DNI know through channels to make sure we deconflict with anything they've got going on, but they'll agree with my assessment."

"Which is?"

"That you should take your ass to Herat. The thing is, Ysabel might even be a better source than the Russian. She seemed like a smart girl to me. If she's calling you, then she's doing it for a reason."

"You won't regret this, John," Ryan said.

"Oh," Clark said, "I'm pretty sure I will. You probably will, too. I've learned a couple of things over the course of my time in government service. No plan survives first contact with the enemy, and anything more sophisticated than a can opener is liable to break when you need it most. Simple things like this hardly ever work out like expected. Anyway, this won't be some Herat holiday, so I'm not sending you over there alone. Ysabel knows Caruso, so he won't spook her. He'll be your backup. I want you traveling under your alias diplo passport. Too many people in Afghanistan are familiar with your family. Now go pack. It's about time you had a little change of scenery—if only to take your mind off Lisanne."

"Lisanne?" Jack said. "I don't know what you're talking about."

"Knock it off," Clark said. "I'm an old spy. I get paid to notice the subtle things. Now go on. I have some calls to make. You'll probably have to fly through Dubai out of Madrid, so see what flights you can find. If you're going, I want you out of here fast. Go tell Sherman to push Dom off his post so he can come see me."

"Crap," Ryan said. "This already isn't working out

like I thought. Waking up Adara scares me more than going to Afghanistan."

Jack wasn't privy to the calls among Clark, Gerry Hendley, and Mary Pat Foley. All he knew was that Clark gave him the thumbs-up to travel. Foley liked to keep as much separation from her office and The Campus as possible, but sometimes they had to talk in order to prevent the team from running headlong into an operation that they knew nothing about. Deconfliction was, after all, one of the main purposes of the ODNI.

Caruso and Ryan made the one-hour Iberia flight from Seville to Madrid, then had a few hours to stock up on snacks before they boarded an Emirates flight to Dubai. They traveled under black diplomatic passports, obviating the need for visas in most countries. Caruso used his own name, but for obvious reasons, Ryan went by an alias. It was standard procedure to pick a legend with the same first name, adding a layer of safety if someone recognized you and called out. Given Ryan's family connections, he decided to go a different route, choosing the name Joseph "Joe" Peterson. "Jack" was just too obvious.

Their connection in Dubai would give the two operatives enough time to navigate the airport and eat something that wasn't warmed up on an airplane microwave. Emirates was a pretty cushy airline, but the Hendley G5 had spoiled them. Commercial travel also put a crimp in their normal loadout of gear. Both men traveled with only a small backpack that they carried on. No weapons, no gear other than their clothing, some emergency food bars, and a satellite phone. Both wore good boots and light jackets. The desert could get chilly at night—and the jackets doubled as extra pillows in their cheap seats.

Ryan had never been on an Emirates aircraft that didn't have a new-car smell to it. The planes were plush, well appointed, and dripping with customer service. Unfortunately, the cavernous A380 was almost full. Jack and Dom had to settle for two economy seats in the rear, jammed against a bulkhead so they didn't recline all the way.

"Sorry about this," Jack said as Dom slid across and situated himself next to the window.

"No worries." The lines around his eyes said he was none too thrilled. "You know me, cousin. I'm always game to help you save the girl."

Jack chuckled at that, picturing the fire in Ysabel's eyes. "Yeah, well, this girl's kind of a badass."

Caruso yawned. "Even a badass needs to be rescued once in a while." He rolled his jacket and shoved it between his head and the window, eyelids already drooping. "Adara and I have an agreement. Sometimes I save her, sometimes she saves me."

39

Ding Chavez had the eyeball. He was having a hard time figuring out if da Rocha and his creepy killer girlfriend were inexperienced or if they just believed they were invincible. Da Rocha kept checking his watch, which was weird, but not overly so. Whatever the deal was, neither of them seemed to be looking for a tail. They'd come out of the hotel a little over a half-hour before, dressed for a casual evening. Fournier wore a loose light jacket over a dark T-shirt, perfect for hiding whatever kind of pistol she'd have under there. Da Rocha, wearing slacks and a long-sleeve paisley dress shirt, carried a leather messenger bag slung diagonally across his body.

Nice man-purse, Chavez thought.

The wily bastard had gone all day without logging on to his computer. Nobody did that. The team had decided that if he didn't pop up online by that evening, something had gone wrong with Gavin's malware. As it was, they were operating in the blind, with no idea of what da Rocha was up to.

A stubby two-car commuter train squealed and rumbled down the tracks in the middle of Calle San Fernando, north of the Hotel Alfonso XIII and the Hard Rock Cafe, where da Rocha and Fournier had apparently gone for drinks. They were inside only a half-hour before they came out and hung a left, hand in hand, looking for all the world like tourists. It seemed odd to Chavez that someone would come to a city as steeped in history and culture as Seville and go to a Hard Rock Cafe, but, he supposed, if you were from Europe, a Hard Rock offered a change of pace—and, at the very least, a cool T-shirt.

It was late evening, and the streets around Seville University and the Real Alcázar park teemed with people heading off for predinner drinks. Flocks of tourists took advantage of the temperate spring weather before it gave way to the incredible heat of an Andalusian summer. The Plaza de Toros was less than a kilometer to the northwest. There had been another bullfight tonight, which added substantially to the crowds.

Hundreds of people, some milling in place, some rushing here and there, broke up the human terrain and made it relatively easy for Chavez to follow without being spotted. It didn't seem to matter. Da Rocha and Fournier were so engrossed in sightseeing that they never even looked behind them.

"Heads up," Chavez said over the radio. "They must have somebody out there running countersurveillance."

"Maybe," Clark said.

"Or maybe they're just dumbasses," Midas offered. He was waiting around the corner, ready to pick up the eyeball if the couple turned past the university onto del Cid.

"Or," Clark said, "they're professional criminals, not intel experts. They might think about somebody following them once in a great while, but they're more likely to worry about personal security in the mano-a-mano sense of things—what is going to try to hurt me in the here and now, rather than who might be building a file on me."

"Not very smart," Adara said, "but it works to our advantage."

"We'll see," Clark said. "They may not be experienced in tradecraft, but I don't get the impression either one of them is stupid."

Da Rocha checked his watch for the fifth time since leaving the hotel.

Chavez reported this to the rest of the team. "This dude has to be meeting someone. He doesn't seem to be in a hurry, but he is concerned about some kind of appointment."

"Maybe he's killing time," Adara offered.

"Right turn on del Cid," Chavez piped. "They're crossing to the west side like they might be going to walk around the Plaza de España or that little park right beside it. Lots of trails there, if I remember my map correctly."

"I have the eye," Midas said, crossing San Fernando on the opposite side of del Cid. Chavez continued walking straight, passing him at the intersection without making eye contact.

"Copy that," Adara said, sounding a little breathless. She was dressed in running shorts and a T-shirt that was loose enough to conceal her copper-wire neck loop and microphone. Her radio was in a small fanny pack. "I'm a block to your east. I'll jog down to the park and get a little ahead."

"They're picking up their pace," Midas said. "Not running exactly, but walking with purpose."

"Are you burned?" Clark asked.

"I don't think so," Midas said. "They're still chatting, but they're definitely walking faster."

Chavez turned right at the next block, working his way through the food stalls and carnival rides of the San Sebastian Park night market. The smell of grilled meat and fried bread made his stomach growl, but he hustled along toward the east side of the park, not following yet, but providing backup for his now diminished team in case things went bad. He wasn't so much upset about Ryan and Caruso heading off to Afghanistan as he was realistic. Even the full complement of six wasn't optimum for a prolonged surveillance op. Four was little better than a wing and a prayer. Still, this was the field. You soldiered on, doing more with less, and grinned about it because, in the end, stopping evil dumbasses in their endeavors to do bad shit was still the best job in the world.

"They've cut into the park," Midas said. "Just south of the Plaza de España."

"I'm jogging loops," Adara said. "I'll head that way and pick up the eyeball."

"Stand by," Midas said. "I'm with a crowd of tourists that happen to be taking the same route they are. No need to switch up yet."

Crisscrossing paths through the orange groves, palms, and jacaranda made it possible for the team to move in a little tighter. Their targets meandered back and forth, stopping now and then to read signs or watch the ducks— as Midas said, killing time.

Da Rocha checked his watch again.

They were on the western edge of the park now, and he pointed north, up the six-lane avenue called Paseo de las Delicias.

"Looks like he might be heading toward the hotel," Midas said.

"I'll keep to the trees," Adara said, "running parallel."

"Copy," Midas said. "Still northbound on—"

"They're crossing the road," Midas said. "East to west."

Chavez broke out of the park a half-block behind Midas, planning to pick up the pace so he could take over the eye. But he could tell that was not going to happen.

It was as if someone had just flipped an on switch. Both da Rocha and Fournier became much more animated. Chavez watched as they waited for a lull in the traffic and then trotted across. There was no more hand-holding or gazing at the sites of Seville. They were going somewhere.

"Are they turning?" Clark asked, as if he already knew the answer.

Chavez figured it out at about the same moment Clark did.

"Well, shit," he said, as their targets continued to jog to the banks of the Guadalquivir River canal and hop deftly into a waiting inflatable boat. Moments later, the outboard growled to life and the little boat sped south into the darkness.

Chavez reported what he'd seen.

"That," Midas said, "was pretty damned slick."

"I should have thought about the river," Clark said. "Midas, how much luggage did you see in the hotel room last night?"

"Not much, now that you mention it. You want me to go check his hotel room while he's not in it?"

"No," Clark said. "If the malware is working I don't want to spook him in case he has someone watching it. We better pray he logs on with that computer, because he could be going anywhere. It's only fifty miles to the ocean. If he wanted to, he could be in North Africa by morning."

40

Elizaveta Bobkova took a sip of mineral water and closed her eyes. Her joints were stiff, her mind lethargic. She probably just needed to get away from the noxious fog of Pugin's cologne and go for a long, relaxing run. Gorev lay asleep on the couch, snoring softly. It was Pugin's turn on post with the laser mic that was aimed across the street at the bedroom window of Senator Chadwick's Arlington, Virginia, condo. What little talking did occur came from Chadwick, and from the sound of things, her young assistant, Mr. Fite, was having trouble keeping up.

Pugin's lips spread into a lascivious grin. "These Americans are strange animals."

"All animals are strange," Bobkova said, after another sip of mineral water. "If they are watched long enough."

Pugin tapped a pencil on the notebook beside his computer. "They are going to be hungry after this round."

The desk in front of Pugin contained a wide assortment of gear, all of it dedicated to sniffing, listening, watching. The laser microphone and receiver, both aimed at the window across the street, sat on tripods to the man's left. A ladderlike Yagi directional antenna was on his right, mounted on its own stubby tripod and pointed at the same condo, collecting cell phone, wireless router, computer information, and two IP addresses Bobkova believed to be Chadwick's "smart" television and dishwasher. The antenna gleaned information from the other condos, along with the IP address of any passing vehicle that had GPS or other connectivity, a phenomenon that was becoming more and more of a reality these days. Bobkova wondered, if the average American suddenly became aware of the digital cloud that followed them around, how many would melt into a pile of emotional goo. If you had a mobile phone in your pocket, grocers could be fully aware of which products you loitered in front of with your shopping cart. Online advertisers knew if you'd looked at a certain type of bra—and bombarded you with adds for that bra if you had the temerity to decide to buy something different. Automobile dealerships knew if you put off that oil change for a few thousand miles beyond their recommendation, giving them a reason to deny your warranty claim. It was probably healthier to be oblivious to the constant intrusion, at least in the short term. Bobkova had taken to disconnecting her own life shortly after joining SVR, placing a small square of electrician's tape over the camera of her laptop while she was still in training. Just as liars found it difficult to trust, watchers were always the most paranoid.

Bobkova was especially proud—and disgusted—at how simple it had been to find out the senator's mobile phone number. The life of a politician and Chadwick's own narcissistic personality made her especially active on social media. There were more close-up photographs of her face on her accounts, perfectly framed in that helmet of hair, than Bobkova had ever seen. It was as if she'd ducked into one of those shopping-mall photo booths and the camera had gone on overdrive, spitting out strip after strip of photos of the same mugging face. Chadwick took care to attach that face to worthy causes, making her, at least in the judgment of her handlers, a more electable senator. Homeless shelters, crisis centers, museum openings, all provided backdrops for her toothy smile. To her credit, she kept her personal life personal—except for her dog.

It was a handsome little thing, as far as dogs went, a mix of border collie and something with a curly tail. Bobkova had once adopted a stray in Afghanistan, where the locals did unthinkable things to the dogs. She'd invested a great deal of emotion, only to have the stupid thing die on her once she got it back to Russia. Chadwick cared enough for her little mutt to share the camera with it on a few occasions—and enough to have it licensed and tagged in case it became lost. It was a straightforward matter for Bobkova to zoom in on one of the hundreds of social media photos and find the mobile phone number engraved on the metal dog tag. Once she had the number, it was simple enough for Bobkova to set herself up as a "man in the middle." Less than an hour later, she was able to "go up" on the phone and begin logging incoming and outgoing calls, collecting packets of information on all Chadwick's Internet sessions. She recorded login data, passwords that the senator would surely use more than once, building the pattern of life that was needed to cause someone's death.

Elizaveta Bobkova did it all through gritted teeth. The pasty sycophant Dudko would soil himself were he to spend one minute in the field alongside her. And still, he pushed her relentlessly to make things happen quickly.

Bobkova reminded him that she knew what she was doing. She was thorough, she was meticulous, and she was good at her job. He did not care. It had to happen tonight. And it could not splash back on anyone from Russia.

Pugin raised his arms high above his head as if he'd just scored a goal. "And . . . they are done."

Bobkova shook her head in disgust, as much for her thoughts of Dudko as this operative with the hairy ears.

Pugin rolled his chair away from the table and pointed his pencil at the session data that was now scrolling down his computer screen. "I told you she would be hungry."

Bobkova walked over and bent down to get a better look. Pugin's cologne was actually quite nice once it had a chance to wear off a bit—or perhaps she was just nose-blind to it.

"See, a table for two at a Morton's steakhouse." Pugin made a note of the login and password she used for the reservation website. They would use it to try and gain access to Chadwick's other applications.

Bobkova watched in real time as Michelle Chadwick—or possibly her carp-lipped boy toy using her phone—made seven-o'clock dinner reservations in Crystal City. Bobkova knew the place well. Morton's steakhouse faced the street but had another entrance inside the underground mall. Her meeting with Reza Kazem had taken place across from the Starbucks in the very shadow of the restaurant. She often ran along the Mount Vernon Trail, which followed the Potomac across the street.

Bobkova folded her arms, pacing the length of the hotel room several times as she thought through the particulars of this location.

There would be enough people to offer the right amount

of panic and melee, making the killing highly visible—as Dudko had instructed. There were several other restaurants in the vicinity—seafood, tapas, noodles, even a place that specialized in bison. Some diners would drive, but many would come and go via the Metro, funneling them right past Morton's to reach the terminal. The crowds would at once provide the necessary witnesses and cover their escape.

Bobkova had studied the security cameras in the Crystal City Underground in advance of her previous meeting with Reza Kazem. Then, she'd wanted to be seen, but such preparation was a habit. She'd send Gorev to check the area again and disable the camera directly in front of the restaurant on Crystal Drive.

Ideally, Bobkova would have liked a little more time to build her file, but Dudko insisted she rush things. Bobkova was smart enough to see what he was up to. Certain news stories were already being written, little flames that thousands of Internet bots would fan into a larger fire across the Web, "liking," tweeting, sharing, commenting. Monday-morning drive-time radio loved a good conspiracy. More tweets would follow, many of these from real people, helped along by the bot army. One story would bolster another until even the most cynical began to doubt their convictions.

Mundus vult decipi—the world wanted to be deceived.

Senator Chadwick would die tonight—and the American people, or at least a substantial portion of them, would blame the man who she accused of having his own assassination squad, the man who stood to gain the most peace from her death: President Jack Ryan.

41

Reza Kazem sat behind the wheel of the stolen Fath Safir—Iran's answer to the Jeep CJ 4x4—and shielded his eyes from the sun as the gigantic plane crabbed into a stiff wind over the makeshift airstrip. A woman in her fifties sat in the passenger seat, hunched over a small notebook in which she made frequent notes with a pencil she kept behind her ear. She wore red lipstick and dark eyeliner, but the pencil appeared to be her only jewelry. A lock of steel-gray hair escaped the scarf and blew across her face, but she left it there, engrossed in whatever she was doing. She hardly ever spoke, except to herself—with whom she carried on many lively conversations that she noted in her little book.

Overhead, the Il-76's engines screamed as it came in on final approach. Carved out of the desert in the valley east of Mashhad, the runway provided an adequate, if not ideal, landing spot for the Ilyushin. The strip was fifteen hundred meters—a thousand meters short of what the airplane would need to take off again had it been loaded to maximum weight.

Reza Kazem didn't care about that. In a short time, it would be some seventy-four thousand kilograms lighter.

The woman in the Safir's passenger seat looked up suddenly at the sound of the engines, startled from her stupor.

"Tell your people to take great caution putting the missiles inside the launch tubes."

Kazem drummed long fingers against the steering wheel. "Two hours and thirty-six minutes until the next American satellite passes overhead. It is better the Great Satan does not see what we are up to, don't you think?"

"This is true," the woman said, her voice dripping with condescension. "But the great accuracy we require will be lost if the components are damaged even in the slightest way. Secrecy will not matter if we cannot hit what we are aiming at." She went back to her book for a moment, then suddenly looked up.

"Do you shoot?"

Kazem nodded. "I have, on occasion, fired a weapon."

"Are you very good?" A professor of engineering, she spoke bluntly, unaware of any possible consequences for the words that escaped her lips.

"I suppose," Kazem said.

"I want you to think of this," she said. "Imagine one of your friends fires an average mortar over your head. This round travels at, say, sixteen hundred meters—or approximately one mile—per second. You are tasked with shooting this projectile out of the air with your Kalashnikov, which shoots a projectile that travels at approximately seven hundred meters per second. The mortar is a larger target, but traveling over twice as fast. You'd want the best bullet possible, would you not?"

"That is exactly what I would want," Kazem said.

"Then please," the woman said, "be careful with the missiles. The analogy I posed is not far off from what you propose we do."

42

Special Agent in Charge Gary Montgomery sent two agents from Presidential Protection in separate cars to park down the street from Senator Michelle Chadwick's apartment as soon as he'd gotten off the phone with President Ryan. Once the trigger was pulled to get things moving, he called his bosses. It took less than ten minutes to be conferenced in with Director Howe and his right hand, Deputy Director Kenna Mendez, and a Service lawyer. There always had to be a lawyer.

There was the usual worry about protecting the good name of the Secret Service. The way the lawyer saw it, this operation could go three ways: nothing happened, in which case all was rosy; Secret Service personnel saved Senator Chadwick from an assassination, and all was rosy; or something got bungled, Chadwick died, and the Service looked inept—or, even worse, responsible. Director Howe and DD Mendez had almost fifty years of experience between them. Both had cut their teeth as post-standers, criminal investigators, protective agents, supervisors, and eventually SAICs of large field offices. They knew the vagaries that an agent in the field had to deal with. The fact that this was a covert detail—Chadwick had not asked for protection, and should not even know she was being protected—added an extra level of difficulty. Without knowledge of her schedule they would lose the ability to conduct advance surveys of locations before arrival. Everything would be a seat-of-the-pants move. Doing this right—and the Secret Service prided itself in providing flawless protection—was next to impossible.

The lawyer pointed out that while there was nothing illegal about Secret Service agents following the senator unannounced as long as they did not spy on her, they were under no statutory obligation to do so. The operation would probably violate policy on several points, and possibly some federal rules in regard to overtime pay, but he would have to research it. Montgomery groaned at that. Given enough time to look, government lawyers could find a way to make anything against the rules.

In the end, Montgomery reminded the director that there was a fourth scenario. The Service could refuse the request, Chadwick would be murdered, and the trust and confidence of POTUS would be lost.

Director Howe said that the phone call was only a way to get everyone on the same page, and there'd never been any question that they would do what the President asked, so long as it was not illegal, immoral, or unethical. Hiding in the shadows to safeguard a hateful woman from potential assassination was uncomfortable, but it was none of those things.

The call ended with the lawyer urging Howe to reconsider—a perfectly safe option, since his words would be forgotten if all went well or he would be vindicated if things went sour. Montgomery found his own position more precarious. No one said it out loud, but if this operation went bad, he'd be the one to take the blame.

Even President Ryan couldn't protect him if he was fighting for his own job.

Where virtually everyone else in law enforcement was trained to seek cover during a gun battle, men and women of the United States Secret Service trained to make themselves the larger target, to stand up and fight while others in the team hustled their protectee away from danger. Shitty position or not, Gary Montgomery knew nothing else. The President had asked him personally to stand up and fight, and that was all there was to it.

Several members of the administration, including the chief of staff, were afforded Secret Service protection. These details were relatively small, just a handful of agents, and stealing even one could jeopardize coverage. Montgomery raided his own team first, as well as drawing from VPOTUS, the secretary of the treasury, the Washington Field Office, and USSS Headquarters. In the end he had a small group of five female and seven male agents. Most of them looked young enough to be Montgomery's children but came with glowing recommendations from their superiors.

Three would work night shift—a basically static post that did little but watch the condominium—while the other nine agents would work days, shadowing the senator wherever she went.

He'd chosen agents who lived near or inside the Beltway. Some of them lived within a few miles of one another, though their schedules made it so they hardly ever crossed paths. The Secret Service was a small agency, and most knew one another, or at the very least had friends in common. There was a certain amount of "smoking and joking" as the detail came together and people caught up on one another's lives.

Montgomery held the first briefing at the nondescript orange brick building on H Street that was Secret Service Headquarters. He'd been honest with everyone, including the lawyer who sat at the end of the long conference table.

"There has been no articulated threat," he said.

"Yeah," Mike Ayers said. "Not to be indelicate, but have you listened to the senator? I'm sure she's got a million people who hate her ever-lovin' guts. Sorry, boss, just saying what everyone is already thinking. It's the ones who don't make a loud fuss who we have to worry about."

The whip-smart supervisory agent from WFO was a natural choice as Montgomery's second-in-command.

"I hear you, Mike," Montgomery said. "But let's not say it outside these walls."

"Copy that, boss," Ayers said.

"One more thing," Montgomery said before everyone deployed to their various assignments. "Normally, we protect from harm or embarrassment. I don't give a shit about embarrassment, but the senator must not be harmed. If you see something brewing, shut it down immediately. If you can do it without her making you, so much the better—but I don't want you to get caught up in that."

The evening turned out comfortably warm, considering what Elizaveta Bobkova had in mind. A low sun behind the hotels and office buildings of Arlington threw Crystal Drive and much of the fountain park across the street into shadow. Bobkova settled back in the park with a half-dozen other people sitting on benches. Most of them probably lived in one of the many nearby apartments adjacent to Reagan National Airport. Some looked like they'd just finished running on the Mount Vernon Trail, others were just out to soak up a pleasant evening. If they stayed around long enough, it would prove to be an evening they would never forget. If Chadwick stayed an hour and a half, she'd be out at about sunset, which Bobkova thought would be just about perfect.

Morton's was directly across the Potomac from D.C. proper via the Fourteenth Street Bridge, so she wouldn't have been surprised to see any number of Washington glitterati. The eateries around Crystal City were favorite places to lobby, be lobbied, solicit funds, or request favors for funds that had already been solicited. It was a dirty business, politics. Dirtier even than espionage, Bobkova thought, so one might as well conduct it over a nice meal.

She'd not been surprised when Chadwick showed up with someone other than her callow aide. Fite was there, but as a driver, not a date. He dropped the senator and her dining partner off in front of the restaurant, and then sped away in her black BMW X5, heading south, presumably to wait until he was called to pick them up again. A happy convenience. The routine would almost surely be repeated in reverse, with Fite pulling up to the curb in front of the restaurant, and Chadwick slowing for just a moment as she got in the waiting vehicle, allowing Gorev the chance to strike.

Tonight the senator was meeting with a strapping lumberjack of a lobbyist for a large pharmaceutical company. Bobkova could not remember his name, but she recognized his bearded face from more than one of the many Washington cocktail parties that everyone loved to whine about but no one wanted to miss.

Both Chadwick and the lobbyist had checked their watches between the BMW and the restaurant, making it a good bet that each had another commitment after dinner.

"Any minute now," Bobkova spoke softly into the tiny microphone clipped inside the lapel of her blouse. Chatting quietly to one's self on a park bench did not see seem quite as bizarre as it had been before the advent of mobile phones.

Both men acknowledged. Pugin from a bench inside the underground mall across from the small post office. His post gave him a vantage point to make certain Chadwick and the lobbyist didn't decide to take the interior exit and go for a walk in the underground without anyone knowing it. The double glass doors gave him a clear view of the street as well and he was close enough to render assistance if Gorev needed it.

Gorev had the trigger job. His youthful face didn't look it, but deep down, he was much more ruthless than Pugin, and Bobkova needed ruthless. Gorev would loiter on Crystal Drive, outside the security camera's field of view, as if waiting for a ride. Bobkova, who could see the front door, would let him know when Chadwick made her exit. At this point, he would walk up and shoot her in the face. Pugin would exit the mall then, acting the good witness and yelling at some imagined assailant up on a rooftop. It took the human mind a few seconds to process surprises, especially violent ones. Most bystanders would follow Pugin's gesture to the vacant rooftop, struggling to make sense of the situation; some of them would have clearly even seen Gorev pull the trigger. Some would stand with pocketed hands while they stared in shock at the broken skull and brain matter that were nothing at all like they appear on television. Overwhelmed senses would be unable to process the input of gore, and blood, and gunpowder. Oh, some Good Samaritan might try and tackle Gorev, but he was strong and quick. Pugin would move in as well, as if to grab the attacker, all the while clumsily blocking anyone else.

This was a good plan. With any luck, it would all be over soon.

Bobkova sat up a little straighter on her park bench, willing her leg not to bounce with nervous energy. Arlington was crawling with police and federal agents. Dozens of them were sure to emerge from the woodwork like termites at the sound of a shot. She wanted to be gone before anyone knew she'd been here.

"CAROUSEL is still stationary," Special Agent Soong said from inside Morton's. Several less flattering code names for Chadwick had been suggested, but Montgomery reminded the team that these things had a way of coming to light and stuck with CAROUSEL.

"Alpha is stationary," said the Secret Service agent on top of the Crystal Place apartments. She lay belly-down behind her Remington 700 rifle, peering through the reticle of a Nightforce scope, cheek against the adjustable comb of the Accuracy International chassis.

"Stay on her, Christie," Montgomery heard Ayers say. Special agents Miller and Woodruff responded next.

"Bravo still stationary."

"Charlie still stationary."

Alone in his maroon Dodge Durango two hundred meters away, Montgomery nodded to himself. He'd liked to have thought the team would have snapped to these threats simply because of their appearance, but he knew the real reason was a friendship that went back to his first days in the Service.

The baby agent who'd sat next to him at the Federal Law Enforcement Training Center during basic criminal investigator school—CI, they called it—had been convinced even in the early nineties that technical measures were the future of law enforcement. Josh Parker had carried around folders crammed full of data on what was then extremely new technology regarding cell phones, digital cameras, and the emerging Internet. He was always eager to share his ideas with anyone willing to listen. Montgomery, who even then looked like a ham-fisted Mickey Spillane character with a clothing allowance and better haircut, had a tendency to depend more on shoe leather than on binary code. But he'd sensed this agent-trainee was onto something. He and Parker became good friends throughout the weeks of CI and then the more specialized Secret Service training course in Beltsville. Special Agent Parker had eventually gone on to head the Secret Service's Protective Intelligence Division, working behind the frosted windows on the uppermost floor of Secret Service HQ.

Parker's drone had provided the first lead.

Strictly speaking, the fifteen-mile circle around Reagan Airport was a No Drone Zone. There'd already been an incident where a small commercial UAV had crashed onto the White House lawn. Few things beyond actual gunfire got the Secret Service quite as animated as remotely piloted aircraft flying up to the window of the President's house. The Service conducted numerous tests, working on methods to stop intrusive aircraft, and coincidentally, how they might employ such aircraft themselves in furtherance of their mission.

Josh Parker headed the research.

He'd launched his newest drone from a park two blocks away from Chadwick's apartment, simply to get some up-to-date aerial video of the neighborhood, possible surveillance vehicles, anything out of the ordinary. He'd suggested launching the drone every hour to look for patterns—and changes in those patterns.

The drone went up for the third time at five minutes after six o'clock, just in time to watch a brunette woman exit the back side of the apartment building across the street from Senator Chadwick's residence and get into a forest-green Ford Taurus. That would not have been abnormal at all, but for the fact that the woman got in the car and did not drive away. Two minutes later, a white male in his twenties came out of the same building but walked to a different sedan. He and the woman pulled away at the same time, heading in the same direction.

Parker had taken his drone up another hundred feet and watched the two vehicles drive out of the neighborhood. They jumped on I-66 heading east. The departure would simply have been logged by the command post, but a third male, this one shorter, darker, and older—one of the agents called him "shifty"—came out the back door of the same apartment building and drove away using the same route.

Chadwick left her residence just before six thirty with her assistant Corey Fite behind the wheel of her Beemer. Seven U.S. Secret Service vehicles trailed, loose enough not to be seen, close enough not to lose one of the most ubiquitous types of vehicle inside the Beltway. She'd stopped and picked someone up at the Clarendon Metro Station Kiss and Ride lot, and then continued on Clarendon Boulevard, generally paralleling the route taken by the three people who'd left shortly before her.

Parker uploaded pertinent sections of the video with the clearest images of each person and sent it to everyone on the detail. The angles weren't ideal, but they were good enough that the "shifty" guy was identified sitting on a bench inside the Crystal City Underground almost as soon as the team arrived on scene.

Montgomery and the others hadn't known where Chadwick was going before she arrived at the steakhouse, so it took them a few minutes to get set up. One agent followed the senator and her male companion inside. This agent, a female who'd be able to check on the women's restroom without being questioned, quietly displayed credentials identifying her as Secret Service Special Agent Madeline Soong, and told the maître d' that she needed to conduct an advance for a visiting dignitary. Protective details were common in and around Washington, so the maître d' gave her the run of the place. The lighting inside the restaurant was dim and Special Agent Soong, dressed in a smart navy-blue suit with an open-collar button-down, blended in with management. Chadwick was self-absorbed enough that she paid no attention to the intense Asian woman checking for would-be threats not twenty feet away.

Shifty's presence on the bench just outside Morton's was enough for Montgomery to put shooters on top of the nearest apartment buildings to the north and south across Crystal Drive. He wanted coverage of the drop-off and pickup point with two long guns as well as two sets of eyes. Parker's drone would have come in handy here, but the proximity to Reagan Airport made that problematic.

Agents on the ground identified the younger man and the woman from Chadwick's neighborhood before the snipers made it to the rooftops. They were given designators that corresponded to the order in which they'd come out of the apartment. All senses humming now, Montgomery couldn't help but wonder if there was some unidentified Delta out there to go with his Alpha, Bravo, and Charlie.

Soong's voice came across the radio. *"CAROUSEL is imminent departure. They're paying the bill now."*

"Okay, boys and girls," Special Agent Ayers said. "On your toes."

43

Montgomery clutched the steering wheel with both hands, leaning forward, fighting the urge to get involved.

Chadwick's BMW X5 pulled up just before she walked out.

"Movement, Bravo," an agent said.

Another piped in. *"Charlie's up, walking toward the street."*

Then: *"Gun Bravo! Gun Bravo!"*

In front of the restaurant, Delray Witherspoon, a six-foot-three rawboned special agent who'd played tight end for Mizzou before joining the Service, bounced Bravo's head off a concrete pillar before he could bring up the pistol. Bravo collapsed on the sidewalk.

Special Agent Soong moved to her right, body-checking subject Charlie at the moment he tried to come through the glass doors, knocking him back into the arms of the two agents who'd sprinted up behind him.

Chadwick and her date got into the Beemer and drove away, seemingly none the wiser that she'd narrowly avoided execution.

"Subject Alpha, running east," one of the rooftop shooters said, calm, sniperlike. His voice held the unique buzz of someone whose face was pressed against a rifle chassis. "She's on the paved trail, heading down toward the airport."

Montgomery hit the steering wheel. Ayers would follow Chadwick's vehicle, staying with her to look out for secondary attacks. With the remaining agents either on the roof or across the street, Alpha was as good as gone.

"Oh, hell, no," Montgomery muttered, slamming the Durango into gear. Flooring the accelerator, he turned quickly off Crystal Drive into the parking lot to his right, cutting between the two apartment buildings. He'd gotten enough of a look at Alpha to see she had long legs and an easy stride. Probably bought her running shoes by the gross. There was no way he'd be able to outrun her. But he was a boxer, and boxers knew how to work the angles.

The Mount Vernon Trail stretched for eighteen miles along the Potomac River between George Washington's estate and Roosevelt Island to the north. The entry onto the trail from Crystal City ran east through the woods as it crossed the tracks and then cut almost due south to follow the George Washington Parkway before finally joining with the trail via a concrete ramp overlooking Reagan National Airport. In other words, if she wanted to run north and stay on the trail, Alpha would have to run south first. Montgomery had run it before with friends from the U.S. Marshals Service, headquartered in Crystal City, and he knew every sickening foot of it.

He took the Durango as far as he could, eventually finding himself stopped by a swimming pool behind the apartments. Out and running immediately, he scrambled over the rusted metal wall along the train tracks. He tore the knee on his khakis when he hit the gravel, but his predatory drive put him past caring. He hit the woods at an all-out run, crashing through dense greenery of oak shrubs and sassafras, half sliding, half bounding down the side hill. The thump of evening traffic on the GW Parkway covered the noise of his approach.

Montgomery slowed a hair as the vegetation began to thin and he neared the edge of the woods. Alpha was to his left, still running as if pursued by demons, just about to go under the bridge. Montgomery dug in, sprinting up the grassy hill to GW Parkway, where he waved at oncoming cars like a madman. Traffic was never good inside the Beltway, but Sunday evening gave him a relative break, and he was able to scramble across in fits and starts like the frog in the video game without getting squished. Energized at having reached the high ground in advance of his target, he stepped into the woods where the Crystal City access T'd into the main trail and waited for Alpha to run directly to him.

He drew his SIG Sauer, but there was no need.

Alpha stopped dead in her tracks and raised her hands when she saw the badge hanging from the chain around his neck.

"My name is Elizaveta Bobkova. I am the Russian attaché for economic affairs and I have diplomatic immunity."

Gun up, Montgomery kept his distance.

Without being ordered, Bobkova knelt on the grass, put both hands on top of her head, and crossed her ankles. She knew the drill. An Arlington PD patrol unit pulled to the shoulder of the road and stopped, pistol out, surveying the scene from behind the safety of his engine block.

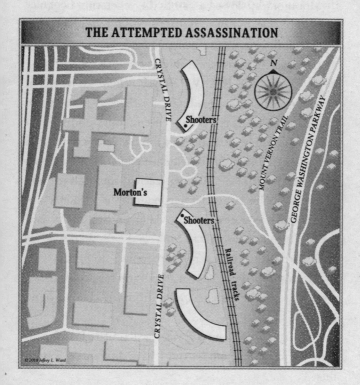

THE ATTEMPTED ASSASSINATION

Montgomery tapped the badge around his neck. "Secret Service. I could use some help here."

Two more APD cars showed up in as many minutes, more relaxed with the situation now that they had superior numbers. Montgomery holstered his sidearm and let the officers, who were accustomed to working as contact and cover, take Elizaveta Bobkova into physical custody.

"Nice Glock," Montgomery said when one of the Arlington officers passed him the G43 they took from her waistband. "Small, but a little much for an economic attaché."

Bobkova cocked her head to one side. Sweat beaded on her upper lip. Her chest heaved from exertion and nerves. It was getting dark now, and the blue and red lights of the squad cars flashed off her passive face. "You are very large man," she said, her Russian accent stronger than it had been earlier. Her eyes were almost shut, as if she were trying to figure out some riddle. "I do not mean to say fat. You are large in good way. But I cannot believe a man as large as you caught up to me on foot. It is . . . remarkable . . ."

44

Urbano da Rocha lay on his back in a plastic lounge chair, reading a car magazine and daydreaming about the new Bugatti he could now afford to buy. An intense midday sun reflected off the white deck and dazzled the blue water of the pool. A heavy gold chain lay across his hairless chest, glinting along with the buckle of his swimsuit. Skintight silk covered with gold brocade, the suit was modeled after *taleguilla*—the breeches worn by matadors. It was complete with tassels—called *machos*—and da Rocha thought it looked ridiculous, but Lucile had bought the suit for him in Seville. As with the actual *taleguilla* of a matador, the suit required da Rocha to arrange his *partes nobles* to one side or the other. In the case of the matador, this was away from the side he used to confront the bull. A wise choice, considering what the sharp horns of a Spanish fighting bull would do to those "noble parts." The suit might look foppish, but it certainly sparked some interesting games in the bedroom. He'd hardly gotten a moment's sleep since the deal with the Russians went through.

Killing always brought out the best in Lucile Fournier.

Groaning now, he set the magazine aside and sniffed the air, taking in the odor of cut grass on the rising heat from the fields below the eighteenth-century villa—his fields and his villa. He gazed down the hill at the olive grove below—his olive grove. And it was only the beginning. Oh, this place was well and good by Portuguese standards, but now he could buy an island of his own if he wished. His estates would dot the globe. If the Russians could be trusted to keep their word—and why shouldn't they—then there would be many more deals to come. Not too shabby for a former Ochoa errand boy.

He caught a flash of movement in the corner of his eye and let his head fall sideways to watch Lucile's tan body arc off the diving board and enter the water with hardly a burble. She was that way with everything, precise, perfect. It seemed she hardly even had to practice. She merely conceived an image of what she wanted to do, replayed it over and over in her mind until she could picture the most minute detail—and then did it. Killing Hugo Gaspard had been da Rocha's idea. How to do it had been hers. She suggested it be public, demonstrating to others in the business that there was a new player in town who was not to be underestimated. Anyone who could murder the feared Frenchman in broad daylight—in front of his armed bodyguards, no less—was surely someone to be reckoned with. The same with Don Felipe. She'd taken special care procuring the toxin and devised a method of delivery that could be carried out under the nose of the Russians without causing them to get overly nervous.

Shielding his eyes against the blinding sun, da Rocha whistled at Lucile. It was not a catcall or a summons. Lucile was not the sort of woman who answered to a snapped finger. It was a whistle of awe.

Both hands on the deck, she pressed herself up and out

of the pool, swinging her leg up in a fluid motion that would have been awkward for most people. She accomplished it with perfect strength and grace. Like a goddess just appearing on earth, her wet skin glowed under the golden evening light. She tipped her head to get all her hair on one side, and then used both hands to wring out the excess water. She wore the same black two-piece she'd had on when she'd shot Gaspard, with the same alluring tear in the cloth over her buttock.

"It is so hot today," she said. "You should come in the water."

"I will," he said.

Her face fell into a frowning pout. She stomped her foot before turning at the edge of the pool, arching her back, looking over her shoulder to taunt him with the ripped swimsuit. "Do not wait too long. The water is making me wrinkle."

"Just a tiny bit of work to do first, my little prune. You know, banking matters." He reached for the laptop on the teak table beside his lounge chair and opened it up. Lucile had kept him so busy that he'd not logged on since returning home. It took only a moment to connect to Wi-Fi.

45

Sixteen hours and three layovers after leaving Seville, the aging Ariana 737 carrying Jack Ryan, Jr., and Dom Caruso made a rapid descent toward the Herat airport, south of the city. There were few missile attacks of late, but the pilots didn't seem to want to try their luck by staying in the air too long at low altitude. The other passengers rocked sleepily in their seats, reading or chatting happily with seatmates, apparently used to the rapid descents. Strong winds buffeted the airplane even after they'd landed, causing it to shake as the pilot took them down the runway toward the sad-looking terminal.

Ryan rolled his neck from side to side, doing little to get rid of the kinks brought on by long hours of sitting, and more than that, the anticipation of seeing Ysabel Kashani. He beat his head against the tattered headrest.

"I swear I saw a cloud of dust fly up from the upholstery when we touched down."

Caruso rubbed his face and leaned forward to look out the window. "This whole place is a dust cloud. I can already feel the grit between my teeth. You think they have any other colors here besides brown?"

The lone Ariana flight attendant stood well back in the galley as the passengers deplaned. Her smile was friendly enough, but she said nothing to the passengers, mainly Afghan men, as they filed past her.

Apart from the constant shove of a wind that seemed made more of dust than air, the first thing Ryan noticed was the smell. The odor of cooked meat and burning plastic reminded him of a time when he was nine or ten and had hidden his G.I. Joe on the barbecue grill. His dad had lit the burners without checking under the lid.

Jack wondered about snipers as he walked across the tarmac but forgot about danger altogether the moment he got inside the unnaturally quiet terminal and saw Ysabel. She wore a loose cotton dress in charcoal-gray and a blue headscarf. He'd expected her to be in a T-shirt and tight jeans, like the last time he saw her, but her clothing was relatively progressive for a severely conservative place like western Afghanistan, where many women wore a burka.

Two men stood beside her, glaring hard at the newcomers. One was darker than the other, with a head that was very close to being shaved and a long pointy beard that reminded Ryan of a billy goat. His head was up, hands at his sides, shoulders hunched forward in a slight crouch, as if spoiling for a fight. The other was taller, better fed, but with an intense sadness around his dark eyes. Like the first man, he had an olive complexion, but this one had a full head of hair, combed straight back, dark, but with a rusty tint in the right light. Ryan suspected he was the Russian. Neither man smiled. For that matter, neither did Ysabel.

She simply nodded in greeting.

"Thank you for coming," she said. "The van is this way."

Caruso and Ryan were shown to a battered minivan across the street in the small lot, a warm dust-filled wind whipping them the entire way. The guy with the buzz cut introduced himself as Hamid as he slid open the back door. He left them to get in the van themselves and walked around to get behind the wheel, apparently uninterested in learning their names. Ysabel sat up front in the passenger seat. The release button that would have allowed someone to reach the rearmost seat was broken, forcing the remaining three men to squeeze in together on the ratty bench seat in the middle of the van. Dovzhenko took the far window, directly behind Hamid, and Jack took the middle, riding the hump. He didn't mind. It gave him a more unobstructed view of Ysabel.

He leaned forward, hands on his knees. Sweating and more than a little nervous at seeing her again after so long.

"I'm surprised you didn't give me one of those Indiana Jones slap-to-the-yap welcomes when you saw me."

Ysabel gave him a sullen side eye without turning her head. "Oh, I would have," she said, completely serious. "But public displays of affection are frowned upon in Afghanistan."

Hamid took the Kandahar–Herat Highway north past the Afghan National Army Base, turning west before entering Herat proper. They drove past fields of saffron crocus and poppies, and orchards of almond and date and pistachio. Stands of willow and cottonwood trees flourished in the valley, in stark contrast to the barren hills.

Jack tried to make small talk, but Ysabel gave only curt answers, so the conversation never went anywhere.

He couldn't help but notice that she hardly even looked at him, and never met his eye.

"You've been here a year?"

She nodded but explained no further.

"How's Avram?"

"My father passed away," Ysabel said. "Jack. I want you to listen to me very carefully. We do not have to catch up. You do not have to pretend to be interested in my life."

"Ysabel—"

She cut him off. "I never would have called and taken you away from your busy schedule had it not been absolutely necessary."

Caruso bounced a fist on Jack's knee, showing his fraternal support.

"Look," Ryan said, "I get that you're pissed at me. But are you sure you want to do this here, in front of everyone?"

"Do what?" Ysabel said, still staring forward. "I am only apologizing for taking you away from your busy life."

Jack fell back in his seat, wedging himself between the two other men. "Suit yourself. It's good to see you, too." He turned to the Russian. "What's your story? Did you get in some kind of trouble in—"

Ysabel wheeled in her seat, finally looking Ryan in the eye. "What was I to you, Jack? Were there other Iranian women after me? Do you have some Persian women fetish?"

"I thought we parted on good terms," Jack whispered. "Your father made it very clear that your safety was paramount—and that any association with me put you in danger."

"My father?" She spat, fuming now. "You would blame this on my father when he is dead and cannot defend himself?"

Jack looked to Caruso for help but got nothing. A silence fell over the interior of the van until Dovzhenko cleared his throat.

"I appreciate you coming," he said. "I have information you might find useful."

"I look forward to hearing it," Ryan said.

More silence.

Hamid kept glancing in the rearview mirror, which, for some reason, was seriously beginning to piss Ryan off.

"Can I help you with something?" Ryan asked.

"No," Hamid said.

"You keep looking at me like you have a question."

"No," the Afghan said again. "Merely an observation."

"And what's that?"

"I find myself surrounded by invaders."

Ysabel looked sideways. "What are you talking about?"

"Persia, Russia, the United States—you have all invaded Afghanistan at one time or another. And now you sit here arguing among yourselves as if I am not even present." Hamid shrugged. "The history of my country in microcosm."

"I'm not invading anybody," Ryan said. "I was invited."

"How could you, Jack?" Ysabel said, ignoring her bodyguard. "You, my father, you were both supposed to be these enlightened men. How could you presume to make such decisions for me?"

"I almost got you killed," Jack said.

"You give yourself too much credit," Ysabel said. "I—"

Hamid cut her off. "I am sorry to interrupt," he said, though it was clear from his tone that he was not. "But there are three motorbikes moving up behind us at a high rate of speed."

Ryan, Caruso, and the Russian twisted in their seats to get a look behind them. The thick cloud of orange dust boiling up behind the van made it almost impossible to see anything.

"Are they armed?" Jack asked.

Hamid gave a grunting nod. "Everyone is armed. This is opium country. The Taliban are active not far to the south. Smugglers and bandits are as common as fleas here."

"That's odd," Jack said. "That a bodyguard would take us through an area thick with opium smugglers."

Hamid laughed, the way someone would laugh at a sophomoric child. "You are in Afghanistan. There are only two types of areas—unsafe and very unsafe."

"Have you got any guns in the van?" Caruso asked.

Ysabel leaned forward and pulled an Uzi from under her seat. She passed it to Jack, keeping the muzzle down.

Hamid glanced in the rearview. "Do you know how to use one of these?"

Jack scoffed. "I do."

"I only ask," Hamid said, "because they fire from an open bolt, and I have seen more than a few Americans shoot holes in the floor believing the weapon is safe, when it is actually ready to fire."

"Thanks," Jack said. "I'm familiar with how to work an Uzi."

"I don't want to come across as a whiner," Caruso said, leaning across Jack and between the front bucket seats. "But do you have a gun for me?"

Ysabel passed him a Beretta 92 but kept a Kalashnikov pointed down between her knees. She looked at Dovzhenko. "I am sorry, but that's all we have."

The Russian held up a hand. "It is fine," he said. "If things get bad, I will take one of theirs, whichever becomes available first."

"They are about to pass us," Hamid said, eyes glued to his side mirror. "They have not unslung their rifles."

One of the motorcycles roared by, throwing up a rooster tail of dust but ignoring the van altogether.

The second bike passed, following the first. An AK-47 rifle was slung diagonally across the rider's back.

The road narrowed some, curving sharply to the north as it followed the meandering course of the Hari River. The third bike kept to the rear, biding his time while his two friends drew farther and farther away. The river straightened, as did the road, and the bike moved up immediately, slowing a hair as he came abeam with the driver's door.

Ryan heard a faint clunk, as if they'd kicked up a rock. The motorcycle rolled on the throttle and sped ahead.

"Sticky bomb!" Hamid said, throwing open the door in an attempt to rid the van of the magnetic device.

It was no use.

The blast lifted the front of the vehicle completely off the ground. One moment Hamid was there, behind the steering wheel, the next his seat was empty, torn to rags. The van lurched violently, the right wheel falling into the ditch that ran along the road and then rolling on its side as it slid along the gravel with a horrific squeal of metal on stone.

With no seat directly in front of him, Jack was thrown

forward during the wreck, landing on top of Ysabel in a tangle of arms and legs and machine guns. Both of them were pressed against the shattered window that was now the bottom of the van and wedged between the dash and the bucket seat. Feet pointing skyward, Jack's weight was on his shoulders and he essentially lay on his back in Ysabel's lap.

"Are you okay?" he asked.

She groaned. "I will be when you get off my ribs."

"Give me the gun!" Dovzhenko barked from the backseat. He'd slid the van door open above him, revealing a bright patch of dusty sky.

Jack passed the Uzi without argument. He wasn't using it at the moment.

"Dom!" he shouted. "You good?"

Dust and smoke poured into the van.

"Dom!" Jack said again.

Nothing.

Dovzhenko had climbed out and now looked down through the open door, the Uzi slung around his neck. "Pass the girl to me! The engine is burning. You need to get out now."

Jack braced himself against the seats and helped Ysabel up. She looked at him in horror.

"You are bleeding," she said.

"I'm fine," Jack said. "Let's get you out of here."

She looked back at him, terror in her eyes.

"No," she said. "You are not."

Ryan pressed up with his legs, pushing on her buttocks while Dovzhenko pulled her up and out.

"We have to hurry," the Russian yelled. "The motorcycles are returning."

"I'm right behind you," Ryan said.

Caruso was only half conscious. He moaned, looked at Jack as if he understood, and then closed his eyes.

"Come on, buddy," Jack said through clenched teeth. He squatted low and looped Caruso's arm around his shoulder, pressing with his legs to drag Caruso up toward the door. "Dovzhenko!" he hissed. "A little help here!"

Nothing.

"Dovzhenko!"

Caruso stirred, his head lolling sideways to look directly at Jack. His eyes were dazed, unfocused. "You're bleeding."

"I'm fine," Jack said.

"No," Caruso said. "I don't think so, buddy. You should see yourself . . ."

"I said I'm fine." Ryan called for the Russian again, then Ysabel, to no avail.

"I can't lift you out of here by myself," he said. "You still got that pistol?"

Caruso shook his head. "Nope."

The sound of approaching motorcycle engines growled above the wind outside.

Jack lowered Caruso gently to the seat. This wasn't working. He cast his eyes around the interior of the van, searching for another way out. He could crawl over the backseat and maybe kick open the rear doors, but Caruso was little better than deadweight.

The *clack-clack* cyclic of the Uzi ripped outside, followed by the distinctive crack of AKs. Acrid smoke began to pour in from the dash as the magnesium engine caught fire. Ryan knew they had maybe a minute before the van would become fully engulfed, less if the heat reached the fuel tank.

"Dom," Jack said, heart racing now in near-panic mode. "We have to get you out of here."

Caruso pointed at the ground. "Here."

"I'm telling you we can't stay here."

Caruso shook his head, squinting now as the initial surge of adrenaline gave way to pain from his injuries. "Here!" He stomped on the window. "We're on a ditch. Crawl out."

Jack saw the butt of the Beretta now, jammed between the side of the seat and the passenger doorframe. He leaned Caruso against the backrest and traded places with him so he was on the bottom. It would be much easier if he went first and dragged his cousin out. The alternative would be like pushing cooked spaghetti. Jack grabbed the pistol and, bracing his feet on the metal frame, put a single round through the window. Fortunately, the van had shatterproof glass and it broke into a thousand tiny squares rather than deadly shards.

They'd come to rest with the wheels on the edge of the road and the roofline resting on the far bank, straddling the ditch. Gun in hand, Jack scrambled through the broken window, feetfirst, sinking immediately to his chest in muddy water. Caruso came behind him, gasping and becoming more animated from the surprise of hitting the muck.

"Can you keep your head up?" Jack asked.

"I'm good," Caruso groaned. "My head feels like shit, though."

"Looks it, too," Ryan said, relieved that Dom seemed coherent enough to assist in his own rescue.

"Oh, yeah," Caruso said. "Just wait until you look in the mirror . . ."

Jack shrimped backward, his back scraping the van, his body submerged up to his neck in the soupy muck. Dom's brother, Brian, had been killed doing this job. Jack wasn't about to lose another cousin. Caruso faced him, crawling along as well as he could, coughing and sputtering from smoke and muddy water.

Jack was vaguely aware of more shots outside, but they were in front of the van. He had a vague plan of staying as deep in the water as he could as he worked his way out feetfirst while making certain Caruso didn't drown or burn to death.

"Stay with me, D—"

Strong hands grabbed Jack around both ankles. He kicked and twisted to try and get away, but, caught on the tunnel-like space between the ditch and the body of the van, he was robbed of any real power. He heard muffled voices and then felt more hands grabbing him, one person on each leg now, dragging him out through the mud. The image of his cousin seared into his brain. His dazed eyes, the crooked jaw, flames licking the van above him.

46

Ding Chavez pressed his spine against the trunk of a gnarled olive tree. He held his short shotgun at low ready. Grasshoppers flew up each time he took a step, wings clicking on the hazy evening air. Birds chirped in the branches. A dead man lay in the shrubs fifteen feet away. It was probably a sentry and whoever had killed him was somewhere uphill, between Chavez and the house.

Ding was not, by nature, a whiner, but just once he'd like to come to some beautiful corner of the world and take a little look around—bring his bride instead of an armed-up team of operatives. She deserved to get out a little, especially since she hardly even knew what he did, let alone where he did it. Growing up with a father like John Clark imbued you with a certain understanding of the way of life. She and Ding had come to an agreement early in their marriage that he'd tell her what he could, and she wouldn't ask questions. It made a conversational dance around the dinner table when JP was younger, but Patsy became adept at jumping in front of any topic that would turn Ding into a liar.

It would be most cool if he could bring them both to this little Portuguese village, but first he had to see to a certain murderous couple—and whoever happened to be trying to whack them at this moment on one of the low hills east of town. Chavez's money was on the Russians, most likely GRU. They'd done a deal with da Rocha and, for some reason, now wanted to back out.

Clark's plan had been to watch and learn, gleaning whatever they could over the course of a few days from watching the activity on da Rocha's computer. Now that they knew where he was, they would get a couple of rooms, act the part of tourists, and see what they could see.

It had been a good plan until ten minutes ago—when they'd seen the body.

Gavin tweaked the malware running in the background of da Rocha's computer so it "phoned home" to him and Midas now that Jack was gallivanting around Afghanistan. The software allowed them to search e-mails, documents, and bank accounts—and to do things to them so long as da Rocha wasn't looking at the screen when they did it. The keystroke-logging feature gave them real-time observation of what da Rocha was doing—which appeared to have a great deal to do with weapons. Most important, though, the hidden program told them where he was.

It was midafternoon by the time the team reached the crossroads village of Alpalhão in central Portugal. Surrounded by fertile fields of wheat and olive groves, the village had fewer than fifteen hundred full-time residents.

Clark had decided they should do a little recon of the location as soon as they got to town, to get a feel for it before finding rooms for the night. The GPS on da Rocha's computer indicated he was located at the end of a tree-lined dirt lane. A copse of pines hid all but the roofline and a few glimpses of white from the road. Adara was the first to see the pair of legs jutting out from the pine trees as she and Midas passed the entrance to the villa lane from the south.

"This changes everything," Clark said over the net. "I'd really like to talk to this guy, but if that happens to be Russians paying him a visit, I'm not hopeful."

"Want me to launch the drone?" Midas said.

"Let's gear up first," Clark said.

Midas and Adara continued north, while Chavez and Clark hung back in the shadow of a large cork oak. They were all traveling heavy now, having brought their weapons aboard the Hendley Gulfstream when they'd first come to Portugal to watch Hugo Gaspard. Clark carried his venerable Wilson Combat .45, the single action being easier for him to operate with the previously damaged tendons in his dominant hand. Everyone else carried Smith & Wesson M&P Shields in nine-millimeter. With a capacity of only nine rounds including the one in the chamber, the little pistols weren't exactly optimum sidearms for a frontal assault. But as Ding had learned from hard experience, when it came to hunting men, no pistol was an ideal weapon. When given a choice, long guns were always primary when there was offensive work to be done.

Both Clark and Adara carried short-barreled Colt M4s on single-point slings around their necks. The 5.56 caliber NATO ammo allowed them to accurately reach out well past four hundred meters. Midas carried an H&K MP7 with three 40-round magazines of 4.6x30, a small but zippy little round meant to rip through body armor that the nine-millimeter MP5 could not. Chavez carried the street howitzer, a Remington Tac-14 twelve-gauge with a ball-like bird's-head grip and a fourteen-inch barrel. The gun was highly maneuverable and devastating at close range.

In addition to their weapons loadout, each carried a Cordura wallet containing a personal trauma kit of clotting gauze, an Israeli bandage, a SWAT-T tourniquet, and a fourteen-gauge needle.

Midas launched the Snipe Nano six minutes after they arrived, taking it up three hundred feet above ground level so it was less likely to be heard.

Adara kept her eyes peeled outbound while the rest of the team watched on the screen as four guys in dark clothing moved slowly toward a buttressed white stucco villa. A man and a woman, probably da Rocha and Fournier, lounged outside by a pool. There looked to be at least two sentries posted near the rear of the house on either end of the pool deck.

"Let's move," Clark said. "I'd like to get da Rocha before they quiet him for good."

Midas recalled the drone, and two minutes later the team spread out in the trees, far enough to get a wider field of view but close enough that they could still see one another in the long shadows. The Russians, if that's who it was, made the classic mistake of forgetting about their six o'clock. Not wanting to make the same error, Clark, Adara, and Ding focused their attention forward with intersecting fields of fire. Midas kept an eye downhill with the MP7.

They found three dead sentries by the time they reached the tree line at the top of the hill—but they'd yet to hear a single shot.

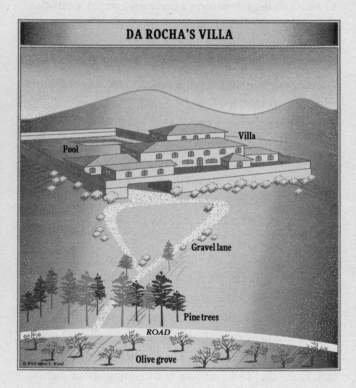

DA ROCHA'S VILLA

Villa

Pool

Gravel lane

Pine trees

ROAD

Olive grove

© 2018 Jeffrey L. Ward

———

D a Rocha pounded the arm of his lounge chair hard enough to spill his beer. "This cannot be right. The product is where it is supposed to be."

Lucile lounged at the edge of the pool. "What? Have they forgotten to pay you?"

"They paid me yesterday." He ran a hand through his hair and then checked a different account. Perhaps he'd checked the wrong one. "Half of it, anyway. I should have gotten the balance today, but now even the first payment has disappeared."

"Odd," Lucile said. "How did they access your accounts?"

Da Rocha heard a muffled grunt and looked over his shoulder to find that Ramirez was no longer at his post. His stomach sank and he found himself overwhelmed with a feeling he'd not had since working the docks. Someone was out in the trees. Someone dangerous.

Lucile felt it, too, and hopped out of the pool, streaming a trail of water as she padded quickly to her folded towel, where she'd left her Beretta. Pistol in hand, she pointed to the far end of the house without speaking and melted into the evening air to see what had happened to Ramirez.

Da Rocha had no weapon. That's what he hired guards for. Feigning disinterest but half expecting a bullet to scream in and blow his head off, he walked nonchalantly until he was five or six feet from the patio door. A single bullet thwacked off the wall in front of him, chipping a perfect half-moon from the white stucco. Another zinged off the pavement, narrowly missing his heel. He heard the staccato cracks of supersonic bullets but no boom from the ignition. They must have been using suppressors.

He didn't wait around to figure it out but ducked his head and ran.

Lucile Fournier tasted blood, as she always did when she was about to spill some. The toe of a leather shoe protruded around the corner, revealing the presence of a man, hiding there to ambush her. She smiled, the pink tip of her tongue moistening her lips, tasting the air, serpent-like. She would have just shot through the wall, but da Rocha believed in solid, near-soundproof houses, and like many of the interior walls, this one was painted concrete. With the Beretta aimed in with both hands, she began to sidestep, cutting the pie, planning to shoot the first bit of the man that she saw and then take care of the rest of the bits as they presented themselves. She'd made it almost all the way around when she realized it was just an empty shoe. Clenching her teeth, she spun too late, catching a powerful fist that slammed her against the wall and sent a shower of lights exploding behind her eyes. She attempted to bring up the Beretta, but her attacker struck her in the forearm with some sort of truncheon. He kicked the gun away when it hit the floor.

Two more rapid blows to the face left her staggered and dazed. She had to use the wall to keep her feet. Her vision was fogged, but she could just make out the Russian with the odd haircut standing in front of her, smirking.

"Tsk, tsk, tsk, Ms. Fournier," he said, a pained expression on his face. "You make things so complicated. Internal piston ammunition, sophisticated shellfish toxins . . . People are not so hard to kill."

As if to prove his point, the Russian raised his pistol and shot her just below the nose. If she'd had any thoughts of arguing, she left them on the concrete wall behind her, along with her teeth.

Clark shot the first Russian twice as he turned the corner by the pool. "Splash one," he said. He kicked the man's suppressed Glock into the deep end of the pool and continued forward. A deafening boom to his right told him Chavez's Tac-14 had spoken. Another Russian staggered backward from behind one of the villa's winged buttresses. Clark and Adara both shot the third Russian as he came out of a bedroom, unaware that the previous gunfire had been at, not from, his comrades. Adara shot the fourth Russian as he was drawing a bead on da Rocha, who wore a bizarre-looking swimsuit that looked like he'd made it from matador pants. The arms dealer was now sprinting as fast as his legs could carry him down the gravel lane toward the main road.

"Stay alert," Clark said. He scanned across the top of his M4, pointing out while Ding covered the interior of the house behind him with the shotgun. "We saw four on the drone, but we might have missed one—and that doesn't count Lucile Fournier. Midas, think you can get da Rocha so we can talk to him?"

Rather than wasting breath on an answer, Midas, who was already running, just waved over his head with his left hand. Clark couldn't help but smile as the retired Delta operator's long strides chewed up the distance between him and da Rocha. He caught up quickly, falling in behind the arms dealer to give him a mighty shove between the shoulder blades. Midas grabbed his quarry by the hair as he went down, riding him to the ground like a sled. Da Rocha took the brunt of the impact on his chest and nose, yowling as he skidded to a stop. Midas rolled him over and slapped him across the ear. Thirty seconds later he was flex-cuffed, on his feet, and trudging back up the gravel road in his ridiculous-looking shorts.

Adrenaline ebbing, da Rocha's shoulders trembled when he looked around his estate at all the carnage. He blinked several times and then settled in on Clark, whom he'd identified as the leader. "Who are you? What . . . what is the meaning of this?"

Adara leaned out the sliding glass door and gave a grim shake of her head. "I found Fournier."

Clark sighed. "Mr. da Rocha. I'm the guy who just saved your life. That means you owe me some information."

Chavez leaned in. "We should go, boss."

"Right," Clark said, his eyes never leaving da Rocha. "I know a place near the coast where we can talk in private." He turned to Chavez. "No shit. The place I'm talking about is soundproof. There's a lake out back that must be a hundred feet deep. We can do whatever we want and no one will ever know."

Completely overwhelmed, da Rocha's face screwed up in a twisted grimace and he began to sob.

47

Dominic Caruso had wandered away from the rest of his family in Shenandoah National Forest when he was six years old. With darkness falling, every tree and bush looked like the other trees and bushes. In no time, he was so turned around he had no idea where he was. He'd sat down on a rock and cried as only a six-year-old boy can cry when he is hopelessly lost. But even then, he'd known that somewhere in the gathering darkness, there were people who loved him and wanted to make him safe.

Now he was slumped on the side of this isolated dirt road somewhere southwest of Herat, covered in mud and blood and bits of broken glass. The charred remains of the van steamed and smoked behind him. There'd been no explosion when the fuel tank caught fire, just a great whoosh and intense heat. The wind had whipped the flames and smoke into a black pyre that was surely visible for miles, but no one came to investigate. Caruso may as well have been on the face of the moon. Not a soul within a thousand miles cared enough to look for him. Hell, no one even knew he was missing. Jack was gone, snatched away along with Ysabel and the Russian. Life was cheap in this part of the world, and if Jack wasn't dead already, it was only a matter of time.

The bandits hadn't seen Dom, belly-down in the muddy ditchwater, or they would have taken him, too.

He dabbed at the side of his head, feeling the bristles of singed hair and blisters of the second-degree burns above his ear. Half his shirt on that side had been burned away as well. The incessant wind coated him in dust, as if he'd been rolled in yellow flour, making it impossible to accurately assess his injuries. One eye was swollen shut, his vision blurred. He could stand, though it made him feel like he might throw up. Both hands seemed functional enough for gross motor skills, but they shook so badly from shock that he'd likely have shot himself in the foot had he been able to find a pistol.

He allowed himself a two-minute pity party and then stood, realizing only then that he'd somehow lost his shoes while crawling through the mud. No one was coming for him. *Be your own rescue,* John Clark always said. That old son of a bitch had a mantra for everything. Caruso took a tentative step on wobbly legs, wincing from the rocks that cut his feet. Facing the wind, he laughed out loud in spite of the situation.

Pain from the burns and sprains and cuts had yet to overwhelm him, but it was only a matter of time. He had to get to a phone. To tell NATO troops or CIA or somebody with big guns and eyes in the sky that Ryan needed help. Caruso realized that as bad as this shit sandwich was, Jack's was far worse. At least Caruso was free, such as it was. Hamid had passed an Afghan National Army base after they'd left the airport, somewhere before he'd turned onto this road. Caruso would walk all night, crawl if he had to. He laughed again. Hell, crawling would probably be faster.

He had maybe an hour until dark—ink dark. The dangers would be exponential once the sun went down, but at least he would be able to hide.

And so he walked, falling forward, catching himself, and then falling forward again. It was painfully slow, but it was progress. A low whine above the moan of wind caught his attention. He held up a soot-black hand to shield his good eye from the dust.

Another motorcycle. Damn it. The rider had surely seen him.

Caruso stepped to the edge of the muddy ditch, closed his eyes, and waited.

J ack awoke unable to feel his hands. He could, however, feel every bone-jarring bump and pothole against his shoulders and hips. He had no idea how long he'd been unconscious, but long enough for it to get dark. The dusty bed of the white Bongo truck provided an unyielding platform, and the three prisoners slammed against it as if on the end of a flail as they sped down the road. Jack thought they were going northwest, but the shifting wind and the inability to see the sun from behind the short rails of the truck made it impossible to be sure. It didn't matter. He had no friends for miles in any direction. Ryan wanted to think Caruso escaped from beneath the burning van, but his rational brain—or what was left of it—told him the odds were against that. Positive attitude was essential for survival, but the bald truth was that they were all as good as dead. Depending on who'd taken them prisoner, burning to death in a muddy ditch might even be the quicker way to go.

The cab light in the truck was on, illuminating Ysabel's face, slack, inches from his. Her scarf was gone. Her head lolled, long black hair pooling against the filthy truck bed. Her clothing was torn, her shoulder bloodied, but her face was amazingly clean. A crystalline trickle of saliva hung from her open mouth. For a time, Jack thought she was already dead, but they wouldn't have bothered to bring her if that were true, let alone tie her up. The three of them were bound hand and foot, faces pressed to the bare metal, heads toward the rear, which only made the ride worse. They'd not been hooded, which was worrisome, since these guys didn't care if they were identified or not.

The bouncing grew less pronounced as the Bongo truck slowed, making a turn.

Ysabel's eyes flicked open. She swallowed hard, coal-black eyes darting back and forth as she tried to get her bearings.

"I am so sorry," she whispered.

Jack tried to shake his head, but found the movement made him sick to his stomach. "Not your fault," he said. "Let's just see what happens."

"You're hurt, Jack," Ysabel said. "You may not know it, but you are really hurt."

The truck slowed.

"Listen to me," Jack whispered. "My passport says my name is Joe Peterson. Whatever happens, you cannot call me Jack. Understand?"

She nodded. "Joe," she repeated. "I understand."

"Remind Dovzhenko."

Ryan heard the growl of motorcycles as the Bongo truck slowed and made another turn. They drove behind a tall fence, and the howling, dust-filled wind was suddenly quiet, replaced by the pleasant smell of new-mown grass and wet earth after a rain. Date palms rose in the shadows on either side of the narrow road. Weeping willow fronds scraped the side of the truck. The barricade wall was tall enough that only the tops of the tallest trees swayed with the wind.

Jack slid forward when the Bongo squeaked to a stop. Men barked in Pashto or Dari, he couldn't tell which. The tailgate fell open and rough hands grabbed first Ysabel, dragging her out by the shoulders. She pretended to be asleep, and the men laughed, slapping her almost playfully on the face. Ryan counted five of them—two from the Bongo and the three murderous bastards on the motorcycles. All of them wore dusty shalwar kameez. Jack guessed them to be in their twenties or early thirties, lean and intense. Two of them grabbed Jack next, dragging him out as well. They looked at his face, shaking their heads.

"You speak English?" Jack asked. He wasn't so much naïve as to believe he could depend on the kindness of these strangers, but he wanted them to see him as another human being and not simply another neck for their knives.

They just looked at him, stone-faced and gaunt, as if sucking in their cheeks.

Jack and the others were taken to a covered veranda, what would have been called a lanai in Florida or Hawaii. Persian rugs covered a concrete pad maybe twenty-by-twenty-feet square. Thick cushions were arranged around a low wooden table in the middle of the space. Earthen-ware pots and intricately stacked rock fountains sat among elaborate shrubs and flower baskets. A fire popped and crackled in a small pit not fifteen feet from the table, just off the edge of the concrete.

A deep voice said something in Russian, and a tall man dressed in a clean shin-length robe called a *perahan* stepped from the doorway. He wore a black turban common to the Taliban. His beard, black as the turban, was long and full. Stylish glasses with an orange Nike swoosh on the earpiece perched at the end of his nose.

Dovzhenko said something to him in Russian, prompting the man to turn to Jack.

"I told him we must get you cleaned up," he said in a decidedly British accent.

"You speak English," Jack observed.

"I do," the man said. He gave a quizzical look. "My men told me you spoke English. So you are not Russian as well?"

"He is," Jack said. "I only just arrived." He thought of mentioning Dom but decided against it. If he was dead, he was dead. There was no sense telling these guys they'd forgotten one of their kidnap victims.

"Ah," the man said. "I see. I am sorry for your treatment. A necessary evil." He looked more closely at Jack now, and then turned to bark more orders at one of the other men. "Do you need to sit down?"

"I'm fine," Jack said. "Please see to my friends."

The man sighed and then stepped back inside his house. He returned a moment later with a tortoiseshell hand mirror, which he held up in front of Jack's face.

"You may feel fine," he said. "But I can assure you,

that is only because you are in shock. We will see to your wounds at once." The man gave him a benevolent smile. "After all, you are not worth much to me with your ear half torn from your head."

Ryan didn't know which bothered him more, the fact that he'd crawled through the nasty muck of the ditch with his ear half torn off or that this man spoke so glibly about how much he was worth on the slave market. He couldn't shake the image of Dom half buried under the burning wreckage, which made his own troubles seem minuscule.

Their oddly benevolent captor identified himself as Omar Khan, a local businessman and a member of the Taliban. He and his men had killed many Americans, he informed Jack with a serene smile, but that was only business—hence his title of businessman. But this was fortunate for Jack, Omar Khan explained. His men were trained fighters, and as such were well acquainted with all manner of field medicine. According to Omar, he himself had sutured on any number of ears.

The Taliban boss was indeed a skilled surgeon. He offered Jack some raw opium to dull the pain. Jack declined and was sweating profusely by the time the suturing was complete. Ysabel assisted, passing scissors and antiseptic pads when Omar asked for them. She said nothing, but watching her in the firelight calmed Jack and gave him something to concentrate on—that and the satellite phone that hung from Omar's belt. She was making some sort of plan. He could see it in her eyes.

An hour later found Jack's head wrapped in a large

gauze bandage and everyone sitting on cushions in front
of a feast of saffron rice, peppers, noodles, and grilled
mutton. Omar seemed pious enough but allowed Ysabel
to eat with the men as long as she covered her head and
did not speak unless he spoke to her. He did make sure
she was seated nearest to him—which put her across the
corner of the table from Jack. Omar sat between the two
of them, barely concealing his lascivious looks.

The surgery had robbed Jack of an appetite, but he ate
anyway, not knowing when he might get to eat again.
Ysabel and Dovzhenko did the same.

"So," the Russian said. "Do you have buyers already?"

Omar tore his gaze off Ysabel and dipped a morsel of
lamb in yogurt before popping it into his mouth. He
nodded thoughtfully, chewing his food before he spoke.
"Women are easy to sell. If they look like this one, then
it does not even matter much if they are virgins." He
shrugged. "If she were, I would keep her for my own
wife, but I can see in her eyes that she is not." He cocked
his head to one side, struck with a sudden thought. "Is
she married to you?"

Ysabel looked up at that.

"What if I said yes?" Dovzhenko said.

"What you are thinking is true enough," Omar said.
"It would not matter. In any case, my men are working
out a ransom for you as well. Russians are a touchy business, but the American will bring a fine reward."

Movement at the edge of the concrete patio caught
Jack's eye. A small, gray gerbil, the kind American kids
kept as pets, scurried in stops and starts toward the rugs,
drawn forward, no doubt, by the smell of rich food.
Omar threw the trembling little animal some rice, coax-

ing it closer. They'd apparently played the game before, and Omar was soon able to scoop the little thing up in his fist.

He nodded to one of his men to add wood to the fire while he caressed the little creature in his palm as the flames grew.

A stricken look crossed Ysabel's face.

Jack frowned. "You're not going to throw it in, are you?"

Omar chuckled. "That would be a waste," he said. "But I am going to make a point." He held the gerbil up in one hand and with the thumb and forefinger of the other snapped the poor thing's rear legs like matchsticks.

Jack winced in spite of himself. He'd never been a lover of rats and their kin, but hurting one just to hurt it made him want to shoot this guy in the face.

Instead of throwing the squeaking animal into the flames, Omar pitched it against a rock planter at the edge of the veranda. Light from the fire cast a long shadow off the crippled gerbil as it dragged itself toward the darkness, crying in distress.

The snake appeared as if by magic, slithering out from between the rocks, tongue flicking, crawling slowly but steadily toward the doomed gerbil.

Ysabel gasped.

"You are evil," she whispered.

Jack had already decided he would not let the man hit her, even if it meant getting shot in the head.

But Omar just gave a dismissive laugh. "A saw-scaled viper," he said, as if watching a nature documentary. "Very deadly. They happen to love my beautiful gardens. In this country, if you find a cool place with shade, there is a very good chance something deadly has found it first."

The viper struck quickly, and then settled back to wait for the gerbil to die. Already stressed from the broken bones, it staggered only a little before falling over. The snake approached tentatively, and then began the laborious process of swallowing its meal headfirst.

"I am fully aware that you are all thinking of escape," Omar said. "But your nearest help is miles away and these snakes are everywhere. You would not even make it to the edge of my gardens. I would hate to lose such a valuable investment to the venom of a viper."

Ysabel looked at Jack and then tugged at the collar of her dress. Omar's cruelty with the animal had pushed her into action. She had a plan, all right, and now he knew what it was.

48

Clark's safe house was on a wooded farm outside Montijo, Portugal, across the Tagus River from Lisbon. He made a call to a friend in the Agency to square the use of the facility, cashing in on a little of the mysterious nature of his reputation. He wasn't active anymore, not on the books anyway. But it was not at all uncommon for active case officers to use trusted retired case officers as instructors or for certain jobs for which they had a particular acumen. The kind of expertise that might be required at a rural farmhouse had Clark's name written all over it.

It was not a long drive from Alpalhão by American standards, just over a hundred miles, and they made it in two hours. Chavez was behind the wheel, with Clark riding in the backseat with a sedate da Rocha. Midas and Adara followed. At first blush, it seemed the arms dealer was distraught over the death of Lucile Fournier, but the more he sobbed, the more it became clear that he would miss her skills far more than he would miss any relationship.

Before meeting Ding Chavez, Clark had frequently worked alone—the pointiest bit at the tip of the spear. But no matter how alone he was, there were always people on whom he depended. People he cared for and who cared for him. He would have died a long time ago if not for Sandy—just burned to a charred crinkle and floated away on the wind. He'd never admit it, but Ding was more like a brother than a son-in-law. If anyone had told Clark he'd be content to have his daughter marry a former gangbanger from East L.A., he'd have put a boot in their ass. But this particular former gangbanger spoke multiple languages, held a couple of advanced degrees, and, more important, busted his ass to do the right thing, all day, every day.

In some small way Clark felt sorry for da Rocha. Guys like him didn't have friends. He had employees, and he had contacts. Lucile Fournier had been neither trusted companion nor comrade-in-arms. She'd been a tool in his hands, a means to an end. This asshole was all about himself—which made the people in his orbit all about themselves. In the end, it made Clark's job all the easier. People fighting for a cause were more difficult to turn. They had to be broken down, and even then, the most zealous might never break, they just came to terms. But if a man's primary goal was money, then money or the idea that they would lose the money they already had would turn them.

Clark let da Rocha stew in his own juices during the drive, asking no questions and ignoring him when he tried to start a conversation. By the time they reached the safe house, the man was ready to vomit information.

Da Rocha's hands were flex-cuffed in front, one restraint around each wrist. A third restraint connected these two cuffs to a chain that was secured around his waist with a padlock, enabling him to raise food or a cup to his lips if he hunched over. Clark shoved him onto a dusty, overstuffed couch that would be hard to get out of without the full use of his hands, and then pulled a dining room chair up close so they were knee-to-knee.

"I gotta tell you," Clark said. "I expected your house to be bigger."

Da Rocha looked up at him, squinting a little, as the room was dim.

"What?"

Clark continued. "I mean, you travel around Europe, wheeling and dealing in illegal weapons, and you're living in a couple-hundred-thousand-euro villa with a handful of bodyguards who might as well have laid down and died for all the good they did you."

Clark stopped and gave time for the silence to close in.

At length he said, "I'm just saying I thought a man like you would have a fortress. Dealing with Russian GRU is dangerous business."

"They were not GRU," da Rocha scoffed.

"Sure they were," Clark said. "I could smell it on them."

"Are . . . are you . . . CIA?"

"Sadly for you," Clark said, "I am not. We have the same interests, to be sure, but I'm not bound by Agency rules."

Da Rocha sniffed, then turned to wipe his nose against his shoulder, like a bird preening its wing. He looked up suddenly. "And what if I tell you everything I know?"

Clark shrugged. "I honestly can't say what's going to happen after this."

"I assure you, I have information you will want."

"We have your computer," Clark said. "Maybe that is enough."

"But that is only part of it," da Rocha said. "By the time you figure it out, it will be too late."

Clark kept his face passive. This guy was trying to bait him.

"I need certain assurances," da Rocha said.

"Specifically?"

"My freedom."

Clark raised an eyebrow. "Depends."

"My money?"

"Your accounts don't reflect any money."

"You could help me get it back from the Russians."

"That's not going to happen," Clark said. "How about you tell me what you know and you might not end up in a very small cell under the Colorado desert for the rest of your life."

"So you are with the U.S. government," da Rocha said smugly.

"Nope," Clark said. "I just believe in doing my civic duty. How about you think about what's really important to you." He stood, then threw the guy a bone. "You seem like a pretty smart man."

"Missiles," da Rocha said.

"I know that already," Clark said. "You're an arms dealer. That's what you deal in."

"Not the kind of missiles you think," da Rocha said.

Clark sat down but said nothing. More often than not, silence was the best tool for extracting answers.

"I have no proof," da Rocha said. He sighed, relieved to be telling his story. "But I believe as you do that those men were officers with the GRU. I had heard, through the grapevine, so to speak, that they needed someone for a very large deal. I . . . I suppose you could say I courted them—as any businessman would."

"Taking out the competition," Clark said.

"In a word. If they were GRU, then the Russian government used me as a go-between to do business with Iran."

In the corner of the room, Ding Chavez sat up a little straighter.

"Russia makes no secret of the fact it supplies weapons to Iran," Clark said.

"Nuclear weapons?" Da Rocha leaned back, sinking into the soft cushions. "The Russians I dealt with obviously want the world to think the weapons came from a third party. I would imagine they have already concocted a story about them being stolen. They promised future business, but I see now that was a lie to keep me compliant until they killed me."

"You're certain the missiles are nuclear?"

"Certain enough," da Rocha said. "Two 51T6 ABMs—you call them Gorgons—and their launch controllers. My people took possession of them in Oman and transported them to Iran."

"Where?"

"These missiles are very portable," da Rocha said. "They have nowhere near the range to reach the United States. But it is not too much of a leap to guess Iran might use them against any number of American bases. They could strike Israel from western Iran."

"Where are they?" Clark asked again.

Da Rocha swallowed. "I must have assurances."

Clark gave a slow nod. "Okay," he said. "I assure you that if you don't tell me where you dropped these weapons in the next fifteen seconds I will cut off your feet. After fifteen seconds, even if you start to talk, you will lose at least one."

"Sir, I . . ."

"Eight seconds."

"All right, all right."

"That's not an answer," Clark said. "Four seconds."

Da Rocha spilled the information. "But they are not there," he said, starting to sob again. "I am sure they have been moved."

Clark snapped his fingers. "The names and contacts of your people. The ones who delivered the missiles to Iran."

Da Rocha wiped his nose on his shoulder again, becoming more animated. He swallowed hard. "I will give them to you, but considering what the Russian bastards had in store for me, I feel certain my men are already dea—"

Ding's phone rang. He stood when he answered it, listened for a moment, and began to pace. Clark could hear only half the conversation, but it was clear from Ding's tone that it was bad.

Ding motioned for Clark to come to him out of earshot. Midas and Adara moved closer, guarding da Rocha.

"What's up?" Clark asked.

"It's Dom," Ding said. "He's hurt pretty bad."

Clark felt as if he'd just taken a sledgehammer to the gut. "Jack?"

Ding shook his head. "Missing. Dom counted five guys, probably Taliban, but possibly ISIS. They hit the van with a sticky from the back of a motorcycle. Our guys were on the way to a safe house. Dom says Ryan was ambulatory when he was taken."

Clark looked across the room at Adara. She couldn't hear the content of the whispered conversation, but the frown on her face said she knew it was about her boyfriend. To her credit, she stood her post beside da Rocha.

"And Dom's injuries?" Clark said.

"Sounds bad," Chavez said. "Third-degree burns, broken ribs, ruptured eardrum. An Afghan pistachio farmer found him wandering on the side of the road a couple of hours ago and took him to the NATO base outside Herat. It only has a small hospital, so they're arranging transport to Ramstein."

Clark closed his eyes, concentrating on his breathing. "Get all the information you can. It's a shitty deal, but I need to let someone know about the possibility of nuclear missiles in Iran. When I'm done with that, I have to get word to the President that his son has been kidnapped."

49

Jack caught Dovzhenko's eye, glancing quickly at the two Afghans who stood over him. The Russian gave a slight, he hoped imperceptible, nod. Both men had been around the block enough to know they'd need to make a move soon or not at all. In his bravado, Omar had released them from their bonds so they could eat. Jack's bloody face and the entire group's generally hammered look certainly made it seem like five guys with rifles were plenty to tamp back any aggressive action. They would be tied again when the meal was over. Jack was certain of that.

There was a chance there were more guards in the house, but no one had been summoned during the meal or the procedure to reattach Ryan's ear. Men like Omar were big summoners, calling servants for this or that to help them feel important. He clearly got few visitors, and this was the rare opportunity for him to put on a show for the foreign devils. Jack felt reasonably sure they were looking at the whole cadre.

The five visible guards were posted around the low table, surely hungry themselves and grumbling inside about why the prisoners got to eat at all, let alone first. Jack could see the two nearest Dovzhenko as well as one on the far side of Omar and Ysabel. The Russian had eyes on the two behind Jack.

Jack gave Ysabel another nod. She blinked and then extended three fingers. She folded one, then the second—a countdown. As she folded the third finger, she began to gag. She fell to the side, clutching her throat with one hand while she pulled the hem of her skirt up with the other, exposing her calf and then her thigh.

Every man there looked down, entrapped for an instant by their accidental exposure to Ysabel's smooth olive flesh. Ryan spun, throwing his shoulder into the knee of the guard nearest him. Ligaments tore and the leg gave way, bringing the man and his Kalashnikov down. Ryan snatched the rifle, still attached to the wounded man by a sling around his neck, and flicked the lever down one notch south of safe to full auto, firing as he rolled. Three rounds slammed into the remaining guard who towered above him, dropping the man before he could bring up his own rifle. The first man attempted to pull away now. Ryan adjusted fire, turning the muzzle of the gun inward, shattering the man's shinbone with two rounds. The guard yowled in pain, grabbing at what was left of his leg. Ryan swatted the arm out of the way and pulled the sling over the screaming man's head. More shots popped over his shoulder. He hoped they were being fired by Dovzhenko. Ryan turned in time to see a third guard bringing a rifle up to aim at his chest. Dovzhenko put a single round in the side of the man's head.

The last guard down, both men turned to find Ysabel had jumped on top of a writhing Omar Khan. She stabbed him over and over in the neck and face with a greasy lamb shank, screaming and sobbing with each thudding blow. Like most meat in the Middle East, the lamb carcass had been hacked into portions with an ax, leaving a jagged bone that provided a sloppy if serviceable weapon.

Strings of black blood flew through the night air each time Ysabel drew back the lamb shank, spattering her face and chest. Omar ceased to struggle, eyes locked open, but Ysabel continued her assault until Jack reached out to put a hand on her shoulder.

"It's me," he said. "We got them. We're good."

Ryan felt his own legs begin to buckle. He took Ysabel by the shoulders and helped her off a lifeless Omar, and the two of them slumped to the cushions together. Rifle bullets at close range tended to rupture skulls like melons. Limbs were left hanging on by thin pieces of tissue, if at all. The carpets and cushions were soaked in blood and gore. Jack tried to cover Ysabel's eyes, but she pulled away.

"It is much too late for that," she said.

Two more shots popped from inside the house. The Russian came out a moment later carrying a rifle.

"The cook," Dovzhenko said matter-of-factly. "Thought he might try his luck with a butcher knife."

Jack took a deep breath. "Any idea where we are?"

"We came west," Dovzhenko said. "We had perhaps two hours until dark when we were taken—and it was dark by the time we arrived here."

Jack grabbed the satellite phone off Omar's body, taking a moment to search for and find the key ring they'd taken. A flashlight might come in handy in the not-too-distant future.

Ysabel found the headscarf Omar had given her on the

ground and used it to dab the blood from her face. "A two-hour drive west from the attack would put us over the Iranian border."

Dovzhenko shook his head. "Eastern Iran is plenty lawless but still receives far more patrols than western Afghanistan. We must have turned off one way or another."

Ysabel got to her feet with an exhausted groan and tiptoed over the pools of blood to step off the veranda so she could look up at the night sky.

"Hey," Jack said, moving up beside her. "What about the vipers?"

Ysabel rolled her eyes. "That poor little gerbil crawled out from under this porch. I doubt it was sharing its home with a snake." She turned to Dovzhenko. "Would you turn off the lights?"

He did, and then joined them at the edge of the concrete pad.

An incredible carpet of stars appeared as their eyes adjusted to the darkness. Ysabel pointed beyond the dying fire with her open hand. "That faint triangle is the zodiacal light."

"Sounds like the name of a cult," Jack said.

Ysabel elbowed him in the ribs. "For one who is so smart, there are so many things that you do not know. The zodiacal light is a reflection on the dust and ice particles within the sun's path."

"Which means that's roughly west," Jack said, trying to redeem himself.

"Exactly," Ysabel said.

"Zodiacal light," Dovzhenko mused. "Didn't Muhammad use that to determine the timing of the five daily prayers?"

"Full marks," Ysabel said. "Finally a man who studies something besides guns."

"Hey," Jack said. "You called me, remember. If that's west, then we were heading north for most of the time after I woke up. You think we're north of Herat?"

"We crossed some mountains," Dovzhenko said. "I felt the truck climbing."

"There is a high ridge that runs north and south just below Herat," Ysabel said. "I doubt they took us across the Islam Qala Highway. There is not much above it anyway by way of roads, and it would mean greater risk. No, they most likely skirted Herat and stayed south of the Islam Qala. The Hari River valley is a sort of greenbelt. I imagine we're somewhere along that. I'll be able to tell more once it gets light."

"That's pretty damn impressive," Jack said. "You're like some Iranian Daniel Boone."

The adrenaline of the fight gave way to the knowledge that they needed to put some distance between themselves and this carnage before Omar's business partners decided to show up. But first Ryan had to make a call.

Omar's computer was in the front of his house, in a small office with tapestries of Persian poetry on starkly white walls. A simple wooden desk faced a window overlooking the tree-lined approach to the estate—beautiful and practical.

"He's a smuggler," Jack said, "so he'll take precautions with his communications. Satellite phones are too easy to intercept."

"Perhaps he pays many bribes," Dovzhenko said.

Jack picked up a white plastic box about the size of two decks of playing cards.

Dovzhenko nodded. "A Thuraya Wi-Fi hotspot."

Ryan connected Omar's sat phone to the device.

Dovzhenko said, "You know a call from this device can be easily tracked."

"The signal can," Ryan said. "But I'm betting this guy's got a method to make it more difficult for anyone to get the content."

He hit the space bar on the open laptop and got the password prompt, and then slid open the lap drawer on the desk. It didn't take long to find what he was looking for. Omar was a proud man—haughty enough to want to show off even to his captives. A Khan—he thought of himself as an emir, a king, surrounded by a phalanx of armed guards, secure from intrusion, when in reality he was a dope-smuggling thug who couldn't remember his password.

Ryan stepped aside to let Ysabel decipher the Persian script on a worn spiral notebook and log in.

"He'll be using a virtual private network," Ryan said.

Ysabel glanced up at him. "You think?" She referred to the list of passwords in the drawer. Her fingers clicked on the keyboard. "He's got all the passwords written here for his VPN and a VoIP."

"The quality of the voice call will be poor," Dovzhenko said. "And, as I said before, the satellite signal will still be visible."

Jack nodded. Apps like Flying Fish or any number of government hardware options could be used to sniff out radio or the poorly encrypted GPS signals from a sat phone. He'd done it many times himself.

"True enough," Jack said.

"I will gather three rifles," Dovzhenko said.

"And I'll find us some keys to a vehicle that's not a Bongo truck," Ysabel said.

Jack tapped a telephone number into the computer. "Okay. I'll make my phone call and get us a ticket somewhere a little less intense. We'll be on the road before anyone has a chance to track the signal."

Dovzhenko went out back while Ysabel disappeared down the hallway toward the front of the house.

Fifty-five kilometers to the east, across the braided streams of the Hari River on the outskirts of the village of Jebrael, Parviz Sassani wiped the blood from his hands with a damp cloth he'd taken from the dead woman's kitchen. The IRGC man with him crouched beside the bodies of the woman's teenage boys, looking for evidence in the eldest one's pockets. The little girl was much too young to have anything of value.

By the time IRGC contacts in London learned that Ysabel Kashani was not there, Sassani had already determined that she worked for the UNODC in Afghanistan. A search of flight manifests departing Tehran revealed Erik Dovzhenko had fled shortly after the raid on Maryam Farhad's apartment. Sassani chuckled softly. The traitor had been at the airport during their phone conversation. IRGC contacts in Dubai and Kabul helped trace the Russian to Herat.

A quick flight over via IRGC aircraft and a few questions around the UNODC office led Sassani to Fatima Husseini, a frequent volunteer and staunch defender of Kashani and her program. According to neighbors in Jebrael, the Husseini woman had walked several kilometers

AFGHANISTAN–IRAN BORDER

TURKMENISTAN

Caspian Sea

N

Mashhad

Tehran

Islam Qala Highway

Herat

IRAN

AFGHANISTAN

IRAQ

PAKISTAN

Persian
Gulf

SAUDI
ARABIA

BAHRAIN

QATAR

U.A.E.

Gulf of Oman

© 2018 Jeffrey L. Ward

just to warn her friend of possible trouble with smugglers. Two of those smugglers were later found in Kashani's office, one dead, the other brain-addled. It was an event big enough to cause a stir even in a war-torn part of the world like Afghanistan.

Fatima Husseini had been no help at all, gnashing her teeth and refusing to betray her friend until Sassani had been forced to threaten the lives of her children. Only then did she tell him of the smugglers, and the man who she was sure employed them—an opium smuggler named Omar Khan. Fatima had no idea where Khan lived, but his brain-addled man was still in the hospital, he would know.

They were close now. Fatima had told him as much before she died. Sassani tossed the bloody rag onto the floor and motioned for his lieutenant to come with him. If anyone knew the whereabouts of Ysabel Kashani, it would be Omar Khan.

50

C lark stood across the room, breaking the news about Jack to Gerry Hendley when Ding's cell phone began to buzz. The voice on the other end made Chavez feel like all his blood drained into his legs.

"We thought you were dead," he said, and then snapped his fingers to get Clark's attention.

Clark held up a hand to tell him to wait.

"It's Jack," Ding said, getting an immediate response.

"I'm going to call you right back," Clark said into his phone. "Sounds like we have a call from Junior . . . Yeah. I'll get you a sitrep as soon as I find out what's going on."

Chavez put Ryan on speaker and the two men went into a back bedroom, out of da Rocha's earshot.

"Speak to me, kid," Clark said. "You all right?"

"We're all alive and free," Ryan said, his voice disembodied, slightly garbled. "But it was touch and go for a while there." He paused, sounding like he was getting choked up. "Listen . . . I have bad news."

"Dom's fine," Clark said. It was one thing to joke, but never about the life of a teammate and friend. "He called us about a half-hour ago from an Afghan Army hospital near Herat. He's got some serious burns but he assures us nothing life threatening. Adara talked to him and threatened to kick his ass if he died. I'd imagine he'll be on his way to Ramstein any minute now."

The relief in Ryan's voice was audible.

"Listen," Clark said. "We've had a couple of significant developments in this end. What kind of a line are you on?"

"VoIP," Ryan said. "I'm anonymized, and I think encrypted, but we're on a satellite link so I have to hurry."

"You think?" Chavez said.

"I can't read Farsi," Ryan said. "But I'm pretty sure."

"That'll have to do," Clark said. "NSA's probably the only ones listening in anyway and they'll know all this soon enough . . ."

Clark gave Ryan the full rundown on the Gorgon missiles, and their last known location in Iran.

"The Russians . . . or at least some Russians, are complicit in this caper," Chavez said. "See if your guy knows anything about where these Gorgons are supposed to go."

"He's right here," Ryan said. "And he looks as stupefied as I am."

"I thought as much," Clark said. "Our guy says they were delivered to an airfield in northeast Iran, near the city of Mashhad. Makes sense. IRGC rocket forces have a missile base there."

"Mashhad . . ." Ryan paused for moment, then said, "That's only a hundred and fifty miles from where we are. We'll check it out."

"Go to Iran?" Chavez said with an emphatic shake of his head. "Not a chance."

"John," Ryan said. "I'm here and ready to go. If the Iranians have nukes then we have to find out where they—"

Ryan stopped abruptly while someone, likely the Russian, talked to him in the background. It was difficult to tell with the latent lag of the VoIP/satellite connection. He came back on a few seconds later.

"My friend on this end says he has a list of Iranian scientists with the potential to use as assets. A couple of them are in Mashhad."

Ding said, "Russian assets won't do us any good."

"He says these guys are vulnerable," Jack said. "It doesn't sound like they have any love for the Russians—just a price. Won't matter to them which way they turn." Ryan paused, listening again. "One of them has a sick kid in desperate need of Western medicine."

"That is promising," Clark said, conceding that much. Leveraging a child's illness was nasty business, but intelligence coups often hinged on just that sort of leverage.

"Then give me permission to go talk to him," Ryan said. "We can be in Mashhad by sunrise."

"I'm sure Iran has methods in place to deter the free flow of people across their border."

"No doubt," Ryan said. "But opium smuggling is big business here. According to Ysabel a large portion of the heroin going into Europe passes through Iran."

Chavez was unconvinced. "That just means the Iranian dope cops will be putting more pressure on the border. Last I read they've increased patrols and are even using drones."

"Shaheds," Jack said. "Ysabel just told me. They're basically knockoffs of our Predator. Her work for the UNODC gave her substantial insight into drug interdiction methods. So she knows the weaknesses."

"And what would that be?" Chavez asked.

"The wind," Ryan said. "And not just any wind. This is

nasty, dusty stuff, but it'll give us good cover. It blows here all summer, making border surveillance with UAVs problematic. It's called 'the wind of one hundred twenty days.'"

"Let's get off this line," Clark said. "Use your best judgment, but do me a favor and check in with me before you do anything rash. I don't need to tell you what kind of a shit storm you will stir up if you're caught in Iran without an entry stamp in your passport."

"Roger that," Ryan said. "Listen. I'm going to e-mail you a photo. It's from our Russian friend."

"All right," Clark said. "I have something else, but it's for your eyes only. Check your messages when you send the pic."

"Roger that," Ryan said. "Outa here."

Ryan logged on to his encrypted e-mail when he ended the call, adding another layer of security to the anonymized virtual private network. He included the link to the photograph of General Alov and the protesters Dovzhenko had put on eBay. A new message arrived from Clark as he was typing. Ryan read it twice, then put it in a virtual burn bag. Information was never really gone, but it could be overwritten so many times as to render it useless—until someone came up with a new program, or the person who invented the original revealed a back door at some hacker conference.

Ryan disconnected the sat phone and looked at the clock on the computer. "Six minutes," he said. "We should get on the road."

"Let me guess," Dovzhenko said. "Your people think I am a dangle and want to put me on the FLUTTER?"

Jack gave an amused nod. FLUTTER was the CIA code name for a polygraph. A dangle was an enemy intelligence officer who volunteered to work as an agent, but was, in reality, a double. All sides used them, so everyone was wary—which made for a tedious process when trying to discern if someone was truly going to switch sides or was merely being dangled by his own government to gauge intelligence capabilities and methods.

"They are wise to think so," Dovzhenko continued. "I would not trust you if the circumstances were reversed. Believe me, I would be glad to take a polygraph test."

"That's exactly what they had planned," Jack said. What he did not say, was the CIA, through Mary Pat Foley, had assigned Erik Dovzhenko the cryptonym—GP/VICAR. Ysabel was already on the books as SD/DRIVER. Each country had a two-letter digraph that changed periodically. At the moment, Russia's digraph was GP. Iran's was SD. These two-letter prefixes were attached to a code name, usually computer generated, and helped keep the individual cryptonyms categorized geographically. It did not matter that VICAR was helping Ryan on matters relating to Iran. He was Russian, so his cryptonym began with GP. It was a rare thing that an agent acting on behalf of the U.S. government ever knew his or her own cryptonym.

"So," Dovzhenko said, "what did they direct you to do? Pull out my fingernails?"

"I told them you'd fought beside me," Jack said. "If you wanted me dead, I think you could have let that happen already."

"Perhaps I wanted to interrogate you first," Dovzhenko pointed out. "And then kill you."

"Do you?"

"No."

"There you go, then," Jack said, checking his watch. The shock of the accident and the fight was beginning to wear off enough that he could think a little more clearly. He thought he heard a car door, and looked up at Dovzhenko. "Hey." He hissed, grabbing one of the Kalashnikovs. "Where's Ysabel?"

Major Sassani hated to backtrack, but sometimes the fastest distance between two points was not a straight line. He ordered his lieutenant to drive him straight from Fatima's hovel to the main Afghan Border Police offices in Herat.

Just as the U.S. Drug Enforcement Administration had agents in Mexico, Colombia, and Europe, NAJA assigned members of their antinarcotics squads and border guard to the Afghan National Police. The Iranian Cyber Police, more routinely occupied with cracking down on dissidents who attempted to circumvent government oversight of the Internet, also had a technician embedded in the Herat antidrug task force. If nothing else, Iranian law enforcement upset the Americans.

There was a good deal of friction between the regular Army and the IRGC inside Iran, but the Sepah were a powerful force that held a tremendous amount of sway over NAJA and, to a slightly lesser extent, the ANP. It took some time due to the late hour, but Sassani was eventually able to get the commanding officer to loan him five men, giving him a ten-man team, counting the three Iranian antidrug task force personnel and him and his lieutenant. Omar Khan was a known bandit, and everyone in the group was jumpy by the time they made the hour-and-a-half drive through a soot-black night to the smugglers' stronghold near Ghourian.

They met no resistance, and it soon became clear why. The officer from Iran's Cyber Police vomited on his own shoes when he saw the shard of lamb bone protruding from Omar's mutilated throat.

Sassani squatted at the edge of the blood-sodden rug to study the carnage. "Ysabel," he said.

The Afghan police captain's face screwed up in disbelief. "How can you be sure?"

"This man has been killed many times over," Sassani said. He stood up and wiped his hands on the front of his trousers, though he'd touched nothing. "Females are emotional creatures. They routinely find it necessary to overkill someone they hate or fear."

The leftover food laid out on the carpets was cool, but not yet too infested by insects. The ashes in the fire pit still gave off heat when stirred.

"They have not been gone long," Sassani said. "Places set for four . . . I wonder who else besides Kashani and Dovzhenko. Surely none of these bodyguards." The major thought on this while he walked through the house. "Seven dead," he muttered as he stepped over the body of what he suspected was the cook. The Russian was more of a man than he'd thought. He turned to the Iranian antinarcotics liaison, a swarthy little man named Malik with arms that looked powerful, if a bit too short for his body. "Please speak to your contacts at the airport," Sassani said. "These fugitives are extremely dangerous."

"Of course, Major," Malik said, but he made no effort to make the call.

"At once," Sassani prodded. "They could already be there."

"Yes," Malik blustered. "I will have to use the satellite phone from the truck."

"Satellite phone . . ." Sassani mused. He nodded to the desk in Omar's office. There was a letter opener, what looked like a functional Soviet F1 hand grenade, and several other knickknacks arranged around the edge of the desk. There was a clear space in the center where there had once been a laptop computer. "He would have used a satellite connection for the Internet. Would he not?"

The cybertechnician looked as if he was about to vomit again, but he'd regained enough of his wits to follow the rest of the group on the search of the house.

"There is no landline," he said. "So he must have."

"Very good." Sassani searched through the desk drawers until he found a file with instruction pamphlets for a Thuraya XT-Pro satellite phone and a Wi-Fi hotspot of the same brand. He turned to the Afghan captain. "Do you have Flying Fish or some other satellite-monitoring capability?"

The man shook his head. "We rely on the Americans for that technology."

"I do," the Iranian cybertech offered. "Not Flying Fish but something similar. We run it continuously, but due to manpower issues do not monitor it unless we are actively hunting someone."

"Outstanding," Sassani said. "Because I am."

"You are what, Major?" the Afghan captain said.

"Actively hunting."

51

"**I**s this conversation being taped?"

Senator Chadwick sat on the couch with her back to the Resolute desk, staring at the President through narrow eyes, like he might jump up at any moment and attack her.

"No," Jack Ryan said. "It's just you and me." He nodded toward the exit to the secretaries' suite. "There is a peephole in that door so people can look in to see if I'm busy. But no tapes."

"We'll see," Chadwick said.

"So," Ryan said, "I thought maybe you and I must have gotten off to a bad start somewhere."

"Nope," Chadwick said. "I just don't like you. You smell bad to me. Your arrogance rubs me the wrong way. I'm smart enough to know it doesn't play well with the media if I refuse a sit-down with the President, but that doesn't mean we have to be friends. So let's get whatever this is over with. I've got a lunch meeting with the chairman of Ways and Means."

"I see," Ryan said. He chose his next words carefully. "You and I both know that thick skins are a requirement in this business. I'm used to people not liking me. But I have to tell you, this incendiary dialogue about the flu vaccine is doing some real damage—"

"Good," Chadwick said. "I hope it cuts your political legs out from under you. If it leaves you unable to hand-pick your heir apparent when the time comes, then I've done my job. The last thing the country needs is another Jack Ryan at the helm when you finally lay down your scepter."

Ryan took a deep breath. "I was going to say this talk about hoarding vaccine is damaging the American people. False narratives and doctored videos very nearly caused a war in Cameroon."

"Well," Chadwick said, "you're the expert when it comes to causing wars."

Ryan waited a beat. He was human and didn't want to say something he would later regret. "What is it you're looking for?"

"I already told you," she said. "I want the American people to see you for what you are."

Ryan nodded at that. "I'm pretty sure they do," he said. "Warts and all."

"Oh, they will, eventually, if I have anything to say about it."

Ryan couldn't help but laugh at this woman's audacity. "I suppose we'll just have to plead our cases to the law of the land."

"That's perfectly fine with me," Chadwick said. "I feel sure the courts will—"

Betty Martin's voice came across the intercom, a blessed interruption.

"Mr. President. DNI Foley is here."

Betty didn't say it was urgent, but Ryan knew it was,

or she wouldn't have interrupted him mid-meeting unless he'd told her to—which he stupidly had not.

Chadwick took her cue and stood. "Well, this has been
real. But it sounds like you have another war to start."

Mary Pat stepped back and gave Senator Chadwick a
wide berth as the two women passed each other at
the doorway. A member of Ryan's "war council," as
Chadwick called it, the director of national security was
every bit as culpable as he was.

"I sure as hell hope you bring good news," Ryan said.
"I could use some about now."

Foley, who was rarely at a loss for words, took a deep
breath. "It's a lot better news than I had ten minutes ago,
Jack. But it's still pretty shitty."

The side door opened and Arnie came in, uncharac-
teristically taciturn. He glanced at Foley and gave her a
distinct *Have you told him yet?* look.

"Okay," Ryan said five minutes later when Mary Pat
had given him a thumbnail sketch. "Let's get the NSC
spooled up again, but I'd like State and Defense in here
ASAP."

"They're on their way, Mr. President," Foley said. "I
took the liberty of asking them to come to the White
House right away. Burgess has someone putting together
an executive summary, but I wanted to let you know
what I know as soon as practical."

She chewed on her bottom lip, obviously having more
to say.

"Go ahead, then," he said. "Tell me." Ryan's stomach
churned with worry—which was nothing new. No matter

how much he trusted Jack and Clark and the others, the world in which they operated was a cold and deadly place. Ryan had made enough calls to surviving parents and spouses to see it firsthand. Bullets didn't care who your father was. People died because they stepped left instead of right.

"He's okay," Mary Pat said, as if reading Ryan's mind. "But we do need to talk."

Burgess all but exploded into the Oval. "Mr. President," he said, breathless, as if he'd sprinted into the West Wing. "Major Poteet is across the hall in the Roosevelt Room at this moment, putting the finishing touches on some slides for you. He'll be in momentarily."

"Major Poteet?" Ryan said.

"He's our foremost expert on the state of Iran's defense capability at present. I find listening to him is like reading a year's worth of *Jane's Defence Weekly*, but I've warned him to turn down the firehose for this presentation."

Ryan stood up and walked across the office to his desk phone, asking Betty to order a coffee service. He had a feeling this was going to be a late night. "We might need a firehose," he said. "This whole thing is a convoluted mess. The Russians love their *maskirovka*, but this . . ."

Scott Adler came in next, followed by a middle-aged man in a white button-down and a pair of starched Wrangler jeans with razor-sharp creases up the front. He carried a closed notebook computer in callused hands.

"Please forgive Major Poteet," Burgess said. "He's on leave, but I happened to catch him stopping by his office after I got the call from the DNI. He worked on his presentation on the ride over."

"Major," Ryan said, shaking the man's hand.

"A real pleasure, Mr. President," Poteet said, his Texas accent as smooth as his hands were rough. "I apologize for being out of uniform."

"Not a problem," Ryan said. "I'm assuming you're up to speed."

Burgess spoke next. "He knows what I know, sir."

"All right." Ryan motioned for everyone to sit while he picked up the phone and spoke for a moment to his secretary. He replaced the handset and took his seat by the fireplace. "I've convened the full National Security Council in half an hour. I'd like to have a framework of ideas started before they arrive, so let's have it."

Poteet spent the next ten minutes going over Iran's known stockpile of rockets and missiles, as well as their abilities to counter any attacks from other countries. Ryan knew much of the information, but the briefing helped to solidify it for the here and now of this situation.

"So," Ryan said, leaning back in his chair and folding his arms in thought, "the Sejjil-2 is capable of reaching targets well over two thousand kilometers away?"

"That's correct, sir," the major said.

"GPS guidance?"

"Yes, sir. We believe it to be Iran's most technologically advanced missile at this point."

"The Russian Gorgons have a range of what, a thousand kilometers?"

"That's about right," Burgess said. "Sources within the Kremlin say more recent variants might give half again that range."

"I see," Ryan said. "That's still nowhere near the range of the missiles Iran already has in her arsenal.

Could they be planning to move the nuclear warheads from the Gorgons to the Sejjil?"

"That's certainly possible," Poteet said. "But it wouldn't be very smart. The nuclear warhead on the 51T6, or Gorgon, is certainly a plum for the Iranian missile forces, but I believe what they're after is the more sophisticated Russian guidance system. Iran has a way of grossly exaggerating the accuracy of their own armament."

"That's putting it mildly," Mary Pat said. "We have satellite footage of them using an explosive charge to make it look like one of their bad boys hit a target during testing three years ago."

"True enough, ma'am," Major Poteet said. "And that's not an isolated incident. We estimate the Circular Error Probable, or CEP, to be somewhere greater than five hundred meters on the Sejjil, even with the internal GPS."

"Half a kilometer isn't what I'd call precise munition," Ryan said.

"Iran has the largest complement of missiles of any country in the Middle East," Poteet said. "If you'll excuse the euphemism, they're fairly bristling with them. But none of them are precision instruments—yet. Sanctions certainly make it difficult for Iran to obtain certain electronics and the finely powdered metals they need for a consistent burn of their solid fuel. Up until now, even the Russians have balked at providing them with the most up-to-date systems. That said, I don't want to understate the threat, either. Lob enough explosive at a target and some of it is bound to fall where you want it to."

The steward from the Navy mess knocked, and then brought in the coffee Ryan had ordered. The conversation fell off until he left and shut the door behind him. As was his custom, Ryan served the coffee himself. It gave his hands something to do while his brain worked on a problem, a trick he'd learned from his father, who would often putter around in his woodshop while he stewed over a difficult murder investigation. He held a cup toward the major, a cube of sugar poised over it between the silver tongs.

"Black is fine, Mr. President," Poteet said, looking more than a little embarrassed at being served by the Commander in Chief. A relatively junior rank at the Pentagon, majors were often the aides who got coffee for generals.

Ryan passed him the cup. "Let's have some best guesses on where they want to hit with this Russian missile."

"The Gorgon is mobile," Poteet said. "So even with relatively limited range, they could reach any number of U.S. bases in central Asia, depending on where they launched from. Iraq is a viable target, as is Saudi Arabia or any number of Sunni countries."

"There's always Israel," SecState Adler said. "It's within range if they launch from western Iran. They've been rattling sabers at Jerusalem for decades. A nuclear warhead will be just the ticket for some of their hardliners."

"Maybe," Mary Pat said. "But that's less likely since they only have two."

"That we know of," Burgess said. "For all we know, they've been slipping missiles across the border for some time now."

"Maybe," Foley conceded. "But odds are someone in Russia would notice too many going missing. Even they have a finite number. Regarding Israel, there is a better-than-average chance that their Iron Dome defense system would stop one or two missiles during their terminal phase. We're not talking MIRVs here."

A MIRV was a multiple independently targetable reentry vehicle—several warheads on a single missile, maximizing the damage from each. A Trident II submarine–launched missile could carry as many as fourteen.

"Besides," Foley continued, "Israel has enough nukes of their own to turn Tehran and every other city in Iran into a lake of fire if provoked. Frankly, I think that's exactly what they would do if they were aware of this present state of affairs."

"You're right about that," Ryan said. "We know the Russians used this Portuguese arms dealer as a cutout for deniability, but what you said about Israel brings up a good point. The Gorgon has a ten-kiloton yield. That's roughly two-thirds of the bomb dropped on Hiroshima. A tremendous loss of life, but even two direct hits wouldn't be enough to cripple any of Iran's enemies."

SecDef Burgess gave a somber nod. "And a nuclear attack would cry out for an immediate response in kind."

Ryan took a sip of coffee. "So what's their game?"

Mary Pat gave a shrug, as if the answer was obvious. "What target would be of the most value to both Russia and Iran?"

Ryan gave a somber nod.

Burgess said, "We would. Mr. President, I know you want to discuss this with the full NSC, but I'd urge you to contact Yermilov and read him the proverbial riot act."

"I tend to agree," the secretary of state said. "There's value in letting Russia know we're aware of their duplicity. You might be able to shame them into remotely destroying the missiles—or, at the very least, rendering them incapable of launch."

"I get your point," Ryan said.

Arnie van Damm stuck his head into the Oval. "The chairman of the joint chiefs is here, Mr. President. The others are waiting in the Situation Room."

"We're on our way," Ryan said. He got to his feet, prompting everyone else to stand as well. "Major Poteet, excellent brief. Mind doing it again for the National Security Council? They can be a tough crowd."

"Not at all, Mr. President." The major closed his laptop. "I'd like to point out one more thing, sir. Apart from supplying Scuds and proxy combatants to places like Lebanon and Syria, Iran customarily uses its rocket and missile forces to intimidate. They *want* the rest of the world to know how many weapons they have and where they are pointed. The fact that they're keeping these nuclear devices a secret leads me to believe they intend to use them."

52

Jack and Dovzhenko watched in horror as the tail-lights on the vehicle carrying Ysabel grew smaller in the distance. The howling wind that blew outside Omar's compound had covered the vehicle's approach. The men, likely Taliban who'd come for Ysabel, had decided to cut their losses and run with the single prize.

Rifle in hand, Ryan ran back inside to grab the laptop and satellite phone while Dovzhenko kept an eye on the lights. Jack found the keys to the Toyota Hilux parked out front, and the pickup was bouncing down the road with no headlights in less than a minute.

Jack drove while Dovzhenko checked the weapons. Neither man spoke until the small station wagon turned off the road and parked in an alley behind a concrete building that looked like a mechanic shop at the far end of the block. Two men got out of the station wagon and shoved Ysabel into the shop. They left the door open to the night air.

Ryan parked the Hilux and eased the door shut.

"Let's go before they lock us out."

"Two with her," the Russian said. "There are probably more inside."

Ryan nodded. "This might get rough. Do you have a problem with that?"

Dovzhenko shook his head. "Do you? You are about to attempt a rescue of a woman you obviously have feelings for, going against an unknown number of assailants, in a place you have never been, with an untried rifle and a man with whom you have never worked."

Ryan was already creeping down the alley, rifle at low ready, scanning. "If you put it that way, this is going to be a cinch. You do know how to run your gun?"

"Russian babies sleep with a Kalashnikov, not a teddy bear. You did not know this?"

Jack rolled his eyes.

"Do you know what Russian intelligence officers think of American intelligence officers?" Dovzhenko asked.

"You got me," Ryan said, homed in on the building ahead.

"They think you are too good," he said. "That you excel at critical thinking, but are not . . . sociopathic enough to be as cruel as you should be."

"Yeah?" Ryan hissed. "Hide and watch. And anyway, you said 'they.' What do *you* think?"

"I think you simply know right from wrong," Dovzhenko said.

Halfway down the block, he slowed, leaning closer, whispering, "Your plan?"

Ryan eyed the Russian. This guy was a philosopher, and for the life of him, Ryan couldn't figure out if that was a good thing or a bad one under the present circumstances. "We're looking at a corner-fed room," Ryan said, stopping in the shadows of a head-high pile of trash, eyes still locked on the door. "That means we'll be able to look down the wall before going in. You know a technique called 'running the rabbit'?"

"Not the term," Dovzhenko said. "But I can guess. I run in and draw fire while you shoot the bad guys."

"No," Ryan said. "I run in and draw fire while we both shoot the bad guys. They should be focused on Ysabel so we'll have the element of surprise. We go in and shoot everyone who isn't her. You SVR guys get some hot-shit training in marksmanship. Right?"

"SVR is an intelligence organization. We are not commandos." He gave Ryan a sideways look. "But do not worry. I can shoot."

The windows at the rear of the shop were covered with wood, but the men ducked as they went by to be on the safe side. Ryan reached the edge of the door first. He began to inch sideways, the muzzle of his rifle pointing where he looked. Each shuffling step brought a tiny fraction more of the room into view without giving away his position. The eastern wall that ran down the side of the building directly in front of the door and to the right was clear. It had a window, but no doors, which meant the bad guys either were to Ryan's left or had gone through some other door in that direction.

A little farther, an inch at a time.

North wall—which was actually a set of rolling garage doors thirty feet away . . . clear.

Wooden toolbox in the northwest corner . . . clear.

Voices.

Metal lift rack in the center of the garage—but no vehicles, giving a clear field of fire.

Ryan froze as the shoulder of one of the men came into view. He was squatting with his back to Ryan, in the approximate center of the west wall. It was one of the men from the station wagon, which meant his eyes were not yet accustomed to the bright light of the garage. Ryan risked another half-step, farther into the fatal funnel of the doorway, bringing Ysabel into view. She was gagged and seated on the dirt floor, leaning against the west wall. She looked up and to her right, at someone who was just out of Ryan's view.

Ryan eased out of the doorway so as not to create a flash of movement.

Shoulder to shoulder with Dovzhenko, he kept his gun on the doorway. "At least two," he whispered, then quickly described the layout. Recon grew stale in no time and he wanted to move while the bad guys were in the same relative position as when he'd last seen them. "Not sure about this wall or the southwest corner." Ryan pointed, in case the Russian wasn't keyed in on his cardinal directions. "The guys closest to Ysabel have to go first. I'll take everyone north, working back to the center. You buttonhook and take everyone south—on this side. Our fields of fire will overlap in the middle."

"What is 'buttonhook'?"

"I go straight in the door," Ryan said. "You come in behind me, hooking around the left side of the door, engaging as I draw fire."

Dovzhenko gave a curt nod. "Understood."

"On three," Ryan said.

"On three," Dovzhenko repeated, bringing Ryan's anxiety level down just a little. He had done this before.

Ryan moved quickly but surely, making it a good fifteen

feet before anyone realized he was there. All eyes—and guns—trained on him as Dovzhenko came in behind him. AKs boomed in the enclosed space, snapping off the concrete-block wall. Ryan turned when he reached the half-way point, putting two rounds into the pelvis of the man on Ysabel's right as he brought up his rifle.

The angle put Ysabel between Jack and the bad guy to her left. Trusting Dovzhenko to take care of that one, Ryan swung farther left. A third target stood in the southwest corner, holding a video camera in one hand and a Kalashnikov in the other. Ryan shot him in the chest, then, using the muzzle rise of his rifle, followed up with shots to the neck and face. The last took off the man's black turban along with half of his skull.

This one down, Jack scanned to his right in time to see the other man near Ysabel fall under two well-aimed shots from Dovzhenko.

Ryan covered the far door. "Any more?" he shouted over the piercing whine in his ears.

Ysabel shook her head.

"We must go," Dovzhenko said, already helping Ysabel to her feet.

Ryan backed out, covering their exit, while Dovzhenko faced forward with Ysabel tucked in between them. Ryan grabbed three extra AK mags from one of the men, and a wood-handled knife from a table on the way out. He paused just long enough in the alley to cut Ysabel's hands free.

The shooting lasted less than six seconds from the time Jack had cleared the door. Just over a minute later, they were in the Toyota Hilux, heading northwest.

53

Hope was not a plan, but Jack and the others had little else.

Ysabel bounced like a nervous cat in the front passenger seat, hyped from being kidnapped twice in a row, and talked nonstop for the next twenty minutes. Dovzhenko drove, and she directed him onto a two-lane dirt path south of the Islam Qala Highway. Ryan took the backseat. They discussed a variety of options as they went—until the adrenaline finally wore off and Ysabel fell asleep.

Rock-strewn smuggling trails crisscrossed the desert, leaving law enforcement and military on both sides of the border guessing. Ysabel had warned of loitering un-manned aerial vehicles, jeep patrols, motion sensors, and cameras, but explained that graft was rampant and staffing was abysmally low. Beyond that, the wind rendered all of it nearly useless.

Crossing the border was the easiest thing any of them had done in the past day. The most difficult thing about it turned out to be putting up with the bumpy ride. The Wind of 120 Days began to blow in the early summer and didn't let up until the fall. It laid down some during the night, but was still stiff enough to cloud the air with dust that could be felt biting the skin. Every crack and surface inside of the Toyota was clogged and covered in a thin yellow patina. Jack had a chronic cough by the time they'd traveled the forty miles to rejoin the paved highway. Taybad lay just a few miles ahead. It was a small city by Iranian standards—around fifty thousand people—just large enough so strangers could blend in, but small enough that there were few people on the road at two o'clock in the morning. Unlike cities in America, it was almost completely dark.

Ysabel stirred when they hit smooth pavement, jolted by the sudden comfort of the ride. Arms over her head, she gave a long feline stretch, which did not go unnoticed by either man.

Dovzhenko took a chance and drove into a quiet neighborhood on the eastern side of town. Toyota Hilux trucks were common and Dovzhenko dropped Ryan off with a screwdriver from the glovebox so he could steal a local license plate. Islam's feelings about dogs made them few and far between in Iran, so he didn't have to contend with any barking while he unscrewed the plate. Dirt all but cemented the license plate to the truck's frame, but the constant moan of wind helped to cover any errant squeaks and clanks when Ryan pried it loose. With any luck, they'd be in Mashhad before the theft was reported.

The new plate attached to the rear of the Toyota, Dovzhenko left Taybad in the blowing dust. Ryan took a quick moment to send a flash message to Clark on the laptop with the satellite hookup. The signal was active for less than two minutes before he powered off the phone and closed the laptop. Headlights cut the blackness ahead and silence settled inside the vehicle.

Dovzhenko knew the name of the engineer they hoped to turn was Yazdani. He knew the hospital where Yazdani's son received medical treatments, but he had no idea where the man lived. They moved forward with only the vaguest of plans.

Pitching a foreign national was touchy, even if one had something tangible to offer, like the promise of medication for a sick child. Some people put patriotism above all else. Even those who might eventually come around had to leap over hurdles of conscience. That took time— something Ryan and the others did not have.

The pitch would have to be made at Yazdani's home, where the rules of Persian hospitality dictated he invite visitors in and offer them refreshment. Ysabel could use her credentials from the UN Office on Drugs and Crime at the children's hospital and, she hoped, find out where Yazdani lived. Then they would simply knock on the door. If he refused . . . Ryan didn't want to think about that.

But first they had to rest.

Dovzhenko knew a place, a woman who he'd worked with in the past, he said. The iffy friend of an unproven Russian spy didn't exactly fill Ryan with confidence. But his ear was starting to throb and probably needed to be looked at. Judging from the muddy slop he'd had to swim through to get out of the burning van, a double dose of antibiotics was in order. The worst part, at least in the near term, was the bandage around his head. Wounds said there'd been a fight, and fights drew unwanted police attention. It couldn't be helped, so he put it out of his mind. He had enough to worry about. Fatigue already threatened to lead to stupid mistakes, and in a country like Iran, they weren't likely to get many do-overs. The physical and mental stress of the past few hours had taken a tremendous toll on all of them.

Ryan leaned forward against the bench seat, resting his chin on the back of his hands. He told himself it was to stretch, but in reality, he just wanted to be as close as possible to Ysabel.

She'd removed the headscarf and now looked like the young woman that he'd once known. The years had aged her, but not in a bad way. If anything, she was more beautiful than before—especially in the eyes. The flippancy of her youth was gone, replaced with a mysterious gravity that made her difficult to read. "Thicker sauce," his mother would say. Life had a way of cooking you down. Jack thought of how they'd first met—right here in Iran, with her screaming up in that little sports car. He turned his head sideways, still leaning on his hands, his eyes playing sleepily over the tiny scars on her jawline and neck. It was difficult for him to distinguish his guilt from the fatigue that pressed him down.

Ysabel suddenly spoke, breaking the silence, causing both men to start.

"Does no one besides me have an issue with what we're doing?"

Dovzhenko looked across the front seat at her, then back at the road.

"It's dangerous," Jack said, "I'll admit. But I don't see a way to find the missiles without crossing the b—"

She cut him off. "I'm not talking about crossing the border. We are about to bargain with the life of a child. Doesn't that bother you?"

Jack took a deep breath. "It does," he said. "But we

didn't give him this disease. We're offering to help him if his father helps us."

"I don't like it," Ysabel said. "We choose to do what we do. This man, Yazdani, has no choice. If he wants to save his son he must commit treason against his country."

Dovzhenko gave a little shrug. "You could say he was helping his country. Nuclear weapons will only bring retaliation against the people. Yes, we are forcing his hand, but for a greater good. And the boy will get help."

"I know all this," Ysabel said. "But I still hate the tactic. We are predators, preying on this man's misery. If he does not help us, his son dies."

"Maybe," Jack said. "But we won't be the ones to kill him."

"No," Ysabel said. "His father's decision will."

"Hopefully," Jack said, "his father will decide correctly. It's a shitty business, Ysabel. But this is the way it works."

Ysabel turned suddenly to glare over her shoulder, her face illuminated in the green glow of the Toyota's dash lights.

"You should sleep," she said.

"I tried," Ryan said. "Can't."

"Then at least lean back," she snapped. "You are crowding me."

Ryan recoiled at the flash of emotion. He'd expected something like this when he first saw her in the airport, but not now, not after what they'd just been through.

"Are you okay?"

She twisted farther in the seat, shaking her head in disgust. "Just so you know, that is not a question women like to be asked. Ever."

Dovzhenko stared ahead, eyes fixed on the road.

"We've all been through a lot," Ryan said, his voice softer. He hoped it sounded less condescending. "In case you didn't notice. I honestly thought you might have discovered some new injury now that we've had time for the adrenaline to wear off."

"I am fine," Ysabel said.

"You?" Ryan asked the Russian.

"No problems here," Dovzhenko said without looking back.

Ysabel took several breaths, composing herself. "I . . . I nearly died, Jack . . . I mean—and you just stopped calling. Dropped off the face of the earth."

Ryan tried to think of a rebuttal, but there wasn't one, not a good one, anyway. Finally, he said, "I know."

The sun pinked the eastern horizon by the time they were just a few miles out of Mashhad. It was a city of almost three million people and traffic began to pick up. Headlights from the vehicles behind them threw Ysabel's face into shadows.

"I thought we had something," she said. "You and I."

"Your father made it pretty clear—"

"You're a grown man, Jack," she snapped. "Stop trying to put this off on my father. I know exactly what happened. I think you merely decided it was time to flip the pillow."

"I don't even know what that means," Ryan said.

"Flip the pillow," she said again. "You wanted something cooler, the other side of the pillow, different from anything I had to offer."

"That's rich," Ryan scoffed. "Your father surrounded you with SAS bodyguards and told me in no uncertain terms you were better off without me."

"I've seen you fight," Ysabel said. "You could handle a couple of SAS bodyguards."

Ryan fell back in his seat. The Toyota suddenly didn't feel like nearly enough real estate for him and this angry woman.

Dovzhenko drove on, the thump of traffic and Ysabel's breathing the only sounds.

Ryan gave a long sigh. "Things are about to get kind of dicey," he said. "You and I should probably clear the air of . . . whatever this is . . ."

"Or we could drive in silence," Dovzhenko said. "That would be fine as well."

Mashhad loomed in front of them. Ysabel stared out her window.

Jack was a fixer, like his dad. He felt sure that most any problem could be made better if properly hashed out. But Ysabel wasn't up for hashing anything this morning. And he was too exhausted to push it—without saying something he knew he would regret. He focused on Dovzhenko instead.

"Mind if I ask you a question?"

Dovzhenko's eyes flicked to the mirror again. "Go ahead."

"You were free and clear," Jack said. "You could have walked into the embassy in Dubai, or any other country, for that matter. Why come all the way to Afghanistan and then risk your life returning with us to Iran?"

"Guilt," Dovzhenko said simply. "It is the best compulsion of all, stronger even than revenge."

Ryan looked at the back of Ysabel's head and understood exactly what he meant.

———

Erik Dovzhenko's friend lived in a cramped apartment in one of the many poor neighborhoods in Iran's second-largest city. Shops selling large chunks of skewered lamb, called shishlik, catered to a constant flow of Shia pilgrims who made their way to the Imam Reza shrine a few blocks to the northeast. *First the shrine, then the shishlik,* the saying went.

Dovzhenko carried a duffel containing the rifles, unwilling to leave them in the truck. Ryan took care of the smaller leather briefcase with the laptop, Thuraya hotspot, and satellite phone. They had no other luggage.

Rickety wooden stairs ran up the rear of the apartment building from the deserted alley. The treads were painted black, but were well worn from constant use. It didn't take long for Jack to realize this wasn't just a fire escape. Dovzhenko stopped at the base and looked up at the barred window beside the door.

"Life has not been kind to my friend," he said. "But she will put on a happy face."

"I understand," Ysabel said.

Dovzhenko looked directly at Ysabel. "I hope you will not judge her too harshly," he said. "I will apologize in advance for her stories."

Ysabel gave a little shrug. "Is she . . . ?"

"A prostitute?" Dovzhenko nodded. "She was between the proverbial rock and the hard spot. Her husband divorced her and she—"

Ysabel raised her hand. "I am not equipped to judge other women. Especially not in Iran. The same clerics who would stone her to death for what she does are only too happy to be her pimps so long as she keeps the money coming in. I might have made similar choices had I not been born into a wealthy family."

Jack started to disagree but stopped himself.

A young woman with mussed hair opened the door, alerted by the squeaking stairs before the group reached the wooden landing on the second floor. The corners of her small mouth perked when she saw Dovzhenko, then she stepped aside, motioning them in before they were seen by too many nosy neighbors. Jack guessed her to be in her mid-twenties. She'd been asleep, and rubbed her eyes with the heel of her hand. She wore black yoga pants and a bright yellow peasant blouse that revealed her long neck and collarbone. The interior of the room was heavy with the smell of tea and talcum.

"Hello, Nima," the Russian said.

She kissed Dovzhenko on both cheeks. "You should have told me you were coming. I have nothing to offer you to eat." She began to putter around the kitchen, putting on the kettle for tea.

"We need a place to rest," Dovzhenko said. "We won't be here long." He introduced Ysabel and Jack, calling him Joe Peterson, then patted his friend on the shoulder, an extremely forward thing to do in Iran. "And this is my good friend Nima. Her family is from Azerbaijan, as is my mother. In truth, she is a distant cousin."

"Iranians treat Azeris like shit," Nima said. "We have to look after each other. Erik is half Russian, but I look after him anyway." She eyed Ysabel suspiciously.

"I love your blouse," Ysabel said, her sleepy smile breaking the ice immediately.

Nima tugged on Erik's arm. "Are you here to crack heads for the protests?"

Dovzhenko looked sheepishly at Ysabel and Jack. "I do not crack heads."

"I am only teasing," Nima said. "But the head-crackers are there, downtown. That is a fact. And I will be there, too, probably getting my head cracked with everyone else."

Dovzhenko frowned. "You should be careful. These people are serious. I understand the Ayatollah is coming to preach at Friday prayers this week."

"The Ayatollah." Nima spat on the floor. "Did you also hear that some mullahs went to the Ayatollah and told them he could be done with the Great Satan once and for all?"

Dovzhenko rolled his eyes in an unspoken apology.

Nima continued in passable English, as if she were recounting a news story and not a joke. "'Oh, Most Beneficent One,' the mullahs said. 'We have discerned that in order to drive the Great Satan from our lands, you must sleep with a virgin.' The Ayatollah thought on this for a moment and then, with his brooding frown proclaimed, 'I see that I must do this thing for the good of all. But I will only do it on three conditions. First, the chosen virgin must be blind, so she cannot see that it is I when she is brought to my bed. Second, she must be deaf, so she cannot recognize my voice. Third, she must have big breasts.'"

Dovzhenko gave an embarrassed smile.

"What?" Nima said. "My walls are thin. I heard you apologize to your friends for my stories, so I told a story. Besides, that one is very popular in Mashhad. Everyone here has heard it before." She gestured to the small couch and a pile of cushions in the corner. "You are exhausted. Please sit before you fall."

"Thank you," Dovzhenko said. "But I must ask, did you stop smoking?"

Nima hung her head. "I did not."

Dovzhenko looked like he might cry. "Good. Because I will go insane if I do not get a cigarette."

Nima reached to the cardboard box she used as a bedside table, and then threw him a pack. "Oh, Erik," she said, "you are already insane."

Jack sat on the edge of the couch, looking around the cramped room. The ornately stamped metal ceiling sagged low, making the room seem smaller than it was. The average Iranian made around two hundred and fifty dollars a month, and prostitutes fared much worse. Nima had very little in the way of material possessions but offered what she did have, giving Ysabel her bed, explaining candidly that she never slept on the sheets on which she worked. Ysabel said she was just happy to lie down anywhere. Ryan made do with the living room floor and was asleep seconds after his head hit the cushion.

In the small kitchen area across the room, Nima Hasanova quietly readied tea. She never had guests and wanted desperately for them to stay for a while when they woke up. Erik was snoring softly, an arm across his face. He was involved in something dangerous. It was written all over his face. Was it not her duty to protect him? But what could she do, a fallen woman. She laughed at that. Fallen woman. Women in Iran had to stand up before they had any room to fall. She eyed the leather case at his feet. Whatever Erik was up to, the answer must lie inside.

54

The engineer who'd been explaining the process to Reza Kazem smiled, seemingly grateful for the opportunity to be near him, and then excused himself to return to his duties. But for the buzz of activity around the missiles and transport trucks this hidden spot in the desert would have been a calm, almost religious place. Both men wore the green uniform and cap of the IRGC, part of what Kazem and his men had stolen from the storage depot north of Tehran. The remote location west of Mashhad hid their activity from the actual military, but the official uniforms would slow any police patrols who happened to approach. It was a big enough lie that few men would have the stones to challenge him directly. No one would want to step on the toes of an official action. Even another IRGC unit would want to check with higher authority before taking any action. Kazem had a small army of his own, nearly a hundred men, all of whom believed themselves patriots, revolutionaries against the revolution, hoping for a new Iran.

Kazem planned to give them one. Just not quite what they expected.

He was a physicist, so he understood the dynamics, if not the minutia of what they were doing. He had the woman for that. She was in her late fifties and carried herself with the arrogance of a man in charge, showing little deference to even Kazem. He didn't care. They needed each other—and mutual need brought a different kind of respect.

She was across the valley floor now, in the lee of a tall escarpment that shielded the trucks from the incessant wind. Wearing pants, her head uncovered, she shouted into her radio, holding it directly in front of her but away from her face—as if she did not quite understand how radios worked. That was the thing about geniuses, Kazem thought, the shine that came in one facet of their lives left other parts lacking. Dr. Tabrizi was among the most gifted mathematicians and aeronautical physicists in the world. She'd come within a mathematical breath of the correct solution for the Poincaré conjecture when she was an undergraduate at the University of Tehran, and might have solved it had the revolution not shunted women to the side of almost everything. She could, with nothing but pencil and paper, make the needed calculations to thread a needle with an antiballistic missile. And still, a simple mobile telephone baffled her. She could draw accurate pictures of radio waves and explain the science to them, but the buttons and knobs on the radio itself remained an uncrackable mystery.

The men on the crane and missile transport trucks leaned out the windows of their respective cabs, looking for relief from the verbal barrage of this crazy scientist. Kazem did not worry. One truck was already loaded, they only had to repeat the procedure.

Everything was coming together. Both launch tubes would be on the trucks before Ayatollah Ghorbani arrived. The tubes themselves had been relatively simple to acquire. Other missiles in Iran required launch tubes, and the manufacturing process was already in place. Orders and designs from the correct government department made it happen. The massive sixteen-wheel MZKT-79221 were also a straightforward purchase. Ubiquitous in the Red Square military parades of the Soviet Union, these huge missile transport trucks were now manufactured in Belarus under the Volat brand. As with much of anything worthwhile, the importation of these vehicles violated UN sanctions—but stripped of their sixteen wheels and broken down to the smallest components possible, they were much easier to ship illicitly than the Gorgons themselves. It took only a team of mechanics to reassemble the trucks, not a rocket scientist.

Kazem tamped back his excitement. Slowly but surely, this was all working out. He wished Ghorbani would have waited another day. But one did not argue with the likes of Ayatollah Ghorbani. Second only to the Grand Ayatollah himself, Ghorbani acted as his eyes and ears— and his contact with Reza Kazem. After all, the leader of the Islamic Republic of Iran could not be seen with the man the entire world thought wanted to bring it down.

The harsh chime of Sassani's mobile phone wormed its way into his dreamless sleep. The mattress in his Herat hotel room was too soft, but it was more comfortable than the couch in his office.

"It is up and running, Major," the voice said when he answered. "I apologize for waking you, but I thought you would want to know at once."

Sassani sniffed and then looked around the room, blinking away the memories of the day before. "What is up and running?"

"The satellite phone you ordered me to monitor."

Sassani sat up a little straighter at that. "At this very moment?"

"Yes," the technician said. "And we have audio. The caller is an Azeri woman, speaking to, we believe, her mother. The caller's name is Nima."

"Origination?" Sassani snapped. He was on his feet now, pacing at the foot of his hotel bed.

"She is calling from Mashhad, Major."

"Mashhad?" Sassani stopped in his tracks. "She is calling from inside Iran?"

"Yes, Major. It is difficult to pinpoint an exact address, but we are reasonably certain the phone is being used not far from the Shrine of the Imam at this very moment."

"Bracket in," Sassani said. "I want as close a location as you are able to give me."

"Yes, Major," the technician said.

"You say the speaker's name is Nima?"

"Correct," the technician said.

Sassani ended the call. He pitched the phone on the bed and rubbed his hands together, thinking. He wondered if Nima would make this easy, or difficult. Fatima had made it difficult. He sighed. Difficult was certainly much more interesting.

55

Something brushed Jack's elbow. His back was painfully knotted and stiff. The shoulder nearest the floor, wedged against something hard, throbbed with a sickening ache, like the time he'd wrenched it out of its socket. The touch came again, accompanied by a distant voice, Ysabel's voice. A dream, maybe? Surely he'd been asleep only a few minutes. Jack tried to open his eyes, but they were glued shut, refusing to cooperate. The pain in his injured ear came next, pulsing in time with his heartbeat. He wondered if that was a good sign or bad.

Ysabel spoke again, closer now, an urgent whisper, pushing aside the fog.

"Jack. Wake up."

Ryan sat bolt upright, searching the room to get his bearings. It took him a moment to remember where he was. Dovzhenko had heard the voice, too, and was up on one elbow, eyes flicking, listening.

"I'm sorry," Ysabel said. She'd showered and covered her torn clothing with a borrowed smock.

Jack saw Nima standing in the kitchen—which was really just a corner of the same room. She was dressed now, in a dark skirt and a knee-length khaki top that reminded Ryan of a cotton pillowcase. Steam came from a kettle set over the blue flame of a two-burner gas stove. People didn't make tea in the middle of an emergency. He rubbed his face, wincing at the jab of pain the movement caused his injured ear.

"Sorry for what?"

"Please don't be mad at her, Jack," Ysabel said. "She didn't know."

Jack stood on wooden legs, feeling a half-dozen more sprains than he'd felt the night before. Whatever this news was, he didn't want to get it lying down.

His neck felt as if someone had tried to twist it off his shoulders, and he was pretty sure he'd chipped a tooth. And that didn't even take into account the fact that his ear was hanging on by nine stitches of catgut put in by an opium smuggler. Old age was going to be a hell of a lot of fun—if he made it that far.

He looked at Ysabel and smiled in spite of the situation when he saw her. "What are you talking about?"

She nodded toward the satellite phone on the table.

A sudden chill washed over Jack. "What's this?"

Dovzhenko saw it, too, and jumped to his feet.

Ysabel gave a sheepish grin. "Nima's mobile phone is broken. She hadn't talked to her mother in months."

Jack took a couple of deep breaths, working to keep his voice calm. "Did she already make the call?"

Ysabel nodded. "She was talking when I woke up."

Jack had to concentrate to keep his voice at a whisper. "How did she—"

"She must have taken it from the briefcase while we were asleep," Ysabel said. "I checked the call log. It looks like she spoke for less than three minutes. She assured me she never mentioned us or said where she was."

Nima glanced up from the kettle. "I will pay for the call," she said. "I didn't think anyone would mind."

"No worries," Ryan said, though he had plenty. He changed the subject. "Did you sleep well?"

Dovzhenko was already tying on his boots. "Nima," he said. "You must leave at once."

She waved off the thought. "I have many appointments today," she said. "The call was only for a moment. I doubt even the Sepah-e Pasdaran are that all-seeing."

"Still," Ysabel said. "Erik is right. You should not take that chance."

"You all worry far too much," Nima said. "I will be fine. I promise."

Ysabel turned to Jack. "You should let me look at that ear before we go."

"Later," Ryan said, turning to head for the bathroom. "We need to go. Now."

D ovzhenko turned on the radio, filling the cab with techno-guitar music. Ysabel, who'd taken shotgun again, turned sideways to glare at him. He reached to turn it off, but not before a deep Persian voice came over the air, sounding somber and somewhat nasal, like a muezzin's call to prayer.

Ryan couldn't understand what was being said, but Ysabel sat up straighter. Dovzhenko shot her a glance, getting the gist of it. And then the traffic began to slow.

"What?" Ryan asked, leaning forward to rest on the seat.

Ysabel held up an open hand to shush him.

The speaker droned on for another fifteen seconds, and then the station returned to Persian pop.

"There are protests ahead," Ysabel said. "We will have to go around."

"Where ahead?" Ryan asked.

"Hard to know," Dovzhenko said. "It is difficult for protesters to communicate with phones and social media dampened by authorities. This announcer was helping, telling people where to show up, but he was interrupted in the middle of his report. Somewhere to the west of the city. That is not enough to know."

"The hospital is west of the city," Ryan said.

Ysabel tuned the radio past more music stations until she found another news program.

"Here," she said. She translated as she listened.

"This is a government radio station so the announcer is urging everyone to stay away. He assures law-abiding citizens that the authorities will be on hand to quell any violence on the part of the protesters."

"Or bring their own violence," Dovzhenko said.

Traffic was at a virtual standstill now.

Ryan had seen video of recent demonstrations. Tehran, Isfahan, Qom—all across Iran. With three million people, Mashhad had enough youth to pack the streets—and they often did.

The Hilux inched along, covering less than a mile in the next twenty minutes. Impatient drivers changed into and out of the lane ahead each time there was an opening. So far, there had been no place to turn off that was not also jammed.

They didn't see the policeman until they'd crested a small hill. By then, it was too late.

A young, clean-shaven man, he was dressed in the black knee boots of a motorcycle officer. His bike, a Chinese BMW knockoff, was parked on the shoulder of the roadway. Another motor officer worked the second lane, each of them scanning the interior of each vehicle, pointing, giving directions to avoid the protests ahead.

"The guns?" Dovzhenko asked without turning around.

"They're covered," Ryan said. "It's going to be tough to explain my ear."

"You don't speak Farsi," Ysabel said. "Your ear is the least of our worries."

The officer gave a friendly but official wave as he approached the driver's-side window.

"Okay," Dovzhenko said. "I will do the talking." He rolled the window down, giving Ryan a blast of sulfur fumes from the dirty gasoline manufactured in Iran.

The officer leaned down to look in the window, at which point Dovzhenko showed him a credential case and barked something to him in accented Persian. He was polite but curt, as if he wanted the officer to clear away the traffic for him.

The officer took the leather case and perused it for a moment before handing it back. He whistled to his partner, shouting something Ryan couldn't quite hear, let alone understand, before pointing to the shoulder of the road in front of the two bikes.

Ryan's stomach fell when he thought they were ordering the truck to pull over. But the officer held traffic long enough for Dovzhenko to inch over and speed along to the next exit, where he passed under the highway, to loop well south of downtown.

"What was that all about?" Ryan asked.

Dovzhenko released a long-captive sigh. "I showed him my embassy credentials and asked where the counterprotest was."

"Counterprotest?"

"Mullahs and other community leaders," Ysabel said. "They are paid by the government to march in counterpoint to these student-led demonstrations. A bunch of old men in white turbans as opposed to a bunch of youth in all manner of clothing. The Basij militia volunteers who aren't busy cracking the heads Nima mentioned will march with them."

"How did you know there would be a counterprotest?" Ryan asked. "Did the radio mention that, too?"

Ysabel shook her head. "There is always a counterprotest. The government makes certain of that." She covered a yawn, then pointed at the sign alongside the road. "The hospital is three kilometers away. Tell me again all that you know about this man Yazdani."

Ryan got in the front passenger seat while they waited for Ysabel to finish her work inside Akbar Children's Hospital. They parked the truck inconspicuously among the buildings of the nearby university. It was the first chance he and Dovzhenko had had to talk out of her presence when they weren't busy in hot pursuit.

"You did well back there," Jack said, his forebrain telling him he should try and break the ice. He was exhausted to the point where his skin hurt, irritable, and in no mood to be social. Still, whatever his credentials, this Russian spy had helped save Ysabel, and for that, Ryan owed him.

"As did you," Dovzhenko said. "You do not appear to be a . . . How should I say this? A garden-variety case officer for CIA."

"Thanks," Ryan said. "I guess. Look, you're eventually going to be debriefed by people well above my pay grade, but just so we're clear, you only know Ysabel because of a mutual friend."

Dovzhenko nodded. "There is no need to worry about my intentions toward Ms. Kashani. I was friends with a friend of hers. Our relationship goes no further than that."

Jack looked at him, thinking. He didn't say it, but those were the exact circumstances under which he and Ysabel had met—and become lovers. He hated to admit it, but the easy way she and Dovzhenko communicated with each other—absent screwed-up more recent events—seriously bugged him. *Knock it off, Jack,* he said to himself. *You stopped pursuing her. Let her do her thing now, whatever it is, and with whoever she wants to.*

"I'm not worried," Jack said. Then, for some inexplicable reason, he shot any possibility he had with Ysabel in the foot. "Dude, you're the one who should worry. You've as much as said you were in love with her best friend, and then, when she was killed, you tossed your own safety to the wind, and went out of your way to save Ysabel's life."

Dovzhenko closed his eyes, swallowing hard. "But you, you came without question when she called for help. Your ear was nearly torn off. Do not forget, you saved her from a kidnapping . . . two kidnappings."

"Yeah," Ryan said. "Forgive me for saying it this way, but you're heartbroken. I can't compete with that."

"Be honest," Dovzhenko said. "Are you really trying to?"

Ryan surprised himself with the answer—and how quickly he gave it. "No," he said. "No, I guess I'm not." He could almost hear John Clark's baritone voice. *You're finally growing up, kid.* Ryan banged his head softly against the side window, suddenly feeling like he'd shucked a tremendous load, despite the rest of the situation. "I just want her to be happy. Happy and safe."

"Happiness does not come from safety," Dovzhenko said.

"You got that right," Jack said, nearly jumping out of his skin when Ysabel knocked on the window.

"I got the address," she said, when he opened the door. She hooked a thumb over her shoulder so Jack would give back her seat. "What are you two talking about?"

"Nothing," they said in unison.

The New York Times had once described the White House Situation Room as a low-tech dungeon. The five-thousand-square-foot complex across from the Navy mess had seen considerable renovation since then. Co-axial cables and cathode ray tubes were replaced with Ethernet, secure routers, and flat-screen monitors, bringing it well into the twenty-first century, but it was still a dungeon as far as Jack Ryan was concerned. It was too maudlin to say aloud, but the decisions made over this conference table were rarely good ones. More often than not, people died—sometimes a lot of people.

The mood today mirrored his own—tense, agitated, spoiling for a fight—and no matter how hard Ryan tried, he couldn't seem to tamp it back. Most of the NSC assumed he was on edge because of the immediate danger of Iran having nuclear weapons. That was certainly a large part of it. They were aware American operatives inside Iran were about to try and turn an agent, but only Mary Pat knew of Jack Junior's involvement.

Ryan studied the flat-screen that took up much of the wall at the end of the table. It displayed a large topographic map of Iran. Major Poteet's tablet computer ran Pentagon encryption and, after some tweaking by the Air Force major serving as the IT specialist on watch, it was connected to the Situation Room system. Poteet used a stylus on the tablet to draw a white circle on the big screen around Mashhad and a smaller red circle around the 14th Tactical Air Base south of the city.

"We believe their radar defense systems reach out at least five hundred kilometers," Poteet said. "Satellite surveillance shows Mirage F-1EQ fighters as well as Shahab-3 and several advanced antiaircraft missile systems are based at this location." It wasn't Poteet's job to say whether or not an air incursion by the United States was feasible at this point, not with at least a dozen people who outranked him in the room. He gave the facts and let them ask questions, which they did. A lot.

Ryan waited for a lull and then looked at Mary Pat, who was seated halfway down the table next to the chairman of the joint chiefs.

"Remind me what NRO has flying over that part of the world."

Foley answered without referring to her notes. "USA161 will pass over again in seven hours. Mentor 6, an Advanced Orion bird, covers that area as far as SIGINT goes."

Advanced Orion, or Mentor, was a class of spy satellite

run by the National Reconnaissance Office. Unlike the Keyhole satellites in low earth orbit, which overflew a given location twice a day, Mentors were parked at various spots approximately twenty-two thousand miles above the earth's surface in geostationary orbit, gleaning signals intelligence such as telephone, radio, and television from an assigned location.

"We're working on the feed from the last USA161 pass so we're ready to do comparisons immediately."

Ryan made a note in his folder. "Let's get a couple more Sentinels overflying Mashhad." He turned his gaze to Air Force Lieutenant General Jason Paul, chairman of the joint chiefs. His background was in intelligence. He was a steady man who thought more than he spoke, and Ryan greatly respected his opinion. "Any new glitches in command and control?"

"No, Mr. President," General Paul said. "The Agency has logged several thousand hours in Iranian airspace. They suspect, but do not appear to know, the birds are up there."

In 2011, Iran claimed to have wrested control of an RQ-170 Sentinel that had violated its airspace. In truth, there had been a glitch on the U.S. end. The stealth technology rendered the bird invisible to Iranian radar, and they'd been unaware of its presence until the computer glitch. Unfortunately, they had been prepared to exploit it once they were. They also claimed to have reverse-engineered an RQ-170 of their own called the Saegheh, or Thunderbolt, but had yet to demonstrate they could utilize their clone to any effect.

"Very well," Ryan said. "I'd like pros and cons of both missile strikes and aircraft sorties within the hour. Let's be ready to act when the KH 161 or one of the Sentinels gives us actionable pictures." Ryan pushed away from the table. "Mary Pat, I'd like to see you in the office."

"How about the medication for the Iranian boy if his father flips?" Ryan asked, once they'd returned to the Oval. Both carried cups of coffee from the Navy mess.

Foley sat down in her customary spot on the couch. "From the sound of things, he's suffering from cystic fibrosis, specifically, the F508del mutation. The illness is controllable with new drugs, but they are extremely expensive—to the tune of two hundred ninety thousand dollars a year here in the States. We'll use PL110 to get the family in the country and to pay for the medication."

Among other things, Public Law 110 was used to fund what was essentially the CIA's version of the witness protection program. High-value assets could be given new identities, backgrounds, and, in the case of Ibrahim Yazdani, necessary medical treatment.

Ryan gave a low groan. Helping a gravely ill child was a laudable thing. The chance that he might have to withhold that help if the father didn't play ball made his bones hurt.

"It's up to them now," he said. "So you've had a little time to mull. I want to hear a pro's thoughts on Erik Dovzhenko."

"Mommy dearest, Zahra Dovzhenko, was a KGB counterintelligence officer until the collapse of the USSR."

"You ever go up against her?" Ryan asked. "Back in the day when you were in Moscow?"

Foley shook her head. "I heard plenty about her,

though. She was a savvy operative. Azeri by birth. Had a bit of a reputation as a vindictive drunk. Her jacket says she was pretty eaten up with the job. Drank, fought, and screwed a lot when she was younger. Reputation of a cowboy. Volunteered for all sorts of dangerous stuff."

Ryan chuckled. "Sounds like somebody else I know."

"Hey," Foley said, acting incredulous. "I was a nice drunk. And except for interludes with Ed, my knees could have held an aspirin in place, they were so firmly closed during that portion of my career."

"I meant the reputation for being a cowboy."

Foley's eyes sparkled with a grin. "I know. I just like to see you blush. My point is, having a superspy for a mother could not have made for an easy childhood. Just like here, intelligence work in Russia is a family business. Not too much of a leap to think mommy pushed him that direction."

"His father?"

"An academic," Foley said.

"One of those," Ryan said, an academic himself.

"Anyway, if he was pushed into a career he didn't want, it would explain his motivation for turning."

"Or it could mean he's an extremely sophisticated operative, setting a trap that will blow up in our face."

"Maybe," Foley said. "But they've been in Iran awhile now. I think it would have blown already if it was going to."

"Let's hope so," Ryan said.

"Foley took a sip of her coffee. "Your son's a smart guy, Jack. No one pushed him into this business. He's got the genes for it, and the drive."

She sighed, closing her eyes for a moment as if deep in thought.

"What?" Ryan asked.

"Doesn't this remind you of the old days, when we were getting Colonel Mikhail Semyonovich Filitov out of the Kremlin?"

"They don't make them like CARDINAL anymore," Ryan said.

"I was thinking about that," Foley said. "Maybe they do."

56

Reza Kazem set the technical manual on the ground, weighting the pages down with a stone against the wind, and looked over the hood of the nearby missile transport vehicle at the approaching Bell 206. Kazem smiled serenely, not because he was happy to see the helicopter, but because he needed the practice.

Ayatollah Ghorbani could not help himself. Though he would stay in the rear of the aircraft, out of sight to the dozens of men working on the missile launcher and transport/erector vehicles, his presence was still a distraction of monumental proportions.

Kazem found Ghorbani to be a necessary evil, a means to an end. The cleric put on a pious face, issuing fatwa after fatwa, extolling the virtues of Iranian manufacturing while decreeing all things Western an abomination before Allah. He instructed his officers in the IRGC to utilize only Iranian-made helicopters such as the Shahed, while he trusted his own safety to nothing other than his personal Jet Ranger.

It was these little things that made Reza Kazem hate the man, but hate him he did.

He patted the sidewall of the huge tire on the missile transport truck as he watched the helicopter land at the edge of the rocky clearing a hundred meters away. No, it would not be long at all. He whistled over the two men he'd chosen to drive the gargantuan vehicle. They'd been eating soup from foam cups that they dropped on the ground immediately when he summoned them.

"You have the coordinates?" he asked once they'd scurried to him. Neither was yet thirty years old, the crystal surety of youth unmarred by the skepticism of age and experience.

"We do," they said in earnest unison.

Kazem wondered what these earnest young dissidents would have thought had they known that the leader of the Council of Guardians, a man second only to the Supreme Leader himself, was on board the approaching helicopter.

"Take a squad of the others and move this truck to the caves," he said. "Wait there until tonight, when the American satellite has passed overhead, and then proceed to the coordinates."

The two men gave curt nods. "Yes, Agha Kazem," they said, using the Persian honorific similar to "Mister" in the English-speaking world.

Ayatollah Ghorbani's helicopter beat the air, throwing up a cloud of dust and gravel as it settled in. Reza Kazem sniffed, gathering up the patience he'd need to show deference to such a prig. On one side of the clearing, Dr. Sahar Tabrizi, the Iranian-born genius of astrophysics, checked and rechecked one of the two Russian missiles that had become her pet projects.

A genuine smile spread over Reza Kazem's lips. Soon he would not need Ghorbani at all.

———

Major Sassani had kept the information about Nima's satellite phone call close-hold rather than turn it over to close IRGC detachment. Too much information was lost when it passed between too many ears and mouths. He wanted to pay the girl a personal visit, to hear from her lips where Dovzhenko had gone.

The 324-kilometer journey from Herat to Mashhad via IRGC Dassault Falcon 20 business jet took less time than the drive from the airport to the neighborhood near the Shrine of the Imam where technicians had vectored Nima's probable location. Sassani arrived less than three hours from the time he first heard of the young woman's call with the satellite phone believed to be in the possession of the Russian traitor, Erik Dovzhenko.

Though the technicians tracking the phone were unable to get a precise location, it was painfully easy to find Nima's apartment. The first person Sassani asked, a scowling woman wearing a black chador and carrying a plastic shopping bag, pointed to the alley stairs.

"*Har jaa'i,*" she sneered. Literally "everywhere," it was the Persian euphemism for streetwalker or prostitute.

The woman had on a considerable amount of makeup, leading Sassani to think she might be turning in her competition. He'd met and even employed the services of plenty of whores who wore the chador. Promiscuous dress certainly led to sinful behavior, but a scandalous heart often hid beneath conservative clothing. Sassani laughed inwardly at the thought. His own blushing bride was a perfect example of the impurity that could hide

under a chador. He was reasonably sure she'd slept with
several men before their marriage—but her virginity
meant less to him than the connection to the general
made possible by their union.

Sassani shooed the woman in the chador away and
then stood in the alley, studying the painted staircase.
He wondered idly how long ago Erik Dovzhenko's feet
had stood on the worn treads, if Ysabel Kashani had been
with him.

The major put a finger to his lips, warning his lieutenant to be quiet as they crept up the stairs.

The door creaked open when they were nearly at the
top. A face peeked out. She was small, looking like a child
next to the door, young and pretty in the worn-out way
that Sassani preferred. A green cotton headscarf was
draped over her head but not tied.

"I am just leaving," she said. She attempted to push
the door shut, but the lieutenant bounded up and put his
foot on the threshold.

She cursed, threatening to cut off vital parts of the lieutenant's body if he did not remove his foot.

Sassani smiled serenely. "Let me speak with her," he
said, stepping up. When her eyes turned toward him, he
leaned in as if to explain why they were there, and then
punched her hard on the tip of her nose.

He followed the punch inside the small apartment. It
smelled like a whore's apartment—tea and makeup and
stale cigarettes. Sassani found there was something
earthy about the odor that deeply appealed to him.

Prostitutes saw more than their share of physical violence, and were not easily intimidated by it. Sassani had
come prepared, and readied a syringe while the lieuten-

ant tied the woman and threw her facedown on the bed. She pressed her broken nose against the sheets, attempting to stop the flow of blood brought on by the punch through the door. The lieutenant put a knee in the small of her back, grabbing her by the hair and yanking sideways.

Sassani found a vein in the side of her neck, not difficult, since fear and exertion caused them to bulge like purple cables under her olive skin. He injected the contents of the syringe, leaving a dot of blood as he withdrew the needle and stepped away. She thrashed for a few more moments, but the lieutenant kept his knee in place.

"Erik Dovzhenko," Sassani whispered. "Is he coming back?"

"No."

"Where is he?"

Nima broke like a cheap clay pitcher when the drugs began to take effect, spilling information so fast that Sassani and his assistant had a difficult time keeping up. The mixture of scopolamine and morphine wasn't exactly a truth serum, but they did induce a state of confused drowsiness that threw the subject off balance, left her feeling out of control—more effective if less rewarding than physical violence.

In less than ten minutes Sassani knew Dovzhenko and the woman had gone to Akbar Children's Hospital to find where someone lived. She did not appear to know the name of that person. Rather than continue with the interrogation, the major decided it was better to finish here and go on to the next location. The Russian was close enough to smell now. Sassani would find him—and kill him—tonight.

Sassani took another vial from his pocket and filled up the syringe.

"What . . . what . . . are you giving me?" The young woman's speech was slurred as if she were drunk.

Sassani cocked his head to one side. "I'm afraid you'll need to be an example."

Tears ran down the young woman's cheeks, mixing with blood and mucus. "You do not have to worry. I swear it."

"Oh, we are beyond worry," Sassani said. "This would have been so much easier had you only answered my questions before I administered the drug."

Nima's face screwed into a stricken grimace as Sassani injected the contents of the second syringe into the same bulging vein in her neck.

"But . . . you . . . you never . . . ask me anything . . . until after you drugged me."

Sassani sat on the edge of the bed. "I didn't?" he said. "Funny. I thought I did." He patted her on the buttocks, giving his lieutenant a conspiratorial nod. "Oh, well. It is better this way. We have what we need and you are nothing but a corruption."

57

Atash Yazdani answered the door on the first chime, as if he'd been expecting them. He was a slightly built man, with narrow shoulders, stooped by the weight of his son's illness. He'd not always been so slight. His slacks were bunched behind two new holes that had been punched in a tattered leather belt as he'd lost weight. A collarless white dress shirt hung off his body, the sleeves rolled up over bony forearms. A quintessential engineer, he had a cheap ballpoint pen and three mechanical pencils in his breast pocket. The forelock of his dark hair was pulled upward to a mussed point, as if he'd been clutching it in thought while bent over a desk or table in his tiny apartment.

Dovzhenko had a pang of conscience when he saw the man's bloodshot eyes.

He'd lost his wife to ovarian cancer, his son was gravely ill. Now they would offer salvation if he would only betray his country.

"May I help you?" the man asked, preoccupied—probably with the vagaries of life itself.

Dovzhenko smiled, hoping the guilt didn't show.

"My friends and I have news that might help your son."

One hand on the door, the other on the frame, Yazdani leaned half out into the hallway, looking to see who Dovzhenko meant by "friends." Ysabel gave a polite bob of her scarf-covered head. The American smiled but kept his mouth shut as they'd planned.

"My son?" Yazdani said. "What do you know of my son?" Hope flashed momentarily in the man's eyes but faded quickly, too overwhelmed with defeat to stay long.

"May we discuss it inside?"

Yazdani stood and stared for so long Dovzhenko was afraid the American might say something, if only to fill the void. Then the engineer suddenly opened the door and motioned them inside.

The interior of the small apartment was as shabby and sad as the harried engineer's countenance. Ryan and Ysabel took seats on the tattered sofa, and Dovzhenko, who was to make the initial pitch, took the faded Queen Anne next to the wobbly dining room chair where Yazdani would sit. As per Persian custom, the host brought out tea and a plate of cake, along with a sharp knife to cut it. He apologized that he did not have more to offer.

"Now," he said, forgoing any tea himself, "please tell me what it is you could do to help my son." He turned toward Ryan. "You are American?"

Ryan nodded, one eye on the cake knife. "What made you guess that?"

Yazdani scoffed. "You have not yet spoken, so I knew you had something you wanted to hide. If you'd been Russian like him, that would not have mattered. Am I wrong?"

"You are not," Ryan said.

"How did you injure your head?"

"A car wreck in Afghanistan," Ryan said.

"I see," Yazdani mused, clearly trying to make sense of these sudden arrivals. "You know much of my son's disease. Are you a doctor, then?"

"I am not," Ryan said.

"None of us are physicians," Dovzhenko said. "We are diplomats who believe we have come upon a way to help your son." He took a sip of tea, letting the man stew on that a bit.

"Diplomats? How would Russian and American diplomats know of the troubles of one Iranian boy?" He glared at Ysabel. "What does this have to do with you?"

"I am a part of it," she said. "But I am not the one who first knew of your child." Her honesty came through loud and clear on her words, obviously impressing Yazdani.

Dovzhenko set the teacup down on a side table. "I am truly sorry about your son. He has cystic fibrosis, does he not?"

"That is so."

"The F508del mutation, to be exact."

"You know a great deal," Yazdani said.

Now Ryan spoke. "That particular mutation responds to a drug called tezacaftor."

Yazdani threw back his head like he was in pain. "What good does this information do my Ibrahim? I earn seventeen million rial each month—roughly three hundred and fifty American dollars. This drug you speak of costs three hundred thousand dollars a year—and that does not even matter, because we could never get it here anyway."

The room fell silent for a time. Everyone sipped tea to be polite, but the cake went untouched.

At length, Yazdani leaned forward, bony elbows on bony knees. "It is obvious that you want something from me," he said. "A quid pro quo in order to help my son. What is it?"

Dovzhenko smiled serenely, the pang of conscience returning with a vengeance. "We can guarantee your son will receive the care and medication that he needs, for the rest of his—"

"Yes, yes," Yazdani said. "I understand what you offer. I want to know what you ask."

Dovzhenko shot a glance at Ryan. The Americans were offering the deal, so it was natural that he should complete the pitch.

Ryan began. "You work with missile control systems at Mashhad Air Base?"

Yazdani threw up his hands. "I knew it would have something to do with my job. You are not diplomats. You are spies. Saboteurs."

"We are." Ysabel nodded at Dovzhenko and then Ryan in turn. "He is Russian, he is American, and I am Iranian. That is the truth. None of us enjoys putting you in this position. But please, for the sake of the people of all our countries, help us so we can help your son."

Yazdani closed his eyes. His narrow shoulders drew back, a little more erect despite this added burden.

But he did not say no.

Major Parviz Sassani eased the passenger door of his rental car shut so it didn't make a noise. Dovzhenko had proven to be an adept quarry, so he would take every precaution. Well, the Russian wasn't truly adept. He'd bested Taliban smugglers, yes, but then he'd allowed some pitiful whore to use his satellite phone, sending up a virtual signal letting Sassani know where to look. The nurse at the children's hospital had been too terrified not to help. Perhaps she smelled the death on him from the recent interaction with the Nima woman. He'd seen the phenomenon before. His own children sometimes recoiled when he approached them after a particularly grisly day— though they could have no idea what he'd done. He'd have to do a more in-depth study, see if he could use it to his advantage during interrogations.

The nurse hadn't recognized the photo of Dovzhenko, but as soon as he'd shown her a photo of Ysabel Kashani, she'd been quick to provide the details of this Yazdani fellow.

They were closing in now. Just as the nurse had smelled death on him, Sassani smelled the tension of the fleeing Russian. Yes. Very close.

"Perhaps we should telephone for reinforcements," the lieutenant said, shoving the keys to the rental into the pocket of his slacks.

"That won't be necessary," Sassani said. "We are talking about one woman and a Russian operative whose heart was never in this line of work anyway. If the two of us cannot handle them, we are in the wrong business."

The lieutenant press-checked the chamber of his SIG Sauer handgun, as was IRGC policy before a raid, and then screwed a suppressor on the end of the threaded barrel. "Shoot on sight, then?"

"I would like to take the time to interrogate him,"

Sassani said, then thought better of it. "No. The Russians would only rescue him. Shoot Dovzhenko on sight. We'll take the girl back to Evin and deal with her there."

The lieutenant looked down the sight of his weapon before returning it to his belt, the suppressor extending out the bottom of the open scabbard holster. "I have been thinking, Major. Perhaps this man, Yazdani, is some kind of spy."

Sassani scoffed. "I do not think so. Our Russian friend is a fugitive. He would have run away to Russia, but I imagine General Alov wants him dead as badly as we do. He's running out of options, and attempting to find refuge with any friend he can."

"But how could Yazdani be his friend? Dovzhenko did not even know where he lived."

"He has recently moved to be near the hospital. Beyond that, Dovzhenko knew the man well enough to know he has a sick son and which hospital he is a patient in." Sassani pulled up a photograph of Atash Yazdani on his phone and held it so the lieutenant could see. "Look at him. He would blow away if he walks out into this wind. He is an engineer of no consequence. We will be doing a service to put him out of his misery."

"It's a difficult call," Ryan concluded. "I get that. We all do. And there will be danger involved. But there's no way this turns out any way but bad without your help."

Ryan wasn't a counterintelligence officer. He knew the basics—from books Clark had assigned him—but the act of turning someone to act as an agent for the United

States was two parts art and one part science. It took time, time they did not have. This pitch had come off more heavy-handed than he'd intended, but that couldn't be helped. He had to be bald about what they needed and hope Ysabel could pull cleanup, appealing to Yazdani's sense of right and wrong, convincing . . . reminding him that he was helping the Iranian people, rather than betraying them.

Yazdani's head suddenly snapped up as he looked at the door.

"What is it?" Dovzhenko asked.

"There is a loose board in the hallway," the engineer said. "That is how I heard you coming before you knocked."

Ryan got to his feet. "Are you expecting company?"

The engineer shook his head. "You are the first visitors I have had in weeks. Did you leave someone outside to keep watch?"

Dovzhenko pulled the engineer to the side at the same moment the door crashed inward, kicked open by a heavy boot.

There had been no handguns to liberate from the Taliban and they'd left the rifles in the car, leaving them unarmed.

"Hello, Comrade Erik," a sneering Iranian man said, his own gun in both hands, pointed at Dovzhenko.

"Sassani!" the Russian spat.

A second man came through the door, a suppressed pistol raised, ready to fire.

The first man started to say something else, but Ysabel flew at him in a rage, batting his pistol aside, screaming, clawing at his face.

Jack made good use of the distraction and closed the distance to the second Iranian, parrying the pistol away with his left arm while he swung upward with his right to plant a staggering hammer fist to the man's unprotected groin.

The extra inches of suppressor on the muzzle of the handgun made it slightly more difficult to maneuver effectively. Jack exploited the lag in speed, trapping the gun in both hands and driving the other man backward against the wall with the point of his elbow. Stunned, the man swung with his left, attempting to hit Jack in the head when he should have tried to secure his gun. One of the blows, robbed of its full power, impacted Jack's injured ear, bringing a wave of nausea.

Ryan growled, clearing his head. With the handgun pinned to the wall, he drove a knee over and over into the man's groin and thigh at the same time, throwing elbows at his throat. The Iranian slid down to protect his groin, then used the wall as a brace as he used the force of his legs to push upward, trying to shake Ryan's grip. The pistol barked, suppressed but not nearly silent, sending a round dangerously close to Ryan's face.

Invigorated by the near miss, Ryan followed the upward transition of movement, twisting his own center at the same time he stepped inward, impacting the man's armpit with the point of his shoulder, spinning toward the gun. The man peeled off the wall as Ryan followed him through the turn, throwing him violently on his back while retaining his two-handed grip on the pistol. He was vaguely aware of the fight going on behind him. He'd heard furniture break, Ysabel's cry as she fell, and

Dovzhenko's frenzied yowl as he attacked Sassani. There had been no other shots, and Ryan had his own hands full.

The Iranian turned out to be a better on the ground than he was standing up. Straddling the man in the mount position, Ryan slammed the gun hand against the floor, sending another shot into the far baseboard. The Iranian bucked his hips upward and to the side, attempting a throw. With both hands occupied against the pistol, Ryan had to post, bringing forward a foot and planting it to the side of the Iranian's body to keep from tumbling over. Instead of returning to the mount, Ryan retained his grip on the gun and continued in the direction of his posted leg, pushing off and around over the top of the Iranian's head, lifting and turning, bringing the arm and the pistol around with him as he went. Ligaments tore, tiny carpal bones snapped. The Iranian's finger convulsed on the trigger again, this round tearing downward through his gut at near-pointblank range. Ryan pressed his advantage, his own finger finding the trigger now and sending two more rounds into the wide-eyed man's belly before wresting the pistol away.

He heard another yowl and spun to find Dovzhenko seated on the ground, bleeding from the nose. Ysabel, too, was on the ground, on all fours, dazed, her scarf gone, trying to get back in the fight. Major Sassani had sunk to his knees, the knife from the cake sticking from the side of his neck. Blood arced from the wound in time with his pulse, painting Yazdani, who stood over him. The IRGC man croaked, unable to speak from the blade that bisected his voice box. He toppled forward a moment later, the arc of blood slowing to a trickle as his life ebbed away.

The other Iranian coughed behind Ryan, causing him to turn with the suppressed SIG. The wounded man shrank backward, shielding his face from another shot. He writhed on the carpet, eyes clenched in excruciating pain.

Dovzhenko helped Ysabel to her feet. She tended to a shaken Yazdani while the Russian stood beside Jack.

"Hospital," the Iranian whispered. "Please."

Dovzhenko knelt. "Lieutenant Gul," he said. He looked at the wounds, then shook his head. "I am afraid there is no time. I will pass on a message to your wife."

"Thank you," Gul said. He coughed again. Pink blood foamed at the corners of his lips now, indicating at least one of the shots had nicked a lung. Ryan guessed another had hit the liver.

"Why?" Dovzhenko asked. "Why was Sassani after Maryam? What was so special about the three students? And why me, for that matter?"

"Alov . . . ordered it . . ."

Dovzhenko's mouth fell open. "General Alov of the GRU?"

Gul nodded weakly. "I am so cold." His voice was like the air escaping a punctured ball.

Yazdani brought a small throw blanket from the couch and draped it over the young man, situating it with trembling fingers.

"Why?" Dovzhenko asked again. "Why Maryam?"

"She saw them . . . together. Like the students."

Dovzhenko groaned. He thought it strange when

he'd seen the picture, but it didn't seem enough to kill over. "Alov and Reza Kazem?"

Gul shook his head. "Not Alov." His lips and teeth were bathed in pink blood. "I . . . I . . . the woman . . ."

The man was drifting now, forcing Dovzhenko to lean forward to hear his words.

Gul's eyelids fluttered. "My son . . . he is only little boy . . ." The coughing came again, more ragged now. He looked up at Dovzhenko, eyes wide, back arched, racked with pain. "Please . . ."

He collapsed against the rug. Still.

Jack looked at Ysabel, then Dovzhenko, assessing them for wounds. He scooped up the suppressed SIG and popped the magazine. Five rounds left. He did a quick peek into the hallway, miraculously saw no one, and then pushed the door closed. The jamb was splintered on the inside, but he hoped the damage wouldn't be too noticeable from the exterior. Blood covered Yazdani's hands and chest. He'd been the one to stab Major Sassani in the neck with the cake knife.

"Thank you," Ryan said.

The engineer sniffed, regaining his composure. "Your thanks are unnecessary. If you are dead, you will be unable to help my son. That is all that matters to me."

"So you'll help us?" Ryan asked.

"I will," Yazdani said.

"I'm a little worried about all the noise," Dovzhenko said. "If your neighbors call the police, we are in trouble."

"Do not worry," Yazdani said. "I am an unhappy man. My neighbors are accustomed to hearing me cry and throw things."

Ysabel ran a hand over the bullet holes in the floor and

doorframe. "Fortunately none of them went all the way through."

"We're interested in two missiles in particular," Ryan said.

"I thought as much," Yazdani said. "Russian 51T6s."

"Exactly," Ryan said. "We need to know where they are."

"First," Yazdani said, "how will we get my son to the United States?"

"It should be straightforward to get you both across the border to Herat," Ryan said. "From there, you'll travel by military transport to the United States."

The engineer pondered this. "I feel as though I should wait to help you until my son is out."

"That won't work," Ryan said. "There are too many variables. We're not even sure who is in charge of this conspiracy. Too much of a chance they'll fire the missiles. We need to figure out their target."

"How will I know you will keep your end of the bargain?"

Ysabel bit her bottom lip, gathering her thoughts. "All we can offer is our word," she began. "But these men saved my life . . . twice."

"I have no choice, do I?"

"I am sorry," Dovzhenko said. "You do not."

Yazdani's stooped shoulders slumped even more. "They've moved the missiles west of Mashhad," he said. "They are on mobile launchers manufactured in Iran, but I wouldn't worry about the targets. I saw the firing solutions."

Ryan waited, but Yazdani just looked at him, waiting to be prodded over the edge—as if he had not quite committed treason until this moment.

"Okay?" Ryan finally said.

"You will think me foolish," Yazdani said. "But the firing solutions I saw aim the missiles at space. These solid fuel rockets are not powerful enough, but it is as if they are planning to launch a satellite."

58

John Clark and the others were still at the safe house in Portugal, waiting for exfil, when Ryan got through.

"Keep it short," Clark said. "You're going to need to move right away after we hang up."

"I'm not on the sat phone," Jack assured him. "This guy has a proxy server he's been using to get around government firewalls so he can look for medication for his kid. I'm using that to jump on an anonymized encrypted VoIP, so we should be good."

"Roger that," Clark said. "Our guest is handcuffed to a chair in the back room. I'm putting you on speaker. We're all here."

Ryan checked on Dom—who was still receiving treatment at Bagram before transport to Ramstein—and then ran down the information Yazdani had given him, using the Iranian's digraph plus code name. "We're trying to work out a way for SD/FLINT to help clear a way for our guys, in case they need to pay a little visit to the missile site."

"Glad you're okay," Ding Chavez said, ever the mother hen, even from thousands of miles away. "We'll have to get clearance from higher, but maybe Gavin can come up with malware he can send you in a zip file or something."

"I'm conferencing him in now," Clark said.

Twenty seconds later, Gavin Biery joined the conversation. Two minutes after that, he was up to speed on the situation.

"I don't need to e-mail him anything," Biery said. "As long as he hasn't lost his thumb drive."

"I lost it," Ryan said. "But I got it back again."

"You're good to go, then," Biery said.

"Seems too simple," Midas said. "Your malware phones home when the computer connects to the Internet. Wouldn't the Iranians be using a closed system for missile defense to guard against online attacks?"

"That is a very good question," Biery said. "To which I have a very good answer. There are a couple versions of malware on the drives I gave you—the one you used in Spain that downloads automatically when you plug it in, and a worm that needs execution. Once the worm is embedded, the system will crash. It should blind missile defense radar for several minutes, depending on what kind of redundant systems they have."

Ryan talked to Yazdani for a moment, then came back on the line, deliberately avoiding the use of the engineer's cryptonym, SD/FLINT, in front of him. "Our guy here says he can slow the backup system from coming online for a half-hour or so, basically by turning off the alarms that would alert staff when the radar goes down."

"We'll need to coordinate," Clark said. "I'll make a call, get marching orders regarding the malware, and specifics on your man's exfil and the medical requirements you've already briefed me on. Check with me in half an hour."

"In the meantime," Biery said, "get a pen and I'll give you the directions on how to execute the worm."

———

The morning national security briefing was just drawing to a close when John Clark's call was pushed through to Mary Pat Foley—though no meeting on national security ever actually finished—and the secretaries of state and defense, as well as the director of national security, the deputy national security adviser, and the chief of staff, were in their customary spots in the Oval.

"I'm not crazy about a military incursion into Iran," Scott Adler said.

Burgess harrumphed. "I say it's long overdue. I'll need to get my people working on rescue contingencies in the unlikely event one of our planes gets shot down."

"That's the least of our worries," Foley said, looking directly at Ryan.

"I agree," the President said. "Let's look at what we know. Russia sold or gifted at least two nuclear missiles to elements in Iran that appear to be linked to Reza Kazem and his so-called Persian Spring movement. We know Kazem had a meeting with our spy and erstwhile assassin Elizaveta Bobkova, and then later with General Alov of the GRU."

"Good catch on her, by the way," van Damm said. "Chadwick's death would have been bad."

"Especially for Chadwick," Foley offered.

"There's that," van Damm said. "But it would have been bad for the country. The tyrant dies, his rule has ended. The martyr dies, her rule begins."

Ryan took a drink of his coffee. "Taking liberties with your Kierkegaard, are you?"

"Maybe I am," van Damm said. "It's true." He looked

down at his notes, ready to move on. "Why would Kazem want a nuke?"

"Maybe his hands aren't quite as clean as he makes them out to be," Ryan said. "It never made sense that Russia was sitting down at the table with him. It's in their best interest to prop up the mullahs."

"So Russia and the Ayatollah use Kazem as a proxy to strike at us and still remain blameless," Foley said. "There's a certain ham-fisted elegance to it that reeks of both regimes."

"That's my guess," Ryan said.

"That still doesn't give us a target," Burgess said.

"No," Ryan said. "It does not."

"I'm not a rocket scientist," Adler said, "but do you think this FLINT might be mistaken in his assessment on the trajectory?"

"That's possible," Ryan said.

Burgess spoke next. "There's a high degree of probability that our Patriots could shoot down both Gorgons when they enter terminal phase, but the likelihood goes up exponentially if we know what the target is and can plan in advance. I suggest we have an expert talk to FLINT, Mr. President, someone who knows the specific questions that need to be asked."

"That's wise," Ryan said, his subconscious mind working in the background on something he couldn't quite put his finger on.

"I wonder," Mary Pat said, tapping a fountain pen on her notepad. "Both China and Russia have been working on antisatellite lasers since my days in Moscow. We know China has the tech to shoot down a satellite. Russia has been testing its Nudol missile for that very purpose. It's possible one of them shared what they know with Tehran."

That's it, Ryan thought. That's what his subconscious had been stewing over.

D ovzhenko and Jack moved Sassani's body along with the other dead IRGC officer into the bathroom so they wouldn't be in full view if someone happened to stop in on Yazdani. For a time, Jack worried that the engineer might be distressed at having to look at the man he'd killed, but that didn't appear to be the problem. Yazdani was a man past distress, beyond tears, numbed by death and illness.

Ryan had had little more than a couple of hours of sleep in the past forty-eight. At least two of his ribs were probably cracked. One of his molars was chipped and each beat of his pulse sent a wave of molten fire through his torn ear. His body desperately needed to rest and heal. But his mind hated these in-between moments. It gave him too much time to think. Like a fool, he'd built up a different end to this story when Ysabel had called.

"So," he pressed Yazdani, "tell me again about this firing solution."

"For the third time," the engineer said, "neither missile is aimed at anything on earth. I suppose it is possible that they are launching satellites into low earth orbit— but they have not removed the warheads as far as I know."

"Why waste a nuclear missile in space?" Dovzhenko mused, his face scrunched, working through the problem. "Why not Israel or some U.S. base in Afghanistan?"

"You got me," Ryan said. "If they're trying to shoot down a satellite, we'll still retaliate."

Ysabel touched Dovzhenko on the arm. "You know that photograph you got from Maryam of those condemned students with General Alov?"

The Russian nodded.

"Let's have a look at it," Ysabel said. "I think there's something we've been missing."

59

Reza Kazem looked away, stifling a smile when Ayatollah Ghorbani had to grab his beard with both
hands to keep the rotor from blowing it across his
face. The cleric glared at Kazem as he climbed aboard the
Jet Ranger, as if the physics of wind and helicopters were
all his fault.

The tour around the missile site had been a quick one,
with Kazem answering questions when he could and de-
ferring to those with more expertise when he could not.
General Alov of the Russian GRU followed along with
his hands clasped behind his back, his face set in a smug
scowl, as if he already knew all the answers but could not
be bothered to voice them. Apparently satisfied, if not
actually happy, Ghorbani had turned toward the helicopter without so much as a word. The Mashhad protests
were going late into the evening, and he'd made it clear
on his arrival that he wished to look at them from the air.

The Bell Jet Ranger lifted off with the pilot and four
passengers—Ayatollah Ghorbani, General Alov. Kazem,
and his trusted lieutenant, Basir. The pilot had served in
the military with Basir and, though Ghorbani was unaware of the fact, was part of Kazem's inner circle.

Kazem and Basir faced aft, while the Russian and Ghorbani were seated facing forward, with the cleric knee-to-knee with Kazem.

The Bell 206 had a top speed of 120 knots, and Ghorbani, his scowling brow the very picture of impatience, insisted the pilot wring out every last knot. They flew in low, two hundred feet over the crowds that had massed in the open area where Navvab Safavi Expressway passed under the Imam Reza shrine. A skirmish line of police and Basij militia against a knot of protesters along Kawthar wall, both sides attempting to use the arched entryways as temporary redoubts. Men and women of all ages had taken to the streets, but the protesters were, by far, youth in their teens and twenties, sick of the present situation. These same young men and women who were often shown on the worldwide media shouting "Death to America!" just as often chanted "Death to Repression!" or "Death to Unemployment!"

The Basij militia—many of them the same age as the student protesters—were particularly brutal in their tactics, answering hurled insults with batons and bullets. Ghorbani took a macabre interest in the action and directed the pilot to move closer to the areas with the most violent confrontations.

"How many do you think?" Ghorbani mused over the intercom, his black turban pressed against the Plexiglas as he peered down at the melee. The cloth headdress necessitated that he wear his earphones wrapped around behind his neck rather than over the top like the rest of those on the helicopter.

"No more than four or five hundred," Reza said. It

was common practice for Ghorbani's advisers to downplay the size of a demonstration—or anything negative for that matter.

"Nonsense," the cleric said. "There are at least two thousand people down there. All of them are angry because they feel they have lost control."

General Alov raised an eyebrow at the insight but said nothing.

"That is true," Reza said.

Ghorbani's head snapped around. "I know what is true and what is not. The government of Iran is ordained of Allah. That truth is absolute. We would put the two thousand presently below us to the sword to protect it— even ten times two thousand if need be." He returned the forehead of his turban to the Plexiglas, gazing downward. "That will not be necessary. The Americans will muster immediately after the first missile hits Bagram—but they will be unsure of who to blame. A stolen Russian missile launched by Iranian dissidents will create enough tension they will not counterstrike with nuclear weapons. They will, however, be very likely to attack a few facilities with conventional weapons. President Ryan will suspect us, no doubt," Ghorbani said. "But absent any definitive proof, the targets will be for show more than anything. And if there is anything our people hate more than misunderstood policies of their own government, it is the interference of the United States. President Ryan's show of force will only give the Iranian people a common enemy."

Kazem bowed, as one should when he is subservient— but this was the last time.

"I have seen enough," the cleric said, prompting the pilot to turn toward the missile site. Ghorbani was customarily cold, but his voice now grew even more icy. "I could not help but notice, Reza, that you have Sahar Tabrizi on your staff."

There was no question there, so Kazem did not respond right away.

"Who is Sahar Tabrizi?" General Alov said, suddenly concerned at Ghorbani's tone. Russia had a great deal on the line here after all. "If there is some . . . how shall we say it? A fly in the ointment, I need to know about it."

"You yourself said to get the best," Kazem said. "Hitting the desired target with a missile of foreign manufacture—"

General Alov cut him off. "If you miss," he said, "it is not the fault of the missile."

"I was going to say," Kazem continued, "hitting a target with a missile of foreign manufacture *from our Iranian mobile launchers* required I find someone better than the best. Dr. Tabrizi is a brilliant physicist and engineer. She is integral to my plan."

"I am well aware of her so-called brilliance," Ghorbani said. "But there is a certain instability that comes with her genius . . ." His voice trailed off and he looked up from the window again. "And what do you mean by your plan?"

"This is all nonsense," General Alov said. "You could lean these missiles against a large tree and they would hit what you told them to hit, so long as you plot the correct firing solution in the command-control system."

Reza gave a nod to Basir, who grabbed General Alov by the collar with one hand while he popped the seat belt with the other. At that moment, the pilot dipped the helicopter sharply to the left, making it a simple endeavor for the powerful Iranian to dump the unsuspecting Russian out over the desert. The general was so surprised by the action, he managed only a startled grunt before he disappeared out the open door.

Ghorbani's face immediately turned ashen, the desired effect.

"What have you done?"

Reza nodded at the empty seat. "An unfortunate necessity," he said. "It was important that you see our commitment so you will listen."

Ghorbani leaned forward and banged his fist on the pilot's seat. "Return to Mashhad at once!"

"I'm afraid that cannot happen, most benevolent one," Kazem said, almost but not quite sneering. "Are you aware of Dr. Tabrizi's most noteworthy hypothesis?"

Not one to be intimidated, even by cold-blooded murder, the cleric glared across the interior of the helicopter. "Of course I am. It is insane."

"I must respectfully disagree," Kazem said. "She is eccentric, to be sure, but she is far from insane. You see, with the help of two Russian missiles and Dr. Tabrizi, you and I are going to change the world."

Jack Ryan, Jr., stood behind Ysabel, looking over her shoulder at Yazdani's computer while Dovzhenko pulled up the eBay site where he'd stashed the photograph of Maryam and the other Iranian dissidents. Ysabel touched the tip of her index finger to her friend's face and then pressed it to her lips. Dovzhenko leaned in—to comfort her or to be comforted, Jack couldn't tell which.

"I suppose Sassani's actions make sense," Dovzhenko

said. "General Alov would not want me to know of his interaction with members of the protests." He shook his head. "But I still do not understand why he was there in the first place. He is too well known to be working undercover. And I cannot picture a scenario where Moscow abandons Tehran in favor of a new regime."

Yazdani stepped closer, peering down at his computer screen. "Perhaps I can help you with that," he said. "From what I saw, Moscow has not abandoned anyone. Reza Kazem is supposed to be the leader of this Persian Spring, but I do not think that is the case. I think they are all working together. The only people who have been abandoned are those who fell under Kazem's spell."

Jack nodded. "So Russia sells nuclear missiles to Iran through a dumbshit arms dealer in Portugal, but since they are supposed to be stolen and going to a dissident group, Russia and Tehran get to skate out from under the blame—even though the whole world knows the story is bogus. Pretty slick, when you think about it."

"I have no idea where they got the missiles," Yazdani said. "But they are Russian and they are nuclear. But this conspiracy does little to answer your question about the targets."

Ysabel touched the screen again, this time pointing to a stocky woman in her mid-sixties who stood talking to one of Maryam's three friends who'd been hanged in front of Dovzhenko. She wore no headscarf and her shoulder-length hair was flat black, as if it had been spray-painted. "I think Sahar Tabrizi could be our answer."

Jack leaned in, wincing, from the throbbing pain in his ear. "Dr. Sahar Tabrizi? Didn't she have some cocka-mamie theory about satellite Armageddon?"

———

"About the time of the revolution," President Jack Ryan said, "there was a brilliant astrophysicist named Sahar Tabrizi teaching at the University of Tehran. She was loud and eccentric and believed women were as smart and capable as men—just the sort of academic Khomeini liked to send to the dungeons of Evin Prison. I believe she fled to teach at a university in South America."

Visitors to the Oval Office customarily dropped their smartphones in a basket out by Betty Martin's desk, but Mary Pat had retrieved hers so she could use it to do research in real time, thumb-typing almost as fast as Ryan could talk.

"There's a Sahar Tabrizi who is the dean of the physics department at University of Chile," she said.

"That's her," Ryan said. "Do me a favor and see if she's traveled to Iran in the last few weeks or months."

Several intelligence agencies routinely kept tabs on the international travel of scientists deemed capable of furthering nuclear, chemical, or biological weapons programs. As an astronautical engineer, Tabrizi fit the bill. Mary Pat made two calls, before CIA gave her the nod.

"That's affirmative, Mr. President," she said. "Tabrizi flew into Tehran twenty-five days ago." She sighed. "I gotta ask, Jack, would you care to enlighten the rest of us hairy unwashed heathens who don't keep up with the world's preeminent rocket scientists?"

"Are you familiar with the Kessler syndrome?"

"A doomsday scenario involving satellites," Burgess said. "Conceived by a NASA scientist in the late seventies."

"Correct," Ryan said. "Donald Kessler postulated that objects in low earth orbit would eventually become so dense that they would begin to collide, causing a cascading event that would form a large debris field that would render low earth orbit uninhabitable by satellites."

"Wait a minute," Arnie van Damm said. "The International Space Station is in low earth orbit."

"It is indeed," Ryan said. "As are most of our surveillance satellites."

"So," Mary Pat prodded. "Dr. Tabrizi . . ."

"She takes the hypothesis to the next level," Ryan said, "Where Kessler thought the number of satellites would domino, leading to a much higher frequency of strikes, Tabrizi theorizes that there is a single satellite in low earth orbit that, if destroyed, would create so much debris that the Kessler syndrome would be greatly accelerated. The collisions would continue to cascade, until everything in low earth orbit is destroyed in a matter of weeks."

"Thankfully, "Burgess said, "our GPS and communication birds wouldn't be affected."

"True," Ryan said. "Those satellites are much higher, but Tabrizi believes that the debris field would be so dense travel through low earth orbit would be like flying through a shotgun blast."

"I'm not a rocket scientist," Scott Adler said, "but you don't think that's overstating it a little?"

"Could be," Ryan said. "But the KH satellites are each roughly the size of a commuter bus. I've seen what a speck of dust can do to a window of the Space Station. Forty thousand pounds of space junk has the potential to do a hell of a lot of damage. And, with each successive collision, we get more space junk. So, no, if Dr. Tabrizi's calculations are correct, we're not overstating it at all. Let's have a look at that photo of General Alov and the protesters from our asset in Iran. It's a good bet those three young men were executed because they saw Tabrizi with Reza Kazem."

Mary Pat continued to do research on her smart-phone. "It looks like she identified a single satellite that would start this chain reaction."

"Yep," Ryan said. "She calls it 'Crux.'"

"Crux," Mary Pat mused. "Which satellite is it?"

"That's the problem," Ryan said. "She never said."

60

"Why?" Ghorbani asked. "What you do makes no sense."

"On the contrary," Kazem said. "It makes all the sense in the world."

"But, Reza," Ghorbani said, trying a conciliatory tone, though Kazem knew full well the cleric would be happy to see him gutted at the moment. "If Tabrizi succeeds, then everyone will be harmed. Russia will be furious, but we have satellites as well—and we hope to have more, to eventually be on par with the West."

"And we will be," Kazem said. "In a matter of weeks instead of the decades that it would have otherwise taken."

Ghorbani shook his head, curling his nose in a mixture of disgust and disbelief.

"You see," Kazem pressed. "Iran depends on satellites for but a small portion of our military and civilian communications—and most of that to counter threats from the West. The United States is almost a hundred percent reliant on their eyes in the sky. Without their precious satellites, they will be blind. They will have no more will to stumble around in this portion of the world without their precious technology. I do not wish to serve as gas stations to the West as the Arabs do. We are better than that. This region has rightly belonged to a Persian Empire for seven thousand years. And this will return to us that history. All the so-called superpowers—Russia, China, the United States—will be rendered impotent. At worst, we will be given an equal playing field. At best, they will leave us alone."

"The sooner I return to Tehran, the better," the cleric said. "Or do you intend to throw me to my death as well?"

"That shouldn't be necessary," Kazem said. "But I'm afraid you must remain our guest for a few more hours. Mark my words, O Guide of Emulation. This will be a boon for us and a hellish nightmare for the West."

"Your mind is gone," Ghorbani said. "You are as insane as the fool Tabrizi."

"We will soon see," Kazem said.

"I need the best astrophysicist in the free world," President Ryan said. "And if he or she happens to be on the East Coast, so much the better. I'd like them in my office as soon as humanly possible."

Foley stood. "On it."

"I may know a guy," Scott Adler said, though this sort of thing was well outside his wheelhouse. "I play poker with some guys from the poli-sci department at Annapolis. A couple of months ago one of them brought an aeronautical engineering professor—a real probability genius who cleaned us all out. I'll have to make some calls to get his name."

Foley was already thumb-typing again. "Dr. Randal Van Orden?"

"That's him," Adler said. "If that son of a gun is half as good at rocket science as he is at poker, he's your man."

"His CV is incredible," Foley said, perusing her phone. "Turned down a job at NASA to teach at the Naval Academy. He's the go-to guy when anyone has a question about satellites. And get this, he's written papers on both the Kessler and Tabrizi theories."

Six minutes later, Ryan had him on speakerphone.

"Dr. Van Orden, Jack Ryan here. We're dealing with a significant problem and would welcome your expertise. I wonder if you would be willing to come to my office?"

"Without question, Mr. President," the scientist said, sounding addled.

"I assume you have a security clearance," Ryan said.

"I do," Van Orden said. "My periodic work with NASA requires me to maintain a TS."

"Top Secret is a little low for this one," Ryan said. "But I'll read you in when you get here."

"Might I ask what the problem is in reference to?"

"Unfortunately, I can't go into too much on the phone," Ryan said. "But it has to do with papers you've written, specifically on Kessler and Tabrizi."

"I see," Van Orden said. "In that case, I have a young protégé here in The Yard who you will want to talk with. He did a recent paper on Tabrizi that was the best I've ever read."

"An associate professor?" Ryan asked.

"No, sir," Van Orden said. "A Youngster."

A "Youngster" in Naval Academy jargon was a sophomore. "Midshipman Alex Hardy is a student of mine, and I have to say, one of the brightest minds in the field of aerospace and astronautical engineering. He personally designed the key components for the guidance system on the satellite we're sending up next fall."

"That might be problematic," Ryan said.

"I assure you," Van Orden said, "if you need answers, he will have more than I do—or anyone else, for that matter."

Ryan said, "We'll read him in as well. This is a matter of some urgency. I'll have a car there to pick you up in . . ." He looked as his watch, then motioned to Mary Pat to get someone on the way immediately. "Shall we say thirty minutes?"

"We'll be ready, Mr. President."

Ryan's hand hovered above the phone. "And, Dr. Van Orden, I realize that you and Midshipman Hardy will have scheduled classes, exams and whatnot. I'll square this with the superintendent. You may tell others with an immediate need to know that you've been summoned to the White House, but as far as anyone else is concerned, the purpose of your visit is classified."

There was no denying it; Randal Van Orden kept a messy workspace. Circuit boards, rolls of soldering wire, plastic boxes of delicate heat-shielding material leaned against an ancient oscilloscope. Stacks of dog-eared papers, some decorated with rings from countless cans of Diet Coke, occupied every place on the desk where there wasn't an electronic component or scientific instrument. Van Orden's thoughts did not come in a linear manner, unlike most engineers he knew. The answers to whatever problem he happened to be working on at the moment appeared like tiny thought bubbles in the cluttered workspace of his mind. But if he needed to work out the load limits of a particular rocket or the right mixture of powdered metal in solid fuel engine—the answers were always there in the bubbles. Just as the soldering gun was where he needed it to be on the table. There was, indeed, a method to his mess.

It did, however, take him a moment to find his cell phone, tucked in the side pocket of the heavy-duty Saddleback Leather briefcase that his wife said looked professorial.

Van Orden himself had never been in the military, but he had a military bearing nonetheless. The midshipmen in his classes were supposed to be professional and squared away. "Locked on" they called it. They were highly intelligent and driven people who deserved the best instruction possible. Dr. Van Orden believed he had a responsibility to be as locked on as it was possible for a man in his early sixties to be. His barber near his home in Crownsville kept his dark hair neatly tapered and groomed. Skinny ties, white shirts, and black frame glasses gave him the look of a man who'd stepped out of the sixties. In truth, he would have been more comfortable in a pullover golf shirt and khaki shorts, but his wife dressed him, using her philosophy that he couldn't be young anymore, so he should go for the coolest old. For an aeronautical engineer, that was NASA mission control in 1969.

He scrolled through his recent calls until he found Midshipman Hardy's number. He'd never had a student with such promise. The young man had such a grasp and recall of numbers that a casual observer might consider him a quirky savant. But that was not the case. The men and women who gained admittance to the United States Naval Academy had to be well rounded as well as smart.

He got no answer on the phone. Not surprising, Hardy could be in class, or in one of the places in The Yard where reception was iffy. He felt a pang of regret at having mentioned the midshipman at all, but if the President's questions were important enough to call an academic like him to the White House, then Hardy's knowledge might be invaluable. He checked his watch. He'd just have to go and find him the old-fashioned way.

Van Orden's office was located downstairs in the aeronautical engineering section of Rickover Hall, at the northern corner of the campus along land reclaimed from the Severn River. He poked his head outside the door to find a pink-faced plebe wearing the white Dixie cup hat and Cracker Jack suit that was synonymous with enlisted Navy personnel. The freshman midshipman had obviously lost a bet with an upperclassman, and now stood "lifeguard duty" next to the water fountain outside Van Orden's office.

"Do you know Midshipman Hardy?" Van Orden asked. He had an abrupt baritone voice that caused the freshman to stand up straighter.

"I do, Dr. Van Orden," the young lifeguard said, coming to attention. "The last I saw him he was going to Dahlgren Hall to make a phone call."

"Thank you," Van Orden said, moving as he spoke. He didn't want to keep the President's car waiting.

He walked quickly, carrying his sport coat so as not to sweat through his shirt in the warm spring weather. Dahlgren Hall was located diagonally across The Yard, at the far south corner, almost at the front gate—about as far away as possible and still be on Academy grounds. Van Orden passed Michelson Hall, and the plaque marking the spot where Albert Michelson had measured the speed of light in 1879. He cut across the grass, almost running as he passed the Mexican War Midshipmen's Monument in the center of the courtyard, aiming for Dahlgren Hall. It made sense Hardy would relax there. He had a girlfriend back in Idaho and the upper deck of Dahlgren was one of the few places midshipmen could get a little privacy to make phone calls.

Unlike other military academies in the United States, Annapolis was an open campus, with visitors simply showing ID and clearing security like that of an airport. The grounds were crowded with sightseers who gave Van Orden sideways looks for not utilizing the sidewalks. He ignored them, entering Dahlgren Hall to the smell of french fries coming from the Drydock Restaurant, and bounded up the stairs. There were several midshipmen in the blue-carpeted lounge area. Unfortunately, none of them were Hardy.

Van Orden checked his watch again. Twelve minutes wasted.

He approached the nearest midshipman, a tall Nordic woman who looked as if she could be an Olympic runner but for her summer white service dress uniform. The fouled anchor and two diagonal strips on her shoulder boards said she was a midshipman second class—a year ahead of Hardy. She was reading, but closed her book and stood when she realized he wanted to speak to her.

"How can I help you, sir?" Her nametag identified her as Midshipman Larson.

"I'm looking for Alex Hardy. Sandy hair, about five-ten—"

"He was here about half an hour ago," Larson said. "I believe he went down to the wind tunnels."

Van Orden groaned. "Thank you," he said, spinning to begin his jog back across campus to the basement of the building where he'd started, just down from his office.

He found Hardy six minutes later, standing beside one of the boxlike wind tunnels in the basement of Rickover Hall, holding a model of a hand with a piece of steel rod sticking through the palm, working with a group of four other midshipmen—who looked nearly identical in their short hair and summer whites. The project was for one of Van Orden's physics classes—the effects of ejecting from a jet aircraft at various speeds and attitudes of flight. The sign on the wall behind them read: "Rocket Science: It Ain't Brain Surgery."

Van Orden plugged his ears, thankful for the scant moment to catch his breath. Hardy looked up when he saw movement and Van Orden waved him over.

Hardy removed his hearing protection. "What can I do for you, Doctor?"

Van Orden looked toward the hallway, mouth closed, shaking his head and indicating they should step out of earshot.

"You and I have been summoned to the White House," he said. There was no time to beat around the bush.

"*The* White House?"

"Correct," Van Orden said. "A car is picking us up in"—he looked at his watch—"less than fifteen minutes."

"All right . . ." Hardy hesitated. "I mean, sir, I still have classes this afternoon."

"Did you hear what I said?" Van Orden said, his deep voice booming down the hallway until he regained his composure. He began to walk and Hardy followed. "By White House, I mean the Commander in Chief. I believe that will count as an excused absence."

Hardy trotted to keep up. "How do they even know who I am?"

"I told them," Van Orden said. "Come. I'll explain on the way."

A man in a dark suit and sunglasses rounded the corner of Dahlgren Hall as Van Orden and Hardy passed the Submarine Monument on their way to the front gate. He gave a slight nod.

"Dr. Van Orden?"

"Yes."

"Special Agent Marsh," the man said. "I'm your ride." He raised a wrist to his lips, then spoke into a mic on his sleeve. "Marsh to CROWN, I have them both."

Hardy balked when they reached the statue of Billy the Goat. "That's Lieutenant Commander Gill, my English lit professor," he said, nodding to a naval officer walking toward them from Lejeune Hall. "He's also my company officer."

"Going somewhere, Mr. Hardy?" the officer asked.

"Yes, sir," Hardy said.

"As a matter of fact, we both are," Van Orden said.

"Funny," Gill said. "I didn't see a missed-class chit for you in my inbox."

"I've not completed one, sir."

"I suggest you make time," the officer said, professional but unyielding.

The Secret Service agent stepped in. "I'm afraid I'll have to ask you to excuse us, sir. Midshipman Hardy is expected at an important meeting."

Gill grimaced, unconvinced. "I have no idea who you are. And who's so important as to rate a disruption of Academy SOP?"

"The President, sir," Special Agent Marsh said.

"The president of what?"

"The United States, sir," Marsh said.

"The President? What's this all about, Hardy?"

"I'm afraid I can't tell you that, sir," Marsh said, displaying the five-pointed star on his credentials. "Now, if you will please excuse us. The superintendent has the information you are cleared for."

"I kind of feel sorry for him," Hardy said when he slid into the backseat of a black Crown Victoria parked in the No Parking area on Randall Street in front of the gate. "He was just doing his job."

"That makes two of us." Marsh shot him a glance in the rearview mirror, smiling. "But you have to admit, this will go down as Yard legend."

Hardy was pressed backward into the leather seat as the agent activated his lights and sirens and punched the accelerator to get them to the White House. For the first time since getting the news, Van Orden saw him act like the excited twenty-year-old that he was instead of a stoic midshipman. "Oh, yeah," he said. "This is dope."

61

President Ryan sat at the end of the conference table in the Situation Room and took a sip of water—his stomach was too knotted over Jack Junior to drink any more coffee. As he waited, he went over what he was going to say when the Russian president picked up the phone.

The plan of action had been a hasty one—as plans always were in response to situations that came out of left field. There were no drills for anything remotely like this.

Two F-22 Raptors, each loaded with two thousand-pound JDAM GBU-32 guided bombs, had taken off from Bagram twenty minutes earlier and were presently topping off with fuel somewhere over Herat. The asset known as FLINT was on standby in Mashhad, ready to upload the malware at a moment's notice. Finally, the Russian known as GP/VICAR was about to make a phone call of his own.

Ryan's telephone call had been arranged through the Washington–Moscow Direct Communications Link set up in 1963 to avoid possible disasters of delayed communication like those that nearly occurred during the Cuban Missile Crisis. Known in popular culture as "the red phone" or "Hotline," the link was never a phone at all. It had first been established over a Teletype machine. Newer technologies eventually led to a computer system over which secure e-mails could be exchanged between the Pentagon and the Kremlin to arrange for voice communication between the two world leaders. There were other methods, but this was the most immediate.

Ryan's tone dripped with diplomacy when Yermilov answered. Ryan spoke passable Russian and Yermilov passable English, but as was always the case in these kinds of delicate conversations, the men spoke through interpreters who had the required security clearances. Ryan described the situation with the missiles and Sahar Tabrizi, leaving out the fact that the United States was fully aware that Russia was behind the sale to Iran.

"Nikita," Ryan continued. "I'm sure you see how dangerous this is. At first we believed the targets to be American installations, but the destruction of a satellite that led to cascading fields of debris in low earth orbit would be catastrophic for both our countries. The International Space Station would very likely be obliterated before either of us could launch an evacuation mission. Honestly, it would be catastrophic for the world. My experts tell me all the resulting junk could make it nearly impossible to send anything into space in the foreseeable future."

Yermilov blustered. "I can assure you, Jack, we believed the missiles were lost during a plane crash on their way for testing in Sary-Shagan in Kazakhstan. I had no idea they somehow made it to Iran."

"I'm not suggesting you did," Ryan said.

"I thought you were calling in reference to another matter."

"Elizaveta Bobkova?"

"No . . ."

"She and her men have diplomatic cover," Ryan said. "But I understand she might be asking to stay."

"Is that so?" Yermilov said, almost a gasp.

"Did you think I was calling about Ukraine?" Ryan said dismissively, as if Yermilov's troop movements were little more than a fly on his nose. "Honestly, my people advised me that Russia might try and invade Ukraine because the Kremlin believes I have my hands full here with domestic matters. I told them you knew me better than that. There was no possible way you would invade, at least any further than you already have. I told them your troop movements simply had to be a bluff. That you and I had discussed this and that you knew I would take drastic action at any further advance, no matter the rationale. And that we both agreed any such action would be tying that untieable knot of war that your predecessor Khrushchev spoke of so eloquently. In any case, we can talk about Ukraine at a later time. This matter with the missiles is larger than that. Wouldn't you agree?"

"Yes," Yermilov said, stunned, on the ropes. "What shall we . . . Do you suggest we contact Tehran?"

"As you are aware, the United States has no diplomatic relations with Iran," Ryan said. "But even if we did, I'm not certain how deeply Tehran is involved. This is likely the work of a dissident group, but it is too soon to say. Beyond that, I fear time is of the essence. I'd hoped you have some method of destroying the Gorgons remotely."

"I must ask, Mr. President," Yermilov said. "How did you come upon this information?"

Ryan chuckled despite the circumstances. "That's classified, but I'm sure you have ways of checking the truth of the matter without tipping our hand with Tehran. Now I must ask you, Nikita, are you able to transmit a self-destruct code to your missiles?"

There was silence on the line while Yermilov muted the call. If Ryan's plan was working, the Russian president was hearing of the plot to destroy a satellite from members of his own intelligence community right about now.

Yermilov came back on the line a full ninety seconds later. "I am afraid the remote destruction of the missiles is not an option, Mr. President."

Ryan sighed. "Not an option or not possible?"

"As you put it," Yermilov said, "that is classified."

"Understood," Ryan said. "Thank you for taking my call."

"What will you do from this point?" Yermilov asked.

"That remains to be seen," Ryan said. "We'll speak again very soon." He gave one last chuckle. "Hopefully not about Ukraine."

"Yes," Yermilov said. "Hopefully."

Ryan ended the call and looked up at General Paul and Mary Pat. "I don't like it, but MUDFLAP is a go."

The chairman tapped a key on the phone on the table in front of him and spoke into the tiny boom mic on his headset. "MUDFLAP is a go."

At the same time, DNI Foley made a call to her asset in Iran, using a more cryptic phrase. "Is this Peperouk Pizza? I'd like to make an order if you can deliver in thirty minutes."

"Wrong number," the voice said in English. "This is Navid Auto Repair."

"Okay," Foley said. "Sorry to bother you."

She replaced the handset and turned to Ryan.

"Here we go," she said, giving him a thumbs-up.

62

Jack Junior and the others followed in the Hilux while Yazdani drove his own car to Mashhad Airbase south of the city. They parked in Toroq Forest Park a kilometer away until Jack received the go signal from Mary Pat.

Yazdani went in without so much as a backward glance, intent on saving his son. He'd assured them he was well respected in the missile defense facility. Years of war with Iraq had necessitated the bulk of any antiballistic missile system to guard against incursion from the west with most protecting Tehran. Few in power expected any attack to come from the east, so the area was lightly defended.

At Ryan's urging, Dovzhenko had made a call to his immediate supervisor at the embassy in Tehran, briefing him of a plot between Major Sassani, Reza Kazem, and General Alov to destroy a satellite in low earth orbit. He had been unable to make contact earlier due to the obvious security issues related to an investigation of a prominent GRU general who surely had spies everywhere. Dovzhenko was, he explained, only looking out for the good name of the SVR—and his supervisor—by separating himself from normal channels. At this point, he told his boss, he would attempt to find out where the missiles were, but he suspected American assets were somehow on scene.

"You think your supervisor believed you?" Ysabel asked while they waited for Yazdani to come back out.

Dovzhenko shrugged. "I think so. If not, they will send someone to shoot me anytime now."

"This is a foolish plan," Ysabel said. "You are going to get him killed."

Dovzhenko put a hand on her shoulder. "It was not his plan," he said. "I am good with it. Really."

"Well I'm not," Ysabel said.

Yazdani's compact sedan rounded the corner and pulled up alongside the Toyota, driver's window to driver's window.

He handed the flashlight/USB drive to Dovzhenko, who passed it over the seat to Jack.

"It is uploaded."

"No problems?" Ryan asked.

"No problems."

Ryan dialed the number to Foley's prepaid burner phone on the mobile Yazdani had given him.

"Is this the person who called about the pizza?"

His use of the word "person" conveyed that the malware had been uploaded. Reference to a "lady" would have meant it had not happened.

"Now I will go get my son," Yazdani said. "And you will keep your end of the bargain."

"Absolutely," Ryan said. "Go get him. I need to wait for word that the missiles have been destroyed."

"That was not our agreement," Yazdani said. "You are to help us get across."

"And we will," Ryan said. "As soon as I hear back."

"And what if something goes wrong?" Yazdani said, eyes flashing. "Is your promise to my son only binding if your aircraft hits the target?"

"No," Jack said. "But plans will change. If we have to, you can meet my contacts south of Islam Qala and they will see to it you both get across."

Yazdani spat something in Persian and sped off.

"What did he say?"

"You do not want to know," Ysabel said. "But it has to do with your balls and a very hot fire."

"Shit," Ryan said. "That's kind of harsh."

"It's not very ladylike," Ysabel said, "but I have to admit that I thought it many times myself over the years while I was waiting for you to call."

"Raptors heading west, Mr. President," the chairman of the joint chiefs said. "At roughly Mach 1.8 they'll be over target in eight minutes."

Bob Burgess clenched both fists and set them on the table. "With any luck at all, the stealth tech and the asset's malware will make the birds completely invisible."

"These are two of the best pilots in two of the most advanced airplanes in the world," General Paul said.

"What about Russian Verba or other man-portable antiaircraft defense systems?" Mary Pat asked.

"They would have to know we're there," General Paul said. "Honestly, with the F-22 I doubt we even needed the malware to blind their system. I think we're good."

The chairman nodded to his aide, who pulled up the pilot's frequency. There was momentary static and then the pilots' chatter came across crystal clear over the speakers in the Situation Room.

"Twenty miles . . ." Haymaker One, the flight leader, said. *"Commence run in thirty seconds on my mark."*

"Roger that," the second pilot said. *"Thirty seconds."*

"Mark," the flight lead said.

"Roger."

General Paul filled in the blanks as the Raptor pilots prepared to drop their ordnance. The assets in Iran—the general had no idea who they were—had provided GPS coordinates for the Russian missiles, giving the JDAMs a positive target to home in on once they were launched from thirty-five thousand feet. With a circular error probable of less than five meters, the four thousand-pound JDAMs would make short work of both Gorgons and anyone who happened to be standing within the blast radius. The Raptors would get close enough to video the attack from a safe altitude with sophisticated onboard sensors and cameras, allowing for a Bomb Damage Assessment, or BDA, in real time before they egressed back across the border to Afghanistan.

"Haymaker One, bombs away," the flight lead said.

"Haymaker Two, bombs away."

Eighty seconds ticked by and the flight leader spoke again.

"Only getting one secondary explosion," he said. *"I repeat. Only one secondary. We plastered the target. The second missile must be in a different location."*

General Paul looked at Ryan, who twirled his index finger in the air.

"Get them out of there," Ryan said.

63

Midshipman Hardy went to Idaho State for two years before he followed through on a dream and gained acceptance to Annapolis. He was considerably older than most midshipmen in his class, but still, being driven up to the side entrance of the White House and ushered past security was enough to make him feel like an excited schoolkid on a field trip to the Smithsonian. Special Agent Marsh waited for the barricades at the northeast gate to the White House to come down. An officer with the Uniformed Division of the Secret Service was expecting them, and waved the Crown Victoria through when Marsh held up the credential card hanging from the lanyard around his neck. Marsh handed both Van Orden and Marsh lanyards of their own, each bearing a badge with a red A, signifying they had an appointment but had to be escorted.

Marsh kept going past the main entrance, parking the sedan at the east end of the circular drive, and led the way down a long walk along what Hardy guessed was the press briefing room. There were no guards on the outside, but they were met by two more officers from the Secret Service Uniformed Division, one standing, another seated at a desk. A sign-in book lay open in front of this one, but Marsh pointed down the hall and the African American officer nodded her head and waved him through. "Hey, Cody," she said. "Busy day."

"You're tellin' me," Marsh said.

Hardy had seen photographs of the White House, and plenty of movies and television shows like *National Treasure* and *The West Wing*—but he was most surprised at how low the ceilings were. Everyone from staffers to the Secret Service U.D. officers spoke in solemn tones. Rich carpeting and antique furniture gave it a reverent, museum quality. What seemed like a palace on film was much smaller, almost to the point of feeling cramped. Historic paintings by Terpning, Bierstadt, and Remington graced the walls. There were even some sketches by Norman Rockwell depicting a visit to the White House, but other than the official portraits of the President and the Vice President like the ones hanging in The Yard, there were none of the Commander in Chief himself.

Marsh turned left at the end of the hall, into a suite of offices crammed full of one too many desks where the President's secretaries and body man sat. A severe-looking woman peered over the top of her glasses and then nodded at the Secret Service agent.

"Go on in, Cody," she said. "He's expecting you."

"Thanks, Ms. Martin," Marsh said. He stopped at the door and straightened his tie before leading the way into the Oval Office.

The President of the United States stood from his chair by the fireplace when Hardy and Van Orden stepped into the room. It, too, was smaller than Hardy imagined, but still big enough to bring more than a little awe. There were others in the room, the secretaries of defense and state, the director of the CIA, the chairman of the joint chiefs, and a couple of others Hardy did not recognize, including a woman who looked to be in her late fifties and sat nearest the President.

"Professor Van Orden," Ryan said, stepping forward to extend his hand.

That is something, Hardy thought. *The most powerful man on the planet and he crosses the room to shake our hands.*

"And Midshipman Hardy," Ryan said. "I'm sure you're wondering what all this fuss is about."

"**S**o you two are my resident experts," President Ryan said after Mary Pat brought the newcomers up to speed with a quick brief. "On the science at least. I want you both to speak freely. Give me your opinions as well as scientific facts—just make sure you make it clear which is which." He heaved something between a groan and a sigh. "So tell me, how real is this threat proposed by Sahar Tabrizi? What are the odds?"

"If Iran is able to hit the correct satellite," Van Orden said, "what Dr. Tabrizi calls 'Crux,' then the odds of a cascading effect are high. She is a gifted physicist. Her theories as well as Kessler's are sound."

"If I may, Mr. President," the secretary of defense asked.

Ryan nodded.

"How quickly would this debris from Tabrizi's Crux affect the remainder of our satellites in low earth orbit?"

Van Orden turned to Hardy.

"My father is a police officer," the midshipman said,

making Ryan like the kid even more. "His ballistic vest is made of Kevlar, but the steel shock plate over his heart and lungs is covered in material to prevent spalling. If a bullet were to hit a metal shock plate that was not coated and angled correctly, then spalling occurs. Metal fragments are sent flying off the plate and become just as deadly to my dad as the original projectile. Even a glancing missile strike on a satellite would create a great deal of debris. I'm sure you've all seen what a particle the size of a grain of sand can do to the window of the Space Station."

Everyone in the room gave a solemn nod.

Van Orden took up the conversation. "There are almost eight hundred satellites in low earth orbit, including some for communications such as satellite telephones, ISR, and the International Space Station, and others. Some of them small cubes just a few inches across. Others weigh several tons and are the size of a bus." He turned to Hardy, giving him the floor to continue.

"We track over eighty-five hundred bits of debris—space junk if you will—that are larger than ten centimeters. China used a kinetic kill vehicle to take out one of their own weather satellites in 2007, creating over two thousand pieces larger than a golf ball. Some estimates put the pieces of junk over two millimeters but too small to track at more than a million. To put that in perspective, a .22-caliber bullet is 5.56 millimeters. Space, even low earth orbit, is a very large place, but the odds of catastrophic damage rise exponentially." Hardy paused, then said, "With each successive satellite creating more and more bits of debris, each traveling at seventeen thousand five hundred miles per hour, it wouldn't take too many days to create a ring that would make low earth orbit a very unfriendly environment."

Van Orden nodded in assent. "And that does not address what would occur when the orbit of that debris starts to decay. Much of it would burn up on reentry, but a significant portion would fall back to earth—right on top of us."

Foley raised her fountain pen. "Since reentry would burn up many of the pieces, would not a nuclear detonation do the same thing?"

"A kinetic kill would be better if their aim is to create more debris," the midshipman said.

Burgess said, "Then we have to assume they were just after the guidance system on the missiles. It wouldn't be difficult to leave the warhead unarmed. PALs should render it incapable of detonation even during a direct, head-on engagement."

A PAL, or permissive action link, was a security system designed to keep a nuclear device from blowing up except when positive actions were taken. As one nuclear weapons expert put it, "bypassing a PAL should be about as complex as performing a tonsillectomy while entering the patient from the wrong end."

"So what do we do about a kinetic kill vehicle?" Arnie van Damm asked.

Hardy gave a solemn nod. "My friends and I worked through this," he said. "You can move a satellite a couple of different ways. Some of them have solar antennas. We could deploy those and move the bird with solar radiation pressure—sort of like wind on a kite."

"Too slow," Van Orden said. "A missile with any guidance system at all would merely reacquire."

"True," Hardy said.

"Can't you just move it?" Foley asked.

"You could," Hardy said. "A lot of satellites require periodic boosts to maintain their orbit. We could boost its orbit to take it higher temporarily."

"Just temporarily?" van Damm asked.

Hardy nodded. "That's correct, sir." Hardy and Van Orden began to talk between themselves, running numbers and scenarios.

Ryan interrupted. "But we can move it?"

"We can, Mr. President," Van Orden said. He muttered what to Ryan sounded like strange incantations about pi and *vis viva*, and orbital decay, while preforming calculations in his head. He looked at his protégé. "A point-five-degree flight path change . . ."

Midshipman Hardy, who'd been working through the same mental calculations, finished the professor's thought: ". . . would mean movement in tens of meters from the original location."

"So," Ryan said, "what you're saying is, we put on the brakes and the missile flies right by?"

"What?" Van Orden said, missing the *Top Gun* reference.

Hardy nodded. "Essentially, yes, Mr. President. As long as the missile didn't reacquire, then it would continue past, eventually falling back to earth."

"Okay," Ryan said. "Nuclear or kinetic, we still have a major problem. So let's have it."

"Pardon?" Van Orden said.

"Crux," Ryan said. "The satellite Dr. Tabrizi talks about in her theory. We can't move it until we know which one it is?"

Van Orden and Hardy looked at each other, then at the President.

The professor spoke first. "We believe there are five that would work," he said.

Hardy added, "Maybe as many as nine. And that's just talking about ours."

64

Atash Yazdani was bouncing in place when Dovzhenko pulled into the parking lot near Akbar Children's Hospital. His son, Ibrahim, stood beside him, looking small and drawn. Arm around the boy's shoulders, the Iranian bent down and stuck his head in the Toyota's window. He showed his teeth in the first smile since they'd met him.

"There has been an attack at the missile site west of the city," he said. "Your plan has worked. The missiles are destroyed. You can now keep your end of the bargain and take my son out."

His face fell when he noticed the mood in the truck. "What has happened?" He put a hand on top of his head and looked skyward. "Do not tell me there is yet another delay."

"I'm sorry," Jack said. "But only one missile was destroyed. There is still one at large."

"That does not matter anymore," Yazdani said, almost in tears. "I have done what you asked. I can do no more." He turned to his son. "Ibrahim, get in the truck. These people are taking us to get you medicine."

"And we will," Jack said. "You have my word—"

"Your word will get us all killed!"

The boy began to cough, hacking until his face turned red. Yazdani pounded on his back and he was finally able to gain control.

"We are still going to help," Jack said again. "But we have to find that second missile."

Yazdani stared daggers at him, then threw up his hands. "There are some caves approximately ten kilometers south of the test site. It is possible they took one of the erector launchers there."

Dovzhenko passed him a map. "Show me on this."

Yazdani pointed out a spot to the west of the city, on a narrow goat track of a road past the village of Noghondar. He took out a pen and drew an *X*. "The caves are here," he said. "I know they are large enough, but that does not mean the missile is there."

"We've got to try," Ryan said, scrawling instructions on a scrap of paper. "Taybad is just a few kilometers from the Afghan border. Take your son and wait there. If you do not hear from us in four hours, then call this number."

"I have no choice," Yazdani said.

Ryan shrugged. "None of us do," he said.

I t seemed that virtually every military and militia vehicle was racing out of Mashhad toward the scene of explosions. Dovzhenko fell in with the parade, speeding west with the group. Ysabel translated the radio broadcasts as they drove.

The official stand was that Israel had fired a salvo of missiles at an Iranian school, killing hundreds of innocent children. That did not explain the massive secondary explosion some were reporting, but the media, accustomed to toeing the government line, made no attempt to explain much of anything.

"Turn here," Ryan said, navigating while Dovzhenko drove.

The Russian left the convoy to head south into a wooded valley when they were close enough to see the glow of flames in the distance. A mile down the road he slowed and turned off his headlights, running on parking lights alone. Continuing toward Yazdani's *X*, they were gratified to see the glow of bright construction lights in the distance.

"Way to go, Atash!" Ryan said. He rolled down his window, letting in the cool air of the mountain valley. "Hear that?"

"What?" Ysabel asked. "I hear the sound of a stream running along the road."

"A generator," Dovzhenko said. "I'll go a little farther, then we should walk up."

Ryan checked the AKs, consolidating all the ammo into four twenty-round magazines. Eighty rounds sounded like a lot—until you were getting shot at.

Dovzhenko parked in the trees, and they each slung a rifle, easing their doors shut to hide any noise of their approach. They crept forward on their hands and knees until they reached the edge of the clearing.

The stark construction lighting, powered by the humming generator, illuminated the area beyond the trees like a stage. A rocky mountain lay beyond the pool of light. The same gravel road on which they now walked led into a black hole in the side of the mountain, while a secondary road forked to the west, continuing down into a dry wadi and then over an adjacent hill. More light spilled from the interior of a squat stone building to the right of the cave.

Three uniformed guards were posted outside—one beside the building, two at the edge of the light nearer the cave entrance.

"I don't like it," Ysabel said. "We don't know how many more are inside."

"True," Dovzhenko said. "We should watch for a—"

Jack put a hand on his arm to get his attention. "Look," he said, a whisper.

Ysabel gasped. "Reza Kazem."

"And Tabrizi," Ryan said.

They exited the cave at the same time, Tabrizi carrying a clipboard, while Kazem carried a satchel over his shoulder. They walked to the stone building and went inside.

"I can't be sure," Ysabel said, "but I think that was Ayatollah Ghorbani in there. And he is bound hand and foot."

"He must not be part of the conspiracy," Dovzhenko said.

"Not all of it, anyway," Ryan said. A plan was already forming in his mind.

Ysabel saw his face. "What?" she asked. "I know that look."

Ryan took the satellite phone out of his pocket and unfolded the antenna, relieved when he got a signal. "First things first. We need to call in another strike."

"Oh, no," Dovzhenko said. "We are much too close. Your bombs will kill us all."

Ryan shook his head. "I'm not suicidal. As soon as we

know for sure the missile is here, we haul ass down the road."

There was no time for anything but a direct call, so he punched in the number for the prepaid he knew Foley had with her as an added layer of security for these conversations. She answered immediately, then passed the phone to his father. It was good to hear the old man's voice, but Jack refrained from calling him "Dad" in front of the Russian. He told him his plan, and then read him the GPS coordinates he got from the borrowed cell phone. "We're moving forward to do a little recon," he said. "I'll call back in ten and give you a sitrep. If you don't hear from me in fifteen, you should go ahead and send it."

He thought he heard the old man choke up a little, so he added. "You'll hear from me. I promise."

Ryan ended the call and folded the antenna down at the same time Kazem and Tabrizi came out of the stone building. They were leading a man with his hands tied in front of him. He had a long white beard and wore the robes and turban of a cleric. Ysabel was right. It was Ayatollah Ghorbani.

Instead of returning to the cave and driving the launch truck outside in the open, Kazem pushed the cleric to a wooden table at the base of the light tree. Ghorbani railed at him, but the generator made it impossible to hear what he was saying. In any case, both Kazem and Tabrizi ignored him. Kazem set the leather case on the table and then opened the flap. All of them recognized it as the launch-control device.

"What is he doing?" Ysabel said. "He can't launch from inside the cave."

Tabrizi was staring at a phone in her open palm. She

raised her free hand, held it there for a moment, and then, still focused on the phone, suddenly let it fall.

Jack looked at the road that disappeared over the next hill and realized too late what was happening. He raised his rifle and fired, killing Reza Kazem at the same moment he finished entering the code into the launch controller.

A searing light flashed in the adjacent valley. The Russian Gorgon streaked upward through the night sky in a bloom of orange and black. The guards, momentarily startled by the gunfire and the missile blast, regained their senses enough to return fire. Dovzhenko and Ysabel fired while Jack rolled onto his back and yanked the cell phone out of his pocket. He'd started a silent count the moment the missile fired and now justified the time with the passing seconds.

Rolling to his gun, he joined the fight, shooting one of the guards at the mouth of the cave as rounds snapped and cracked overhead. Dovzhenko shot Tabrizi as she picked up one of the fallen rifles. The other guard near the opening of the cave was already dead. The third fell a moment later, brought down by Ysabel. Jack had learned long ago that protracted gunfights were rare. This one ended quickly—and badly for the untrained guards. The sound of the humming generator settled across the valley along with the odor of burned metal from the rocket.

Ghorbani stood alone, blinking under the bright construction lights.

No other shooters ran from the cave, but Dovzhenko moved laterally, ordering the Ayatollah to walk toward him just in case.

Ryan moved the other way, keeping to the trees as he

pulled the sat phone from his pocket. Ghorbani didn't need to know he'd ever been there.

Foley picked up immediately.

"Missile launch at 12:06:32 Iran time," Jack said. "We couldn't stop it."

65

"**D**r. Van Orden," Mary Pat Foley said, letting the cell phone fall to her side. Her face had gone pale. "How long will it take for a Russian 51T6 to reach a satellite passing overhead?"

"A little over three minutes," Van Orden said.

"Mr. President," Foley said, "we're launch plus fifty-four seconds and counting."

General Paul had Air Force Satellite Control Network near Colorado Springs on an open line in anticipation of this very event.

"Why don't we move all our satellites if we're not sure of the target?" Ryan asked.

"We could move any or all of ours, Mr. President," Van Orden said. "But it's a risk moving all that metal at once. It will take some time to do calculations so we don't cause a collision ourselves. And we might move the wrong ones first."

"Okay, gentlemen," Ryan said. "I'm thinking you have about ninety seconds to pick me the correct satellite."

Hardy sat at the conference table, hunched over a laptop computer with access to satellite information that was not available outside those with a specific need to know. His voice was calm and cool though he was surrounded by men and women who outranked him by factors of ten. "A launch actually helps us," he said. "These Russian missiles travel at 5,328 miles per hour, while satellites orbit the earth at around 17,500 miles per hour. The 51T6 as we know it has max altitude of five hundred miles. Even if this is some new variant and we give it an extra hundred miles . . . To score a head-on kinetic kill, they'd have to account for"—he drummed his fingers on the table—"eight hundred forty miles of movement from the time the missile launched until it reaches . . ." He scanned the computer screen. "That leaves only five satellites within range."

"Anytime now," Ryan prodded.

"Two of them are Chinese, one Russian, one from Thailand, but none of them are big enough but this one— an ISR bird that I've never heard of." Hardy looked up. He turned the computer toward the chairman. "This is it, General Paul. It has to be."

"Let's get it done," Ryan said.

The chairman of the joint chiefs relayed the message to AFSCN at 12:09:12 Iran time, two minutes and forty seconds after missile launch.

"We don't have long to wait," van Damm said, stating the obvious.

Midshipman Hardy closed the laptop and then his eyes. His lips moved slightly, whispering a quiet prayer. Dr. Van Orden gave him a paternal pat on the shoulder. No one spoke. Few breathed. Everyone in the room, including Ryan, mumbled prayers of their own. All eyes eventually fell to General Paul. Fifty-four seconds later, the general leaned back in his chair and held up a thumb.

"Looks like we're good, Mr. President," he said. "AF-SCN tracked an unidentified missile launched from Iran as it passed within a quarter of a mile from our ISR bird. Satellite signals are still being received five by five."

Ryan got to his feet, prompting everyone else in the Situation Room to stand. "Midshipman Hardy," he said. "Dr. Van Orden. I know it's kind of a letdown after all this, but how about you come to my place for dinner?" He grinned. "It's not far."

66

Two days later, Senator Michelle Chadwick was in her kitchen, filling two bowls with butter-pecan ice cream. She wore a fawn-colored negligée and a pair of fuzzy slippers. *"L'état c'est moi,"* she said, licking the scoop before she dropped it in the sink. "No, Jack Ryan, you are not the state." Her run-in with the President had left her feeling celebratory. Sure, he'd somehow convinced Yermilov to pull his troops back from the Ukrainian border, but the public still didn't trust him. His smarmy ass thought he was so much smarter than everyone else. No, that wasn't it. He thought he was better. More honest. Less corruptible. Less prone to the temptations mere mortals fell prey to. There was no one thing that Michelle Chadwick didn't like about Jack Ryan— there were a million of them.

"Hey!" Corey yelled from the bedroom.

"Hold your horses," she yelled. "I'm just getting the ice cream."

"Forget the ice cream," Corey said. "You're going to want to see this."

"What?" Chadwick said a moment later, flopping down on the bed beside her boy toy and handing him the bowl with the lesser amount of butter pecan.

When she looked up at the television, she nearly bit off the end of her spoon.

When Jack Ryan said he'd take their case to the highest court in the land, he'd not been talking about the Supreme Court. That son of a bitch meant the American people.

"*. . . the danger of lies, telling them, believing in the echo chamber of social media,*" Ryan said, from behind his desk in the Oval Office. "*We could, as some nations have done, curtail free speech or criminalize sensationalism that is masked as satire. Congress could pass legislation that called for heavy fines or even prison terms for spreading lies—even when these lies are done with a wink and a nod toward entertainment. There is no question that many lies damage real people. And if real people are hurt, should not the government step in?*

"*My fellow Americans, you . . . we, are smarter than that. I believe we deserve better.*"

As Ryan spoke, the screen split in half. Both images showed him sitting behind his desk, giving the same speech, but in one he wore a charcoal suit, in the other his suit was black. The screen split again into four and then six images. Ryan gave the same speech but in different suits and from different venues. One of them depicted expertly manipulated footage from the commencement address he'd given at the United States Military Academy at West Point the year before.

"*Unfortunately,*" all the Jack Ryan images said in unison, "*technology makes deception far too easy.*"

"Son of a bitch," Chadwick whispered.

Corey put a hand on her knee. "What do you think he's—"

"Shut up," Chadwick said, pushing his hand away. "Just shut up."

I n the Oval Office, the real President Ryan stepped in front of the green screen to sit on the edge of the Resolute desk. Behind him, the images of him in various venues wearing different suits froze, and Ryan continued his address uninterrupted. The demonstration of manipulated videos was far better than any explanation he could have given.

"It is not always up to those in government to decide everything that is true and what is a lie. That responsibility falls to us as individuals. In this age of digital manipulation and artificial intelligence, voices can be mimicked so well that those closest to us believe it is the real thing. There are far too many who would use technology against us—too many foreign powers, and too many here at home, whose primary goal is not to joke or prank but to destroy and degrade. We cannot allow ourselves to be deceived. We must study, read, make informed decisions by weighing things for ourselves before we rush to judgment. And I'm not just talking to you, I'm talking to myself as well. Together, we must be vigilant . . ."

In the hallway outside the Oval, adjacent to the Roosevelt Room, Special Agent Marsh leaned in close to Gary Montgomery as Ryan wound up his address.

"POTUS never mentioned the actual doctored videos of him talking about hoarding vaccine or backing a coup in Cameroon. He never said a word about Russian bots."

Montgomery grinned. "Like he said, Americans are

smarter than that." He paused, eyebrows furrowed, lips pursed. "Most of them, anyway . . ."

Two old men, fishing along the Sofiyskaya Embankment, were the first to see the body. One of the men was a former apparatchik and kept a bent and bony finger on the pulse of the present administration. Hungry fish had already begun their work, but he recognized the lipless corpse at once as Maksim Dudko, aide to President Yermilov. "What have you done, comrade," he whispered to himself, "to end up fish food in the Moscow River?" Better not to know, he thought, and used his walking stick to push the bloated thing back into the swirling current.

Jack, Dovzhenko, and Ysabel crossed into Afghanistan with Atash Yazdani and his son, following the same smugglers' route they'd used to enter Iran. The Wind of 120 Days, still blowing hot and strong, gave them cover from border security force surveillance.

Considering what happened on their last trip through Herat and the likelihood that they'd made some lifelong enemies, Ryan opted to fly on to Dubai. There were still plenty of Russian and Iranian operatives in the UAE, but the U.S. intelligence community was also strong there and provided more places to lie low than western Afghanistan.

Two case officers from CIA, who were also registered nurses, took custody of the Yazdanis. Public Law 110 would ensure that both father and son got new names and a new place to live. Medical treatments for Ibrahim's cystic fibrosis would begin as soon as he'd seen a pulmonary specialist. Atash Yazdani would eventually be given help finding a new career, but as an engineer in Iran's rocket and missile forces, he had enough information to keep debriefers from several U.S. intelligence agencies busy for months.

Jack's part in all this was still a ticklish issue, so it was decided that CIA case officer Adam Yao, who'd worked with Ryan before, would make initial contact with Erik Dovzhenko, debrief him, get a feel for his veracity, and then put him on the FLUTTER before accepting him into the fold as double agent GP/VICAR.

Russia had provided nuclear missiles to Iran from the beginning, but as far as they knew, Dovzhenko was unaware of anything beyond the plot by Reza Kazem and General Alov to shoot down an American satellite. Ayatollah Ghorbani corroborated his report, with the stories of his daring rescue from the insane dissident who had murdered General Alov and kept him captive. Dovzhenko was a heroic, if plodding, SVR operative just doing his job. He'd pursued other dissidents into Afghanistan, where he'd lost them among the Taliban. Rather than returning directly to the embassy in Tehran, he was to fly back to Moscow along with his new friend, Ysabel Kashani.

They'd arrived in Dubai eight hours earlier than Dovzhenko had told his supervisors, and, after a lengthy surveillance detection run, met Yao in a suite at the Crowne Plaza Dubai. The CIA case officer stood in the corner of the room, chatting with Dovzhenko, making small talk—and observations on his new, though battle-tested recruit.

Jack and Ysabel stood in the front alcove by the door to give the two men a little more privacy.

Ysabel had changed from her headscarf and smock into jeans and a blue silk blouse that perfectly accented her olive skin.

She scuffed the tile floor with the tip of a white tennis shoe. "You okay?" she asked.

Jack nodded, meaning it, but feeling a little down just the same.

"I was pretty hard on you," she said.

"So," Ryan said, attempting to change the subject. "You're going to work in Russia."

She nodded. "For a while. That's my expertise."

"Dovzhenko is a good dude," Ryan said. "Brave. Solid."

"He is." Ysabel looked up. "But we're not . . ."

"I know," Ryan said. "I'm just saying he's a good dude, that's all. And if you were . . . you know . . . that would be okay."

"Listen," Ysabel said. "Do you know the story of the Bibi Khanum Mosque in Samarkand?"

Ryan chuckled. "Can't say that I do."

"Well," Ysabel said, "tamerlane hired a Persian architect to design and build a mosque for his favorite wife, Bibi Khanum. It is said that this architect and Bibi Khanum fell so deeply in love that when the Persian kissed her, it burned her cheek, leaving the imprint of his lips."

Ryan raised a brow. "Okay."

"What I'm saying, Jack"—Ysabel waved a hand low in front of her lap—"is don't look for someone who only sets you on fire here. Find someone who burns your cheek with a simple kiss."

Dovzhenko walked up before Ryan could respond.

"Hope I am not interrupting," he said, hooking a thumb over his shoulder. "My case officer had to make a few calls."

"Not at all," Ryan said. "I was just on my way out. The fewer people that see me with you, the better."

"Understood," Dovzhenko said.

Ysabel leaned in, kissing Ryan on the cheek and then giving a little shrug. "See," she said. "No burn there, my friend."

Dovzhenko looked sideways at her. "What?"

"Nothing," she said.

"It was an honor," Ryan said.

"The honor was mine," Dovzhenko said. "Two weeks ago, we may have tried to kill each other, and now . . ."

"You're sure about this?" Ryan asked. "SVR counter-intelligence line is going to work overtime trying to trip you up the moment you get off the plane."

Dovzhenko glanced quickly to the left and right, and then leaned in with a secret. "We should probably not mention this to your friend, but if there is one thing I learned from my mother, it is how to beat a polygraph."

Dovzhenko smiled and shook Ryan's hand, drawing him close and patting him on the back in a brotherhood hug. "I feel like our paths will cross again, my friend."

"Seriously," Ryan said. "Maybe you should let us check this out through our channels before you return to Moscow. It may not be safe."

"Ah, Jack Ryan, Jr.," Dovzhenko said with a wry smile. "You know better than I, happiness does not come from safety."

Ready to find
your next great read?

Let us help.

Visit prh.com/nextread